QUIET GUILT

THE STATE OF MICHIGAN v. STARR

To Jim & Joyce —
Enjoy Chuck's story.

CLARE ADKIN

Clare E. Adkin Jr.
3/2/2011

Warren Publishing, Inc.

Published by Warren Publishing, Inc.
www.warrenpublishing.net

ISBN 9781886057586

Library of Congress Catalog Number: 2010933551

Printed in the United States of America

The events in this book are fictionalized. Any resemblance to persons living or
deceased is purely coincidental.

ACKNOWLEDGMENTS

Quiet Guilt has lain in the shadows, dust covered by the sands of time. Yet, this story is played out every day in our homes, our streets, our courtrooms. It's an old story, one laced with laughter, hope and calamity. Make no mistake, this is a work of fiction, but the events, times and places ring familiar.

Thank you Sally (wife) for allowing me to discover the sequestered twists and turns of this mystery unencumbered by the daily trappings of life. You have been and always will be a treasure for us all.

Thank you Katie (daughter) for your good counsel in the wake of home, school, work and children. I look forward to returning the favor.

Thank you Lorana Kauffman and Salome Souder, my high school English teachers. Your shared love for literature and poetry have inspired and comforted generations of students. You will be fondly remembered forever and ever.

Thank you Melody Cannon for your incisive advanced reading and your thought provoking suggestions for improving the manuscript. As your students always say, "You're The Best!"

Thank you Cathy Brophy (Publisher) and Tasha Yehuda (Editor) for your suggestions, directions, and corrections. But most of all, thank you for your unrelenting encouragement.

Thank you George S. Keller for setting the standard high as a small town trial lawyer. Also, thank you for sharing your love of the law with me and my high school students.

And, thank you to all of my students—you know who you are!

DEDICATION

For Sally and our children Andy, Katie and Blake

**"Three things shall I have till I die:
Laughter and hope and a sock in the eye."**

By Dorothy Parker, from *Vanity Fair*, January 1920

I
THERE GOES MY HEART

"Hey Chuck! How long 'till quit'n time?"

"Shut-up and keep pick'n!" hollered back a tall sandy haired young man coming down his pole ladder with yet another picking sack overflowing with apples.

"What do you mean, it's at least four thirty ain't it?"

Chuck wiped the late summer sweat from a tanned brow with his black and white plaid shirtsleeve. "Listen-up Josh, you'll have to learn how to tell time yourself. This is my last time picking these Jonnees."

"Oh yeah, until next year this time," Josh sassed back.

"This time next year I'll be somewhere else."

"Where's that, big man?" Ken, the third boy and middle brother, matter-of-factly questioned while dumping a full sack of apples into an empty field crate.

"I don't know yet, just somewhere else. Now keep picking you two. We get to quit when we finish up this orchard, in an hour or so I'd guess. You know Dad doesn't want to come back out here in the morning."

"So we're pick'n 'till we're done?" Josh moaned as if giving up to the inevitable.

"Smart boy," quipped Chuck as the teenage brothers continued their toilsome late afternoon harvest.

That summer of '38, the sight of bushels of Jonathan apples lining the orchard rows for yet another season would forever remain etched in my memory. The trees I had picked with my brothers stood a little straighter, signaling relief from their heavy burdens. I shared that emotion. A bridge of sorts, between the boy I'd been and the man I would soon become. Two summers out of high school, and still I could see no clear path before me. It was a time of eager apprehension, restless anticipation for what lay ahead, and blissful ignorance of the tremendous heartache that life's desperate situations can sometimes bring.

Apple time had once more come and gone on the Scott farm. As our last seasonal harvest, it symbolized family relief, especially for me. My two younger brothers, Josh a junior and Ken a senior, had gone back to school three weeks earlier; Fennville High School. I was 19, had finished school a year earlier but still lived and worked at home; an increasingly uncomfortable situation.

There existed an unspoken expectation within my family, and within our community, that after a person completed their schooling they should branch out on their own. Since graduation, I'd been made more and more aware of that expectation. Mom's wishes were quite plain, "Get married and settle down," though not quite that blunt. Dad's wishes were less overtly defined but leaned directly toward financial independence. I was in the market for a destination, a desire that was growing with each passing day.

The Scott family was in its third generation of Allegan County farmers and, if left up to me, three generations was as far as we Scotts would go. Make no mistake; I was proud of my Dad as a good farmer, as were his father and grandfather before him. The sweat shed in working their fields and orchards had been legendary throughout the county. No member of the Scott family was a stranger to strenuous physical labor. In my view, "Scott" and "sweat" were synonyms.

Because I had parents that were both the products of large farm families, I realized at an early age that I was related to half the people in the township and many more in the greater county area. I had an abundance of aunts, uncles and cousins. With few exceptions, all were farmers and although not wealthy, none were living at a subsistence level. While not ostentatious, all of their farms gave the appearance of order and stability. There was a lone exception to the rule, the farm of my Great Uncle Otto Barnes, Mom's uncle. His farm always appeared in want of repair, with orchards that needed tending and scattered rusting equipment lying about. I remember Dad saying as we passed the Barnes' place, "Doesn't look like a Scott farm to me." We all understood.

Our 102 acre piece of land was primarily fertile sandy loam. Its proximity to Lake Michigan, less than three miles, and the rolling nature of the property made our farm an excellent fruit site. The lake effect caused the land to warm slowly during the spring and cool slowly during the fall. Thus, sap didn't start running too early in the spring, which would result in susceptibility to tree freeze damage and frost during pollination. The rolling landscape facilitated good orchard air drainage which also defended blossoming fruit trees from killing late spring frosts.

Since I was 13, I'd worked on the farm fulltime during the summer months, and most weekends during the early fall and late spring of the school year. I never dreaded this work; actually, I sort of enjoyed it, most of the time. My least favorite assignments were digging stumps, picking up rocks—which seem to grow in the soil like weeds—and thinning peaches. Dad's gusto for these toilsome tasks escaped me. That said, I shared his sense of accomplishment after completing a full day's work.

One August day Josh, Ken and I each picked 100 bushels of Hale Haven peaches. We helped Dad load them on our flatbed Ford truck and he drove two loads to the nearby Michigan Fruit Canners plant in Fennville and one load to Benton Harbor. The load to Benton Harbor was the first in the morning and went to the famous fruit and vegetable market there, one of the largest open-air fruit markets in the country. Dad believed that getting to the market early assured him a better price.

When Dad returned from Benton Harbor, he told us about an enormous cold storage plant that had opened at the foot of the market. He claimed that the storage facility would extend the life of highly perishable farm products, which in-turn, would stabilize volatile market prices for the farmers. Had he not possessed such a disdain for Wall Street, we would have thought Dad owned stock in the business. He had the impression that a religious group of little old men with long hair and white beards owned the new storage. "They call 'em Holy Rollers."

His voice escalated as he related how he sold our peaches. "Brokers crawled all over the truck yelling prices at me. I sold the whole load to the highest bidder!"

Even though Dad spent over four long hours in the truck that day, we still gave him credit for picking 40 bushels. The four of us picked 346 bushels of peaches in one day! I would remain proud of that and the many other accomplishments we've made on the farm. However, I didn't want to make a career out of it; for me it would be *The Road Not Taken*. I'd much rather read Robert Frost than pick peaches.

Life on the farm had been a challenge for my parents and maybe more so during the difficult economic times. However, as a team they had managed the farm efficiently for all of our benefit. In addition to cooking, cleaning, washing and ironing, Mom canned everything that could be canned and some things we thought she should not can, but avoided telling her so. We all agreed her canned dill pickles were the best.

Mom could be obstinate in her self-proclaimed stewardship of the Scott's proper relationship with God. My brothers and I complained about going to church as if it was our sacred duty and the manly thing to do. Our chiding remarks drew exasperating cold stares at times. Nevertheless, there was no negotiating with our mother, whose goal in life was to have each one of us well presented before God and everyone else; by her standards. Mom loved morals. Dad loved dogs.

In addition to managing the house and our spiritual lives, Mom helped in the field whenever needed. By any measure, the Scott family farm provided each member a solid quality of family life. But, as mentioned earlier, a life on the farm was not in my future.

There must be more to life than worrying about the weather or the market, or any one of a myriad of mundane things that are out of mortal control. Farmers always yearn for the proverbial bumper crop, but when it comes, they can't sell their crop for what it cost them to raise. Many are the stories of crops rotting in the fields; even during hard times. What a waste.

Dad continually sang the praises of being self-sufficient. From my vantage point, the Scotts had become less and less self-sufficient over time and increasingly dependent on outside sources for our well being and livelihood. For example, Dad grew only four fruits: apples, peaches, pears and tart cherries—all cash crops. No livestock; he claimed they were too time-consuming. With the exception of Mom's garden behind the house, no vegetables were ever grown on our farm. Dad said vegetable farming was too tedious, even though his grandfather pioneered the cultivation of Michigan cauliflower.

Dad did not practice what he preached. However, it never bothered him any more than it bothered Ginger, our family Irish setter and Dad's faithful hunting companion. Every fall when Dad started cleaning his 12 gage shotgun, Ginger would go crazy. She would literally jump in Dad's lap. To witness true happiness was to watch Dad and Ginger heading out past the barn to hunt pheasant.

By the time we finished picking-up the last of the cider apples, I had saved enough money to start looking for a car of my own. Asking to use the family car was never easy for me. I knew that I wouldn't be able to buy the best car on the market, but I'd seen several good second-hand automobiles. I inherited the conviction that a person should spend less than they make, especially as they plan to strike out on their own. This was a rather ubiquitous Scott family belief; for generations. Dad and Mom never purchased anything they could not pay for in cash. I was surprised to discover that this frugal principle was not a law founded in the United States Constitution.

My savings account had reached just over $500; $516.22 to be exact. It had taken me two years to amass this personal fortune, and it was not burning a hole in my pocket. But, I wanted a car of my own.

On the first Sunday in October, Dad and Uncle Bill—who owned the adjoining farm to the north—took me for a ride over toward Allegan. Dad had heard of a traveling salesman living near the Allegan Dam who had a car for sale. It made me feel adult that Dad recognized my desire and need for a car. Also, I felt grateful for his and Uncle Bill's assistance, but never told them so. I was nervous, but tried not to show it. Owning a car was a big step toward freedom.

We found the car and it was for sale, a 1929 Ford Model A Coupe. It looked a little rough and worn, but Dad whispered to me that it was sound. The way he said "sound" made me know he liked it. Its rumble seat and stylish whitewall tires were to my liking, as was the artificial leather top that made the Coupe look like a convertible with its top up.

A vision of riding through the countryside with Miss Maxine Martin seated next to me, while friends bounced up and down in the rumble seat behind, passed through my head. How long would it take me to unload the friends so that I could get Maxine alone? Wasn't what I had in mind what Henry Ford had intended when he created this marvelous mobile location for romantic misconduct? A car afforded limitless possibilities.

We did a little haggling with the owner, mostly Dad and Uncle Bill haggling, but finally agreed on a price; $235. Dad wouldn't let me drive "my" car on the road until we were able to get the title notarized. Therefore, he drove us back home, all the time complaining that he thought we could have gotten the car for $225. Uncle Bill followed us in his old Chevrolet.

Once home, Dad told everyone he couldn't believe what a good deal we had made for the car. I immediately took my "little" brothers for a ride around the farm. Later, Mom wanted me to take her and Dad for a ride. Funny, she wanted to ride in the rumble seat with Dad's arm around her. Slightly embarrassing, but Dad and I accommodated her.

Taking Maxine out in my new car filled my head with alluring contemplation. Two weeks earlier she had invited me to go with her to the Allegan County Fair; she would drive her parent's car. Maxine had arranged this outing with the condition that we take Hilda, her little sister, and Hilda's two girl friends. I was eager to go, but unsure of Maxine's motive. Had she simply wanted to see the fair, had she wanted to take Hilda and friends to the fair, or was going to the fair an excuse to go out with me? I suspected the latter, since Maxine could have driven to the fair without me.

It had been over a year since Maxine and I had gone out together, so I didn't know exactly what to expect. We had a good time at the fair, but a clearer picture of feminine intention developed toward evening's end. When we were almost home, Maxine insisted on dropping the little girls off at the Martin home, and then she would drop me off before returning back to her home. She said her father needed the car first thing in the morning. Her justification of this driving pattern defied Scott logic. What happened while dropping me off confirmed to my satisfaction that Maxine had wanted to go out with me. I liked her logic and wanted to be the recipient of more.

Although not close neighbors, the Scotts and the Martins were members of the same rural Methodist church, and Maxine also had attended and recently graduated from Fennville High School. We had dated a little; nothing steady. We went to the prom together my senior year. I hoped she might ask me to her prom last spring. She had been dating the high school sports hero and went to the prom with him. Since then, I had lost track of Maxine until she approached me at the church picnic about going with the Martin girls to the fair.

The evening of the county fair had rekindled my interest in Maxine and once I had my own car, I pined with desire to get up the nerve to ask her out. No complaints about going to church the following Sunday. When I happened to literally bump into Maxine, I compulsively asked, "Do you want to go to the movies?" I ended my sentence with, "I'm sorry, I didn't mean to run into you." I felt energized by the encounter, but in an uncomfortable, self-conscious sort of way. That feeling disappeared when she answered with a perky, "I'd love to!"

I thought of little else until church the following Sunday. In the narthex we agreed I'd pick her up at 1:30 to go to a matinee movie in South Haven. I washed my little Ford Coupe inside and out. Dad, my brothers and I tinkered around with her at every opportunity. She seemed to be in perfect running order. We, the Coupe and me, were ready to take Miss Maxine Martin to the movies. Yes.

I marked my calendar to commemorate the event. **FIRST DATE, Sunday, October 16, 1938. Pick-up Maxine Martin at 1:30 P.M. Must have her home by 10:30 P.M.** I had gone out on dates with girls before, but this one was different. This was a real date—one male, one female, one car; my car.

Stopping about a mile from the Martin house, I first looked at myself in the rearview mirror and then double-checked my watch to make sure I arrived at the correct time. When I entered the Martin's gravel driveway Hilda ran into the house, undoubtedly to announce my arrival. Mrs. Martin answered the front door eight seconds after I knocked.

"Hi Chuck, please come in. Has your mother finished her canning?"

"Uh, yes, I think so," I stammered back nervously.

Mr. Martin waved hello from the kitchen. Hilda watched, sitting at the top of the stairs petting the family's Calico cat.

I felt like a 4-H exhibit at the county fair until Maxine bounced into the room smiling and declaring, "Let's go, Chuck!"

I tried to be polite, like Mom had taught me, but I couldn't wait to get out of there. I think that feeling was encouraged more by not wanting to be on display than the anticipation of anything Maxine and I might do when alone. After all, the most we had ever done we did in her parent's car following the fair. I enjoyed kissing Maxine, twice quite passionately, but nothing ever really happened, like an exploit to share with fellow comrades. Nothing brag worthy.

We had a good time riding in my car down U.S. 31 along Lake Michigan to South Haven, passing through the tiny hamlets of Ganges and Glenn. All the way to South Haven we reminisced about events, places and people we knew along the route; laughed a lot.

The summer vacationers had long since departed for their year-round homes, mostly in Chicago. I turned into an alleyway directly across from the Michigan Theater marquee. Last summer I had parked in the same ally with a church youth group attending the annual South Haven Peach Festival. The town was teaming with festival goers and Jewish summer resorters. We were just high school kids, more interested in checking-out the summer people than eating peaches & cream. Try as I may, I couldn't remember if Maxine was part of that group, and didn't dare ask her.

The title of the movie was **There Goes My Heart**. I wondered which my heart liked best; Maxine or my Coupe. Maxine was a luxury; my car was a necessity.

A ticket lady with a five o'clock shadow told us that the feature would not start for another 20 minutes. Since we had the time, I suggested we take a quick drive down to the beach. I wondered if I wanted to impress Maxine with the romantic vista or if I just wanted to drive the Coupe around town. Probably both.

A deserted windswept beach blocked the cold dark blue water. Summer cottages were closed and shuttered tight. Threads of sand snaked aimlessly before a cool, damp west wind. The sun hung midway to the western horizon, accented by low line-like gray clouds. Holding hands, we took in the view, silently. The chilling wind gave Maxine's nose and cheeks a faint pink accent, which complemented her tanned face and dark green eyes that glistened in the breeze. I recall my futile search for something profound to say. Nothing.

Back at the theater the smell of popcorn made me hungry. It must have affected Maxine in the same way. I asked if she would like a snack and she suggested we share a bag of popcorn. We agreed to have it lightly buttered and salted. Maxine picked up a couple of extra napkins.

Try as I might, I couldn't pay attention to the movie. I kept glimpsing out of the corner of my eye at Maxine and marveled at how well she filled out her blouse. Her bright red lipstick made me wonder if I would get lipstick on me. I wasn't sure if she was wearing perfume, but the subtle scent that cloaked her was at once alluring and mysterious.

As we watched the movie, I could feel her shoulder and arm next to mine. I held firm. She didn't seem to mind. Whenever something happened on the screen that particularly impressed her, she grabbed hold of my arm with her opposite hand and squeezed. Each time this happened, I instantly tried to stiffen my biceps and triceps, but knew that wasn't my best attribute. Internally I smiled at my lack of a Superman physique. However, I was a sinewy six foot tall, had light brown hair, blue eyes, and my grandmothers had convinced me that I was good looking. Maxine handed me a napkin which I used, unsure of an implied message.

Finally, the movie ended and we moved closer to my ultimate objective. As we exited the theater, I noticed that the sun had gone down and the yellow street lights sharpened an already exhilarating mood. Instead of walking to the car, we walked up Center Street to the corner bank, crossed the street and started back the other side. Maxine chattered continuously about the movie. She raved about Virginia Bruce and her beautiful long blonde hair.

"I really liked the leading actress, Virginia Bruce, wasn't she wonderful? Could you believe how gorgeous?" I think she's the most popular actress in Hollywood.

"Yeah, I guess, are you hungry? We could stop here at the Dairy Diner and grab something." Maxine agreed, so we entered the little diner.

"Don't you just love black and silver?" I poked fun at the only colors inside the diner. Knowing we would be closer to each other, I suggested we sit at the counter.

Maxine giggled, "You're funny," as she spun around on her stool. It looked like fun, so I joined her for a spin.

Maxine ordered a cherry soda and I had a blueberry malt. Her teasing gestures with the maraschino cherry topping tantalized me. My reciprocating blue mouth didn't achieve the same effect for her. But, again she giggled and spun, playfully bumping against me.

There were several other patrons present, although the restaurant was by no means crowded. Maxine observed that one of the ladies seated near the front window looked similar to the actress in the movie. How could I notice, Maxine's light babble and occasional mischievous touching held my attention. She continued talking while I savored the blueberry malt and her company. It was fun to be with her. I hoped she felt the same.

She asked me what I planned to do: "You know you've been out of school over a year now."

I didn't have an answer for this too frequently repeated and increasingly irksome inquiry. I supposed it was logical for anyone to want to know. Before I could craft an acceptable answer, Maxine reported that she would attend County Normal in January and planned to start teaching in one of the rural K-8 schools next fall. Both of us had attended country schools through the eighth grade. So had each of our parents, and in my case, my parents and one grandmother attended the very same little one-room, red brick school house that I had attended; Peach Belt School.

She continued to expound on her future as I drifted, lost on a seemingly empty road ahead. I wondered at that time where the little Coupe would take me; maybe to California.

From the Dairy Diner, we walked while Maxine talked, back to the patiently waiting little black Coupe. I found myself inattentive to what Maxine was saying; distracted by things I might do the rest of my life. I didn't want to farm. I hadn't particularly excelled in any area of school. Teachers liked me, I got by, and no one gave me a hard time about my poor study habits. Though never revealed formally, my personal goal in high school was to never be caught carrying a book or doing homework. Graduating with a rank in the exact middle of my class was never my objective, but as fate would have it, that's exactly where I ranked. I likened myself to the center post of a carrousel—everyone was moving, but me.

As we drove towards home, the curtain slowly closed on Maxine's vociferous commentary. Had she grown tired of me? I confess that my attentions had become preoccupied, until we were about a quarter of a mile from her house. Then, Maxine suggested we turn into an orchard lane to see if the cherries had been trimmed properly. The orchard belonged to her father and at first I was confused at Maxine's interest in or knowledge of pruning quality. Suddenly, realization overwhelmed me. I could feel my heart rate speed up. Maxine had brought me back to life.

Almost before I could stop the Coupe and turn off the head lights, Maxine had turned around in the seat and was facing me with her hands on my shoulders, as if wanting to have a serious discussion. Within a heartbeat we were locked in the most sensuous round of kissing I had ever experienced. Her lips were pleasingly moist and wanted to devour mine. Mine were willing and eager for full participation. I tasted her lipstick...well; luscious. Although possessing only limited previous experience, the irresistibly intense little noises that accompanied her ambitious embrace left me confidently out of control. I wanted to go further.

Exploration of the front of Maxine's blouse was not possible with her pressing so tightly against my chest. As we struggled, I felt her damp breath lingering in my ear. Her tongue and lips playfully pulled at my left earlobe and slipped down the side of my neck. The more we caressed, the more desirous I became, pushing myself toward the center of the seat. I speculated what her reaction would be if I put my right hand on her leg near the bottom of her dress. *No guts no glory*, repeated in my head. But, I couldn't bring myself to try, fearing Maxine's rejection. Maybe she wanted me to, I thought.

My feverish fumbling with the top button of her blouse brought our wonderful session to an abrupt end. I felt the sting of impending embarrassment, rejection or both.

"Not now, Chuck," she whispered in my ear. "I think I'm late and you know my dad."

Smiling with relief stifled by frustration, I whispered back that I did know her dad, and we slowly disengaged. Maxine straightened her dress and repositioned herself on the seat beside me. I took a deep silent breath. As I started the car, I noticed that trimming had been done and brush had been neatly gathered in every other row, ready for pushing and burning.

Two minutes later we were on the Martin's front porch. Maxine made the good night kiss one worth remembering. She looked up at me with eyes sparkling in the moon light, "Chuck, I had a great time tonight."

"Me too," I clumsily replied. It seemed too little, too late and too stupid.

I noticed an upstairs light. Had someone watched us inspecting the cherry orchard? A warm feeling enveloped me all the way home. Ginger greeted me at the kitchen door; tail slamming repetitively against the cupboard. I patted her firmly on the shoulder and told her to go lay down. Mom was reading in the living room. She asked me how the movie was as I headed for the stairs. "I'll give you a review in the morning."

Had Maxine kissed her old high school hero like that? This had been the best date of my life; and not the last—with any luck.

II
SPORTS REPORTER

Morning came instantly. The scent of Maxine still lingered. Quickly I examined the shirt on the floor next to my bed to make sure there were no lipstick tracks. Then I washed my face twice, again making sure no residual evidence remained. Looking in the mirror I smiled, recalling the night before and thinking about re-inspecting the Martins' cherry orchard in the near future—very near future.

At the breakfast table, Mom started grilling me about my date. "Did you enjoy the movie?" she demurely inquired.

Remaining true to my policy of never volunteering information to parents, I answered matter-of-factly, "Yes, the movie was enjoyable." I pretended not to notice the stupid, immature looks and noises that came from Josh and Ken and added, "Mrs. Martin asked about your canning. My car ran perfect."

Curious what came out of my mouth when my mind was fixated on something entirely different; Maxine. I knew my brothers had Maxine on their minds as well. That notion gave me internal satisfaction.

"Will you drive us to school?"

"Oh, alright." Again I pretended to be less than enthused, but all the time harboring a desire to show-off my little black, almost a convertible, Ford Coupe with white sidewall tires.

Before we left for school, Mom handed me a list of three job possibilities Dad had heard of, and thought I may be interested in following-up. I told her I was, and that I would. One involved clerking in a Glenn farm supply store, one a permanent farm hand on the state game reserve two miles south of Fennville, and one a position with the *South Haven Tribune*, the closest daily newspaper.

After dropping Josh and Ken at school, I decided to go to the newspaper first since I was sure this job had nothing to do with farming, and was by far the longest drive. I could also bask in the afterglow of the previous night's journey.

Maxine's scent permeated the Coupe, which caused my mind to meander over our recent struggle in the cherry orchard. I thought to myself, "This young lady could become habit forming."

The office of the *South Haven Tribune* was just a couple of doors down from the Dairy Diner. Again, pleasant memories of the day before wafted over me. What I would encounter or say upon entering the newspaper office never entered my mind. There was absolutely no sense of urgency from my perspective or preparation on my part. No matter how increasingly uncomfortable these personal traits made me feel, I lacked the will power to change.

The front window was stenciled with six inch block letters, **THE SOUTH HAVEN DAILY TRIBUNE.** A small bell above the door jingled when I entered. A short stout bespectacled man, mid 40s, with as much salt and pepper hair growing from his ears and nose as on his head, emerged from a deafening back room. He was wearing oversized cuffed gray pants, white shirt with sleeves rolled-up, wide yellow and green flowered tie, and charcoal vest one size too small; all 80% covered by a black bibbed apron tied at the neck and waist, and hanging below the knees. In a questioning voice he said: "Hello?"

I introduced myself, my reason for the visit to this man, who I soon found to be the proprietor, editor, the man in charge—Irving D. Mendelsohn. Mr. Mendelsohn, the Editor in Chief, wiped his ink-stained hands on an ink-laden apron, shook my hand vigorously, and suggested we interview immediately. He acted as if he'd been expecting me. With that, he invited me into a cluttered office to sit. Agitated and harried was my first impression of this comic strip caricature.

Before I could be seated, he asked, "What experience do you have with papers?"

"I was a staff member of the Fennville High School student newspaper, the *Black Hawk News*; printed twice each semester. In addition to contributing articles, I set the type for the front page of *The Hawk*, as we students referred to the paper." The only other thing I could think of, but didn't add, was that I enjoyed reading the funnies in the Sunday paper; never missed "Little Orphan Annie."

The Chief, as Mr. Mendelsohn preferred to be addressed, asked if I knew anything about sports.

"I played three years of baseball, winning major letters as a junior and senior. Also, I played football my junior year. I like sports."

"Why didn't you play football your senior year?"

"I knew better."

The Chief grinned. "What was your favorite course in high school?"

"English my junior year. We studied American Literature. I liked our teacher. She really liked poetry."

"Who's your favorite author?"

"Mark Twain." Finally a question I could answer with conviction.

"Why Samuel Clemens?" Asked the Chief with a rather pedantic tone in his voice, as if surreptitiously testing me. That's good, if you understand his meaning and have an answer.

"Because he told the truth, mainly." I loved that line from *Huckleberry Finn* and had waited a lifetime for an opportunity to use it. Perfect, I thought.

The Chief smiled, stood up and held out his hand to shake mine. "Times-a wasting. You got the job." Then he told me what the job entailed: covering and writing stories about school events taking place within the paper's circulation area of Van Buren and Allegan counties. My focus was mainly high school athletic contests, but other stories as they occurred, such as interesting honors and achievements, fires and vandalism, proms, picnics, graduations; whatever.

"What you find of interest will probably be of interest to our readers. If it isn't, you must report it so that it *will* be of interest to our readers. You understand?" The Chief had made an exclamatory statement sound like a question, with both tone and body language.

"Yes sir." Frankly, he left me a bit confused. Was the Chief practicing economy of words? He obviously expected me to read between the lines. Also, I wondered if he intended to pay me for my services. I'd heard about the Jewish tourist arriving in town Sunday night with a clean shirt and a ten dollar bill, and not changing either one all week. Jewish thrifty jokes were common around South Haven.

"Be ready to cover other special events as assigned. We work with a shoestring staff around here. From time to time you may be asked to help with printing and/or newspaper delivery. You have a car?"

"Yes." I could feel myself also becoming a man of few words. A strange attribute for a newspaper reporter, I thought.

"Alright already, you'll start your one-week probation day after tomorrow. Be here at nine sharp and we'll discuss games for you to report on this weekend. We expect a fifty-hour week. You'll receive $35.00 plus expenses after turning in a weekly voucher." The Chief handed me a stack of pink one-page mimeographed "Staff Voucher/Expense" sheets.

"Thanks Chief." And I left the newspaper office, not exactly sure what had just happened or what was going to happen. Not good, not bad—just going somewhere at 70 cents an hour; better than Dad paid me.

On my way back to the car, I picked-up a recruiting poster for the Civilian Conservation Corps. Dad and I had talked a year ago about my joining the CCC. One of FDR's New Deal programs, the CCC put young men between the ages of 18 and 25 to work conserving the nation's natural resources in national parks and forest by planting trees, stocking fish in lakes and rivers, and building fire lanes and wilderness trails. For a dollar a day plus room and board, the CCC attacked national unemployment by promoting long-range conservation projects. If this job as sports reporter didn't work out, I thought I'd give the CCC a try. The pressure was mounting inside me to move on with my life.

Mom squealed and hugged me when I entered the house announcing my new career. "How much does it pay?" Dad wanted to know. Josh and Ken asked if I'd write about their football team and put their pictures in the paper. Each in a personal way paid deference to me. Good feeling.

Following supper, I drove over to the Martin place to tell Maxine that I was going to work for the *South Haven Tribune*. My ulterior motive was to ask her to go with me to the Saugatuck October Fest Saturday night. She said yes to Saturday night, and then suggested that we go for a walk so that I could tell her all about my new job. I almost responded that there wasn't much to tell, but caught myself, thinking she might have had things other than walking or my employment on her mind. I certainly did.

I had very little to talk about, a man of few words, and there's not much a guy can do walking with a girl down an orchard lane on a brisk fall evening. Fortunately, Maxine had lots to tell me. She had her life perfectly mapped out. She would teach in a rural school, marry a farmer and raise four children— pretty much a shadow of our parent's lives. She didn't want to move very far away, either.

Once out of sight of the house, I held Maxine's hand as we walked. Our held hands were warm but we each kept the other hands in our pockets; it was getting cold outside. We stopped to kiss two or three times, but nothing like Sunday night. Our heavy coats insulated us from meaningful physical contact. Eventually we arrived back at the house and agreed that I'd pick her up at six on Saturday night.

Kindling a relationship with Maxine was not something I had initiated, but I definitely enjoyed it. Mom made no effort to disguise her pleasure in our dating. Maxine's reputation was the very best.

Maxine Faye Martin graduated eighth in her high school class of 47, was president of the Future Homemakers of America, secretary of the debate club, voted most likely to succeed by her classmates, taught K-2 Sunday school, talented seamstress, and was twice named Allegan County Cherry Pie Baking Champion. No disrespect or jealousy is implied in repeating these well deserved laurels. Maxine was capable, enthusiastic, and very pretty. I told myself I was lucky to be going out with a young lady of her quality. Would my intentions test her moral certainty? Did she have intentions that involved me? Not if she planned to marry a farmer.

I was having a good time working with the Chief organizing how best to cover the weekend football games. I could see right away that I had both freedom and responsibility. Chief readily approved my suggestions that I cover high school games on Friday nights and a college game or two on Saturdays. Articles about the Detroit Lions and Chicago Bears would be featured every

Monday. Special interest stories, coming events and minor sports would be appropriate during the middle of the week.

I read old sports articles, made phone calls, visited schools, and even conducted four formal interviews during my first three days on the job. Just give me the final score and I'll write the story, became my silent mantra. In the past I had found sports pages dull. They seemed to be the same story over and over again, with just names rearranged. In small schools you hardly had to rearrange the names or the statistics.

Maybe I could add new life to this drab picture. How would I sign my articles? Charles Andrew Scott? Charlie Scott? Chuck Scott? I chose the third, thinking it had a sporty ring.

Taking Maxine to the October Fest was a nice reward for getting off to a good start at the *Tribune*. The rowdy festival was held in the spacious Saugatuck Pavilion overlooking Lake Kalamazoo. Mountains of potato salad, bratwurst and sauerkraut followed by dancing and the possibility of being alone with Maxine; what could be better? As the night progressed, Maxine and I had the time of our lives between polkas and square dancing. She was an arm full of happy swings and spins, and I kept getting better, I thought, as I became more confident in complementing her.

Toward midnight I realized that I was rolling in sweat. Maxine was very warm too. Her kelly-green blouse with tiny white accents clung to her body in all the right places. During the closing number, a waltz, she pressed her warm damp body so tightly to mine that I thought people might be observing us. Discretely, I took a fleeting glance around the dance floor. I didn't see anyone particularly holding us under surveillance. They didn't care, nor did I; I realized. I loved it.

By the end of the last dance, my anticipation rose to a new level. We were heading for the pavilion exit when a couple of Maxine's girl friends asked her if they could catch a ride home with us. She turned to me with a questioning look in her eyes. Happily I said, "Of course. You guys can ride in my rumble seat. It'll be cold, but fun." To myself I thought: "There goes my time in the cherry orchard!"

It turned out that I was right. We had such a good time laughing and joking with the two in the rumble seat that we rode around until everyone felt they had been out too late and had to get home. After we dropped the girls off at their homes, I suggested another orchard inspection for the two of us. Maxine laughed and snuggled next to me: "Maybe next time." Never had I heard anyone say: "Maybe next time" in a more suggestive, sexy way.

On my way home, I repeated out loud: "Maybe next time." I tried to sound like Maxine. I made up my mind, there would be a next time, or I would die!

The first week of November found me working more hours in and out of the newspaper office than I thought possible. The probation period was never mentioned. My typing improved markedly. Days passed quickly, and almost before I noticed the high school football season was drawing to a close. League championships hung in the balance, and the University of Michigan and Notre Dame were both pursuing postseason bowl bids. The fact that Chief had allowed me complete autonomy in the focus of my articles had served to push me beyond the required fifty hour week; no salary adjustment.

The role of "Chuck Scott, Sports Reporter for *The South Haven Tribune*" suited me. So much so that Maxine dropped out of sight and out of mind. Until, that is, the completion of my second full week as sports reporter. Just before the start of church services one Sunday, Maxine, appearing unable to find a seat, sat down in the pew between Dad and me. This took me by surprise, but I was happy to see her; a little embarrassed that I had sort of forgotten about her.

Maxine's comfort level with my father amazed me. Other than the Chief and close relatives, I had personally never been truly at ease around older people. Dad was all smiles, obviously enjoying Maxine's attention. Who wouldn't? She was pretty, no doubt about that. Whispering to each of us, and occasionally to Mom, she fit in like a bug-in-the-rug.

Following the first hymn, Maxine leaned toward me and whispered: "How's your job been going? I've been thinking about you. Please come over and tell me all about what you've been doing."

Maxine had a way of talking to me that caused me to sit a little straighter. Blood rushed near the surface of my skin. She thrilled me and I searched for a suggestive response. All I could think of, but didn't say, was: *"Maybe next time."* Fortunately, the Morning Prayer saved me. A simple smile served as my reply.

During the remainder of the church service, I thought of nothing else but my next conquest of Miss Martin. The usual intermingling and conversation between friends and neighbors followed the church service. I found it difficult to maneuver into a position where I could discreetly ask Maxine out. Thankfully, that opportunity presented itself just before heading for home. Maxine asked me how the Coupe was doing. Smiling, I asked her if I could take her for a ride and possibly a soda Tuesday night. "Make it Wednesday and you can come by around six thirty."

"See you then," I smiled as I wondered at Maxine's reason for Wednesday instead of Tuesday. Did she simply want to make our going out happen on her terms, or did she have some other commitment?

Moving through November and into December I fell into two routines, work and Maxine. Maxine and I would see each other two or three times a week. I'd typically drop by once during the week, and Friday or Saturday we'd go out on a more formal date. We saw each other in church every Sunday, usually sitting next to each other. It seemed to me that our parents were spending a little more time with each other than usual. Work was falling into an anticipated schedule of basketball games and holiday events. I enjoyed the work and the added sense of independence it afforded me.

However, the exhilaration that accompanied the first few weeks began to dissipate, and I began to map out alternative destinations in my mind, not aware of the turn that my life was about to take.

III
JAKE WINTERS

I will never forget that frigid Tuesday morning in mid December. Tuesdays and Wednesdays had become routine, and honestly, rather dull. The jingling bell above the door announced my arrival and seemed to serve as reveille for the Chief. He immediately called me into his office and asked me to sit down. More stressed than usual, I sensed that he had something important on his mind. Rarely had I observed a staff member or even the Chief, sitting in his office. His summons appeared serious.

"Chuck, we've got a problem. Ben Summers has come down with pneumonia. I need someone to cover that murder trial down in St. Joe. You haven't handled this type of assignment before, but your work has been good; you can do it. So, you will do it?"

Ben was our lead reporter, a true professional, and the only fulltime staff member with an academic journalism pedigree. "I'm ready Chief. When does the trial start?" I gallantly blurted out.

"Yesterday," came the Chief's irresolute reply complete with raised eyebrows and voice inflection. He stared at me for two very long seconds. I wondered if he thought he might have made a mistake, assigning an ill-prepared rookie to a high profile assignment.

"Be at the county courthouse in St. Joe by nine in the morning. Give us a trial article at least every other day. Here's your press pass. There are reserved seats for newspaper reporters."

Standing to receive the pass, I responded, "Thanks Chief. I'll do a good job." I said with some conviction, wanting to reassure him while internally jumping at the opportunity.

Not expecting further instruction, I turned and left the Chief's office. Embarrassed that I didn't know more about the case, I grabbed yesterday's paper off the front office counter to see if anything had been written about it. This assignment energized me. I looked forward to a new experience, variety, and a change of scenery. I was intrigued to be a part of a trial that I soon discovered had been widely publicized. The trial of Mary Ann Starr dominated local headlines in recent weeks. I had to admit, the "Rah Rah" circuit of sports reporting was getting old.

Before I got to my desk, the Chief hollered after me. "Keep up with your sports articles. The games won't interfere with the trial."

"Right Chief."

At 8:55 A.M., I drove around the Berrien County courthouse in St. Joseph, Michigan. A bitter wind blew in off the lake and swept over the knoll above the river bluff that supported the dark, menacing courthouse. There were several heavy coated citizens milling on the landing at the top of the steps leading to the main entrance. A few people entered the building by a side door, probably employees.

I searched for a convenient location to park my car and found a space on Church Street. From there it was just a two and a half block walk. I chanced to meet two middle aged women hastening toward the trial. They informed me that they had not missed a single day and eagerly competed to bring me up to date on the two days I had missed. "The star witness, no pun intended, has yet to take the stand." They smiled knowingly at each other, obviously enjoying the little play on the defendant's last name.

The enthusiasm of my first two St. Joe acquaintances was shared by the two-dozen or so spectator hopefuls first to be admitted into the main courthouse hallway. I tried to capitalize on their excited conversations for possible insights or leads that I could use in my submissions. Bailiff Gordon Pile had cordoned off the stairway to the top floor courtroom. I scanned and evaluated the rapidly gathering crowd for perspective characters and points of view, of which there was no shortage.

Pile sternly and repeatedly announced that only 120 spectators would be admitted into the courtroom gallery. "At 9:00 A.M., the sheriff's deputies will admit, and count, spectators they allow to ascend the staircase to the courtroom."

As the hour drew near, the crowd pressed against the restraining rope and the deputies guarding the staircase. Several carried sack lunches, some women brought along knitting bags, and all sought a gallery seat. I stood tall gazing over the crowd, smugly confident I would be accorded "press seating."

I proudly displayed my official pass, as did several others who could easily be identified by the note pads they carried. As emotional anticipation grew in the crowd, a feeling of self-importance came over me—being an essential ingredient of something really significant. Fortunately, a well deserved feeling of self-doubt soon followed. I recalled telling the Chief that I would not let him down. Now I had my fingers crossed, hoping that my prophecy would come true.

Upon entering the courtroom, I identified myself as a reporter for the *South Haven Tribune*. A sheriff's deputy directed me to the second row of the gallery, reserved for members of the press. The first row appeared to be reserved for close relatives, people working for the legal adversaries, and others making a strong effort to look important. I introduced myself to those around me, making mental notes of names and affiliations. An impressive courtroom I thought. I was thrilled to be a part of it.

If ever a Midwestern trial scene could, or should, be captured for a touristy-style postcard, it was the Berrien County Circuit courtroom. A movie set could do no better. The glassy hardwood floor possessed a deep luxuriant shine and permeated the air with a faint odor of fresh varnish. The floor provided the appropriate judicial squeaks when traversed by litigants. A 20 foot high white ceiling, complete with four evenly spaced cut glass hanging chandeliers, featured a vine and leaf plaster relief that added an aura of stature and dignity. The walls opposite and to the right of the judge's bench each held six tall, though proportionately narrow, oval topped windows growing from generous blue and white marble sills. The slanting columns of light they emitted were bright and clear, no evidence of dust in the air. Five foot oak wainscoting accented all four walls that surrounded this cavernous 50' x 55' hall. A massive elevated judge's desk occupied the front and center of this spacious third floor room. The witness stand bisected the distance from the bench to the jury box on the left. To the right was designated space for the court officer/bailiff, the court recorder/stenographer, and sheriff's deputies as needed. Behind the bailiff's chair stood an elegant seven-foot tall grandfather clock crafted from cherry wood.

A three-foot high oak bar 15 feet in front of the judge's desk separated gallery space for up to 150 spectators. The exact center of the wall to the right of the gallery featured 12 foot solid oak double doors with balancing intricate constitutional etchings. All desks, tables, chairs and complementary furnishings were highly polished dark stained oak. The wall behind the judge's desk displayed a 10' x 20' mural depicting the French explorer Rene LaSalle trading with Indians. In 1679 LaSalle established a fort at the mouth of the *Riviere des Miamis*, the St. Joseph River, and traded with Potawatomie Indians. This very location was reported to be LaSalle's final rendezvous before launching his Mississippi Valley exploration. The mural was both impressive and appropriate. Hidden behind the mural were two separate rooms, the judge's private chamber and the jury room. All in all, this was a proper setting for an artist's rendering of American jurisprudence.

When an eclectic assemblage of characters was added to this backdrop, the quintessential depiction of American justice, or possibly an American tragedy, was created. First, there was a young out-of-town judge, joined by a defense team made up of a disinclined, stody old lawyer in need of work, and a flamboyant latecomer determined to free the oppressed and downtrodden. A complementary set of attorney players made-up the prosecution team. A Chief Prosecutor, whose dual ancillary objectives were to defend himself while exonerating his schoolboy mentor, and his prosecuting assistant, who had recently won election for Chief Prosecutor and was on a mission of self-aggrandizement. Completing the main cast of characters competing for neon billboard recognition was the defendant, the most attractive woman in the county, perhaps in all of Michigan!

There were numerous uniquely fascinating members in the supporting cast, but most important was the ever present, rambunctious gallery of local citizens. Made up of an equitable cross-section of Berrien County's electorate, there were farmers, merchants, homemakers, tradesmen, newspaper reporters, bankers and service workers in the crowd. Women took up over half the gallery seats, but represented only two of the jurors and none of the courthouse staff with the exception of the court stenographer; reportedly left behind by LaSalle. All dressed professionally in what was colloquially described as "preachin' cloths", or Sunday best.

"All rise!" Shouted Bailiff Gordon Pile, followed by his reverberating preamble in honor of the inflowing presiding judge and the great State of Michigan. Before I could catch my breath, "Whack," the judge's gavel smacked the top of his desk. Thus began day three of the murder trial of Mary Anne Starr—my first.

Judge Tobey D. Jackson, 33, a lean, clean, severe looking man was reported to be the youngest circuit court judge in the state. He received his first judgeship in 1934, an appointment to fill a vacant Hillsdale County position. The sitting Berrien County Circuit Judge, Freeman Warren, had requested to be removed from the trial due to a blurred conflict of interest. Jackson was appointed to replace Warren as the presiding judge for *The People of the State of Michigan v. Mary Anne Starr.*

Before the prosecution could call its first witness, Judge Jackson decided to review his expectations for proper courtroom decorum. He cautioned the gallery about reacting in any way to questioning and testimony. Their proper place was to "be seen and not heard. The gallery properly served the court by remaining invisible. If I have to, I will not hesitate to clear the courtroom of all spectators."

"He threatened to do that at least twice yesterday," whispered Mike Halamka, a reporter for the *St. Joseph Herald* Press who was seated on my right. Halamka was to become my confidant and significant source of relevant information. Everyone sat quietly, if not attentively, impatient to get on with the trial; me too.

When finally permitted to do so, the Chief Prosecutor, W. C. Foster, called his first witness of the day. A murmur passed through the press corps, anticipating that the person called may be the conclusive eyewitness to the shooting.

"The prosecution may rest its case by noon." Halamka fed me a constant translation of what was transpiring, as if I didn't understand. Self-consciously, I borrowed some paper from him to take notes. A fear of looking out of place encouraged me to imitate those around me. The other reporters were vigorously writing in their notebooks.

"Chuck," I whispered to myself, "you aren't covering a reserve football game in Bloomingdale. We're not talkin' from a final score here!"

"The State calls Benton Harbor Police Sergeant Jake Winters to the stand." A uniformed Sergeant Winters marched stiffly toward Bailiff Pile, who waited with his Bible and swore in the witness. Winters took his place in the witness chair.

Foster covered the basic questions of name, address, employment, but then came straight to the heart of what prosecutor and witness were there for—to prove the defendant guilty of premeditated murder.

"Sergeant Winters, where were you on the morning of October 17?" Foster began his questioning in earnest.

"I was the duty officer at the Benton Harbor Police Station located in the city municipal building."

"Can you tell us what you experienced shortly after midnight?"

"Around twelve twenty, Bob Eastwood came into the police station and said, 'Winters, I want to see you. I want to see you alone.' Then Mrs. Eastwood came down the stairs."

"By 'Mrs. Eastwood' you mean?" the prosecutor interrupted.

"Mrs. Starr. I've always known her as Bob's wife. So, I took Bob into the Chief's office. He said his wife was bothering him."

"Was Bob sober?"

"As far as I could tell, he was."

"What was the nature of his complaint?"

"He said his boy came to see him from Kalamazoo. When he went to his law office, Mrs. Starr told him his dad was out of town. She started swearing at him and told him to 'get the hell out of town.' Then she tried to lock him in the office, but the boy escaped."

Defense Attorney J.P. Pinehurst objected. "This is all hearsay, Your Honor, not in the presence of the witness." Judge Jackson casually overruled the objection, permitting the questioning to continue. The defense team was clearly upset concerning the admission of hearsay testimony. However, from the defendant's body language, no one would have suspected she was anything other than an interested, pretty woman.

"Could Mrs. Starr hear what Bob was saying?"

"Yes, she stood outside the door yelling, 'It's a lie!' He said he and his son had spent Saturday night at the Dwan Hotel, bowled some, and on Sunday when he wanted to take the boy home, he couldn't find his car. So, he got his friend Izzy Genoa to take them to Kalamazoo and Mrs. Starr chased them all the way."

"What did he say then?"

"He said he wanted to get some rest at the hotel, and wanted me to make sure she didn't bother him. Mrs. Starr started to come into the Chief's office and Bob pushed her out. When she tried again, Bob started for her and I stopped him and told her to stay out. Then Bob threatened her, and I told him that if she caused trouble he should do nothing but call me. Then I told Bob to go to the hotel."

"And what did Mrs. Starr do?"

"She started to follow him, but I stopped her. I told her that if she went to the hotel and started anything, I'd have to arrest her. I asked her if she understood, and she said: 'Yes, I heard you.'"

"Was she angry?"

"Yes."

"Would you say she was very angry?"

"Yes, I would."

"How long did you detain Mrs. Starr at the station after Bob left?"

"Oh, two or three minutes. I told her to go home and the next day she and Bob could patch things up. I thought it just another family row."

Judge Jackson interrupted and called for the morning recess. A well-timed break as the questioning appeared to be moving into the actual shooting episode. The defense team was still festering over the admission of hearsay testimony.

During the 15 minute recess, Halamka pointed out to me some of Starr's relatives. Her son Donald, and daughter Ruth Anne, were accompanied by a sister LaVonda Rogers from Ligonier, Indiana. Donald and Ruth Anne were 17 and 15 respectively. They were both high school students at Cromwell High School in Cromwell, Indiana and living with the defendant's parents, William T. and Mary Adams of Kimmell, Indiana. The defendant's mother, who walked with a limp, had attended the first two days of the trial, but didn't seem to be present. I felt proud of my success in acquiring and recording these kinds of details, in addition to actual testimony.

I reviewed the facts before me: Eastwood had been killed in the middle of Wall Street between the front steps of the police station and the front steps of the Carnegie Library across the street. The library faced the intersection of Sixth Street and Wall Street, while the municipal building faced Wall Street. Fellow reporters worked feverishly. On my borrowed paper, I sketched the street layout of the murder scene.

Following recess, Judge Jackson reminded Deputy Winters that he was still under oath. Prosecutor W.C. Foster—W.C. stood for William Carlos—continued a rather tedious questioning of Winters. His questions, Halamka informed me, were designed to corroborate the testimony of four previous eyewitnesses to the shooting death of Robert Eastwood and its immediate aftermath. I thought about asking my new mentor if it was possible for me to review the testimony I had missed.

After hearing what sounded like gunshots, Deputy Winters testified, he prepared to go investigate. Before he could strap on his holster, three men rushed into the station. One of them, Fireman Dutch Van Horn, brought Starr into the station.

"What did you do then?" questioned Foster.

"I asked what happened. She said, 'I killed him.' I took her into the Chief's office. Then she said, 'He had it coming to him for a long time. I had to eat dirt; now he's going to eat dirt.'"

"Your witness," a self-assured Foster abruptly concluded.

On cross-examination, defense counsel Glenn Biglow probed Winters for inconsistencies, but found little. Then he asked, "Was Eastwood drunk?"

"No, not that I could tell."

"Had Mrs. Starr been drinking?"

"I don't believe either had been drinking; they were both mad as near as I could tell."

"Was Eastwood mad?"

"Yes he was."

"You say he shoved her out the door. Did he hit her?"

"No, he did not."

"Was he gentle, or did he use considerable force?"

"Well, he wasn't gentle."

Winters's answer brought a smattering of light laughter from the gallery. "Whack!" went the judge's gavel, followed by yet another severe gallery scolding. "This won't happen again or I'll clear the court!" snarled Jackson. I sheepishly glanced around to see if anyone had noticed me jump when Jackson smacked his gavel.

Biglow asked Winters to explain the circumstances concerning the Eastwoods reporting of a prowler at their home. "Last summer, two of us were sent to investigate a report of a prowler at 400 Parker Avenue. Since that address is outside the city limits, we did it as a favor for the county. Some clothes hanging on a clothes line had been vandalized."

"Was that the extent of this matter?" Biglow continued.

"Pretty much. Anne said they had seen a prowler in front of their office on Pipestone St. She gave us a license plate number."

"And did you follow-up on the license plate?"

"No, I don't believe so."

"Why not?"

"They were supposed to come to the station and file a formal complaint the next day. They never did. We don't keep records on complaints outside the city limits."

Biglow pressed Deputy Winters further. "Do you believe they were seriously concerned about the prowler?"

"Maybe. Bob said he was going to get a gun because he worried about Anne being alone at home on several nights."

"I notice you have referred to Mrs. Starr as Anne."

"Yes, I think I said several of us at the station knew her as Anne Eastwood, Bob's wife."

"Did Mrs. Starr have a black eye when she first came into the police station the morning of October 17?"

"Yes, the left one."

"Was there a change in her condition when she was brought into the station following the shooting?"

"She had a goose-egg over her left eye."

"Thank you, Deputy Winters. That's all." With that Attorney Biglow concluded his cross-examination and the deputy was excused.

Prosecuting Attorney Foster turned to a young man seated behind him in the first row of the gallery. They spoke quietly for a minute.

"Call your next witness Mr. Foster," the impatient judge bellowed.

Foster told the young man to take the gum out of his mouth, and then turned to face the bench. "The State wishes to call Houston Eastwood." Judging from Foster's facial expression, new trial revelations were on the horizon.

IV
THE BLONDE

"My name is Houston Eastwood. I live with my mother and three sisters at 2000 Monroe Avenue, Kalamazoo. I'm 16 and a sophomore at Kalamazoo Central."

"Thank you."

Assistant Prosecutor, Robert M. Spears, commenced the questioning of young Eastwood. "Please tell this court what you recall of your last meeting with your father, Robert Eastwood."

"Well, on Saturday I hitchhiked to Benton Harbor and went to my dad's office. The blonde told me to 'get the hell out of town or I'll call the police.'"

"By the 'blonde,' do you mean the defendant, Mrs. Starr?"

"Yes, she's sitting right over there," the witness pointed at the defendant.

"Did she say anything else to you?" Spears continued.

"She called me names that I can't repeat here."

"Did you say anything to her?"

"Yes, I told her it was my dad's office and I had as much right as she did to be there."

"What happened then?"

"She and her friend left the office. I left at the same time. I think her friend is sitting right over there. The..."

Spears interrupted, "Please Houston, just answer the question I ask you. What did you do then?"

"I went looking for my dad over at Uncle Harley's, but he wasn't there." Huston paused expecting another question that didn't come. He continued, "Aunt Maude and Uncle Harley were home. I went with Uncle Harley to hang campaign posters around the county. When we got back, he dropped me at the police station to have the police take me to my dad's house. Uncle Harley said he was afraid there would be trouble if he went there with me."

"Was there trouble when you went there?"

"No. The blonde was there. She told the policeman that Dad was downtown. Then he took me back to Uncle Harley's. Dad was there."

Judge Jackson interrupted, noting that it was approaching twelve-o-clock. He requested the witness to step down and for Pile to call for a noon recess. Complying, Pile reminded us that court would reconvene at 1:00 sharp.

Before I could get up, Halamka, once again seated next to me, informed me that Harley Eastwood was the younger brother of Robert Eastwood and at the time of the murder, Harley was running for election as Berrien County Prosecuting Attorney against Spears. Spears, a Republican, defeated Harley in that election as had Foster defeated him in the previous two elections. "Harley Eastwood won't give up."

I needed the break. Leaving the courthouse, I approached a sneaky looking but well-dressed gentleman, earnestly smoking a cigarette near the front steps. "Excuse me sir, which way to the lake?" Obviously amused by my query, he sneered and nodded his Fedora-covered head, "Walk three blocks that way, you can't miss it."

"Thank you," I replied, but from the amused expression on his face, I thought he should be thanking me for bringing a little levity to his day. Following his instructions, I discovered Lake Michigan from the bluff in front of the famed Whitcomb Hotel. I sat on a bench next to a water fountain protected by two half-naked nymphs. Hungrily I devoured the roast beef sandwich and piece of apple pie—with a slice of cheese—Mom had packed for me. I gulped down the lunch oblivious to the cold. From there I found a nearby drinking fountain to wash everything down.

St. Joe was a quaint town at the mouth of the St. Joseph River. I spent most of the noon recess scouting out places I wanted to show Maxine. Day dreaming about our last rendezvous could have easily taken up my entire afternoon. She had a quixotic way of weaseling into my thought process. While walking around the compact business district, I realized I was freezing; intermittent slivers of determined snowflakes blew past me from the lake. I headed for my car.

The Coupe handily accommodated my desire for a short sightseeing tour. We headed towards the lake. No directions required the second time. At the beach I got out and walked through a deserted amusement park. Nearing the piers that channeled the St. Joe River into Lake Michigan, I stopped in front of a large globular building. The sign read, **Shadowland Ballroom**. Closed, cold and desolate, it possessed a spectacular setting. I could have wandered here all afternoon, but I knew if I didn't hurry, I'd be late getting back to the courthouse.

By the time I got there, the staircase to the top floor was closed; Pile's sentries posted. If I hadn't had the press pass, I would never have been readmitted. I entered the courtroom as quietly as possible and excused my way back to an open seat next to Halamka, all the time enduring the cold stare of Judge Jackson. Fortunately, he constrained himself as the trial proceeded. I felt I had dodged a bullet or much worse.

Halamka had saved me the seat. He told me that Jackson called the court to order at precisely 1:00 P.M. and assistant prosecutor Spears recalled Houston Eastwood. I could see Houston basking in his time on stage answering Spears' questions. The grandfather clock registered one-fifteen. Not too late, I self-vindicated.

"Uncle Harley loaned Dad his car and we drove out in the country to interview a client. Later that afternoon, we went to the office and Dad had a meeting with the same man. From the window I saw the blonde drive by looking up at the office." Houston was explaining what he and his father did on October 16, Sunday. I felt confident I hadn't missed anything important. Just give me the score and I'll write the story, I confidently thought to myself.

"Did you see Mrs. Starr again that day?" Spears guided Houston's memory.

"Yes, while we were waiting for Dad's friend to take me home. We were sitting in front of the hotel and she drove by looking at us."

"And what did your father do?"

"He got real nervous so we went inside."

"Is that all?"

"Well when we started for Izzy's car, which was parked where they are repairing pavement, she spotted and followed us."

"Wait a minute, I'm confused. I thought you and your father had your Uncle's car."

"We did, but Dad had to give it back and the Blonde had Dad's car."

At this point Spears clarified, "Let the record show that Izzy is one Isadore Genoa, and that Mr. Genoa's car was parked on West Main Street approximately one city block south of the Dwan Hotel." This all seemed odd to me, but was of no great concern.

"Is that all, Houston?"

"Well, she followed us to Kalamazoo and passed us several times. Dad gave me seven dollars when he dropped me off at home."

"Was that the last time you saw your father alive?" Spears asked in a low sympathetic voice.

"Yes."

Spears turned towards the defense team, "Your witness."

Attorney Biglow rose from behind the defense table, "I have just a few short questions for this witness. First, Mr. Eastwood, did you ever call Mrs. Starr names?"

"No, I never did."

"But you never addressed her as Mrs. Starr. Is that right?"

"I never knew her name before..." Houston stammered.

Biglow quickly continued, "Did Mrs. Starr lock or try to lock you in your father's law office?"

"No, she never did."

"Did you tell anyone that Mrs. Starr locked you in that office?"

"No, I never did."

Halamka leaned toward me and whispered, "In his opening argument, Foster claimed that Starr locked the boy in the office."

"When was the first time you saw Mrs. Starr after arriving in Benton Harbor October 15, Saturday?"

"At my dad's office. She and another lady were preparing to leave. Everything was quiet, and I thought something was fishy. I walked out between the two women."

"Mr. Eastwood, you previously testified that Mrs. Starr was swearing at you and telling you to get the hell out of town! Have you forgotten?"

The boy flushed in the face weakly responded, "She did swear."

"Where did you go from the office?" Biglow asked.

"To Uncle Harley's, and I went with him to hang posters, like I said this morning."

"You eventually found your dad and spent Saturday night with him at the Dwan Hotel?"

"Yes."

"He took you back to Kalamazoo Sunday evening?"

"Yes, Dad and his friend."

"I have no more questions for this witness, Your Honor."

"The witness may step down." Judge Jackson looked down at an inattentive prosecuting team. With noticeable annoyance he inquired, "Does the State wish to call its next witness?"

Attorney Foster stood-up, hesitated as if unsure of what to say, and then announced, "The State of Michigan rests Your Honor."

A perceptive rumble of revelation passed through the congested courtroom. The tension in the air was palpable, as anticipation of future courtroom drama soared. Most were skeptically surprised by the early resting of the prosecution's case, but eager to move forward; with the possible exception of the Starr defense team. Pinehurst and Biglow sat stoically; motionless.

"I hope the defense is ready to present its case?" Not a wish, but a command from an impatient judge. Observing no instant response from the defense attorneys, Jackson firmly stated his expectation that significant progress would follow the afternoon recess. Then Jackson requested Bailiff Pile to announce recess, with a reconvening at 2:25 P.M.

During the recess I took a quick bathroom break, and then returned straight back to my second row seat. I had no intention of ever being late again. In the down time I must have fallen asleep at my post because when I woke Bailiff Pile was calling the court back into session.

"State your name and occupation for the court."

"Aaron H. Barth. I'm the Chief Deputy for the Berrien County Sheriff's Department. County Sheriff Donald L. Diamond is my immediate superior officer."

No more that 30 seconds after the proclaimed start time, and Biglow had already called and launched the defense's questioning of its first witness. "How long have you been on the force?"

"Nine years."

"Deputy Barth, do you recall where you were and what you were doing at approximately 8: 00 A.M. the morning of October 17?"

"Yes sir, I was at the county jail preparing to fingerprint and photograph Anne Eastwood; I mean Mary Anne Starr."

"Did Mrs. Starr say anything to you at that time?"

"She said, 'How's Bob?' I was adjusting the camera and had my back to her. I said, 'He's dead.' I heard a thump and when I turned around, she was laying on the floor; fainted."

Five of Barth's photos of Starr were then entered into evidence. However, no pictures were taken of her as she lay unconscious.

The proceedings did not make perfect sense to me. But, starting with their first witness, the defense's strategy materialized picturing the defendant in an altered state of mind, allegedly the result of Eastwood beating her. I couldn't see how a person's state-of-mind mattered one way or the other. Self-defense, sure; if someone is trying to kill me, I have the right to do whatever is necessary to save my own life. But, Starr shot Eastwood in the back, twice, and then finished him off with two bullets in the head. That had been common knowledge from the time of the murder. What's insanity got to do with it? This issue became the source of lively debate within the press corps.

To me, an insanity defense was itself pure insanity. An outline for a feature newspaper article began to take shape in my mind. By the time I could get my focus back to what was transpiring between Biglow and his witness, several questions and answers had escaped my notice.

"What did you do then, Deputy Barth?"

"I took Mrs. Starr to her home. I told her to get a good night's sleep and she could work things out with Bob in the morning."

This was the last question and answer of direct examination, and it left me perplexed. Hadn't Deputy Barth just told Starr that Bob was dead, and now he is telling her to work things out with Bob in the morning? I was lost, but too embarrassed to ask Halamka for what I had missed.

On cross examination, Foster asked Barth if he had understood that Mrs. Starr and Attorney Eastwood had worked out their differences in the past. "Had they previously patched things up after arguing?"

"Yes, they must have. I recall two or three additional altercations between them."

"To your knowledge, they always worked things out didn't they?"

"I don't know differently."

Barth was allowed to step down from the witness chair. Everyone but me knew what was going to happen next. An indescribable unrest came over the courtroom. I felt as if a runaway locomotive was racing through the dark straight towards me. As I looked around the room for a clue, the notion passed through my head that I had unwittingly wandered onto the train's tracks...and was utterly unprepared.

Judge Jackson swung his gavel. "Order!" The raucous commotion dissipated as if he had turned-off the volume of a blaring radio. Quiet, and then..., "Next witness!"

V
NEXT WITNESS

"Next witness!" the judge's command reverberated throughout the great room. Even though he wasn't watching me, I carefully watched him. He looked too young to be a judge. I didn't know if there was an age requirement, but he seemed boyish and his high-pitched voice undermined his desired air of authority. He glowered down toward the cluttered defense table over sterile horn-rimmed spectacles. His piercing voice had broken the uneasy silence of anticipation that bound the breathless courtroom, which was filled to capacity. The gallery's anxious suspicions were confirmed when a soft-spoken, brown-bearded defense attorney leisurely rose to his feet.

"May it please Your Honor? The defense wishes to call Mary Anne East...sorry Your Honor, Mary Anne Starr to the witness stand." The stylishly attired attorney's carefully crafted partial name miss-statement sparked an irritating sensation among the prosecution team. No vocal response—just an arched eyebrow or two.

A muffled flurry of excited whispers accompanied the strikingly attractive young defendant as she strode confidently in front of the judge's bench. "Order!" shouted the black-robed jurist, in yet another dubious display of resolute authority. The courtroom hushed as the young woman avowed to tell the truth and assumed her place in the witness box. She sat straight, legs crossed, her back not touching the chair. Slowly she turned her head and reviewed the entire courtroom.

"Please state your full name and current address."

"Mary Anne Starr. I live at 400 Parker Avenue."

"Is that a Benton Harbor address?"

"Yes it is, but it's in St. Joseph Township."

"What is your occupation?"

"I manage my husband's law office at 139 Pipestone St. in down town Benton Harbor."

"Objection!" Cried the Chief Prosecutor, springing to his feet and slamming both thighs into the bottom of the prosecutor's table. A startled audience stared in unison as an incompatible echo followed; the prosecutor's chair toppled over behind him.

"Sustained!" Shouted the judge of the same opinion, but not to be up-staged in his own courtroom. "Mrs. Starr, in the future please refer to the deceased by his formal name, not an alleged marital status."

The defendant, tilting her head forward and eyes slightly upward toward the judge, replied softly but clearly: "Yes, Your Honor. I'm sorry."

And so began the testimony of Mary Anne Starr, on trial for murdering Walter Robert Eastwood October 17, 1938, just 30 minutes after midnight. The stately grandfather clock peering over Bailiff Pile's right shoulder read nine minutes past four. The conclusion of day three approached.

Defense attorney J.P. Pinehurst was in charge of the direct examination of his client. Even though he had just recently joined in Starr's defense, he had confidently assumed the position of lead attorney. Prefaced by only a cursory examination of her childhood and first marriage, Pinehurst swiftly moved to questions concerning the defendant's relationship, alleged and otherwise, with the deceased.

"When did you first come to know Robert Eastwood?"

"I first became acquainted with Bob in 1929, the very last day of December. I had charge of the soda fountain and dining room for the Madison Drug Store in the Hotel Burdick building. One morning when I came in, one of the girls handed me a note. It said: 'I would like a date with you.' It was signed Robert Eastwood. I didn't know him, so I threw it away. About two days later the same girl handed me another note. This one said: 'I will call you Saturday night. I **must** have a date with you.' I threw that note away, too.

That Saturday night our landlady called me to the phone twice. She said the caller was Robert Eastwood. I refused to take the first call, not knowing a Robert Eastwood. He called again and she insisted I answer it and tell him to stop calling. When I answered the phone, Bob introduced himself to me and suggested that he take me for a drive and out to dinner Sunday. I said: 'I'm sorry Mr. Eastwood, but I don't know you. I'm not in the habit of going out with men I have not met and been properly introduced to.' He said: 'I'm coming over Sunday to take you for a ride.'

I repeatedly said no, that I did not go out with people I did not know. He persisted. I finally said: "All right, I'll go if you take my two children along," thinking that would discourage him. He surprised me and said he'd pick the three of us up at one on Sunday. I remember it was the last day of the year the stock market crashed." [During a careful investigation, it was discovered that Starr's recollection of her first meeting with Eastwood was off by two days.]

"What did you do during that first meeting?"

"We went for a drive over to Paw Paw. Bob wanted to call-on a fellow attorney he had been doing some work with, a Mr. Bill Barnard. We stayed in the car while the two of them met in Mr. Barnard's office. Then we continued a nice drive through the countryside and when we returned home, my children got out of the car and ran into the house.

As I tried to follow them, Mr. Eastwood took hold of my arm. 'Please sit down a minute. I want to talk to you. I'd like to take you out to dinner tonight.' I told him I didn't think I should go under the circumstances."

"What was your impression of Robert Eastwood?"

"I felt sorry for him. He was dirty. His face was dirty. His body was dirty and I was not in the habit of associating with that kind of people. I think he slept in his clothes. I soon found out he was sleeping in the back of his office. It was clear to me that he was down on his luck. But, he persisted. He was smart, charming and kind to me and my children."

"Were you concerned about Mr. Eastwood's marital status?"

"Yes. When I eventually agreed to go out to dinner with him, the first question I asked, 'Mr. Eastwood, I don't know you. Are you married? If you are, I don't want to go.' At that time Bob told me that he was not married. I asked if he had ever been married and he said yes but that he was divorced. I asked if he had any children and he said no. After that he continued to come to my apartment frequently."

As Pinehurst prepared to ask his next question, the judge interrupted. "Due to the lateness of the hour and without objection, I'm going to recess for today. The witness may step down."

As the defendant gracefully descended from the witness chair, returning to her two attentive attorneys, her presence mesmerized the spellbound courtroom. *Did she really do it? Why? Where did she come from? How did she wind-up here?* The intriguing young woman had piqued community curiosity and emotions while sharing newspaper headlines with such contemporary notables as movie star Bette Davis, Nazi dictator Adolf Hitler, and writer/actor Orson Welles and his "Martians."

Mary Anne Starr's brief 20 minutes, more on stage than on a witness stand, proved an enticing foretaste for future trial drama. Because of constant newspaper notoriety, in less than two months she had emerged from virtual anonymity to the most widely recognized person in Southwestern Michigan. Had the situation been less ominous, Mrs. Starr would have reveled in all the attention. She reported later that, "A pleasurable adrenaline rush stirred me to the quick." Everyone looked forward to the next day's trial session.

The judge had paused briefly to allow the defendant to return to her seat. Then he requested the bailiff to declare court adjourned until 9:30 A.M. and banged his gavel to the desk. The raring-to-go bailiff smartly complied, jumping to attention and ordering all to rise as the judge briskly retired to his chamber. The trial was adjourned for the day.

Instantly the courtroom erupted into a cacophony of excited voices. A swarm of reporters rushed to the respective adversaries, but primarily to the defendant and her attorneys. Starr possessed a natural proclivity to meet, greet and socialize with people. However, her attorneys had counseled her that she must not speak with reporters. "Reporters are not your friends." Pinehurst, no stranger to the public eye, definitely preferred handling the public relations chores personally.

"Harlot! Shameful harlot!" screamed a pasty middle-aged woman with burning black eyes standing next to the gallery's center aisle. This prim and proper lady had crocheted quietly in her third row seat throughout the day's proceedings, seldom looking up from her needlework. Her seeming trial disinterest unexpectedly morphed to a wrathful demonstration. This incongruous outburst was not lost on thirsting reporters, two of whom instantly descended on her for additional quotes. She timidly complied.

Two uniformed sheriff's deputies quickly and politely maneuvered the defendant between inquiring reporters and other engrossed spectators, and out of the courtroom. The three traveled down a back staircase, out a side door and across the street to the Sheriff's House. This was the normal route followed by incarcerated trial defendants.

The Sheriff's House served as living quarters for the county sheriff and his family. It was connected in the back to the county jail that butted up against the St. Joseph River. Once inside the foyer, the defendant was allowed a few minutes to meet and talk with her children and sister. Following a short visit, the deputies escorted Starr directly to her cell.

Starr seemed to enjoy her courtroom role and was clearly not ready to adjourn. Most anything would be preferable to the austere concrete cell that had become her home for the last two months.

I remained seated, awestruck by what I had witnessed. Feelings of inadequacy and self-doubt swept back and forth in my head like Lake Michigan waves lapping at the nearby ice-encrusted beaches. The judge was such a little would-be Napoleon. The attorneys appeared well educated and articulate, but blindly polar in their interpretations, which struck me as amateurish. And what was I to make of the long hair and beard sported by Pinehurst? Newspaper reporters were too aggressive, too self-confident, too self-important, and too numerous. What were they, we, competing for anyway? I remember feeling confused.

Admittedly, a "new" newspaper reporter, I found the defendant fit none of my preconceived notions for criminal trial defendants, which I'll confess didn't go much further than Al Capone or Lizzy Borden. It was my opinion that a criminal stands trial to be proven guilty and if not, they got off lucky. Criminals were people like Clyde Barrow and Bonnie Parker; bank robbers, killers. Mary Anne Starr did not fit my image of a Bonnie Parker or a Lizzy

Borden. But she did shoot and kill Robert Eastwood; no doubt about that among row two occupants.

Mary Anne Starr had hair the color of the spun gold of childhood stories and nursery rhymes. Her clear, blue eyes seemed radiant when she gazed in my direction. Her voice was smooth, enchanting. Try as I might to be sophisticated or professional about such matters, her form, tightly packaged in a 5' 6", 125 lb. frame, was every man's dream. I had to find out more about this lady—it was my job—I'm Chuck Scott, investigative reporter for the South Haven Tribune.

I distinctly remember living this daydream following my first day of trial.

It wasn't the first time I'd seen an attractive woman. At the time I'd been dating Maxine for over two months and thrilled at hearing her referred to as my girlfriend. And it wasn't my first job either. Before I went to work for the Chief, I'd worked fulltime on my dad's farm for over a year.

Until the trial, I'd been reporting high school sports and a variety of other K-12 school related events. My job and my life had become increasingly routine. This trial made things different. I could feel it from the moment I stepped into the courtroom. Maybe the trial was destiny, covering an important case, a chance to make a difference, and as Dad said, "live up to your potential."

The exhilaration of the courtroom left my head spinning. And, the apparition of Mary Anne Starr left an embedded impression beyond my inexpert ability to describe.

Blood pounded through my veins as I left the St. Joseph courthouse and headed for home, our farm a few miles west of Fennville; 43 miles all totaled. I had a million questions about the trial and its defendant. I couldn't wait to start digging into my first real journalistic assignment. The most troubling question was where to begin? As I drove, my mind was awash with the day I had just experienced. A newly acquired investigative inspiration, coupled with diminished driving concentration, resulted in three near accidents; driving off the road twice and once stalling the motor because I had forgotten to downshift while ascending a steep hill. I simply couldn't concentrate on anything but the Mary Anne Starr murder trial.

While passing South Haven, I stopped off at the office hoping to catch the Chief and tell him about my amazing day. The Chief, as usual, worked late. Bursting into his office, "Chief, you'll never believe what happened in court today!" I proceeded to fill the air with a trial description that clearly rivaled last year's famous radiobroadcast of the Lakehurst, New Jersey Hindenburg disaster.

The Chief, seated at his desk, looked up at me with an atypical calm demeanor. "Chuck, relax already. So, tell me what you know."

"That blonde, Mary Anne Starr, shot and killed her boss, lawyer Robert Eastwood, on October 17, 1938 in front of the Benton Harbor Police Station. Case closed," I reported with as much detail and finality as I could muster, and a flare I thought sure to please the Chief.

"Chuck, sit." The Chief became even less emotional and addressed me with a comatose expression exaggerated by his thick stationary forehead furrows. "Chuck," he repeated softly. "You are telling me less than I knew before I sent you to the trial. You tell me nothing." His empty stare perfectly complemented his low, steady, melodious voice.

I felt like a birthday balloon mortally penetrated by a blunt ice pick; nothing to say, and my spinning head suddenly felt like a slowing, wobbling toy top. I searched the Chief's wisdom-creased face for a sign of approval. Nothing. Just seconds earlier I had wanted to share my excitement over an assignment well done, only to find that my boss viewed what I had accomplished as an utter failure; zilch.

"Chuck." He looked down at his desk, still expressionless, and whispered, "Chuck, would you walk out of a police station and murder someone on the front steps? Can you tell me?" Then he methodically listed questions as he handed me a pencil and pushed a tablet towards me. At that moment and for reasons I can't explain, I could feel air creeping back into my deflated soul. Chief took his job seriously. And, I still had mine because he still wanted me; I rationalized.

"Chuck, questions I want answered." He listed them off in Tommy Gun fashion, and I wrote quickly, trying to keep pace.

1. Who is Mary Anne Starr?
2. Who is Robert Eastwood?
3. Why did Starr kill Eastwood?
4. What is the defense's strategy?
5. Is this a fair trial?
6. Do you know the outcome?

With each question, I realized I too wanted to know the answer. And if I wanted to know the answers, so would my readers. I scrambled to get down on paper each idea, each nuance that the Chief had offered. He gave me the structure I had been searching for on my drive from the courthouse.

"I'm sending you back again tomorrow and every day until this trial ends. And one last point, this case is not closed for this paper until I say it is! Now, get-the-hell out of here and let me get some work done. I'm late for supper already! Oh, by the way, I think Eastwood started his law career here in South Haven."

"What? Thanks Chief. I'll do better this time, I promise." I immediately turned and left the office, closing the office door quietly on my way out. Passing through the outer office, I noticed back issues of the Benton Harbor *News Palladium* bundled by month. I grabbed the October and November bundles as well as copies of December. Once safely back in the Coupe, I mulled over the events of the day. I kept returning to the Chief's unanswered question, "Chuck, would you walk out of a police station and murder someone on the front steps? Can you tell me?"

VI
INVESTIGATIVE REPORTER

My first day as an investigative reporter had been long and tumultuous, yet I felt as if I had just hit the winning home run in the World Series. I was alive and ready to go. Events of day one flashed through my mind like a theater newsreel. Up early, I had driven to St. Joe; the longest trip ever on my own. I had covered an important murder trial for the *South Haven Tribune*, just like reporters from papers in Kalamazoo, South Bend and even Chicago; and I was expected to write about it, just like they were. I had taken notes on trial witnesses Jake Winters, Houston Eastwood and Aaron Barth. I had seen the murder defendant Mary Anne Starr testify in her own defense. I had survived a scolding by my boss and was a better man for it. That was the crux of my euphoria; I had gone to work immature, childlike, and returned a changed person, more serious, more responsible. And, even if overstated, I savored the fresh feeling of accountability.

On the drive home from South Haven, I experienced an incessant ringing in my ears. The substance of the Chief's scolding had been totally unforeseen, but after further consideration, totally deserved. Hardly ever had I been reprimanded, but although hurtful, I felt supported in a professional sort of way. What did he say, "This story isn't over until I say it is!" That's a show of confidence; maybe a command? I resolved to count it as a positive, and the Chief's suggestions as a road map. I'll do more than answer the Chief's questions, I told myself. I wanted to know Mary Anne Starr and her murder trial inside and out.

Before I arrived at the farm, snow began falling. I worried that it may be difficult driving to St. Joe in the morning. The bundles of newspapers on the seat next to me now represented a tormenting treasure waiting to be discovered. Logically, there would be information about the case starting from the day of the murder. Why couldn't I remember that date? My head was packed with details and starving for more, and I couldn't remember the starting point. Get home and get to work, I thought. Then a strange possibility entered my mind; was homework in my future? And, I looked forward to it!

There was a car sitting in our driveway that I recognized as the Martin's. After putting the Coupe in the barn and giving token chase to Ginger, I went to the house. An inch of light powdery snow had fallen. A broom strategically placed by the kitchen door reminded me to sweep off my shoes before entering. Ginger thought it a game and tried to bite the broom as I swept the snow from my shoes. A faint jump toward her and she spun around and came back for more. Good to be home.

Ginger pushed between my legs to enter the kitchen ahead of me, as if announcing my arrival. The warm kitchen and supper engendered a comfortable feeling. The smells of baking filled the air with a cinnamon aroma.

"Hey, are you working nights now?" came a greeting from Maxine.

"Hey," I smiled back. "Fancy meeting you here."

Wow, did she look good. In a long tight black skirt, white form fitting blouse, one of Mom's old faded bib aprons, and her usual bright smile accented with shocking red lipstick, stood Maxine by the stove. She was apparently putting the finishing touches on a crust for an apple pie, with Mom overseeing. By all indications, they were having a good time.

"Maxine dropped by after supper and brought us a pie for dessert. Too bad you missed out," Mom teased.

"I hope not. You've eaten already?" I said turning to look at the wall clock over the sink. "Is it 7: 30?" I questioned in disbelief, looking back at Mom and Maxine. The trial had recessed at 4:30, which seemed like only minutes ago.

"Yes, but we've saved your supper." Mom salvaged a plate of meat loaf, mashed potatoes and gravy from the oven and sat it on the table, motioning for me to sit down. Maxine took a cherry pie she'd been warming in the oven and sat it on a hot pad.

"Hurry up and eat your supper. We've waited to have dessert until you got home. Where have you been?" Maxine asked as she put a fresh apple pie in the oven and set the temperature to 400 degrees. "Mrs. Scott, we'll need to take this pie out to cool in one hour."

"Thanks Maxine," Mom smiled. I wondered if my mother wished she'd had a daughter, instead of three boys. Her obvious pleasure in Maxine's company seemed to indicate that. "Go on Chuck, eat your supper. We can't enjoy Maxine's dessert until you're ready. We've been waiting patiently."

Both women joined me at the kitchen table. "Tell us about the trial," Maxine giggled as if she contemplated hearing a most interesting piece of gossip.

"Yes, I'd like to hear about it too," Dad said as he entered the kitchen and sat down with us.

As I ate supper, I thoroughly enjoyed sharing my courtroom experiences. Fascinating, I mused, not half an hour earlier there was not one single thing I could say that interested the Chief. Now, it was difficult, but not impossible, for me to eat the meatloaf while reminiscing about the trial. Both activities were pleasurable.

Josh and Ken joined the four of us at the kitchen table for a slice of cherry pie. They had been working on their homework in the living room. The dessert was very good, as was the pleasant surprise of Maxine's company. Relatives and neighbors frequently made early evening social visits and company usually arrived unannounced, but welcomed. Maxine's surprise visit flattered the Scotts, each one of us.

As we finished the pie, Maxine suggested that she had better head for home. Saying goodbyes around the table became a noisy event unto itself. "I'll walk you to the car," I said as Maxine was getting her coat.

"Best pie I ever tasted Maxine," was Dad's jovial farewell and Maxine responded with a wink and a smile, "Thanks, Mr. Scott."

Maxine pleaded softly as I opened her car door, "Can you get in for a second?"

"Slide over." We were instantly locked in an emotional embrace, almost as if we hadn't seen each other for a year and were ravenous for the feel of intimately close physical contact. When finally our lips reluctantly parted, I luxuriated in Maxine's heavy breathing, her smell, her taste.

"Shall I pick you up about seven-thirty Saturday night?"

"I can't wait to show you my new dress?"

We were planning to go to a Christmas Ball in Fennville on Saturday night. Maxine had been extended an invitation and, of course, had invited me. "I can't wait to see you in your new dress. You had better get going. Be careful, the roads are slippery."

She sighed, "I know, I told Daddy I'd be home by eight and it's way past that."

"And I've got homework," I coughed knowing how strange that sounded. A quick kiss on the lips, a squeeze and I jumped out and closed the door. We exchanged waves as she drove out the driveway. The snow had stopped. Good.

Cold. With no heat in the upstairs, I woke to a very cold bedroom. I could barely read my alarm clock from what little moonlight crept through the curtained window. It was ten minutes to five, as near as I could tell in the dim light and through sleepy eyes. I had stayed up past two reading back issues of the *Benton Harbor News Palladium*. Never before had I read newspapers with such interest and attention to detail. I found myself going far beyond the object of my research; following additional stories and newsworthy items completely unrelated to the Eastwood murder. It was reassuring to acquire a better sense of time and place.

I discovered that on one night in early November, violence against Jews erupted across Germany. It appeared to be the result of German anger over the assassination of a German official in Paris at the hands of a Jewish boy. There existed a clear suspicion that the assassination was an excuse used by the Nazis to inflict violence against Jews, their homes, businesses and synagogues.

Although I previously knew nothing of this event, it seemed analogous to the distant thunder of an approaching storm.

I wondered if the Chief kept himself abreast of European events. A hypothetical Chief retort, "You know I'm from Poland?" I could hear the Chief proclaim: "You want we should expand to an international coverage already?" An intriguing and complicated man, the Chief.

My room was cold, but I was not. Sleep had been fretful due to a busy mind. No time to waste. Downstairs to the bathroom, shave and clean up. Back upstairs, dress. On with a clean white shirt, one of two Mom had washed, ironed and hung in my closet; a solid light tan colored tie. The same brown suit I wore to court yesterday. It was my only suit—a graduation gift. A quick look in the bathroom mirror; combed my hair and straighten my tie.

Mom had taught the Scott boys, Dad included, how to properly tie a double Windsor knot. She said you could tell the character of a man by how he tied his tie. I felt good about my professional appearance and was raring to go to work on what I considered a "real" assignment, albeit, not a world event.

By five I was at the kitchen table with my notes and old newspapers, trying to glean a little more insight concerning the Eastwood murder case. Drafting a plan for research into the background of this murder and the characters involved had weighed on my mind since talking with the Chief. He had set my course. With his six questions written on top of my notebook and indelibly etched in my brain, I was determined to know everything possible, but I needed an organized plan of attack.

I started by writing down what I had learned during my first day in court, which didn't take long because it wasn't much. Basically, on October 17, 1938, a lady shot a lawyer in front of the Benton Harbor Police Station. Victim's name: <u>Walter Robert Eastwood</u>, deceased. Suspect's name: <u>Mary Anne Starr</u>, defendant, who everyone knows did it, but for whom a proper identifying label had yet to appear. This was the extent of my knowledge, and I felt uncomfortable even with this little, without further validation. Nothing certain.

How could so few facts conjure up so many questions? <u>Goal</u>: find out why Starr killed Eastwood. The next trial session may hold the answer.

Next, I wrote down the names and titles of all players remembered from yesterday who were related to the case. In several instances, the name, the title or both were left blank. Blanks must be filled. I created a timeline of events which consisted of <u>October 17, 1938</u>—the murder and <u>December 15, 1938</u>— current date. From the newspapers I developed an informational foundation, but feared misinformation from faulty news reporting and contradicting facts. Obviously, I had a lot of work to do if I expected to develop a relevant timeline, one that would help make sense out of Robert Eastwood's murder.

So much didn't make sense. Most importantly, if you planned to kill someone, would you kill him in front of a police station? After seeing Mary Anne Starr on the witness stand, I didn't want to believe she had killed anyone. But, she had indeed killed Robert Eastwood; that was an irrefutable fact.

Dad entered the kitchen about five thirty on his way to the basement to stoke the furnace. During the winter months, it was his routine to bank the coals before going to bed and get the fire going again first thing in the morning.

When he returned to the kitchen, Dad asked what I'd like for breakfast; not, "Why are you up so early? Breakfast was the only meal we were regularly allowed to start without everyone seated at the table. "A couple of eggs and bacon." I knew that was what he was going to make regardless of any request. He would fry the bacon first; baste the eggs swimming in rendered bacon grease and liberally salt and pepper the result. I loved it, and so did Dad. Dad often prepared breakfast for, as he put it, "anyone ready to go." We all understood his meaning—"go to work." You could depend on Dad's schedule, his habits and acute sense of right and wrong. He preferred having the last word, and liked to end conversations with "What's fair is fair."

He didn't ask why I was up so early, but I knew he was curious. He knew that my inspiration would eventually materialize. Well, he didn't have to wait long before I hungrily blurted out, "I'm going back to court today, and I intend to find out why this murder took place. Reading these old papers is helping me gain background."

Dad concentrated on splashing hot grease over the frying eggs to get them just right, whites hard—yokes runny. He was thinking, I could tell. Then he casually commented, "A few less lawyers wouldn't be a bad idea."

"Well," I chided him playfully, "With an attitude like that, you would be dropped from the jury panel."

From there, I launched into a complete reenactment of my courtroom observations from the day before, repeating several things from last night's discussion over cherry pie. Of course, I left out the physical description of the defendant; I didn't want Dad to form an opinion of my motives as less than of the highest standard. It pleased me that he asked me questions about the trial and what exactly I would be doing. With the little I could give him, it whetted his appetite for more; mine too.

After raising my voice in an animated account of the Eastwood murder, I suddenly feared being interpreted as self-important. I knew better, we all did. In an attempt to reign myself in, I changed the topic, and asked Dad what he had been doing the past week. It came as no surprise that he was trimming the Macs, but that he had been working completely alone left me feeling a little guilty, since I could have been working alongside. Typically, he would hire someone to help or a brother or two would come over to assist. My dad and uncles frequently went back and forth between their farms helping one another.

It was hard for me to equate what I was doing as work, when compared to what farmers did, and I knew Dad felt the same way; adding to my guilt. Our area of Michigan had received an unusually heavy snowfall the week before Thanksgiving. The depth of the snow made it next to impossible for Dad to move around the orchards trimming. "I'll catch-up," and he would.

It never mattered whether it was hot, cold, raining or snowing; Dad would be out of the house by 7:00 A.M., doing what needed to be done. He never complained, but seemed to thrive on inclement conditions. I complained. We had all heard him say, as he was going out to work in sub-20 degree temperatures, "Cold is good for the cuts. Trees heal better. I never get cold, but if I did, I'd just come in and sharpen saws. They always need sharpening."

Everyone was up before seven. As usual the house, especially the bathroom, became a beehive of activity. There was always an intense gravitational pull toward the kitchen. Warmth and hunger collaborated to create this mystifying force.

It energized me when each family member expressed an interest in what I was doing. I seized the moment, promised a full report on my return, and assured Mom I'd be home for supper. Still pitch black outside, I headed straight for the barn to crank-up the Coupe. Ginger raced back and forth past me, absorbed in some imaginary game that made life good. I couldn't wait for the trial to start.

VII
UNDER THE MOON AND STARS

It took me almost an hour to drive from the farm to the courthouse in St. Joseph. U.S. 31 all the way to Benton Harbor, same route as yesterday; the only route. I mentally reviewed what I knew about Mary Anne Starr, the murder, the witnesses, and what my goals were for the day. The drive gave me plenty of time to hash and rehash. The road was a little icy in spots, but on the whole, better than anticipated.

Arriving in Benton Harbor at approximately ten after eight, I noticed that I had passed the Dwan Hotel. Quickly, I circled the block and passed by the hotel again on Territorial Road. I determined where Starr claimed she parked her car on that fateful evening. Then I slowly drove the route Starr and Eastwood walked from the hotel to the police station. Testimony images passed through my imagination as I attempted to reconstruct the murder scene. Driving between the police station and the Carnegie Library, where the shooting had taken place, I continued west on Wall Street and soon came to and turned right on Pipestone. There I found 139 Pipestone, the office of W. Robert Eastwood, Attorney At Law—the shingle still in place. It impressed me how close these key locations were to one another. Also noted was how far from where the actual shooting took place to where alleged eyewitnesses had reported their initial locations. I questioned myself, "Did anyone really see the shots being fired?"

Spotting a small diner near the east end of the bridge between Benton Harbor and St. Joe, I stopped and went in, seating myself at a small table near the door. It didn't take me long to realize why that table sat empty, cold and drafty. At the earliest opportunity, I took my coffee and Bismarck to a rear booth. There, I sketched the streets and important buildings that were connected to the murder event.

Thinking as an investigative reporter and taking the measure of the waitress, I asked, "Have you heard of the murder of a lawyer a couple of months back?"

"You talk about 'Office Wife.' It in all papers long time," she answered with an interesting accent as she warmed my coffee.

"Yah, that's the one."

"I not know much, but nice officer come here every Friday at eight. He tell you about murder."

The clock over the counter approached nine. I became impatient, wanting to be in the courtroom with time to spare.

"Do you think he'd talk with me if I came in tomorrow? I'm a newspaper reporter," I pronounced with a mild air of authority.

She smiled, giving the impression of being unimpressed by my credentials. Staring straight into my eyes, she spoke in a serious monotone, "I think yes. He is humble man."

Her message was understood, but I didn't acknowledge it. I thanked her, paid at the register near the door and hurried for my car. Being late for court was not an option.

The parking place on Church St. awaited us—me and my Coupe. Actually, there were very few cars parked along this quiet St. Joe street. We could have parked almost anywhere, but preferred the security of the familiar. The weather was more of the same, cold and windy. A shiver passed through me on my short walk to the courthouse. I was thankful to get inside the warm and already busy hall of justice. My mind blinked twice briefly, first on Dad, alone, trimming the Macs on the back forty, and second on the Chief, "...not over until I say it is."

The gallery was over 75% full fifteen minutes before the scheduled court reconvened. I introduced myself to two more fellow reporters, one from Niles and the other from South Bend. The one from the *Niles Star* gave me a copy of yesterday's *Palladium*. The headline read: **SILVER SLAYER SOBS LIFE AND LOVE OF OFFICE WIFE.**

As the aging grandfather clock struck nine thirty, Bailiff Pile brought all to attention. Judge Jackson hurried in and banged his gavel to bench. With only a moderate undirected admonishment of yesterday's gallery behavior, he granted permission for the defense to proceed.

Attorney Pinehurst indicated a wish to continue questioning his client, Mary Anne Starr. Starr returned to the witness chair. Stylish, but not flashy, she wore a black skirt with a white blouse closed at the neck by a black wooden Scotty broche, reminiscent of President Roosevelt's pet Scottish Terrier. Her long, silver blonde hair was combed back tightly above her forehead, braided and wrapped into a crown adorning the sides and lower back of her head. On her head she wore a black pillbox hat slightly cocked right. Hose seams rising from her medium height black pumps were in perfect alignment up the back of her legs. Over her shoulders hung a short black fur stole. Men gazed at her too long, then turned away in disguised indifference. Women stared at her too long, then turned away in silent envy; a few scoffed their disapproval.

Pinehurst picked up right where he had left off the day before, continuing the evolution of the Starr/Eastwood relationship.

"As you became better acquainted with Bob Eastwood, did your opinion of him change?"

"I really came to like him. He was a very thoughtful person, kind to me and my children."

"How often would you go out together?"

"During that spring Bob would stop by our apartment two or three times a week and we would usually go out, just the two of us, once on a weekend."

"Did you ever go anyplace special?"

Starr smiled, "Bob took me to Chicago once to see a show. We had a great time. I remember he bought me a bouquet of red roses." Starr answered with a dreamy lilt in her voice.

"How would you describe the bond between you and Bob Eastwood?"

"Bob and I fell in love with each other. He asked to move in with the children and me. I thought we should be married first. That's when he admitted that his divorce was still pending, but it would be finalized soon."

"Did he mention having children?"

"I asked him if he had any children and he said he had one. I told him, 'I will not live with a married man.' A week or so later Bob told me his divorce came through."

"What did you do then?" Pinehurst continued.

"I asked to see proof, so he took me to his office." Starr hesitated.

"Please continue."

"It was the most awful place I ever saw. It was dirty. The bed was full of bedbugs. I cleaned it up, and cleaned his office." Starr's manner in answering indicated a willingness to assume responsibility.

Pinehurst shook his head. "After he kept company with you for some time, did he ask again about moving to your apartment?"

"Yes, about a month later. He said he needed to be with me."

"Did you say anything more about marriage?"

"I insisted that we be married first, before he could move in."

"What did he say?"

"He said, 'We'll take care of that.'"

Following this exchange of questions and answers, the defendant relived for the jury her common law marriage to Robert Eastwood. She testified that following a visit to her parents' farm in Indiana, she and Bob stopped at the family church on their way home. There in front of the Sparta United Church of Christ, "under the moon and stars," the couple exchanged marriage vows crafted in the moment.

Pinehurst pressed his witness, "At that point, did you believe you were legally married to Robert Eastwood?"

Answering, Starr's voice sounded questioning; pleading, "Yes, he told me we were, he was a lawyer, I trusted him." Seemingly torn between romantic memories and harsh realities, Mary Anne Starr sat even straighter, as if girding herself against an invisible force.

I was so focused on the witness and the answers she gave, the first hour of trial passed in a flash. Never before had I taken notes with such purpose. Unlike my first day, I came prepared. Each nuance held significance. Before the morning recess, I had developed several personal shorthand techniques, not wanting to miss a single word. During each break in the action, I proofed notes or crudely sketched courtroom scenes.

Pinehurst led his witness through the story of her life in Kalamazoo as it was connected to Robert Eastwood, that period of her life filled with romance, turmoil and contradictions. From what I surmised, she fell deeply in love with Robert Eastwood, a loveable lawyer who possessed a troubled mind. Although bright, typically engaging and charming, he was undisciplined, unorganized, and in the most basic professional sense, unethical.

As Starr told the court of her relationship with Eastwood, she wove an increasingly tumultuous tale. Unlike her life with first husband Marty Starr, a steady downward spiral from the beginning, her life with Robert Eastwood was one of peaks and valleys. During their first year together they shared many happy, even glamorous times together. They enjoyed an occasional movie, picnics with her children, dining with friends, and small trips—once to Detroit and once to Chicago.

However, from the very beginning, Eastwood experienced difficulties attracting and retaining clients. His law practice never thrived. Shortly after moving in with Mary Anne, Eastwood became aware that he was being investigated for possible disbarment. When information of this investigation ultimately found its way into local newspapers, their landlady became convinced they were living together out of wedlock and kicked them out.

Not long after being evicted, Mary Anne lost her managerial position of the lunch counter and soda bar at the Madison Drug Store. Since she was their only regular means of support, they were evicted again, this time for failure to pay the rent. Mary Anne felt forced to leave her children, at least temporarily, with her parents in Indiana. Her effort to protect her children served to add the strain of separation to her life. These financial and family circumstances weighed heavily on the couple and their suspect common law marriage.

During the fall of 1931, notice of Eastwood's impending disbarment appeared in the *Kalamazoo Gazette*. From that day forward, his frazzled law practice virtually ceased to exist. Eventually, he found menial employment in Sturgis. Mary Anne followed him to Sturgis, but their struggles compounded along with the slowing economy.

The official disbarment of W. Robert Eastwood came January 25, 1932. Mary Anne left Eastwood a month later, and moved by herself to Albion, Michigan. She found work as a domestic in a private home for little more than room and board. According to her witness stand testimony, she had left Eastwood several times previous to this, but he always convinced her to come back. This time she was determined not to reunite.

After living in Albion for several weeks, the local Chief of Police contacted Mary Anne through her landlord. He told her he had an official request asking him to locate a Mrs. Eastwood. She admitted to begging the police officer not to reveal her whereabouts, but that he claimed it was his duty.

"The next day Bob called; he was crying. He wanted to know if I'd come back to him in Kalamazoo. He said it was impossible for him to go on without me. After I heard his voice, I broke down. I said I would come back to him. He telegraphed me $14 to take the bus, and met me at the Burdick Hotel where he had engaged a room." Starr began weeping softly.

"Please continue," Pinehurst sympathetically encouraged.

With tears running down her cheeks, she went on, "We went up to his room. He sat beside me on the bed and prayed. I've never heard such a beautiful prayer—he asked the Lord to make him good enough for me." The witness lost her composure for a moment and sobbed openly for 10-15 seconds. Then, regaining control she continued, "He asked me never to leave him again. He made me put my hand on a Bible and promise never to leave him no matter what he did. I promised."

Starr began crying convulsively. Pinehurst requested a few minutes to help his client regain her composer, to which Judge Jackson willingly complied.

The morning recess followed; ten forty by the courtroom clock. The normal noise and conversational din of recess was noticeably restrained. Pinehurst's picture of a young defenseless woman, emotionally entangled in a strange and increasingly violent web, began to take shape.

Prior to Pile's releasing us for recess, I had already mapped my path to intercept Starr's children. I had been watching them intermittently throughout the morning session to see how they reacted to their mother's testimony. Disturbing strain darkened their facial expressions, especially the daughter's. Approach them quickly but calmly, I thought.

VIII
LATE FOR SUPPER

Meeting Donald and Ruth Anne Starr for the first time did not live-up to my expectations. However, I was sure they had no reason to believe I was just another reporter pouncing on them. I introduced myself as they were exiting the courtroom, and asked if I might walk and talk with them for a few minutes. It played to my advantage that I was only two or three years older. They told me that during the morning recesses they usually were allowed to talk alone with their mother outside behind the courthouse. "Today mother is meeting with Pinehurst to work on our strategy," Donald remarked in a manner of support.

As we talked, we walked downstairs and outside. I realized I had Donald, who wanted to be called Mickey, and Ruth all to myself. Ruth barely said a word, and although Mickey talked freely, I learned very little. For that I held myself responsible, as I feared offending them by probing too deeply into their relationships with their mother and Robert Eastwood.

I seemed to hit it off well with Mickey. He was interested in how I got my job. We all laughed when I confessed, "This is only my second day, and judging from my boss's reaction last night, I might not be back tomorrow." After I asked the two of them numerous questions about life in Indiana, Mickey suggested that if I ever got down that way, he'd be happy to show me around. "Thanks, I may take you up on that. I don't think I've ever been to Indiana." Too soon, we had to get back to the courtroom. It had started snowing.

As court reconvened, Judge Jackson recognized Attorney Pinehurst. Pinehurst requested that he be allowed to expedite trial time by calling several corroborating witnesses before recalling Starr and completing her direct examination. Jackson appeared ready to allow anything that would speed the trial along.

"If it please the court, the defense wishes to call Richard Pence." While Pence was being sworn in, the reporters around me thrashed out this divergence from normal witness succession. We tried to calculate an unusual strategy or hidden Pinehurst agenda. Although no one was able to offer a consensus explanation, all were watchful for some strange twist of events.

"Mr. Pence, what do you do for a living?"

"I'm the president of the Watervliet National Bank."

"How did you come to know the defendant?" Pinehurst asked.

"She came into the bank last May or June requesting a $500 loan so she could have her husband institutionalized. She said, 'I'm afraid he is going to lose his mind.'"

"Did you give her the loan?"

"No, would you?" That response amused several spectators and irritated a scowling Jackson.

Following Pence to the stand was Stanley Zederski. Zederski stated that he served as the county coroner and owned a mortuary business in St. Joseph. Pinehurst began questioning, "When did you first meet the defendant, Mrs. Starr?"

"Last May she came to my office and requested help in getting her husband, Bob Eastwood, admitted to the University of Michigan Hospital for mental health treatments. I told her the hospital required a family physician's recommendation."

"Why would Starr approach you in getting Mr. Eastwood medical assistance?"

"I think she had heard that my brother was on the medical staff at the University of Michigan Hospital."

"Did you assist Mrs. Starr with her request?"

"Yes, I asked Dr. Andrew White for such a recommendation letter and he agreed."

"Mr. Zederski, would you comment on Mrs. Starr's appearance when she came to your office?"

"The first time she came she had a black eye and bruises on her arms and her legs below the knees." With an embarrassed expression, he added, "That's all I could see. She was in bad shape."

Following Zederski to the stand was Dr. Andrew J. White, Starr and Eastwood's regular doctor. White told Pinehurst that he wrote a letter recommending Robert Eastwood for admission to the University of Michigan Hospital at the request of Zederski. In addition, he stated, "Prior to that, Mrs. Starr called at the office several times requesting that Eastwood be sent to a hospital for observation and treatment. She told me that his practice was slipping badly, that he was acting peculiarly to some of his clients, and that he drove one client out of the office physically."

After consultation with Eastwood and Starr, Dr. White concluded, "Since Eastwood was a Great War veteran, I arranged to have him admitted to the Hines Memorial Hospital in Maywood, Illinois. Eastwood agreed to go and personally picked up a copy of my recommendation letter. I was informed he never followed through." At that point, Pinehurst offered a copy of Dr. White's referral letter, which was admitted into evidence by Judge Jackson and read into the trial record.

The last witness called prior to the noon recess was Attorney Clarence Butler. Biglow handled Butler's direct examination. Butler gave testimony that during his last year as Justice of the Peace in Benton Harbor (1936), "Mrs. Starr came into my office with an ice pick and a torn dress and said, 'Bob attacked me with this ice pick.'" Butler described injuries about her neck and head, but that she didn't appear to be bleeding. "Starr wanted a warrant for Eastwood's arrest. She said, 'He tried to kill me with this ice pick!'"

"I told her, 'You will have to post security for costs or get an authorization for the warrant from the Prosecuting Attorney.' Later I talked to Prosecuting Attorney Foster about it, but no warrant was issued. Foster said they'd be back together again in a few days."

"Really?" Turning to the prosecutors Biglow grumbled, "Your witness."

"Isn't that just what happened?" Foster demanded without moving from his seat.

"What happened?"

"They got back together."

"As far as I know, they did."

"No more questions Your Honor."

Judge Jackson requested that Butler step down. He announced that the noon break was overdue. "Gentlemen and ladies of the jury, please remember my earlier admonition not to discuss this case with anyone, including among yourselves. Mr. Bailiff, let's have the noon recess with court to reconvene at 1:30 P.M."

I was hungry. Mom had packed a chicken salad sandwich, a generous cheese slice, a jar of fresh apple cider, and two chocolate walnut cookies. I relished my lunch while sitting with spectators on the floor of the first floor hallway. By doing so, I could listen to what the locals thought about the trial and the main characters involved in it. There was no shortage of opinions about Starr and Eastwood. Until the night of the murder, neither was well known outside the law enforcement and the legal communities. The couple had resided in Benton Harbor little more than four years.

The afternoon session began promptly at 1:30 P.M. with Mr. Pile replaying his part to perfection. Pinehurst recalled Starr. The judge reminded Starr that she remained under oath. Among the second row scribes, the consensus was that Starr would be asked to describe the eccentric behaviors exhibited by Eastwood, as well as the physical abuse she had endured. I sided with the prevailing opinion, giving me a new confident feeling.

"Mrs. Starr, will you tell this court when you first suffered physical abuse at the hands of Robert Eastwood?"

Starr put the fingers of her right hand over her mouth and cleared her throat; eyes somber. "I think it started when Bob received the official notification of his disbarment [January 25, 1932]. Bob became very angry when he received that letter. He grabbed me by both arms and shook me wildly. It hurt and left black and blue bruises on my upper arms. I thought little of it at the time. I knew Bob was suffering; not being able to practice law anymore."

"On what grounds was Mr. Eastwood disbarred?"

"Objection! Your Honor. Relevance?" questioned Foster.

"Sustained."

"Can you think of a time prior to his disbarment that Mr. Eastwood struck you?" Pinehurst asked.

"I had tried to separate from Bob several times before that. Sometimes he would become very angry, yelling and cursing at me. I'd leave him, but he would always talk me into coming back. He could be so sweet and considerate. I don't believe he ever actually hit me during those times."

"After Mr. Eastwood was disbarred, when do you next remember him physically abusive towards you?" Pinehurst continued.

"Shortly after we moved to Benton Harbor and he went to work for his brother."

Pinehurst interrupted his witness, "Let the record show that Robert Eastwood's brother is Attorney Harley Z. Eastwood, Berrien County Prosecuting Attorney from 1933-1935. Please go on Mrs. Starr."

"In March of 1934, Bob and I were returning from a visit with my family in Indiana, when we got into an argument. He slapped me and pulled a gun from under the seat, and threatened to kill me."

"Was that the end of it?"

"No, then he drove straight to the sheriff's office and turned me in, handing the gun over to an officer there. I was put in jail on a charge of assault with a deadly weapon. That's what they told me."

"How did this episode end?"

"Several hours later I was released. I suspected at first it was all a joke, and later they said it was a joke; bad joke. They told me the gun didn't work."

"Was this before Eastwood became Assistant Prosecuting Attorney?"

"Yes, the week before." A small commotion rustled through the gallery triggering a smack of the judge's gavel.

Pinehurst asked, "Did the physical abuse abate once Eastwood became a law partner with his brother and second in command at the prosecutor's office?"

Starr became emphatic, "No, if anything his spells became more frequent, often slapping or punching me."

"How would you account for this behavior?"

"Objection!" cried Spears. "Calls for a conclusion of the witness for which she is wholly unqualified."

"Sustained," replied Jackson in an uncharacteristically restrained voice. "Please sit down Mr. Spears," as he glared at Pinehurst.

"Sorry, Your Honor. Please let me rephrase the question?"

"Please," echoed the judge.

"What was Robert Eastwood's reaction to working for and with his brother?"

"Not good. Harley continually caused Bob aggravation. Bob's spells repeatedly came when he was overworked and irritated. Bob was aware that this happened to him."

"Do you recall anymore incidents of abuse?"

"Several," Starr stated emphatically. "Once, while we were staying at the Michigan Hotel here in St. Joe, Bob came in cursing Harley. He walked back and forth cursing and swearing. Then he picked up a glass and threw it at me. It struck me in the back of the head and cut me. The maid helped me comb the glass out of my hair. Later Bob came back crying. He said 'Mary Anne, can you ever forgive me for the things I do to you?' As usual he took me in his arms and begged for forgiveness," Starr answered, staring impassively over the jurors' heads. After a long pause, she continued, "Another time at the Denis Hotel, Bob threw a chair at me and then tore my dress. I still have the scar on my lip from where the chair hit me in the face." Pinehurst had Starr step down and walk to the jury box to show the jurors the scar on her upper lip as well as the remnant of a lump above her left eye.

After returning to the witness chair, Pinehurst encouraged Starr to continue her catalog of abusive events during her life with Robert Eastwood.

"While working late at the office one night last year, Bob went into one of his spells cursing the Berrien County lawyers. When I tried to calm him down, he picked me up and threw me into the hot water register. I think I may have broken a rib. It was very painful for several weeks."

At this time, Pinehurst introduced documentary proof that Eastwood's mother, Mrs. June Pearl Eastwood, had been committed to the state hospital in Toledo, Ohio on March 7, 1903, and that she died there on July 18, 1913. She had suffered from dangerous and uncontrollable mood swings. These documents were submitted into evidence and included in the trial record.

Satisfied that he had well established physical abuse, Pinehurst altered his line of questioning and asked, "What was Robert Eastwood's normal attitude, typical demeanor?"

Starr smiled, "He was very, very kind to me except when he was in one of his spells. He frequently expressed concern for my health."

"Mrs. Starr, I know this is difficult for you, but now I need to ask you some questions concerning the week prior to Mr. Eastwood's misfortune, and the reason we are here today."

"I think now would be a good time for our afternoon recess," Judge Jackson interjected before Pinehurst could frame his next question. The courtroom took a synchronized breath of relief.

The recess that followed was once again quite subdued. It gave me time to write a rough draft for the trial article I'd submit to the Chief on my way home. Fellow reporters confirmed for me the spelling of witness names. If nothing too significant happened during the last hour of court, writing the final copy would take less than thirty minutes once back at the office.

Returning to the witness stand, Mary Anne Starr showed signs of stress. Her eyes were tired, and she didn't sit as straight or with as much comfort as usual. If this had been a hard day for her; the prospects of the next day's cross-examination loomed ominously.

I also noted a weary deportment in Pinehurst's typically vigorous charisma. There were bags under his eyes and his shoulders stooped forward slightly.

Pinehurst started, "Mrs. Starr, will you tell the court what happened the evening of Wednesday, October 12 at the law office of W. Robert Eastwood?"

"We worked late getting the paper work completed for an estate settlement Bob had been handling. I thought he was taking inappropriate short cuts and offered suggestions. One thing led to another, and we started arguing. Suddenly, Bob flew into one of his spells. He hit me hard a couple of times, grabbed me, tearing off my dress, and threw me on the floor; he was on top of me slamming my head against the floor. Finally, he got off me and walked out of the office."

"What did you do then?"

"I gasped for air. My nose bled and I had blood in my mouth. At first I could hardly move, just withered in pain. When I regained enough strength to stand-up, I called Stella. When I told her I needed her help, she said, 'I'm on my way.'"

"Are you referring to Stella Stallwell?" asked Pinehurst.

"Yes, Stella Stallwell." Starr nodded acknowledgement toward her friend seated to the right of Attorney Biglow at the defense table.

"How long did it take Mrs. Stallwell to get to the office and what was your condition?"

"I think five to ten minutes at the most. She helped clean me up and get me dressed. I had two black eyes, a painful jaw, a swollen forehead above the left temple, and bruises and scrapes on my back and both arms. I could barely walk, see or talk. Stella drove me home and put me to bed."

"Was Mr. Eastwood at home when you arrived?

"No. Bob didn't come home until around noon the next day."

"Did you see Mrs. Stallwell that Thursday?"

"Oh yes. Stella came over in the morning to check on me. She doctored me and wanted me to go to the hospital. I told her she could fix me some soup. We had soup together."

"Did you consider going to the police?" Pinehurst asked.

"Stella wanted me to, but it hadn't helped in the past," Starr answered matter-of-factly.

"How did you feel the day after suffering such a vicious attack?"

Starr sighed, "I felt awful. My left eye was swollen completely shut. I could barely see out of my right eye. I had the worst headache of my life; throbbing. My forehead was swollen. When I first tried to get out of bed in the morning, I had a small nose bleed."

"What did Mr. Eastwood say when you first saw him again?"

"He started crying and begging for my forgiveness. He said he didn't understand why he hurt the person he loved more than life itself."

During this last session of the day, Foster and Spears sat unmoved. The jury listened intently, observing Starr's every move, every expression. From their outward appearance, the jury was well engaged in their patriotic civic duty. Pinehurst intermittently consulted his notes and his co-counsel.

Now, Pinehurst turned to address Judge Jackson. "Your Honor, due to the lateness in the day and the likelihood that we will complete direct examination of Mrs. Starr by the morning recess, the defense would like to request a recess for today."

"Agreed," proclaimed the Judge. He then requested Bailiff Pile to announce a recess until 9:30 A.M." Pile did the judge's bidding with his usual enthusiastic flare.

A gust of bitter cold wind from off the lake took my breath away as I walked out of the courthouse. Dark blue slivers with specks of white could be seen through the leafless trees to the west. A shiver climbed my spine, thinking of the cold water. I wondered if the lake was going to freeze over. The beaches and bluffs needed more shore ice for protection against the looming winter storms. One was brewing, from the looks of the heavy black cumulous clouds approaching from the west.

Since I had walked straight out of the building without talking with anyone, it surprised me to see Attorney Pinehurst already getting into a car at the bottom of the courthouse steps. It looked as if he was being chauffeured by two tall sturdy young men, also sporting long braided ponytails and full beards. One of the men held the car door open as the defense attorney got in. They drove a brand new silver-gray Oldsmobile.

I walked swiftly to my car, started her up and headed for home. If lucky, I could be home in less than two hours. I still had to stop at the office and submit a trial article. Also, I wanted to catch the Chief so that I could report to him directly. Surely he would observe professional growth in his rookie reporter.

While driving Main St. through Benton Harbor, I passed the diner where I intended to bump into the police officer in the morning. Continuing, I noticed two businesses displaying "House of David" signs. One on my left was an Oldsmobile dealership, and one on my right was a hotel. Attorney J.P. Pinehurst may be connected to these businesses too, I thought to myself.

It took me 35-40 minutes to get to the newspaper office in South Haven. I went straight to my desk and typewriter, and started pounding out the story of the day's trial. Headline, **"Mary Anne Starr Defends Self."** My story focused on the defendant's testimony as it was interspersed by corroborating witnesses. I suspected, but didn't include, the victim suffered from mental illness. The article ended with the promise of a spirited cross-examination to follow.

I read the article out loud to myself. The Chief had suggested that I do that to acquire the sound in the reader's head. At first I didn't really grasp the Chief's meaning, but as I gained experience, I became a believer in this technique. If I thanked and complimented the Chief on his sage advice, I could hear his response, "I was born yesterday?" Again, a statement ending in a question mark.

After rereading the second time, I took my article into the Chief's office. It appeared he was up to his neck reviewing copy for the next day's paper. "Hi Chief. Interesting trial today. Do you have time to look over what I've written?"

He peered over the top of his glasses as I handed him my article. Without looking at me or uttering a word, he began reading carefully.

"You're getting better kid. You changed your name? Nice touch. Now, go home and get some rest. Sounds like tomorrow's trial may be a big deal."

"I think so," I said. "I can't wait. See you tomorrow."

As I was leaving the office, the Chief said, "Try to be back by five thirty tomorrow. Rose wants I should go with her to the synagogue."

"I'll try. I don't think it will be a problem on a Friday; the judge wants to get home to Hillsdale."

As I turned into our driveway, Ginger flashed by the Coupe at full gallop. She's going to get hit one of these days, I thought. I parked the Coupe in the barn. Ginger greeted me griping tightly in her teeth an old waterlogged softball she'd found; wanting me to throw it for her. I obliged by throwing the ball over the barn roof. Undaunted, she tore around the corner of the barn like a March hare. She was excited and so was I.

Before I could get to the kitchen door, Ginger was back, holding the ball in her big smiling mouth. I patted her on the shoulder and she dropped the ball, wanting to slide through the door ahead of me. Mom permitted Ginger in the kitchen, but no further, and no begging.

Everyone looked up from the supper table. "Come on, you're late. We were forced to start without you," Dad said. I washed my hands in the bathroom sink, Mom not allowing us to use her kitchen sink for such, and returned to sit down in my place. Mom sat on the end closest to "her" sink and Dad on the end opposite. I was on Dad's left, along the interior wall with the heat register, and Josh and Ken sat side by side across from me. This seating arrangement was never assigned; it just was, as long as I can remember.

Mom had made meatballs and spaghetti. I worried that none was left, but she had successfully fended off Josh and Ken. It was great spaghetti, with lots of garlic in the meatballs. Mom's canned dills made a perfect complement. "Don't call me late for dinner," I mused.

Since the rest of the family had almost completed their supper, they started grilling me about the trial while I ate. The trial had become the main topic of family conversation. Josh had reported on it in his history class. If I didn't answer their questions immediately, someone else would answer for me. "Do you think she's guilty?" Mom asked as she passed me the bread.

"She shot him in the back! What do you think?" Ken smugly retorted.

"Everyone's innocent until proven guilty in a court of law," Josh pretentiously quipped.

To which Dad sagely added, "To be found innocent does not mean proven innocent, or even that one is innocent. It just means not found guilty."

The exchange continued with no one leaving the kitchen, even long after the meal was finished. As we talked everyone pitched in clearing the table, doing the dishes and putting them away. It made me feel good that all were so interested in what I was doing. But I wanted to run over and see Maxine. She had been in the back of my mind since leaving South Haven.

Turning to Mom, I said, "Do you think it'd be too late to drop by and see Maxine?"

"I don't think so, but why don't you give her a call to let her know you're coming," Mom replied. I went into the living room to give Maxine a call. After cranking the phone twice, Miss Hess, the forever disgruntled Glenn operator, finally answered. I gave her the Martin's number.

I heard their phone ring, two long and three short rings; they, like everyone else in the township, were on a party line. On the first ring, Mrs. Martin answered, "Hello."

"Hi Mrs. Martin. This is Chuck. May I speak with Maxine?"

"I'm sorry Chuck. Maxine is not here and I don't expect her for a couple of hours. May I take a message for her?"

"Please tell her that I called and that I'm looking forward to Saturday night."

"I'll do that Chuck. Max is also looking forward to the dance. Good night."

I wondered where Maxine was, and why she was out on a weeknight. Oh well, I had lots to do and thought my brothers could help me. I offered them a dollar apiece to make a couple of phone calls to county schools for me. Their help could make my keeping up with high school sports teams a little easier. They were both mildly receptive to my offer, so I gave them each an outline of what information I needed them to find.

We talked about Christmas and gift possibilities. Mom suggested two or three possible Christmas presents for Maxine. "What color dress is Maxine wearing to the Christmas Ball?"

"Green, it's her favorite color," I said, still considering Mom's interest in my giving Maxine a gift. "May I make you a corsage to give to Maxine?"

"That'd be great, Mom."

I headed for bed about ten, good and tired. As I got between the blankets, my thoughts returned to the trial. How would Pinehurst conclude his examination of Starr? How would she hold up under cross-examination? Before I went to sleep, I reminded myself of my unofficial morning appointment at the Benton Harbor diner.

IX
MURDER WEEK

At five thirty, the alarm clock jolted me from a sound sleep. I instantly rolled out of bed, wide-awake, ready to attack the day. By the time I had shaved and dressed, six registered on the kitchen clock. Dad greeted me, "What do you want for breakfast?"

"The usual," I yawned. Ginger, with her hindquarters swinging from side to side, bumped against my left leg. Her head shook and her rusty eyes pleaded for a pet; I obliged roughing her shoulders.

Dad and I ate together and talked about things. "Remember taking some peaches to the Benton Harbor Market?" I asked.

"Yes, got a pretty good price I recall."

"You told us about a cold storage plant there run by some little old men with long hair and whiskers,"

"Yes?"

"Well, do you remember if they were part of a religious organization known as the House of David? I've been hearing a lot about that organization lately." Dad wasn't sure but thought that sounded right. "One of the defense attorneys is the business manager for the House of David," I informed him.

"I don't think they'd be lawyers, but I couldn't say for sure."

"I'll see if I can find out more today," I said. "How do I find that market? I want to take a look at it and the cold storage you told us about."

"Doubt much is going on there this time of year, but if you're in Benton Harbor, go south along the river. You can't miss it."

"I've got to get goin' Dad. I want to try to meet-up with one of the Berrien County police officers before court starts. He may be able to help me."

"Well, don't let me hold you up. We'll see you for supper." Ginger jumped to her feet proudly displaying her intention of going with me.

Benton Harbor was one of the larger towns in southwestern Michigan and growing. But finding its famous Fruit and Vegetable Market and the House of David Cold Storage proved easy. The long rows of loading docks stood empty. It was essentially a cold ghost town during the winter months, but I could imagine what it looked like during the height of the harvest season.

The massive House of David Cold Storage stood between the foot of the market and the St. Joseph River. There were three or four trucks backed up to loading bays. From strictly a drive-by observation, the activity seemed lively, especially considering the time of year and hour of the day. Some of the laborers wore long beards, but I couldn't tell about the length of their hair because they all wore flat bulky touring caps that concealed their unshorn tresses.

It was still early, only seven forty-five, so I parked the Coupe on West Main St. near the Pegasus, the Greek diner I had stopped at the previous morning. On the roof above the entrance stood a plaster winged carrousel horse. It could have been a Coney Island refugee, judging from a chipped hind hoof displaying the partial label lettering "SLAND."

Once inside, I quickly spotted a uniformed deputy sheriff seated alone at the back booth. If it was the officer I wanted to see, he must have been early. This was good. The same waitress from the day before tended the counter. I asked her if she remembered me, and if that officer seated in the back was the one she said may help me. She smiled, responding, "Yes and yes, his name Aaron Barth."

Not looking at her, but heading directly for the officer's booth, I said, "Nice to see you again." Catching myself, I turned my head and smiled, but kept walking. I had a mission.

"Excuse me sir, are you Deputy Aaron Barth?" He looked up from a sheath of official looking papers and nodded. "I thought I recognized you. My name is Chuck Scott, and I'm a reporter for the *South Haven Tribune*. May I talk with you a minute?" I stammered with nervousness.

"About what?" he grunted and squinted as if sizing me up.

"Sir, I saw you testify in court Wednesday. I've just been assigned to cover the Starr murder trial and want to learn as much as possible."

Barth smirked and motioned with his eyes for me to sit across from him. "Have you read the papers?" he asked.

From the sound of his voice, I suspected he was either making fun of me, or newspapers in general, but I let it go, magnanimously. "Sir, do you have an opinion about what's been written about this case in the newspapers?" I asked in all sincerity, trying to look the officer straight in the eye.

"If I did, I wouldn't want to read about it in the *South Haven Tribune*," he dispassionately replied, and took a large swallow of his black coffee.

The same waitress—the only waitress—reappeared, serving Barth two eggs, fried potatoes and a generous slice of ham. While warming his coffee, she asked if she could take my order. "I'll have a cup of coffee and one of your soon-to-be famous Pegasus pastries."

"How you know pastries famous?" she grinned at me while placing her left palm on her left hip.

I thought about winking at her, but decided that would be stupid and immature. So I said, "Because if they taste half as good as they smell, I'll be back for more."

"Be back soon with your order," she said moving to the next table to warm the coffees for a couple of sailors.

"Penny works here every morning before school," Barth said. He may have noticed my interest in her or possibly, just reporting the facts.

Steering us back to my wide-ranging mission, I asked, "You testified that Starr appeared to have suffered from Eastwood's physical abuse. Do you think Eastwood actually beat her?"

"I don't talk about cases I handle with the public or the press." Barth ardently stated in a strong commanding voice.

"I'm trying to get to the truth, and I think you can help me." I couldn't help thinking of myself as a defender of truth, justice and the American Way.

"We're all trying to find the truth and you...what's your name?"

"Chuck Scott."

"You Chuck, need lots of help, but you'll not get it from me," Barth replied deflating my noble quest.

Penny returned with my coffee and pastry. As she sat the cup in front of me, she asked, "So, you two know each other?"

Deputy Barth smirked at Penny, "Why do I think you set me up, Penny?"

With a bogus look of shock, Penny replied, "Deputy Barth, why you say that? I'm just dumb high school girl working in dinky diner." Penny nearly laughed as she continued her transparent confession turning towards me, "Don't he look like he need some good help?" Penny cheerfully moved on to another patron, exhibiting an artificial lack of interest in hearing any response from me.

"She's right, Deputy Barth, I sure could use your help. What can you tell me about Pinehurst, Starr's attorney?"

"Tell you what Chuck, why don't you swing by the Eden Springs Amusement Park after trial today. You'll find more information about Pinehurst than you can shake a stick at. I will tell you this, his best friend was hit by a car and killed night before last." Barth stood-up, "I gotta go, I'm already late." With that Barth headed for the cash register to pay his bill.

"How do I get there?" I hollered after him.

"Just ask anyone at the courthouse."

Judge Jackson struck his gavel on his desk, declaring that court was in session. I didn't have to look at the faithful grandfather clock to know the time; we were right on schedule—Jackson's schedule. The judge peered toward the defense team, "Mr. Pinehurst, how would the defense like to proceed?"

As Attorney Pinehurst rose deliberately, I couldn't help thinking of what Deputy Barth said about Pinehurst's friend being killed. Maybe it had affected his court presence.

"Your Honor, the defense wishes to recall Mary Anne Starr." Mrs. Starr again assumed her accustomed position in the witness chair, holding the attention of the full to capacity courtroom once more. She wore essentially the same clothes she had worn on Wednesday. I found myself growing tired of the constant newspaper attention being given to the defendant's appearance, more reminiscent of a beauty contest than a murder trial. Admittedly, her appearance interested most.

"Mrs. Starr, please continue reviewing the events leading up to your arrest, starting with Friday, October 14."

"I felt much better on Friday. The swelling around my left eye had gone down enough that I could see out of it. Still stiff and sore, but not too bad. Stella came by, said I looked like a recovering prizefighter. I did some work around the house. Ida Jean DiMaggio called around noon and asked if we were still going to the Republican rally? We agreed she'd pick me up about six."

Pinehurst interjected, "Let the record show that the Republicans held a rally at the Benton Harbor Naval Armory the evening of Friday, October 14."

"Where was Bob Eastwood on said Friday?"

"He went to the office before noon and hadn't returned when Ida Jean picked me up to go to the rally. Bob met us at the Armory, and after the band stopped playing, the three of us went to the Green Cottage in St. Joe. We all had a good time."

"Your Honor, again we'd like Mrs. Starr to step down for a few minutes while we call corroborating witnesses. We believe it will clarify testimony and save this court's valuable time," pleaded Pinehurst.

Judge Jackson looked towards the prosecuting attorneys, but found no objection. "Without objection, permission granted. The witness may step down."

The defense then called Ida Jean DiMaggio who identified herself as owning and operating a beauty shop not far from Bob Eastwood's law office. She stated that she was a good friend of Mary Anne.

Miss DiMaggio testified that one day last summer when she dropped by the law office, "I heard Bob Eastwood shouting, 'These Berrien County lawyers are the crookedest I ever saw. You can't rely on any of them.' Bob frequently complained that he was '...so desperately tired.'"

Her testimony was brief, basically corroborating the evening with Mrs. Starr at the Republican rally and then with Starr and Eastwood at the Green Cottage tavern. She testified that Eastwood had acted strange at times, "...moody, one day he was happy to see you, the next he might not even recognize you. But, we all had a good time at the Green Cottage that Friday night."

Pinehurst then summoned Benton Harbor police officer Albert Lewis. Lewis recounted that in late August he and fellow officer, Ellis Hull, investigated a prowler complaint at the Eastwood's home, 400 Parker Avenue. Pinehurst's objective was for the record to show that the land contract for the purchase of 400 Parker Avenue had been signed by Robert Eastwood and Mary Anne Eastwood—husband and wife. He offered a copy of that contract to be placed in evidence.

"Were the Eastwoods alarmed about this prowler? Pinehurst asked.

"Definitely, Bob said he was going to buy a gun for protection. His wife said she was missing clothing from off the clothes line where other items had been vandalized. They both reported seeing a prowler once before at their home and once in front of their law office on Pipestone."

"Did the Eastwoods appear fearful?"

"Yes, especially Bob. He mentioned at least twice that he had to get a gun for protection."

On cross-examination Foster asked Lewis if he was positive of the facts he testified to. "Yes, absolutely."

"Are you sure you didn't investigate this prowler complaint with Deputy Jake Winters; not Deputy Ellis Hull?"

Looking about sheepishly, "Well, it was a long time ago. Hull, or maybe it was Winters."

That concluded Lewis' testimony. Foster had waived his right to cross-examine DiMaggio until later if the need arose.

With Starr reassuming the witness chair, I realized my fingers were stiff from unrelenting, frantic note-taking. For a moment, I sat back and surveyed the courtroom, massaging my hands and fingers. The legal environment filled me with an exhilarated sense of being present at an important place and time, of playing an essential part in something significant; Mary Anne Starr's life hung in the balance.

"Let's move to Saturday October 15," Pinehurst directed his witness.

"I remember Saturday. I've always liked Saturdays. It was a bright crisp fall day and Bob decided to rake leaves in our front yard. He asked me to run downtown and get a paper. While there, I dropped by the office. Stella stopped in and I suggested we go for a ride north of town. I wanted to show her a house Bob and I had been thinking about buying. When I returned home early-afternoon, Bob was not there."

"Did you know where he had gone?"

"No, but I knew he had clients to see."

"Then what happened?"

"Bob didn't come home that night. When I got ready for bed, I thought of the prowlers we'd had and got scared. So I took the gun from Bob's top dresser drawer and put it in my pocketbook near our bed."

I took notes frenetically. When I looked up, I noticed attorneys Foster and Spears doing the same, undoubtedly for different reasons.

"Please tell the court," Pinehurst requested, "how you came to acquire that gun."

"After having prowlers around our house, Bob told me to go to South Bend and buy a gun. On a shopping trip to South Bend, I saw a pistol in a pet store and bought it."

"Did you have ammunition for the weapon?"

"Bob had told me to buy that in a different store. He didn't want the police to know he had a gun."

"Interesting."

"Well, now we come to Sunday October 16. Please tell us what you did on that day Mrs. Starr. Please recount the events of your day starting from the time you got up in the morning."

Starr drew a slow deliberate breath and then exhaled. She obviously wanted to collect her thoughts for what she knew could be a lengthy report.

"I did not sleep well, and when I got up it was almost noon. Bob had not come home. I got cleaned up and drove down to the office to see if Bob might be there working. He wasn't. I decided to drive to South Haven to see a movie I didn't want to miss. In South Haven I ate lunch at a small diner about two thirty or three, and then went to the movie. Following the movie, I had a soda at the same diner, and then headed home.

When coming into Benton Harbor about seven or seven thirty, I passed the Dwan Hotel and saw Bob sitting on a chair out front. I drove around the block and came back, but he was gone. From there I went to the office and worked for an hour or two. A little after nine, I drove past the Dwan Hotel again hoping to find Bob. I saw him talking with Izzy Genoa and some other men. I didn't stop; I don't like Izzy.

Being hungry, I decided to go to Phil's Place in Coloma for a ham sandwich. However, I got worried about Bob, and turned around in Coloma, and came back passed the hotel looking for Bob. Not seeing him, I drove around for a while, over to St. Joe and back. Finally I parked on Territorial Road, across from the Recreational Gardens, near the back of the Dwan Hotel. I watched the people coming and going until almost midnight.

I started the car to go home when I saw Izzy Genoa drive up beside the hotel and drop Bob off. I got out of my car and crossed the street. I said something like, 'Bob, are you ready to come home?' He said something like, 'I'm not going home.' He turned around and started across the street. I walked with him down 5th Street, across Main, and up Wall Street to the library. There he crossed the street and went into the police station; I followed him."

"Did he say anything as you walked to the police station?" Pinehurst interrupted his witness.

"No."

"Did you say anything to him?"

"No."

"Did you know where he was going or why?"

"No."

"Were you quarreling?"

"No."

"Were you angry at Mr. Eastwood?"

"No. He looked very tired, haggard. I just wanted him to come home and get some rest."

Then Attorney Pinehurst requested that Starr explain what transpired in the police station. She again took a deep breath, and then began reciting the dialog that took place between Eastwood and Deputy Jake Winters.

"Bob said, 'Winters, I want to talk with you, alone.' Jake said, 'We are alone.' Then Jake led Bob into the back office. As I followed them, Bob pushed me back and closed the door."

"Could you hear them talking?" Pinehurst asked.

"I could not make out what they were saying, so I got a drink at the fountain and sat down on the corridor bench."

"Did Eastwood and Winters talk long?"

"No," Starr responded and continued, "When Bob came out of the office, he walked past me and out of the police station. When I started to follow him, Jake said he wanted to talk with me. He said something about going home and working it out in the morning. I said, 'Mr. Winters, I have done nothing to talk to you about,' and turned and left the station."

"Were you chasing Mr. Eastwood?"

"No. I had decided to go back to my car and go home. As I came up the station steps to cross Wall Street to 6th, I saw Bob standing a short way up Wall towards 5th. I was almost across the street, nearing the library, when I heard hurried footsteps coming toward me. As I turned my head, I saw Bob coming at me." Starr's frantic voice trailed off.

"Please describe his face," Pinehurst requested.

With body language and facial replication emblematic of a dreadful memory, Starr gasped, "His eyes, his face, I really can't describe it. It was hideous, so horrifying."

"What was your reaction?"

"Bob intended to kill me!"

"Did you believe that?"

"I did when I saw his face. His fist came towards me—," the defendant's voice ebbed, and a vacant expression covered her face.

"Objection, Your Honor" Foster implored. "This line of testimony would better serve a Broadway stage than this honorable court of law."

"As I feel we are nearing the end of direct examination of this witness, I'm going to allow it. The objection is overruled. Mr. Pinehurst, I trust you will bring this line of questioning to a speedy conclusion," Jackson cajoled Pinehurst.

"Thank you for your indulgence, Your Honor. Just a few more questions."

Pinehurst turned again to the witness, "Then what took place?"

"I don't know. The last thing I saw was Bob's fist," Starr's voice again faded as she stared blankly above the heads in the jury box.

Pinehurst considerately asked Starr if she needed a minute to compose herself or possibly a glass of water. Judge Jackson offered that he would be calling for a morning recess soon. From the sound of his voice, he clearly wanted to move the questioning along.

"No, I'd rather go on," Starr spoke in a steady voice, responding to the judge's wishes.

Addressing Jackson, Pinehurst said, "I think the defense can finish with this witness in just a few more minutes, Your Honor."

"Proceed."

"If it pleases the court, the defense has prepared a portable blackboard showing the street and building layout between the Dwan Hotel and the police station. We would like for Mrs. Starr to point out for the jury, hers and Mr. Eastwood's movements on the night and hour in question."

"Please proceed," the judge responded in what could be interpreted as an interested and pleasant voice—a rare occurrence indeed.

Starr, assisted by Pinehurst, stepped down from the witness chair. Pinehurst provided her with a blind man's white cane to use as a pointer. Starr, with the encouragement of her attorney, indicated on the blackboard where she had parked her car on Territorial Road, across from the Recreation Gardens. From that starting point, she proceeded to recount Genoa dropping Eastwood at the south side entrance of the hotel, meeting and walking with Eastwood to the police station, leaving the police station separately, and concluded with her location when she observed Eastwood's fist coming towards her.

Starr looked questioningly at Pinehurst. He thanked her and suggested she return to the witness stand. She handed him the cane and abided by his request.

I found the map testimony both interesting and perplexing. From the looks on the jurors' faces, they were experiencing a similar reaction. The route outlined, times and locations of witnesses and their previous testimonies, failed the logic test. At the very least, previous eyewitnesses gave statements incompatible with one another as well as with Starr. I remembered my high school Civics teacher telling us that following presidential elections more people claimed to have voted for the winner than actually did. I wondered if some twisted variation of that analogy applied here.

Attorney Pinehurst thoughtfully stroked his neatly combed beard while scanning his notes. "Mrs. Starr, what is the next thing you remember after you saw Eastwood running towards you with his fist held high?"

Starr reflected for a moment, then answered, "Mr. Johns had hold of my shoulders, shaking me."

Q. —"Did you hand him a gun?" A. —"I don't remember."

Q. —"Do you remember being taken to the police station?" A. —"Someone held my arms; that's all I remember."

Q. —"Do you recall smoking a cigarette?" A. —"No sir, I don't smoke."

Q. —"Have you ever smoked cigarettes?" A. —"One or two since we moved to Benton Harbor."

Q. —"Had you been drinking?" A. —"No sir."

Q. —"Were you angry at any time?" A. —"No, I was not."

Q. —"What was the next thing you can remember?" A. —"I remember Sergeant Winters sitting me in the Chief's office. That's when I felt the bump over my eye."

Q. —"Was that bump over your left eye there when you first visited the police station that night?" A. —"No. I couldn't understand where it came from."

"Your Honor, this concludes our direct questioning of Mrs. Starr."

"Good. Mrs. Starr, you may step down." Looking from Starr to the bailiff, Jackson continued, "Mr. Pile, let's take a 20 minute break before moving to cross-examination."

Starr and her attorneys were locked in an intense whispering discussion at the moment recess began. Obviously they believed that Starr's handling of her impending cross-examination was crucial to the trial's outcome.

X
MR. FOSTER

I sat reflectively for a few minutes, trying to digest the defendant's testimony. She certainly found herself in a desperately precarious situation. Was the shooting the culminating event of her increasingly desperate life? As I considered these thoughts, I wrote down a few more notes before getting up to stretch.

During the recess, I asked Halamka if he had met J.P. Pinehurst. "Yes, I met him a year ago when he hosted the Michigan Press Association's annual meeting at his Grande Vista restaurant. Quite a place, you should go see it— another House of David business. Pinehurst is the business manager for the House of David religious colony headquartered east of Benton Harbor. They tell me that guy that was killed Wednesday night was Pinehurst's best friend."

Checking the previous day's paper, I found an article about House of David florist Karl Friedman being hit by a car and killed in front of his home on Lake Shore Drive. The accident took place between Pinehurst's home and the House of David Greenhouse across U.S. 12. By asking around, I confirmed that Pinehurst and Friedman were in fact close friends and neighbors. They had just finished supper together in Pinehurst's home before the accident.

Following recess, the prosecution recalled Starr to the witness stand for cross-examination. Judge Jackson glanced at Pile, as did I, thinking the bailiff was going to once again mistake activity for accomplishment while duplicating his swearing in services. Seeing no movement from Pile, the judge reminded Starr that she was still under oath.

"Yes sir, I know."

Standing and waiting patiently W.C. Foster was ready to take responsibility for Starr's cross-examination. He wasted no time. "Mrs. Starr, you testified that you would not go out with someone you did not know, but you went out with Robert Eastwood. Isn't it a fact that you did know him previously?"

"Why, Mr. Foster," she answered in a soft, patronizing voice, "as I said yesterday, I tried to put him off by insisting that my children come too. Bob surprised me by agreeing to take my kids, and I didn't want to go back on my word."

Foster abruptly turned to the matter of Eastwood's marital status, trying to get Starr to admit that she had knowledge of Eastwood being married when she allowed him to move in with her. He approached this subject from several angles, but Starr, though a bit confusing in her answers, maintained her ignorance.

"Surely," Foster protested, "when Eastwood was under investigation for disbarment, you must have heard something about his being married?"

"Yes I did, and I asked him again if he was married. He took me to his office to prove to me that his divorce was final."

"But, you said you wouldn't live with a man out-of-wedlock."

"That's right, and that's when we said our wedding vows in front of the church I grew-up in."

Foster snapped, "When was that?"

"Why Mr. Foster, I don't remember the date for sure."

"Was it in the spring or fall?"

"I don't remember."

"Isn't it true, Mrs. Starr, that when you and Mr. Eastwood lived in Niles with his sister, Mrs. Jessie Harrington, she told you Eastwood was still married?"

"No Mr. Foster, she said she was pleased that Bob had met someone that could help him. Jessie and I became good friends and often worked together on household chores. We traded cooking duties back and forth. I like Jessie and have every reason to believe she likes me."

Attorney Foster's face plainly showed his skepticism and annoyance with Starr's vague, rambling answers. Then, the prosecutor walked over to the evidence table and picked up Exhibit #1, a four barrel, 22 caliber Derringer pistol. Returning to the witness, he commenced a series of rapid-fire questions.

"Do you remember sticking a gun in Eastwood's ribs, making him promise to get a divorce?"

"I never threatened Bob, and besides, Mr. Foster, I thought Bob was divorced."

"Isn't it a fact that on that fateful night, you followed Mr. Eastwood out of the police station and pulled a gun on him? When he started to run, shouting 'help, help, don't shoot!' you shot him in the back?" As Foster's voice got louder and louder, he brandished the pistol in front of the witness.

Waiting for the sound of the prosecutor's voice to fade, the witness answered in a smooth even monotone, "Why, Mr. Foster, I can't remember very much. I can't remember enough to tell you anything. The last thing I remember was Bob's fist coming towards me and then being told the next day that he was dead."

"Judge," Foster asked, "please instruct the witness to quit stalling and simply answer my questions with a simple yes or no." Judge Jackson nodded, but said nothing.

"After shooting Robert Eastwood twice in the back and twice in the head, did you say, 'Take that you son-of-a-bitch! Take that you son-of-a-bitch!'"

"I don't remember. It doesn't sound like me."

"Merchant police officer John Henry Johns testified you did!" Foster boomed.

"After being escorted into the police station, did you say, 'I'm not sorry. I'd do it again!'"

"I don't remember."

"Fireman Zane Johnson testified you did!"

"When talking to a deputy in the office of the police station, did you say, 'I killed him. He had it coming to him for a long time.'"

"I don't remember."

"Sergeant Jake Winters testified you did!"

"You testified that Mr. Eastwood abused you physically on several occasions. If he beat you as you say he did, why didn't you leave him?"

"Why didn't I leave him? Because I worshipped him. I loved him very much. He was sincerely sorry for what he had done to me. Bob and I planned to build a happy home together."

"You testified that you and Robert Eastwood purchased a home at 400 Parker Avenue on a land contract. You signed that contract as husband and wife, with you signing your name as Mrs. Mary Anne Eastwood." Foster shouted, "Didn't you know you were committing a fraud?"

Before Starr could answer, Pinehurst leaped to his feet objecting to the question. Judge Jackson ruled the question stricken from the record, and instructed the jury to disregard it. The two defense attorneys had already lodged two previous objections, attempting to break the prosecutor's momentum and intimidating behavior toward their client. Both were summarily overruled.

As the morning session drew to an end, I found myself amused, and sometimes tickled, by Starr's unflappable fielding of Foster's hammering questions. The interchange between the two of them reminded me of actors in a high school play—Foster too angry, Starr too tender. It was hard to take either one of them seriously. Foster tried to paint a picture of Starr as a mean-spirited, devious woman. Starr attempted to portray herself as the patiently suffering little lady. The jury was left with an unenviable responsibility.

Without prompting, Judge Tobey Jackson asked for a noon recess, reconvening at 1:30 P.M.

Immediately, I hurried from the courthouse, jumped into the Coupe and headed out Lakeshore Drive to see if I could find Pinehurst's home. It didn't take long before I came to a large greenhouse with a House of David sign in front. With the noon recess fleeting, I needed to make the most of my time.

Upon entering the greenhouse salesroom, I witnessed a vigorous holiday business. A rather picturesque little fellow with neatly braided hair wrapped tightly and tucked beneath another one of those bulky flat hats, waited on me. I didn't want to spend much money, but neither did I want to look like I was snooping. I decided to buy Mom a Christmas bouquet; the least expensive possible.

I took advantage of the selection process to inquire about the religion of House of David members. The clerk's explanation came at me like an avalanche. Before we had decided on the make-up of the bouquet, I knew more about the Israelite faith than I needed, and also, that their business manager, Senator Pinehurst—as he preferred to be addressed—lived in the beautiful new home across the highway and set back from the road.

Pinehurst had come by his unofficial title while serving as a state senator in southern California. He had earned a law degree in college, served as a school superintendent, and newspaper editor in Illinois before health considerations forced him to move his family to California. Approximately twenty years ago, the Pinehursts moved to Michigan to joined the Israelite House of David. The Senator scaled quickly the religious colony's leadership hierarchy. He was now the man responsible for their many and varied business enterprises.

By the time I had paid for the flowers and drove up Senator Pinehurst's driveway, accidentally on purpose, my time was running short. The Pinehurst family lived in one of the nicest private homes I had ever seen. Curious, I thought, for members of a celibate religious colony that believed in giving up all worldly possessions and living communally.

I got back into the courtroom just before Jackson called the afternoon session to order. As he did he announced, what several had suspected, that the trial would continue on Saturday morning. Being my first trial, I thought nothing of it. Then he quickly recognized Attorney Foster, who in turn recalled Mary Anne Starr for continued cross-examination. Foster informed Jackson that he anticipated completing his questioning of Starr by the afternoon recess.

"If not sooner." It was the first time I had seen Jackson smile.

Following a brief whisper to Spears, Foster began, "Mrs. Starr, do you normally carry a gun?"

"No, I've never carried a gun."

"But you carried one the night you shot and killed Attorney Robert Eastwood."

Mrs. Starr replied, "I forgot I had put it in my pocketbook."

"Do you mean to tell this court that you lugged a gun around all day, and didn't know you had it?"

"I left my pocketbook on the car seat," answered Starr.

"Not when you killed Eastwood!"

For the second time, Foster picked-up the fatal little four-barreled pistol from the evidence table, and walked with it toward the witness.

"Objection!" Blustered Pinehurst.

Judge Jackson instructed Foster to be careful; "Remember, counselor, you are the one who suggested we avoid theatrics."

Hefting the murder weapon in his right hand while looking at the witness, "You say you purchased this cute little gun, one that would easily fit into a nice lady's purse, in a pet shop. Why?"

"Because I like birds and animals. Birds are one of my hobbies."

"Why the gun?" an agitated Foster barked.

"Oh, because Bob told me to and it was the only one I saw." Starr again played the naive little woman.

Condescendingly, Foster followed in a soft, mimicking voice, "How did you know it wasn't one of those guns that are filled with candy?"

"Are guns sold with candy?" a wide-eyed Starr asked. Her inquiry pleased the gallery, further irritated Foster and drew a cold frown from Jackson.

"Where did you buy the bullets?"

"In the Cutler & Downing store."

"Why did you go to another store to buy cartridges?"

"Because Bob told me to and besides, they didn't sell cartridges in the pet shop."

Attorney Foster paused, glaring at Starr. Then he looked at the pistol he held in his hand. "Mrs. Starr," he said looking slowly up at her in the witness chair. "On Sunday October 16, 1938, did you not in fact put this weapon in your purse, and go out looking for Robert Eastwood?"

"Why Mr. Foster, you know it never happened like that. I had forgotten the gun was in my purse," Starr answered again in a patronizing tenor.

Prosecutor Foster turned around, returned the gun to the evidence table, and walked back to confer with Attorney Spears; possibly to regain a noticeably shaken poise. Returning again to address the witness, he proceeded to ask the following series of short questions, covering a wide range of previous testimony.

Q. —"You stated during direct examination that you separated from Robert Eastwood several times. Isn't it a fact that he left you to return and live with his lawful wife and family?" A. — "No, never."

Q. —"You and Mr. Eastwood have been evicted multiple times because you were not legally married, true?" A. —"No."

Q. —"Is it true that you were fired as head waitress at the Benton Harbor Vincent Hotel?" A. —"I was discharged, but never given a reason."

Q. —"Have you ever assaulted or threatened Mr. Eastwood with a gun?" A. —"No."

Q. —"Would you know if a March 5, 1934 warrant charging you with assault with a deadly weapon was lost, destroyed or stolen from the office of Justice J. W. Cullinine?" Pinehurst's objection to the question—lack of a warrant—was overruled. A. —"No, I think you are talking about a joke Bob tried to play on me."

Q. —"You testified to combing glass from your hair after being hit in the head with a bottle. Is it not true that you acquired that glass in your hair after you rammed your car into the Preston Lumber Company?" A. —"No."

Q. —"Wasn't your jealousy of Robert Eastwood's family the root cause of your contentious relationship with Eastwood?" A. —"I've never been jealous of people I don't know."

Q. —"Do you remember Mrs. Mabel Eastwood, with her children, meeting you at the Hotel Eastland in Benton Harbor to complain that she was no longer receiving Robert's monthly $50 military disability check?" A. —"No, I don't remember meeting them."

Q. —Did you write a letter to Washington, requesting the Robert Eastwood's disability check be sent to his office in Benton Harbor?" A. —"No, I never did."

Q. —Did you send a letter to Mabel Eastwood with a picture of you and Robert?" A. —"No."

Q. —Do you recognize this letter in your handwriting?" A. —"It looks like my handwriting. I must have written it, but I don't remember doing it."

Q. —"Did you send this snapshot to Mrs. Mabel Eastwood?" A. —"I have a snapshot of Bob and me just like it, but I never sent it to anyone."

Q. —"Since you have red or dark colored hair in the photo, it appears that you've changed the color of your hair. Is that true?" A. —"No. I've always been a silver blonde."

Q. —"Did you send this letter with this clipping to Mrs. Mabel Eastwood?" A. —"I did not write this letter nor mail it to anyone. I did read this article in the newspaper. It's about Bob and me attending my baby sister's wedding."

Q. —"Did you write a letter to Mrs. Mabel Eastwood and ask her to divorce Robert Eastwood?" A. —"No."

Q. —"Following your arrest for the murder of Robert Eastwood, did you not ask Mrs. Diamond for medical help?" A. —"Not that I recall." Defense Attorney Biglow objected to the prosecutor's use of the word "murder," suggesting "homicide" would be appropriate. "Overruled."

Foster suspended questioning to confer with Spears. "Please, Mr. Foster, do you have more questions for this witness?" Jackson inquired.

"Yes, Your Honor, we do." Returning to the witness, "Mrs. Starr, if you would please answer one final question?" Foster then read a long question and answer statement taken by County Stenographer Beatrice Solis of Sheriff Donald L. Diamond's interrogation of Starr. This record was completed at the Benton Harbor Police Station approximately 40 minutes after the shooting. "Do you remember these questions and your answers?" Foster asked.

"I do not remember any of this," Starr moaned.

Foster turned to face the bench; "We have no more questions for this witness, Your Honor."

Without hesitation, Pinehurst stood and requested permission to redirect examination of Starr.

"Your witness," the judge responded.

"Mrs. Starr, when you were furnishing the law office at 139 Pipestone for you and Mr. Eastwood, please tell the court what the local furniture salesman said to you."

"Mary Anne, you may have whatever furniture you want, but nothing for Bob or Harley Eastwood."

"Objection! Your Honor, where did this come from and how is it relevant?"

"Sustained."

Pinehurst then produced a copy of a forfeiture notice for a land contract and handed it to Mrs. Starr. "Do you recognize this document?"

After looking the document over, Starr answered, "I do. The house Bob and I were buying has been foreclosed on while I've been in jail."

"Are you without funds at this time?"

"Yes"

Pinehurst requested that it be noted in the record that during the second week following the homicide, Mabel Eastwood applied for and was granted appointment as administrator of W. Robert Eastwood's estate. Mary Anne Starr was left destitute.

"Request granted."

"No more questions, Your Honor."

Judge Jackson instructed Starr to step down. The witness was obviously relieved after almost two straight days in the spotlight. As she rejoined her dutiful attorneys, her gate and posture drooped ever so slightly, but she still commanded the courtroom's full attention.

Jackson again announced that court would be in session the next day, Saturday, and that he would call the trial to order at 9:30 A.M. Halamka quietly informed me that Saturday sessions were highly unusual. Following the announcement, Jackson called for the afternoon recess; a much needed respite. I had scribbled so many notes that second stage rigor had invaded my right hand.

XI
UNCLE OTTO

While Judge Jackson was reconvening court for the last session of the day, I did a quick check of the clock above Bailiff Pile's scrawny head; three thirty exactly. The judge snappily summoned the defense to call their next witness.

Attorney Pinehurst rose deliberately, straightening the long braided ponytail that ran from the back of his head down between his shoulder blades. He delivered a concise, but poignant preamble for the importance of expert medical testimony in trials of this nature. Then he painstakingly, and with dramatic flair, outlined the order and significance of each pending defense witness. I scanned the courtroom thinking an ovation might be in order. The nonchalant countenance displayed by the prosecution team indicated they did not share that sentiment.

"At this time, Your Honor," Pinehurst announced, "the defense request that Dr. Henry Roebuck assume the witness stand."

Dr. Roebuck was sworn and gave a larger than expected autobiographical review that began with: "Dr. Henry Roebuck, Kalamazoo, Assistant Superintendent of the Kalamazoo State Hospital. I've been with the hospital for seven years..."

As Pinehurst began direct examination, he reviewed further with Dr. Roebuck the evolution of his impressive academic and medical credentials. After completing an undergraduate degree at Dartmouth, Roebuck went on to medical school at NYU, served a one-year internship at Northwestern Hospital in Chicago and was a second-year resident at Johns Hopkins. With degrees in both psychiatry and internal medicine, he had practiced eight years privately in Chicago before accepting his current position.

While this transpired, the old newspaper hack to my left leaned over and whispered, "Do you think the Senator wants us to fall on our knees and worship silently in the presence of the good doctor?" Suffice it to say; before Pinehurst completed the doctor's resume appraisal, I wanted to scream "Alright already!" I amused myself thinking of the effect the Chief was having on me.

"Dr. Roebuck," Pinehurst asked, "have you had the opportunity to examine Mrs. Starr, the defendant?"

"I have. One week ago I evaluated her in the county jail."

"What was your impression of Mrs. Starr at that time?"

"I found her to be of good mental condition, above average in intelligence, and displaying no evidence of a criminal predisposition." Roebuck's confident, precise answer indicated self-satisfaction with his courtroom position. Also, judging from the smile on her face, Mrs. Starr approved of the doctor's flattering evaluation.

"As a professional psychiatrist Dr. Roebuck, would you explain Mrs. Starr's lack of memory for the events surrounding the early morning hours of October 17?"

"Mrs. Starr suffered temporary amnesia."

"Doctor, from your experience, please list for the court the probable causes of such amnesia?"

"Extreme panic, terror, possibly a head injury. Amnesia is frequently associated with injury to the orbit frontal cortex."

Pinehurst had prepared a series of hypothetical questions for his first expert witness.

Q. – "If the deceased was running towards the defendant, eyes glazed over, bloodless face, and fist held high, could temporary amnesia occur?" A. — "If she feared for her life, it's entirely possible."

Q. —"What if she had been struck by the victim before; a history of previous beatings?" A. —"Yes, that could trigger temporary amnesia."

Q. —"What if, at that time, the defendant received a severe blow on the head?" A. —"Yes, amnesia may result."

Q. —"What if she had received a hard blow to the head five days earlier, and now received an additional severe blow to the head? A. —"If we put all of these events together, severe blow on the head, extreme fear, prior beatings, and a previous severe blow to the head; taken together these events increase the propensity for temporary amnesia."

The rejuvenated crispness in Pinehurst's voice revealed a sense of pleasure in both his questions and Dr. Roebuck's answers. He proceeded to remind the witness of the victim's history of physically abusing the defendant, basically information Roebuck had gained during his jailhouse examination of Starr.

Then the debonair attorney summarized Starr's testimony of what happened moments before her claimed memory failure—Robert Eastwood rushing toward her, his face colorless, his eyes glazed-over, and his fist upraised. Dr. Roebuck confirmed that he was fully aware of all of these details. "Dr. Roebuck, do you believe the defendant, Mrs. Mary Anne Starr, is completely candid in her amnesia claim?"

"Absolutely, and judging from the forehead that still shows evidence of swelling, I've determine that she received a hard blow to the head just prior to the actual shooting."

Pinehurst requested permission for Roebuck to step down from the witness stand, and escort Mrs. Starr to the jury box so that each juror could see and feel the swelling on the defendant's forehead. The duet of Foster and Spears shouted in unison, "Objection!" And Foster soloed, "We've done this before!"

Jackson sustained the objection. "Unnecessary counselor, let's move on."

Unperturbed, Pinehurst continued with his witness. "Dr. Roebuck, in your expert opinion, on the night in question was the defendant acting in self-defense?"

"Yes, she believed her life was in imminent danger."

"Could the defendant shoot the victim in the back, and still be reacting in self-defense?"

Roebuck explained, "It makes no difference. Acting in an emergency while suffering from temporary amnesia, the conscious mind is gone, and only the subconscious mind is acting. The subconscious mind knows no distinction between right and wrong; in the front or in the back, it makes no difference."

It appeared the direct examination of Roebuck was concluded. Pinehurst turned from his witness to address the bench. However, he requested a sidebar meeting between the judge and the legal adversaries. After five minutes of whispered discussion between the four attorneys and the judge, the attorneys returned to their respective tables.

Judge Jackson then addressed the courtroom. "Defense will resume the examination of witnesses at 9:30 A.M. The cross-examination of Dr. Roebuck will be deferred until Monday due to a funeral obligation on the part of the witness. Therefore, Bailiff Pile, will you do the honors?"

"All rise!"

I felt a strong urge to go straight home. By the time court adjourned for the day there remained less than two dozen spectators in the gallery. Not much interest in expert witnesses, I thought. What would attendance be tomorrow, only a half-day, Saturday, and all technical medical testimony?

It took me only a couple of minutes to get to the Coupe and head for home by way of the South Haven office. The wind off the lake was cold and strong and the sky was stuffed with menacing dark purple clouds. It was well after five by the time I entered the newspaper office. A pining Chief had on a clean gray suit, starched white shirt and colorful tie, as if he had an important appointment.

"So where've you been?" he greeted me.

"I've been in court all day," I answered questioningly, thinking he knew the answer to his question.

"Did you learn something new today?"

"I think so. We ended the day with a Kalamazoo psychiatrist on the witness stand. They're really getting into self-defense, temporary amnesia and I think temporary insanity is coming."

Just then the Chief's wife came through the door, "Irving, come now, we're late already." She noticed me, "Who this nice-looking young man? You don't pay him enough," she said smiling with one eye on me and the other on the Chief.

A mid-calf brown fur coat and white neck scarf covered what I suspected was a neatly tailored dress. Her high heels made her stand slightly taller than the Chief. With sparkling dark eyes to accent a white pearl necklace, straight collar length black hair, warm friendly face, and bubbling voice, this middle forties lady was impressive; the Chief did well, I surmised.

The Chief, in his most formal manner, introduced me to his wife, Rose, as our new number one reporter. I was pleased, if not a bit overwhelmed by this unexpected, and I thought, sincere compliment. Rose smiled, "Well, I knew that. Tell me something I don't know." The Chief seemed at a loss for words, but, as previously reported, he's a man of few words.

"Irving we're late," Rose cajoled my boss. As the two of them hurried for the door, I asked the Chief if he wanted to proof my trial report.

"Just leave it on my desk. I'll take a quick look before we put it in. By the way," he looked back over his shoulder, "get that story coming out of Fennville. See you tomorrow." And, Rose and the Chief were gone. I liked Rose.

I promptly went to work on the trial report. It took me about 45 minutes and I kept it between 400 and 500 words; this had been the Chief's suggestion. I titled the piece, **"EXAMINATION OF STARR COMPLETED: Expert Medical Witness Called."** I knew the title couldn't compete with the sensational headlines that were typical of other papers, but this was my choice.

When I finally turned into our driveway, I was bone tired, so drained from the hectic day that I felt like just staying in the Coupe and taking a nap. Snow was falling in slow motion, millions of tiny white butterflies drifting to earth. Not a breath of wind, quiet and dark except for the light coming from the house. I walked from the barn to the house in what my high school literature teacher defined as "a picture of serenity." I was relieved to be home and even though I had to work in the morning, I was glad it was the weekend and I'd be going out with Maxine.

Just as I opened the kitchen door, I thought to myself, where's Ginger? She must be inside. Something was wrong. Ken was seated at the table, aimlessly shuffling a deck of cards. Josh stood, butt against the sink. Ginger got up from under the table and hesitatingly came to welcome me, but with head stretched low and none of her usual unbridled enthusiasm. "Hey girl," I patted her shoulder while looking around. Several voices came from the living room, talking in soft tones.

"What's going on?" I asked. Both brothers blankly looked at me.

Ken stopped shuffling, "Haven't you heard?"

"What?" The memory flashed through my brain of what the Chief said as he and Rose left the office; *Get that story coming out of Fennville.* "Heard what? I haven't heard anything."

Ken looked toward the living room and then at Josh, as if asking permission to speak. In a hushed voice he said, "Uncle Otto killed Aunt Arlene, wounded Kelly, and then committed suicide."

"What?" in a quiet shout of disbelief. Ken frowned at me, indicating with his hands to keep my voice down.

Mom was in the living room with Nana Hunter, Aunt Jane, and one of Aunt Arlene's close friends, Nellie Peterson. Putting my coat on a hook by the door, I sat down across from Ken. Josh joined us. Then my brothers began to take turns telling me the story of a neighborhood and family tragedy, a tragedy that surpassed our immediate comprehension.

They related to me that sometime around noon, Uncle Otto and Aunt Arlene had an argument. Uncle Otto got his 12-guage shotgun and shot Aunt Arlene in the face while she was sitting at their kitchen table. Kelly saw it happen and ran out of the house, heading for the Woodley place to get help. Uncle Otto chased her part way, and shot at her, wounding her in the lower back and left leg. He then went back into the house and shot himself. Kelly didn't know she had been hit until Mrs. Woodley found blood on the back of her shirt. Her wounds were more than superficial, but not life threatening.

Josh and Ken were a virtual tag-team of information about the shooting. Most of what they knew came from Mr. Woodley who stopped by, shortly after Josh and Ken got home from school, to tell Dad and Mom what had happened. As near as I could tell, Mr. Woodley got his information from Kelly, and the officers from the county sheriff's department. Mrs. Woodley looked after the hysterical Kelly. Mr. Woodley met Kelly's brother, James, when he came home from school. Her brother John had stayed at school for play practice. Aunt Arlene's kitchen was a bloody mess.

Ken told me that Mom, Nana and the others were trying to figure out what they could do to take care of Kelly and her brothers. Kelly, my age, had dropped out of school her sophomore year, and her brothers were currently attending high school.

Josh said, "Dad and them are over at Uncle Otto's cleaning up the place."

"I never liked Uncle Otto," I said. My brothers agreed with my terse assessment in one way or another. Each of us shared stories of Uncle Otto's crotchety character. We all agreed he had been a troubled, mean-spirited man.

While we were sharing memories of Uncle Otto and his tumultuous family relationships, Dad, Uncle Bill and Grandpa Hunter came in, stamping their feet on the doormat. They all looked quite serious and no one said a word. Finally, Grandpa broke the ice, "It's starting to build-up out there."

Grandpa had a penchant for lifting spirits; he always looked on the bright side. I remember him advising me to always walk on the sunny side of the street. At the time I took his meaning literally and always tried to walk in the sun when in town, and probably always will.

"Chuck, I hear you're becoming quite the newspaper reporter," Grandpa quipped while massaging my neck. Even at that tragic moment, I was happy to see Grandpa and quickly stood up saying, "Just call me C. Drew Scott, investigative reporter for the *New York Times*; sorry, I mean *South Haven Tribune*."

There were a few forced chuckles as Grandpa repeated my new handle, "C. Drew Scott, hey, what am I supposed to call you?"

"You can still call me Chuck."

"I guess you've heard, but we've got an awful story for you to investigate right here," Uncle Bill chimed in. Dad headed off further discussion as Mom came into the kitchen carrying what was left of a fruitcake. The other ladies followed her, each one carrying something—a cup and saucer, small plates, silverware; something. All were crestfallen. Nana's red eyes indicated she had been crying.

Uncle Bill suggested that he had better be getting home, and that he could drop-off the others. There was an unusually long round of somber hugs and barely audible words of encouragement, and then they were gone. The kitchen became quiet. Ginger remained under the table, listening, but pretending to sleep.

For what seemed like five minutes, but was more like five seconds, we all just stood there in silence, waiting for someone to say something. Finally, I broke the stillness; "I need to know everything you can tell me about what happened at Uncle Otto's today."

"We are all worried about what's going to happen tomorrow. Do you realize that we have three orphans that need our help?" Mom compassionately exclaimed with tears forcing their way to the surface.

"You are absolutely right, Mom, but"—I hate using 'but,' I thought—"I need to write a story about this for tomorrow's paper. Better me than someone else."

"Newspaper aside, let's all sit down right now and talk this over," Dad suggested in his typical authoritative manner. Josh and Ken looked a little too eager, and I saw a questioning glance from Mom to Dad and back again. Then a nod of okay passed between them. My parents could carry on a conversation with each other without ever saying a word aloud. We all sat in our places around the kitchen table. I took voluminous mental notes, well more than enough to write the following article that appeared in the December 17, 1938 issue of the *South Haven Tribune*.

FENNVILLE FARM TRAGEDY
No Inquest Necessary In Murder-Suicide
By C. Drew Scott

Fennville, Dec. 16—The Allegan County Sheriff's Department is completing an investigation into the tragic deaths of Otto and Arlene Barnes, at their farm four miles northwest of Fennville. The apparent murder-suicide took place while eating the noon meal in the kitchen of the couple's farmhouse. Kelly Barnes, 20-year-old daughter of the deceased couple, witnessed the shooting of her mother and has given the following account.

"My parents had been arguing most of the morning. While at the kitchen table, they started shouting back and forth and my dad went and got his shotgun, came back to the table and shot Mama. I ran to the neighbor's house, calling for help. Daddy started shooting at me too."

Neighbors, Henry and Edna Woodley, took Kelly in and called the sheriff. When officers arrived, they found both Otto and Arlene Barnes dead on the kitchen floor of their home. Both had received gunshot wounds, Mrs. Barnes in the face and Mr. Barnes in the heart. From what police officers learned interviewing surviving daughter Kelly and their surveying of the crime scene, preliminary findings indicated that Otto Barnes shot and killed his wife, shot and wounded his daughter, and then turned his gun on himself. Kelly Barnes' wounds required hospital admission but are not life threatening.

It was common knowledge among the neighbors that the Barnes couple experienced a contentious relationship during the past year. There are unconfirmed reports that Arlene Barnes had, on

**previous occasions, reported to the authorities her husband's
violent behavior towards her.**

**Otto Barnes (53) and Arlene Barnes (49) had been married 25
years, and have owned and operated their farm for the past 20
years. They leave behind three children, Kelly (20), James (15),
and John (17). In addition to their children, Arlene Barnes is
survived by a sister, Mrs. Arthur Stevens of Kibbie, and a
brother, Albert Roberts of Elgin, ILL. Otto Barnes leaves behind
his aged mother, Mrs. Olive Barnes of Allegan, one sister, Mrs.
Wilma Hunter of Pullman and two brothers, Dr. Harry Barnes of
Kalamazoo, and Roy Barnes of Spring Grove.**

**A double funeral service will be held for Otto and Arlene Barnes
at the Fennville Burch funeral home, 2:30 Monday afternoon.
The funeral service will be followed by burial in the Casco
Township McDowell Cemetery.**

Completing this article caused me to think about the Chief's declaration,
"This story is not over until I say it is." Now I had two stories. From what I
knew and what I learned during our family discussion, I certainly hoped the
Allegan County Sheriff's Department would conduct a thorough investigation.
Basically, everyone could clearly see what had happened, but why did it
happen? That was the question that needed answering.

From what Mom said, my Nana Hunter had been aware of her baby
brother's mistreatment of Aunt Arlene, and had talked with him about it at least
twice. Nana felt guilty for what happened because as she says, she had only
hoped Otto had changed, she never checked-up on him. Mom said, "Even Dad
and I talked about Uncle Otto's spiteful behavior, but we never did one thing."
It was clear to me that Nana, Dad and Mom were second-guessing themselves
and their complicity in this family tragedy. "Mark my words," Mom said,
"Uncle Otto's death did not end the problems."

Surprising to all of us was what Josh had to say. Josh and James Barnes
were about the same age. Although not close friends, they were second cousins
and did talk occasionally at school. Josh said that James had told one of his
teachers about his dad hitting Aunt Arlene. James said that his mother often
had bruises on her arms and face.

Mom asked, but Josh didn't know, if the school or other authorities ever
contacted Uncle Otto concerning the matter. Meddling in the affairs of others
was a community taboo.

"Kelly and I talked at the graduation party you had for me. I thought about
what she said, but always just crossed it off as an excuse of a poor student," I
confessed. I went on to tell them that Kelly told me that the reason she dropped

out of school was because her dad had spanked her. She said he had cut her lip and she was embarrassed to be seen in school. I didn't take her seriously because she was 16 or 17 when she dropped out, and too old to be spanked; besides, I reasoned, you don't get a cut lip from being spanked. "Considering what has just happened, I feel certain she was asking for help. I feel sick about all of this. She could be dead too!"

"Hold on a minute," Dad said. "I don't want anyone leaving this table blaming themselves. None of us know exactly why this disaster has happened. I do know that there is nothing more dangerous than an angry man." With that, Dad indicated that our little family meeting had adjourned.

I thought about what Dad said and would probably think about it again. One thing for sure, Dad speaks emphatically. He doesn't mind if you have a different opinion, just keep it to yourself.

When the family conference broke-up, I think we all left the table a little more confused about life, and each with a tinge of personal guilt. This story was not over.

I asked Josh and Ken if they had their sports articles for me. "Please, you've got to give me the drafts before you go to bed. I need your help." They said they would and even though they wrote their drafts longhand, it saved me lots of time.

"Mom, is it okay if I type in the kitchen? I've got lots to get done before I sleep."

"Yes, I know, and promises to keep," she sadly smiled completing my thought. "Would you let Ginger out for awhile? And, be sure to turn out the lights when you go to bed. I'm going to bed. Good night."

Less than an hour later, Mom came back into the kitchen in her faded red bathrobe and slippers. She sat down at the table where I was typing away. Mom wanted to talk.

"I can't sleep. This thing with Uncle Otto and Aunt Arlene is weighing on my mind."

"Mom, Uncle Otto was a mean man."

"Otto was the last of four children and was quite a bit younger than the other three. As his big sister, your Nana helped raise him. She has always felt responsible for him, even protective."

"Mom, I don't think Nana has anything to do with this. Uncle Otto was always upset, always arguing with someone. He did the shooting and there is no excuse."

"What I want to say is, there was good in Uncle Otto too. It was sometimes hard to find because he had difficulty relating to other people. He didn't have a close parent-child relationship; his parents were older. He was always trying to measure-up to others, especially his older siblings. He didn't feel respected, and..." Mom paused, searching for how to express her sense of Uncle Otto. "And maybe we thoughtlessly didn't show our respect. He must have felt helpless, or worse yet, hopeless."

Impatiently listening to Mom while not wanting to lose my train of thought for what I was writing, I responded without looking up, "Don't turn Uncle Otto into a sympathetic victim here. He killed his wife and tried to kill his daughter." Thinking I had succinctly boiled the excess rhetoric out of our conversation I looked up to find Mom's face full of tears.

Embarrassed to see Mom in such a sorrowful state, I got up to get her a glass of water. Then I encouraged her to go back to bed. She hugged me and headed quietly toward hers and Dad's first floor bedroom.

Upon hearing the door close behind her, I got back to work, but sluggishly so. She had left me thinking. With just a small twist of fate, Uncle Otto could have killed his entire family. Also, I couldn't help but consider the many similarities between the story coming out of Fennville and the one coming out of Benton Harbor.

XII
CHRISTMAS BALL

It was far too early for a civilized person to be out, I thought to myself as I drove along the dark and wintery U.S. 31 south towards South Haven. But there was so much that needed to be done before the trial reconvened. The road ahead lay snow covered, with about an inch and a half of build-up over night. Judging from the tracks down the highway, there were a few other crazy people up and out early on Saturday morning. It was a comfort to know that I was not the only one going to work at six 'clock. At least there was a good track to follow, and as long as I was careful, the road didn't seem too slippery. The Coupe sat high and handled surprisingly well in the snow.

The Barnes family tragedy dominated all other thoughts. It was good that Uncle Otto was dead; at least he had done something right. Common reason told me that conditions within that family must have been much worse than anyone outside ever suspected. I wanted to know more. I felt an urgent need to understand what caused Uncle Otto to explode, and not just because I was an "investigative reporter," but because this was my family.

It took me two hours in the newsroom to complete sports and special holiday event articles for the day's paper. The article I left last night for the Chief to read still lay on his desk. So I left the "Farm Tragedy" piece next to it, along with a short note, **Chief, this is the story coming out of Fennville, by C. Drew Scott.** With deadlines hanging over my head, I had been forced to concentrate and work swiftly. A sense of pride in accomplishment took my mind off my personal relationship to the Fennville story.

Before leaving the office, the thought struck me that the Chief may appreciate a bit more information. I returned to the note I'd left for him and added, **P.S. Otto Barnes is my Great Uncle and I think the Fennville and Benton Harbor cases are similar.**

As I got back into the Coupe to head on to St. Joseph, I noticed something lying on the passenger side floorboard—Mom's bouquet. I picked up the flowers to have a look. They had apparently wilted and frozen. With everything that had happened since their purchase, it wasn't surprising to me that the flowers had slipped my mind. They served as a reminder to steady my focus and avoid running around like a chicken with his head cut-off, one of Nana Hunter's favorite expressions.

From South Haven to Benton Harbor, the Eastwood murder trial replaced the Barnes' shooting in my mind. Analyzing the separate players in this courtroom drama had become my persistent pastime. I found myself mentally listing the simple facts of the case: Starr went looking for Eastwood, Starr had a gun, Starr shot Eastwood in the back, and Starr is on trial for a murder she does not deny. Sympathies aside, this was an open and shut case, and no "expert" could modify the unadorned facts.

The closer I got to Benton Harbor, the barer the road became, until evidence of last night's snow disappeared completely as I drove through town. I was hungry. My stomach ached as I passed the Pegasus. I could taste the now famous Pegasus pastries and smell the freshly brewed coffee. I wondered if Penny worked on the weekend. But Judge Jackson and his madcap accomplice, Bailiff Pile, would reconvene court in less than 20 minutes with or without me.

Before nine thirty-five Senator Pinehurst had completed a lavish introduction of Dr. James A. MacIntosh, prominent longtime Benton Harbor physician and highly acclaimed psychiatrist. It brought to mind Friday's preamble to Dr. Roebuck, and the caustic comment made by the old timer that had sat next to me; nowhere to be seen. Guess he had his fill of "expert" testimony. Apparently, so had everyone else. Less than 20 spectators sat in the gallery and less than half a dozen sleepy reporters showed up.

As with his first medical witness, Pinehurst posed several hypothetical questions for Dr. MacIntosh. Recalling the testimony of officers first at the scene of the shooting, the urbane defense attorney asked, "If Mrs. Starr was beating the prostrate Eastwood with his hat, was non-responsive when first confronted, and had a bewildered, distant expression on her face, would that indicate that she was in a state of temporary amnesia?"

"Yes," Dr. MacIntosh replied. "I would say she was suffering from what we term as 'punch drunkenness.'"

"Was she able, at that time, to discern right from wrong?"

"I would say she was not," the witness answered. He elaborated that a state of temporary amnesia frequently follows a blow to the head, particularly one on the forehead because the brain in the front of the head is the seat of cognitive processing in decision-making.

Pinehurst's request to have MacIntosh step down and show the jury the defendant's swollen forehead was denied, as expected.

Subsequent questions and answers brought out that Dr. MacIntosh knew personally both the defendant and the victim. He had known the couple for four years, and had most recently examined Mrs. Starr two days before the trial began. When asked to describe Mrs. Starr, the doctor gave the following description:

"I found Mrs. Starr to be a selfless sort of personality, wanting to do for others as opposed to doing for herself. In reviewing her family history, I found that she was born into and brought up in poverty, being required to work long hours in the fields at a tender age. In view of her limited formal education, I'm surprised to find her to be above average in intelligence, with an excellent memory, and good writing and speaking skills. She possesses normal good judgment, with no predisposition to persecute others."

Satisfied with MacIntosh's description of Starr, Pinehurst asked, "How well did you know Robert Eastwood?"

"I would say quite well. I've known him personally since he and Mrs. Starr moved to Benton Harbor." When asked, Dr. MacIntosh described Eastwood as follows:

"I would term Robert Eastwood as a constitutional psychopathic personality. This personality disorder frequently manifests itself in aggressively antisocial behavior. A person is born with this mental make-up, and it continues through life. Characteristics of this personality type are: wandering, irresponsible, disorganized, frequently failing to pay bills, and requires someone else to constantly give them direction. I have observed Mr. Eastwood wandering aimlessly around at odd hours of the day and night. He had great mood swings, from significant depression to euphoric highs, an abnormal swing of the pendulum. Periodically, he would fail to recognize people he knew quite well, and have a peculiar staring look in his eyes. Such a person might be exceedingly dangerous to the community."

As Pinehurst continued questioning Dr. MacIntosh, he maneuvered the doctor toward taking a position with regard to temporary insanity. MacIntosh proved more than cooperative, suggesting that in his opinion, "Mrs. Starr responded subconsciously in a self-protective and reflexive manner to Eastwood's threatening posture—most indicative of temporary insanity."

Skillfully, Pinehurst wove together Dr. Roebuck's testimony supporting temporary amnesia, Dr. MacIntosh's testimony supporting temporary insanity, and the testimony of both doctors supporting the self-defense theory. Evaluating his body language, made difficult through his heavy facial hair, it was clear that the Senator was self-satisfied. However, the success of this unusual and technical defense strategy would depend on how well it satisfied the 13 citizens occupying the jury box.

Following the mid-morning recess, Attorney Foster began his cross-examination of Dr. MacIntosh. The no-nonsense prosecutor made it plain from the start that the defense's theories were just that, theories, with little relevance in the real world.

Unfortunately, when Foster questioned Dr. MacIntosh at length about Starr being "punch drunk" when she shot Eastwood, he failed to raise the specter of doubt in the doctor's mind or his testimony. The resolute witness stuck to his position and further explained that "Boxers in the ring, although 'punch drunk,' will continue to instinctively strike out to protect themselves. They act only through the reflexes of their subconscious mind."

Unruffled, Foster asked, "Would a woman suffering from temporary amnesia go to her purse, take out a gun she had forgotten she put there, and shoot another person?"

To the pounding prosecutor's surprise and chagrin, the witness answered, "Yes," in a firm, authoritative manner.

Seeing that he was getting nowhere with MacIntosh, Foster spoke briefly with his associate prosecutor. Then he suggested to Jackson that this may be a good time to recess until Monday at which time the prosecution would like to cross-examine both Roebuck and MacIntosh. Judge Jackson concurred with Foster's assessment, and observing no objection from the defense, instructed Dr. MacIntosh to step down. Before excusing the jury for the weekend, he reminded them, "Remember my earlier admonition and instruction to you about discussing this case with no one. That includes not only fellow jurors, but family members as well."

Then Judge Jackson turned and requested Bailiff Pile to recess the court. Pile sprang into action. "All rise! This court now stands in recess until 9:30 Monday morning. God save the State of Michigan and this Honorable Court!" Judge Jackson disappeared in a manner reminiscent of Washington Irving's headless horseman.

Not yet noon, recess came as a pleasant surprise. I figured Judge Jackson probably had some Christmas shopping to do and was anxious to start for home. I was hungry, very hungry. I wasted no time leaving the courthouse, with the Pegasus diner as an urgent objective.

On the windy courthouse steps stood Mickey and Ruth Starr, talking in a small group. With professional agility I quickly shifted objectives, from food to a fortuitous interview opportunity. Mickey introduced me to his Aunt LaVonda Rogers, who he and his sister had traveled with to the trial. Try as I may to get them to go somewhere so we could talk, the visibly pregnant Mrs. Rogers was determined that they go straight home. She did suggest a willingness to talk with me on Monday. I walked the threesome to their car. Before they left, Mickey reminded me of his invitation to visit in Indiana. I felt he sincerely wanted me to come—as a friend. As they drove away, I thought to myself how hard it must be on the three of them; attending their mother's and sister's murder trial.

Thoughts of the trial consumed me as I walked back to the Coupe. Again and again I asked myself, where did Starr come from? Why did she send her children away to be raised by her parents? Why did she become so attached to Robert Eastwood? Why did she come here? Why did she kill Eastwood? In a general sense, my interest in this rather obscure subject was unbounded—the focus, Mary Anne Starr.

Before I got to my car, I heard someone call out, "Hey Chuck, got a minute?" It was Billy Moore, a reporter for the *Chicago Tribune* Press Service. We had talked several times over the past three days. A man in a hurry, he wanted to know if I could help him out by covering for him on Monday. He would call me Monday evening, if I would share what I picked up at the trial. I told him I'd be happy to help, knowing that he would be able to share the insights of a seasoned reporter. He thanked me, saying it would save him time and about a 90-mile drive each way.

As we parted, he offered to make me copies of trial pictures he had taken. "Terrific, my editor hasn't supplied me with a camera yet, and I could use a picture or two to go along with some of my submissions."

Still starving, I headed straight for the Pegasus, less than a mile away. As I entered, Penny checked-out a customer at the cash register. She flashed me a big smile, "Be with you in sec, Chuck." The restaurant was busy and noisy, with all tables and booths occupied. I found a stool at the end of the counter next to a squeaky swinging door separating the kitchen from the dining area. Penny hustled past me and through the swinging door, "Back to take order." I watched her disappear into the kitchen, marveling at how good the waitress outfit looked on her; or was it the other way around?

Seconds later she came back through the door carrying a steaming plate in each hand, "What you like?"

You, I wanted to say, but settled for, "Breakfast, can I still get breakfast?" I waited for an answer as she served a noon meal to two construction workers seated at a small table directly behind me.

When she came back, she asked, "How you like eggs?"

"How do you know I want eggs?"

"Because they like sausage and fried potatoes."

With raised eyebrows I said, "Okay, basted. Do you baste eggs here?"

"Well, we no send out," she laughed amusing both of us. "What you like to drink?"

"Coffee's fine as long as you brew it here and its today's," I snickered.

Penny was busy, virtually waiting on all the costumers by herself, 21 by my count. A slightly older woman brought orders out from the kitchen, and intermittently assisted Penny by covering the register. Attractive, I wondered if this lady might be Penny's mother, but she seemed too young, thirty at most.

In less than five minutes, Penny sat a plate of three eggs, two large linked sausages and a pile of fried potatoes in front of me, and without asking, warmed my coffee. This breakfast was long overdue, very good, and very much relished. The sausage had a little bite, and the potatoes were laced with garlic, onions, and red and green peppers.

I attacked my breakfast, all the time thinking that it wasn't going to be enough. Penny reappeared with buttered toast, and slid a jar toward me. Its label read, **House of David Jams and Jellies St. Joseph, Michigan**. Another mystery connected to Senator Pinehurst, I thought. Being hungry in a hectic diner left me little opportunity to talk with Penny, but I wanted to.

Before I paid my bill, the clientele had thinned some, allowing me to capture Penny's attention. I told her that I really needed to talk with Officer Barth again, and I didn't want to wait until next Friday.

"Why you need to talk to him?" Penny questioned with pinched eyebrows. I noted that Penny had a habit of putting her hand on her hip when she asked a question.

"I absolutely must learn more about Mary Anne Starr, the defendant in the trial I'm covering."

"Well, why not say what you need? There is lady who comes here Tuesday following hair appointment, about five. I know she good friend lady on trial. They come here together many time. I think she talk with you, and I introduce you so I not accused of trickery." Penny smiled knowingly.

"Thanks, Penny, I'll try to drop by around five Tuesday." I wanted to talk more, but I didn't know what to say without looking foolish. When I paid my bill, I said, "I'll see you Tuesday, for sure."

Penny's eyes sparkled, "Hope so." And I was out the door.

The road was perfectly clear all the way to South Haven. When I entered the newspaper office, the Chief reminded me of Nana's "chicken with its head cut off." I had never seen a chicken with its head cut off, but now I had a better grasp of the meaning; Chief Mendelsohn.

"Do you have your trial story ready? We have space and time!" the Chief exclaimed.

"Can I have 20 minutes? I can have it for you."

"Good, go to work. It's as good as your story out of Fennville?"

"I'll try," and hustled to my typewriter. Had the Chief just complimented me?

When I walked into the kitchen, the clock above the sink showed five straight up. The last three days had simply disappeared. Mom hurried into the kitchen from the living room carrying a small cardboard box in her hands. "Supper will be ready by six. Maxine is expecting you at seven thirty and we have decided to have you open your Christmas present early this year." I had to smile at her as she reminded me of schedule details, and was amused and confused by the present announcement.

"Is that it?" I nodded towards the box she in her hands.

"No," she said. Remembering how I had ruined the bouquet I purchased for her, encouraged a quizzical grin on my face.

Something smelled good, "What's for supper?"

"Corn beef and cabbage."

"Good. What's in the box?"

"Oh, a little something for Maxine."

"May I see it?"

Mom smiled, handing me the box. Opening it I found a delicate corsage designed in the shape of a holiday wreath of holly vine, evergreen and tiny red berries. This piece of art had been held together with a small, obscure piece of wire, and a spot of glue beneath each berry. Adding additional support, and a touch of class, was the small piece of red ribbon fastened around the wreath and tied in a miniature bow; a perfect present for Maxine. I knew Mom had gone out exploring around the farm, and selected each ingredient with care.

"Mom, this is beautiful!"

"Do you think Maxine will like it?"

"Like it, she'll love it! Thanks Mom."

"Come see your Christmas present! I want to make sure everything fits," Mom said as she pulled me by the arm into the living room. Lying over the sofa was a new gray tweed suit.

"Wow, you shouldn't have done this Mom."

"Well, you needed it, and besides it's from all of us," Mom explained unwittingly letting me know that it was expensive.

Mom had me try it on immediately. For what seemed an eternity, I let her fuss over me, tell me where she bought it, how much it cost, other suits that she had considered, why I needed another suit, and on and on and on. I truly liked the suit, and out of respect for Mom, I patiently repeated over and over how much I liked it. "Of course I'm wearing it tonight. Do you think I should take it off before I take a bath to get ready for the dance?"

"Oh, you hush," Mom said as she playfully hit me on the arm. "Now go take it off, and get washed-up for supper. Will you bring Maxine by on your way to the dance so we can see the both of you all dolled-up?"

Honestly, it was hard for me to concentrate on corsages, suits and the dance. I kept thinking of Uncle Otto and Aunt Arlene. I asked Mom if she knew anything more about what had happened. She said that Dad and Uncle Bill had been over there most of the day, and that after supper they would all meet over at Nana and Grandpa Hunter's place. If she learned anything new, she would let me know. "I feel so sorry for that family," Mom lamented.

Just two hours later Maxine and I were standing in Mom's living room. Mom bubbled over with pride, profusely complimenting Maxine on her appearance. Maxine would not be outdone, raved about how much she loved the corsage, how perfect it was.

"Dad, get your camera. We need a picture of this lovely couple," Mom said not taking her eyes off Maxine. Josh and Ken were just hanging around, not taking their eyes off Maxine either.

The Christmas Ball was held in the Fennville High School gymnasium. The dance featured a colorful winter wonderland theme. Everyone *ooohed* and *aaahed* over the lavishly decorated gym. A dance band from Grand Rapids had been hired, positioned on the stage at one end of what had become a dance hall. Each member of the band wore a black tuxedo with a gold or red cumber bun. The chic bandleader gave diminutive but professional introductions to each piece, and following each number recognized featured solo musicians. A talented and willowy female vocalist accompanied the band. In appearance, she reminded me of Mary Anne Starr, although not quite as tall or attractive.

At the end of the dance floor opposite the band was a twenty foot brightly decorated Christmas tree, and a large multi colored papier-mâché archway welcoming all "Good Little Boys and Girls" to Santa's Workshop. Huge crystal punch bowls filled with red or green punch, along with an assortment of light refreshments, were available in the workshop. Santa Claus held court listening to Christmas wishes and posing for pictures. Mistletoe hanging in the center of the archway caused the biggest commotion. The high school students had the most fun with the mistletoe, girls wanting to be kissed, and then trying to avoid being kissed. Boys just acting stupid.

The two sides of the dance floor were bordered with round nightclub tables covered by white cotton tablecloths. Each table had a red, green, or white-lit candle in the center of an evergreen wreath, several small candy canes, and small festively wrapped boxes of candies as favors.

All the evergreen decorations couldn't completely mask that ubiquitous gymnasium smell, but almost. The gym seemed much smaller than when I had been in high school. However, everyone agreed that it was a beautiful setting. The Fennville VFW Ladies Auxiliary had gone all out in their efforts to make this Christmas Ball one to remember. Several member ladies were dressed as elves, serving as Santa's helpers during the evening's festivities.

A cold clear sky teaming with millions of twinkling stars, a still snow covered rural landscape, a beautifully decorated dance hall, nostalgic holiday music wafting over an excitedly joyful crowd, I thought it was the ideal setting for a Currier and Ives lithograph. A more perfect evening would challenge the most gifted imagination.

However, all paled in the presence of my date, Maxine Faye Martin. When I escorted Maxine through the papier-mâché archway, I could feel other partygoers holding their breath as they caught sight of her. Walking beside her made me stand a little taller. She was no high school Harriet, not anymore.

Maxine's shiny green satin dress had a hint of dark burgundy running deep beneath the surface. The sleeves that reached below her elbows, and a simple collar encircling her neck, were each accented with creamy white lace. The flawlessly fitted waistline emphasized both her small waist and mature bust line. Coupled with a hemline swishing just above her shins, it gave her shape an hourglass illusion.

While admiring Maxine, I discovered a curious match between her lipstick and the ribbon bow of her corsage. Could a surreptitious collusion have taken place? Parted on the left, her glossy brown hair fell in natural curls to her shoulders. I wondered if her dazzling green eyes were as gripping to others as they were to me. She could have passed for a Hollywood movie star.

As perfect as all this may have seemed, I remember feeling edgy. The Barnes' shootings and the Starr trial were never far from my mind. Throughout the evening, several people asked me what I knew about the Barnes' killings. Two had actually read my article in the *Tribune* before coming to the dance. No one seemed to add anything new, but opinions about what happened at my Uncle Otto's were plentiful.

As Maxine and I navigated the dance floor, we tried to avoid gossip about the shootings; a difficult task considering how recently it had happened and how close to home. Also, several friends wanted to know about my work, and if I liked it. If I mentioned the Starr trial, it automatically triggered many more questions. Understanding my connection to the trial, I should have anticipated their interest.

I felt certain that many of my old male friends wanted to say hello, just to get a closer look at Maxine. I couldn't blame them, and Maxine certainly didn't discourage or disappoint anyone. She was having fun and it was infectious.

When the band played Artie Shaw's "Begin the Beguine," Maxine tried to teach me how to Fox Trot. I liked it, but before I really got the hang of it, the band played Count Basie's "Jumpin' at the Woodside," and we...well, we had a great time.

The dance was scheduled to end at midnight. Maxine and I left slightly before the bewitching hour. I looked forward to a little private time with

Maxine, but I really had no plan for how I could make that happen. The way we were dressed presented me with additional complications. Before I had a chance to "run out of gas" or "get stuck in a snow bank," Maxine suggested that we go to her place. "Everyone will be asleep, and I can make us a sandwich and some hot chocolate."

"Let's go," I anxiously agreed.

Entering Maxine's front door, we took our shoes off, trying to make as little noise as possible. Maxine took my coat and threw it over a chair, put her arms around me, and gave me an absolutely delicious kiss followed by, "I'm having a terrific time."

"Me too," I whispered as she pulled away.

"Make yourself at home. I'm going to run upstairs and change out of this dress." Back in a flash, she invited me into the kitchen to help. Taking me by the hand, she playfully pulled me behind her. Maxine had changed into a baggy pair of old pants and a heavy red and white woolen sweater. She still looked good, and now I wasn't afraid to touch her for fear I might break something. Maxine welcomed my arms around her as she made us a cold chicken sandwich and hot chocolate with lots of melted marshmallows. "Take off your tie, Chuck, relax."

She motioned for me to help her carry our midnight snack into the parlor where we could close the double oak doors and sit next to each other on a spacious sofa. The sandwich was good, but I couldn't give it my full attention, being completely distracted by Maxine's presence. I found myself constantly using a napkin to wipe off my lips, as I sipped hot chocolate.

"Do you like your hot chocolate?"

"It's very good," I complimented while taking another sip.

"See what you think of this," she said as she took a big sip of hers, sat her cup down and turned into my arms. As our lips met and slowly parted, I could feel a warm sticky marshmallow being forced into my mouth. Before I realized what was happening, our faces were sticking together in what will undoubtedly be the most memorable, and sweetest, kiss I had ever been a party to.

Giggling, Maxine drew back and reached for a napkin. She cleaned both of our faces, and then in a breathy whispered, "Want to try that again?" As we passionately embraced, I slid my right hand under her sweater and was thrilled to discover that she had neglected wearing any undergarments. Searching with my hand across her bare back sent a pleasurable shudder through my entire body. Maxine's lips moved forcefully back and forth across my face, as did mine across hers, exploring and tasting more of each other.

As we shared a delirium of frenzied kissing and petting, I consciously desired to touch more of Maxine's curvaceous, warm body. Slowly I brought my right hand around her rib cage until it was just below what I knew must be her left breast. For what seemed a euphoric eternity, I moved my hand ever closer while sensing no resistance from my feminine collaborator. Finally, I cupped what I had only dreamed of. Maxine emitted a soft moan, pushing her body firmly against mine.

I interpreted her physical signals as an unspoken, welcoming consent. We continued our passionate struggle while I fondled the womanly anatomy hidden beneath her sweater. Summoning up the nerve, I pulled back and looked at Maxine. "Maxine, may I look at your breast?" I asked, gazing into her glistening emerald eyes. To my amazement, she sat straight and pulled her sweater over her head. What I saw had to be the most amazing set of female breast ever formed; breath-taking, alive. I caressed the warm delicate pyramids in my hands, tenderly felt the nipples move beneath my fingertips, and then eagerly tasted each of them in succession.

Slowly, I felt myself becoming apprehensive. The thought of where we were and what I was doing slowed my romantic course. I whispered in Maxine's ear, "Are we safe? Is everyone sleeping?"

"I'm pretty sure no one will walk in on us," she whispered. That wasn't quite good enough to restore my eroding comfort level. Although we continued to caress each other, I worried that someone would catch us.

Eventually Maxine pulled back, "What's wrong, Chuck?" My feeble explanation was unavoidably inarticulate, not wanting to appear less of a man. As I tried to cover my ill at ease predicament, I explained to her that I couldn't help thinking about family and work problems.

Maxine pulled her sweater back on. I could tell she was annoyed, but trying to save face by engaging with me in artificial relevant conversation. We continued for a short while in meaningless interaction; the mood hopelessly lost. What began as a perfect evening was ending on a sour note.

On the drive home I remember feeling utterly frustrated with myself. Not knowing how to overcome that condition, I was at a total loss as to how I would deal with Maxine at church in the morning.

XIII
LIGONIER

I woke early after a fretful night of worrying about how to deal with Maxine when I would see her in church. After dressing quietly, I headed for the warmth of the kitchen. It was not yet seven, but I met Dad coming up from the basement. He had already stoked the fire and, of course, wanted to know what I wanted for breakfast.

"Don't you ever sleep late?"

"No, why would I want to do that?" came a positive reply.

"I don't know, it's Sunday, and you don't have anything you have to do today."

"What do you want for breakfast," he repeated, "and why are you up so early? Church isn't for another three hours."

"Well," mumbling on, "Dad," stalling, "I'm going to Kimmell, Indiana to see if I can talk to some of the trial defendant's family."

"Your mother's not going to like this."

"There's a human-interest story there that I want to tap." I explained to Dad that they were farm people just like us; subconsciously soliciting his support for my missing church. His interest in farmers plainly surfaced, but he informed me that he felt certain they were not fruit growers.

"You may be right, but I really want to see the country and the people that Mary Anne Starr came from. It may shed light on why she committed murder."

"Does your boss know what you are doing?"

"No, but he'll be okay with it."

Since we had opened the subject of human-interest stories, I asked if he knew anything more about Uncle Otto, and what was going to happen to the surviving members of the Barnes family. He told me that it had been decided that James and John would live in town with a friend and classmate of James. Aunt Jane was going to have Kelly live with them for a while. Dad reminded me that Kelly faced many personal challenges, but had a good heart and was a hard worker. Those two character traits ranked high in the county, and especially so among the Scotts.

"Do you know what enraged Uncle Otto enough to do what he did?"

"You know he has always been an angry man. I never remember him happy, ever." Dad said as he pondered just how to tell me more:

"As I understand it, your Aunt Arlene and Kelly have been working at the Fennville Cannery through most of the fall. In fact, they had just finished-up last Tuesday. Otto accused Arlene of running around with some man at the cannery. We don't think there was anything to his accusation, but he just kept getting madder and madder. According to Kelly, who had difficulty explaining all this, the two of them were yelling and screaming at each other at the kitchen table. Otto jumped up, went out on the back porch, got his shotgun, came back in and shot Arlene. Kelly was sitting at the table when it happened. She jumped up and ran out screaming. She was yelling for help when she realized her dad was shooting at her. She ran all the way to Woodleys who said they heard gunfire, and came outside to see what was going on. They saw Kelly running towards them, and Otto standing in the yard with his gun. Hank Woodley said he saw Otto go back in the house. That's when he heard the last shot. Mrs. Woodley said that Kelly was so scared and upset that she didn't even know she had been wounded. A pretty bad wound, Hank took her to the hospital, but she's okay."

"Dad, do you know if anyone had ever reported problems in Uncle Otto's family to the authorities? Josh mentioned that he thought teachers at school knew about the problems, and at the dance last night, one of my old classmates told me that he was sure there had been a complaint made to the county sheriff."

"I can't say for sure, but we all knew they were not getting along. No one could get along with your Uncle Otto for very long. As I've always said, there's nothing more dangerous than an angry man."

I hoped that Dad might be able to confirm some of my suspicions. He gave me the name of a deputy sheriff from Fennville that may be able to help me, and he also thought that if I waited a few days, we could drive over and talk with Nellie Peterson, who was Aunt Arlene's closest friend. Dad's choice of the word "we" sent me a mixed message. First, he wanted to help me, which was good. Second, he had suspicions. This could be good or bad, depending on what the two of us found.

Conversations with Dad had become more mature. They supported an emergent awareness of personal manhood, a feeling I wanted to embrace. He visibly believed that what I was doing was important, and he was not only willing, but also wanted to help. Those moments of camaraderie added to my growing sense of responsibility, somewhat paradoxical in light of the fact that I was both avoiding Mom and an impending uncomfortable meeting with Maxine.

"Dad, I gotta go. I want to be in Indiana by the time church lets out, so I can make the most of my time. Also, I want to be gone before Mom gets up." At least I acknowledged one of the two women I was avoiding.

Dad smiled knowingly, "You'd better gas-up here. It may be hard to find a station open on Sunday. I hope the paper pays for your trip."

I crossed the state line just north of Middlebury, Indiana, barely a wide spot in the road. Passing through this village gave me a feeling of turning back the pages of a history book. There were lots of horses and buggies on the street; few cars; several Amish families lived in the area. I stopped to ask directions from three boys in heavy dark coats standing beside a horse drawn wagon. They were interested in me and my car. They told me that to get to Kimmell I'd have to go through the town of Ligonier, about fifteen miles ahead.

I wished I had had time to talk with those boys, but I wanted to find Mickey Starr as quickly as possible. They said they were Amish and that several Amish families lived in the area.

The drive from Middlebury to Ligonier took me through fertile farm country interspersed with wood lots and a small lake or two. Farmhouses were plentiful, along with their complementary barns and silos, and from my observation, quite a bit of dairy production. The land went from flat to rolling, and the farms well laid out, but no real fruit orchards. I wondered as I drove what the main crops were. Old cornfields were obvious, but what I suspected to be other grain fields were not so obvious.

As I drove along the single lane country roads, I thought of Maxine and last night. She was beautiful. We had been very close to going all the way. I was certain that impression was not just wishful thinking on my part. Wasn't that what I wanted to do? She appeared willing. Now, I wasn't sure. Was I afraid of getting caught? Worried about getting her pregnant? Avoiding the commitment, responsibility? And, what about Penny? Why would a waitress at a small Benton Harbor diner be crossing my mind? I recall thinking, "too much to worry about now, I have work to do."

Pulling into Ligonier, I saw large silos that dominated the skyline next to an east/west railroad line. I parked in the middle of town, in front of the Gill Hotel, and walked the length of the main business district up and back. I greeted each person I met, usually asking a question that I hoped would stimulate conversation. In spite of the cold, that strategy did work about half of the time.

Inquiring about the Adams family resulted in a general location south of Kimmell, about five to six miles. However, I was told that the youngest Adams girl married Zeb Rogers and lived in Ligonier.

"Do you know her first name?"

"They call her Vonda, but I don't think that's right."

When I told my informant that I was trying to get in touch with her, the directions were accompanied with an animated flurry of hand gestures. Five minutes later I entered the drive to the Rogers house.

To my surprise, Mickey answered the door. He was just as surprised to see me, and hastily invited me in. Mickey took me to the kitchen to let Vonda and Ruth know they had company. The two women were busy preparing a midday meal and immediately invited me to stay and have dinner with them. I tried to decline the invitation, explaining that "I only intended to travel around the countryside and learn as much about the area and the Starr family as I could. I had not intended to impose on anyone, but Mickey had invited me to visit, and I was just sort of rambling around to see if I could find him."

They would not consider my declining their invitation. Ruth put an extra plate on the table saying, "Please call me Ruthie; Ruth sounds so formal." Before I knew it I was breaking bread at the home of Zeb and Vonda Rogers, who had one small child and one on the way in January. The Rogers had taken in Mickey and Ruthie Starr, their nephew and niece, and intended to give them a home at least until both graduated from high school. Zeb called on me to return grace before we started eating, and I gladly obliged; Mom had prepared me well for just such emergencies.

This lucky turn of events was the most serendipitous of my fledgling career. Although the Rogers lived in a modest home, their gracious generosity was boundless. They were a wealth of information, and willingly and candidly shared it with me. Mindful of the family's relationship to the defendant, I evaluated their candor as creditable.

Vonda had vivid memories of growing up in the Adams family. Her stories of how they lived and the things that she and her brothers and sisters did were very interesting to me, and Mickey and Ruthie as well. Naturally, the three of us were most interested in stories of Mary Anne. Judging from the touching way Vonda related her memories of their formative years, Vonda and Mary Anne shared a very close relationship. Ruthie noticeably enjoyed the way her Aunt Vonda compared her to her mother, Mary Anne.

Zeb grew up near the Starr family. He knew Marty Starr before Marty married Mary Anne. Marty was six years older than Zeb, but the families lived on adjoining farms, and came to know each other quite well. In fact it was because Mary Anne married Marty Starr that Vonda and Zeb met each other.

Before we knew it, Mickey reported that it was almost three, and that his basketball team was meeting for practice at three-thirty in the high school gym. "Chuck, would you like to go to practice with me?"

"Only if I can drive," I said not knowing what I was getting myself into.

"That's great. We can drive past my Grandpa and Grandma's farm, and I'll show you where my mother and Aunt Vonda grew up. The gym is in the same school they both attended," Mickey said. He also told me that he had some extra gym clothes for me to wear.

With that, Mickey got ready and I said my goodbyes to Zeb, Vonda and Ruthie, thanking them profusely. Vonda said she planned to drive Mickey and

Ruthie to the trial tomorrow and would probably see me again. I smiled, "Yes, if you are there, you will probably see me."

Mickey liked the Coupe. He directed me past the Adams farm, and on to Cromwell High School. All the time he talked to me about living with his Grandpa and Grandma Adams for the last several years. He also liked the farm, was the president of Future Farmers of America at school, and hoped to own his own some day.

Practice reminded me of the Fennville gym, not the festive hall I danced in last night, but the one I played in during my days in high school; albeit, one in the same. The Cromwell gym was even smaller. The basketball center circle and the keys at both ends intersected. The key at one end intersected higher on the midcourt circle than the other, which I knew couldn't be right. Also, there was a post about three feet inside the sideline out-of-bounds line at one end. Mickey explained that his team used the post as a sixth defensive player during the first half and as a pick during the second half. "Just call it a home court advantage." He laughed, while I considered how to write it up for *Tribune*.

As I was driving Mickey back to the Rogers' home, he shared some of his memories about his dad. The first thing he mentioned was that his dad had passed away almost three years earlier over in Ohio. His memories of his father were not happy, although he did love his father. Mickey revealed that Ruthie didn't remember much about their father, but that she had nightmares about Robert Eastwood. When I asked him to explain more, he looked at me somewhat conflicted and said, "I'd rather you ask Ruthie yourself. She hates it when I speak for her."

By the time I dropped Mickey off, it was already five and beginning to get dark. Mickey wanted me to stay for supper, but I felt I needed to get on the road. I told him I'd had a great time and would really like to visit again. He said, "I hope so, and plan to stay overnight next time."

I started straight for home, knowing it would be at least eight before I got there. It was dark by the time I crossed the Michigan border. It was also cold, but at least it wasn't snowing. Snowing made driving at night difficult because my headlights were largely ineffective, being reflected by oncoming snow.

By the time I entered Kalamazoo, I decided to stop and get something to eat. Over a sandwich, I reviewed and added to my notes. There were several poignant memories of childhood experiences and insightful comments about Mary Anne's character, and the multitude of people and events that played upon it. A good start had been made into understanding a very complex person, even though I knew I could and would find more. Learning about Marty Starr's upbringing and character was an unexpected bonus. Most importantly, I felt confident that lines of communication between the defendant's family and me were open and invaluable. *What were Ruthie's nightmares all about?*

The downstairs lights were on in every room when I put the Coupe in the barn. Ginger welcomed me with a fly by, little yips and squeals of pleasure. When she came by the second time, I lunged at her, which only encouraged her to run faster loops and bark more. What a great dog.

Mom, Dad, Josh and Ken were all in the living room trimming the Christmas tree. Without pause, I fell right in with this annual tradition, complete with arguing with my brothers over who could hang certain ornaments, and where they should be hung.

Mom said, "Maxine called and wanted you to call her when you got home. Did the two of you have a good time last night?" I had anticipated that Mom would bring Maxine up and found myself feeling a little uncomfortable with her matchmaking tendencies.

"We had a great time. Saw a lot of old friends. The Ladies Auxiliary did a terrific job of preparing the gym; and yes, Maxine was the belle of the ball. I'll call her in a minute. I have to hang Grandma's delicate silver bell before anyone else does."

"Where have you been? I thought you would have at least stopped by today?" Maxine scolded playfully over the phone.

"In a way I was working. Can I come by now and tell you about it?" I asked.

"You can help us trim the tree if you come right over. Hurry."

Mom was not real happy with me and I could sense it. I had missed church, I hadn't been home all day, I had missed most of the trimming of the Christmas tree, and now I was going out to see a girl friend. However, Mom loved Maxine. When I told her again how much Maxine enjoyed the corsage, and how many compliments she received on it, I think Mom was okay with my running out again.

Over the phone, Maxine gave me no indication that she held any negative memories of last night's conclusion. She sounded very jovial, her old self, and I was eager to see her.

When I got to her place, the Martins were trimming their Christmas tree. "Only a week until Christmas," Mrs. Martin said as she opened the door for me. "Have you picked out your Mother's present yet?"

I told Mrs. Martin about the bouquet of flowers I had purchased for Mom, and had forgotten all about. "Well, I know you can do better. Come in and help us trim our tree. Maxine is expecting you." With that, she led me into the parlor and memories of the night before.

On a stepladder, Maxine attempted to put an angel at the very treetop. In my mind, "wow, what a vision," but from my mouth, "Hi Maxine, I understand you had a good time at the dance last night."

Maxine smiled, winked and retorted, "That's what someone told me about you!" Everyone laughed.

The Martin family reminded me of my own. We all enjoyed trimming the Christmas tree. Mr. Martin brought out a few wrapped presents he had been hiding and placed them under the tree. "I'm priming the pump, so to speak," he smiled, suggesting that he expected some pretty nice presents this year.

Hilda ran up stairs, returning with two more presents, one for each of her parents, and placed them under the tree. "What about me?" Maxine pouted.

"We made presents for our parents at school, not for our sisters," Hilda came back.

Before we finished decorating the tree, Mrs. Martin had gone to the kitchen to pop some corn. Maxine offered to make hot chocolate, if anyone would be interested. I was certain she addressed the question directly to me, although she continued hanging strings of silver tinsel.

"I sure would like some hot chocolate, especially with a little marshmallow," I answered sending Maxine a sly message. The knowing glint in her holiday eyes gave me to know the message was well received.

While Maxine and her mother were in the kitchen and Hilda was upstairs, I asked Mr. Martin what he made of the Otto Barnes shooting. He expressed his sympathies, but really didn't add anything that I didn't already know.

However, when I asked him if anyone could have anticipated such a thing happening, I was shocked by his answer. He told me that early last spring Otto had taken Arlene to the hospital with a broken arm, and several bruises and scratches on her shoulders and face. Arlene reported falling from a ladder in the barn. When I looked at Mr. Martin questioningly, he looked back seriously. "That's what my sister told me. She's worked at the hospital for almost 20 years. Never saw an accident quite like it."

I wanted to talk more with Mr. Martin, but popcorn and hot chocolate arrived. It was a pleasant time that evening with the Martins, but I grew increasingly tired. Try as I may to give Maxine the attention she craved, I ultimately excused myself, saying that I had had a long day and tomorrow may be longer. Maxine walked me to the front door. She told me that some of her friends were organizing a toboggan party for later in the week.

"That sounds like fun. I'll give you a call when I get home tomorrow night." A quick kiss and I headed home. My mind quickly shifted from Maxine to my work.

While driving I contemplated what to expect during the next day of trial. I looked forward to finding out how the medical witness testimony would hold up under cross-examination. More importantly, I looked forward to Pinehurst calling Ruth Anne Starr to the witness stand. From what Mickey had intimated to me, his sister's testimony may be startling. What if she had witnessed beatings, or worse yet, what if she had been a victim? Whatever she had to say, I knew I would be there to hear it.

XIV
EXPERT WITNESSES

Ten minutes prior to Bailiff Pile's call to order, I was seated and ready for the trial, as were several fellow row-two scribblers. A quick visual survey of the courtroom failed to locate Mickey, Ruthie or Vonda. However, I did see an unfamiliar face that worked-up my curiosity. She sat in the first gallery row, directly behind the prosecutor's station. Word rapidly spread that the mystery woman was none other than Mrs. Mabel Eastwood, widow of the victim. During my surveillance, no acknowledgement or recognition passed between the defendant and the widow, if indeed they had ever before met each other.

As the seventh day of trial got underway, Pinehurst recalled Dr. McIntosh to the witness stand and reminded the jury of the physician's impeccable medical credentials. McIntosh confirmed that the answers he had given to hypothetical questions were based on information he had personally obtained, in addition to the facts assumed in the questions.

Attorney Foster objected, requesting that such testimony be stricken from the record. McIntosh assured Judge Jackson that his answers would have remained the same regardless of his independent personal knowledge of the defendant. "Objection overruled," Jackson proclaimed. "Let's get on with the questioning."

Continuing under direct examination, the doctor repeated that he had observed Robert Eastwood on at least a dozen occasions walking aimlessly, at odd hours of the day and night, with a vacant, strange expression on his face. These observations spanned two to three years.

On cross-examination, a dubious Foster paced McIntosh back through his answers to direct examination.

Q. —"Is a person a constitutional psychopath if they walk aimlessly at odd hours?" A. —"No."

Q. —"What if they have a vacant expression on their face?" A. —"Probably not."

Q. —"Doctor, you stated that you observed Eastwood aimlessly walking alone late at night on the beach. At the very least, you described this as strange behavior." A. —"Yes, I did say that."

Q. —"What were you doing on the beach at that time?" A. —"Well, I wasn't alone."

Q. —"Dr. McIntosh, did you then, or have you ever examined Robert Eastwood in your medical office or anywhere else? A. —"No, I have not."

Q. —"Did you examine Mary Anne Starr in your office?" A. —"No."

Q. —"Have you ever examined Mrs. Starr?" A. —"Yes, during the first week of December I examined Mrs. Starr in her cell at the county jail."

Q. —"Would a person suffering amnesia want to know where they were?" A. —"No."

Q. —"Would a person suffering amnesia want to know why they were there?" A. —"No."

Q. —"When you examined Mrs. Starr in her cell, how would you describe her?" A. —" As a person suffering from mental depression, as if she had lost a close friend."

Q. —"Would an extremely hard blow to the head cause a lesion?" A. —"It's likely."

Q. —"Did you find a lesion on Mrs. Starr's forehead?" A. — "No."

Q. —"Now, isn't it a fact doctor, that if a woman was struck such a blow as you've described, she'd now be in a hospital or a sanatorium?" A. —"That's not true at all."

Q. —"Isn't it a fact that a person suffering amnesia never does anything abhorrent to their character?" A. —"Of course they would. That's what amnesia is."

Q. —"Now, isn't it a fact doctor, that temporary amnesia for a short duration might easily be pretended by a smart person?" A. —"Yes."

Q. —"And if struck by a blow, as you say, wouldn't she, to use the terms of the layman, have gone out like a light?" A. — "No, not necessarily."

Q. —"Could a reasonably intelligent person feign amnesia?"
A. —"Yes."

To this question, Pinehurst stood and objected saying, "Your Honor, this question has been asked and answered, and others are quite redundant."

Jackson agreed, and requested Foster not waste the court's time repeating. "Yes, Your Honor. Thank you."

Q. —"Does the front part of the brain control the power of speech?" A. —"I think so."

Q. —"You don't know for sure?" A. —"I think so, but I'd want to look it up."

Foster made it emphatically clear that the public had the right to expect that a physician of McIntosh's caliber know such fundamental medical information. Judge Jackson had grown weary and requested Pile to recess the court. For once, I appreciated Pile's unrestrained efficient enthusiasm.

During recess, the occupants of the second row participated in an intense discussion analyzing the merits of the trial. I reticently contributed. One middle aged hack proudly boasted, "I'm going to ride this horse for as long as possible!" With unabashed confidence, he listed sordid trial headlines he had developed. Newspaper headlines were made-up and tossed about in a one-ups-man contest for most humorous. Halamka claimed that he had participated in the first newspaper interview with Starr less than eight hours from the time she shot Eastwood. He asserted it had taken place in the county sheriff's office, and that there were at least six other reporters taking Starr's picture while peppering her with questions. Yet another expressed the fear that he may be laid off when the trial ended. I covertly took notes, on everything.

Rumors circulated that Starr's daughter, Ruth Anne, would soon take the witness stand in defense of her mother. Some thought it a logical defense tactic to counter the prosecution's use of the victim's son as their final witness. Others saw it as a weak imitation. Conjecture about possible rebuttal witnesses ran from the outlandish to the humorous. One way or the other, we were about to find out. Halamka assured all who would listen, "Closing arguments will start tomorrow."

Recess ended quietly with McIntosh reassuming the witness chair and Foster resuming his witness interrogation. "You say Mrs. Starr was punch drunk. Is that the same as slap happy?"

Unfortunately for McIntosh, he had to claim he had never before heard the term "slap happy." His voice cracked as his confidence waned. In an attempt to reestablish himself, he tried to explain temporary amnesia as a form of insanity, but was abruptly cut-off. "Doctor, please, simply answer the question I ask." Foster had once again cast the shadow of doubt over McIntosh's creditability.

"During direct examination, you testified that Mrs. Starr pulled out a gun and shot Robert Eastwood as a 'dissociative reaction' or an 'irresistible reflex'—something outside her control; an automatic reflex. Is that correct?"

"That is correct. She reacted subconsciously to a perceived threat to her life."

"My God sir, she shot him in the back while he was running away yelling 'help, help!'" Foster shouted while turning pleadingly towards the jury.

"Objection!"

"Withdrawn!"

When Foster challenged the doctor's credentials, McIntosh corrected Pinehurst's introduction of him as a noted psychiatrist. He said, "I should be considered a specialist in internal medicine." The articulate, and again composed, physician did this with such humble grace that his creditability survived with minor blemishes.

"No more questions."

On redirect Pinehurst asked the witness, "Was Mrs. Starr in a state of amnesia?"

"She must have been. Amnesia may be caused by shock or by fright alone."

"Thank you, doctor. No more questions, Your Honor," Pinehurst concluded.

Foster addressed the judge, "The State would like to recall Dr. Henry Roebuck for the purpose of cross-examination." Roebuck reassumed the witness chair. He then thanked Judge Jackson for allowing him the privilege of delaying his cross-examination in order to attend a family friend's funeral. Jackson acknowledged with a nod and a pleased expression.

Foster wasted no time in confronting Roebuck with the crucial question. "Would a woman suffering from temporary amnesia go to her purse, take out a gun she had forgotten she put there, and shoot another person?"

Pausing to think, the doctor spoke deliberately, "Well, it's possible, but perhaps not likely."

Smelling blood, Foster rapidly moved through a review of the defense's hypothetical questions. Finally, "Doctor, if the facts of the hypothetical questions were changed, would that change your answers?"

"I would reserve my right to change my answer if the facts of a question were changed," Roebuck confidently responded.

"Could a smart person fake amnesia?"

"Yes. In fact, they might even wish for it; something like a self-fulfilling prophecy."

The state continued its cross-examination of Roebuck, but with some confusion as to whether they were supporting or attacking his creditability. In short, the court plodded through a rather ho-hum session filled with convoluted questions and esoteric medical language.

The midday recess mercifully arrived. It was a good bet that the afternoon session would feature a sparse gallery.

I decided to swing by the Pegasus. Mom had not packed lunch and I was hungry. On my way out of the courthouse, I met Mickey, Ruthie and Vonda coming up the steps. I asked them to join me for a bite to eat. They thanked me but declined as they were on their way to meet their mother. I expressed my hope to one day meet Mrs. Starr in person and wished them a pleasant visit. "I had a great time yesterday. Maybe we could talk after court this afternoon?"

The diner provided a comfortable familiarity; bustling with workmen eating their noon meal as if their longevity depended on it. Tantalizing aromas enticed waiting customers, and none left hungry. My order was taken by a thickly built, matronly woman who spoke broken English. The food was good and the price was right—and the Chief would reimburse me.

Satisfied, but still having some time before the trial reconvened, I left the diner and drove east on Main Street, turned south on Fair Avenue, and left on Britain. As I crossed Eureka Avenue, I shouted out, "Eureka, I've found it!" Several large buildings of the House of David religious commune lined Britain Avenue on the left, and there was a miniature train station and ice cream parlor on the right. I took the liberty of driving around the grounds, which were mostly snow covered, but still impressive. I made as many mental notes as possible, then headed back to the courthouse.

On the drive back, I thought about the House of David. What an amazing place. Maxine would love to see it. There appeared to be a stage and amphitheater, amusement park, miniature trains, ball diamond, zoo and in general, tourist type attractions. I hadn't observed much activity, but I surmised that it must be a lively place during good weather. The extent of the business empire controlled by Senator Pinehurst was impressive. However, I was left perplexed as to why the leader of this commune lived privately and several miles from colony headquarters.

Court came to order promptly at 1:30 sharp. Judge Jackson announced his intention to accelerate the trial by calling for an evening session to convene at 7:00 P.M. "There will be evening court sessions until this trial is concluded."

The legal adversaries appeared surprised, and somewhat perplexed, but made no objection. Several reporters were outwardly disappointed, preferring to drag out their trial stories as long as possible. From my vantage point, the little black robed Napoleon was determined to dispatch this case before Christmas.

"The State wishes to recall Dr. Henry Roebuck, Your Honor. We have just a few more questions for the learned doctor." As the witness returned to the stand, the two prosecution attorneys conferred and exchanged notes. "Dr. Roebuck, are you familiar with Sigmund Freud and his theories?"

"Yes, of course."

"Is it possible that Mrs. Starr's temporary amnesia could have been caused by her wish not to remember?"

"Yes, people have been known to purposefully forget disagreeable events in their lives."

After two more questions concerning Freudian theory, that seemed more about demonstrating Foster's academic pedigree than soliciting the witness' answers, the prosecution finished with Roebuck.

Pinehurst rose and requested permission to redirect. "Your witness," grumbled the ever-impatient judge.

"Dr. Roebuck, assume that a woman shoots a man half an hour after midnight. That she immediately admits to the shooting. That she talks freely about her past life. And then, she goes to bed and sleeps the remainder of the night. When she awakes in a jail cell the following morning, she asks, 'How's Bob?' By Bob, I mean the shooting victim. Would that person be suffering from amnesia?"

"Yes."

"No more questions of this witness, Your Honor." The self-assured attorney stared confidently at the jury, nodded, and unhurriedly reseated himself.

"The witness may step down."

The topic of Freud and Freudian psychology had perked my interest, thinking sex was on the docket. No such luck. Disappointed, I hoped for no more expert witnesses. Again, no such luck.

"The defendant calls Dr. Weldon Guminski." Dr. Guminski, a Benton Harbor physician, was sworn and ascended to the witness chair. To the surprise of no one, his introduction was longer than his testimony. No new information, simply corroboration of the previous physicians. During cross-examination,

Guminski agreed with Roebuck that if any of the facts assumed in Pinehurst's hypothetical questions were false, his answers would not stand.

Following Guminski on the stand came two additional witnesses of Eastwood's emotional eruptions. One was a past Van Buren County Sheriff, and the other was an unemployed Baptist minister and current neighbor of the Eastwoods. Both volunteered stories of Robert Eastwood's bad temper. A third witness, yet another Benton Harbor physician, said that he had treated Starr for what she reported as lumbago, but which he thought resulted from a blow to the back.

At four forty-five Glenn Biglow called defense witness Mrs. Stella Stallwell. Stallwell identified herself as a freelance court reporter and public stenographer. Well dressed, well spoken and confident, I judged Stallwell to be in her early forties. Certainly no stranger to this courtroom, she had sat at the defense table with Pinehurst, Biglow and their client throughout trial. She had, on several occasions, been observed offering moral support and encouragement to the defendant. Although she did not say as much, it was common knowledge that Stella Stallwell, a divorcée, and Mary Anne Starr were best friends.

When Stallwell was asked to tell the story of Mary Anne and Bob Eastwood as she had come to know them, she related an account that pointedly corroborated that of the defendant's testimony the previous week. Biglow read each question for Stallwell from a list he held in his hands. The questions and answers marched in perfect sequence in support of Starr's recollections. Biglow's obvious preparation for direct examination of this witness improved his evaluation in the opinion of the press corps.

Stallwell recalled stopping to see Starr when Starr was in bed with a kidney ailment. Stallwell believed the ailment had been the result of Eastwood kicking her in the back. She testified that Eastwood admitted to her, "Oh, I kicked her in the side. I guess I nearly broke her back."

"I asked Mary Anne why she put up with it, and she said, 'I care too much for him to leave.'"

Judge Jackson asked the witness to step down, but to be ready to resume testifying at seven when court would reconvene. He then called on Pile who was anxiously waiting to take the stage, like a hungry school boy waiting to be excused for lunch. I hoped that someone would feed Pile. Unfortunately, malnourishment was only one of the bailiff's many curiosities.

As court recessed for supper, I made my way over to Mickey, Ruthie and Vonda. Mickey was not with the girls, but talking to Houston Eastwood near the bailiff's desk. I spoke with Ruthie and Vonda, and suggested we have supper together. Ruthie thanked me, but said she and Mickey had permission to eat supper with their mother at the jail. At somewhat of a loss for what to say next, I turned toward Vonda who said, "Where are we going?" I had to smile, realizing she felt confident enough to tease me, but also knowing I only knew one place, the Pegasus.

"I have this special place, I think you'll like it."

Mickey returned to tell us that he had introduced himself to Houston Eastwood, and that he seemed an all right guy. A sheriff's deputy came by to take Mickey and Ruthie to meet their mother. Vonda told her niece and nephew that she would meet them back in the courtroom at a quarter to seven.

As Vonda and I walked out of the courthouse, I told her that it was a little more than two blocks to my car, and I'd be happy to go get it and come back for her. She smiled, "Chuck, the walk will do me good, but thank you. I warn you, I'm eating for two, and we're hungry." We laughed.

I found Vonda a sociable, cheerful person, but I felt sure that she and Zeb experienced a challenging life. Now they had the additional expense of Mickey and Ruthie living with their, soon to be, family of four. It was hard for me to understand how she could be so undeniably positive and compliant with the fate that had befallen her. Vonda and Mary Anne shared many admirable character traits, but one I found mysterious. They both experienced fleeting moments of withdrawing into their own private world, as if thinking about something from another place and time.

We drove across the bridge into Benton Harbor, my intention being to take Vonda to the Pegasus. Before I could park the Coupe, Vonda suggested that we go on to the dining room in the Vincent Hotel. I wondered at the time if I could afford it, but the Vincent was only a few blocks further, and I wanted to please Vonda as best I could. After all, she had welcomed me into her home just the day before.

The Vincent Hotel was an imposing eight-story building, prominently located on Main Street in the heart of downtown Benton Harbor. I wondered how Vonda knew about the Vincent, and why she had such a keen interest in going there. Nevertheless, supper with Vonda alone afforded me an uninterrupted chance to ask several burning questions.

XV
MURDER AFTER MIDNIGHT

In the well-appointed confines of the luxurious Vincent Hotel dining room, Mrs. LaVonda Rogers poured out the story of Mary Anne Starr's early life. Vonda possessed a wealth of recollections, which she fervently shared with me. Indeed, she displayed a need to do so. Adding to her account what I had already discovered in public documents, legal records, and courtroom testimony enabled me to construct a substantial record of my subject's life. I carefully organized all such evidence and kept it in a journal I titled, "Murder After Midnight." Coupling my journal entries with Vonda's reminiscences, I penned the following unfinished freelance essay. I felt I had discovered a praiseworthy bond between two devoted sisters.

There isn't much that would distinguish Noble County, Indiana from the rather ubiquitous turn-of-the-century Midwestern farming communities. If the county had been in Kansas, it could easily have been mistaken for the setting of L. Frank Baum's allegory The Wonderful Wizard of Oz (1900), currently being made into a Hollywood movie, "The Wizard of Oz," scheduled for release next year. Small villages, lakes, woodlands and open prairies dotted the gently undulating landscape of north central Indiana. This fertile land provided a living for both the men and beasts who teamed to work it. For most it was an adequate, though not so comfortable existence.

On June 28, 1904, Mary Anne Adams was born to parents William T. and Mary Adams. The Adamses were grain and mint farmers. Little Mary Anne was their third child and at the time of her arrival, the Adamses had taken up temporary quarters in their barn, while they built a new house. This fact is the source of a much latter scornful accusation that Mary Anne was "born in a barn." By 1915 the Adams family had grown to six children, a total of eight all living under the roof of a small farmhouse. Unfortunately, family prosperity did not keep pace with family growth. During that time, the mint industry moved north into Michigan; mint had been the family's primary cash crop.

It never occurred to the Adams children that they were growing up in intimate proximity to stark poverty. Their lives were quite similar to the lives of all other Noble County children. They always had each other, if not much more. Mary Anne's sisters, Betty Jane, two years older, and LaVonda, three years younger, were her primary playmates until she reached high school. A close bond was forged with Vonda, who became a willing and happy participant in many of Mary Anne's imaginary adventures. The sisters always shared a warm emotional connection.

Mary Anne's father openly hoped for a second son when Mary Anne was born. Unfortunately for her, she was made aware of this fact at an early age and suffered a struggling, at times contentious, relationship with her demanding father. As a little girl, her father frequently addressed her as Mike, exacerbating a less than affectionate relationship. Mary Anne carried a lingering suspicion that she never quite measured-up to her father's expectations.

By Mary Anne's sixteenth birthday the six Adams children, ranging in age from five to twenty, were all still living in the same cramped farmhouse a few miles southwest of the tiny hamlet of Kimmell. The Great War had been over for more than a year. The deadly Swine Influenza, which caused more casualties than the war, had all but run its course. Republican presidential candidate Warren G. Harding called for a "return to normalcy." If his campaign slogan meant that Americans should return to a previous comfortable life, it rang hollow in the ears of the Adams family. This family had experienced little more than a subsistence quality of life during the first two decades of the twentieth century.

Maturing early, Mary Anne possessed a keen awareness of the world around her. Growing up within a close-knit farm family, her circle of life consisted of family, farm, church and school. Along with her brothers and sisters, she had attended a one-room rural school, first through the eighth grade. At sixteen, Mary Anne had completed one year at Cromwell High School. An above-average student, she liked school and, like many her age, paid increasing attention to personal grooming and social acceptance. She enjoyed reading magazines, mimicking fashion trends, movie star Mary Pickford's glamour and George M. Cohan's music. Most importantly, she reveled in the peer level social interactions that going to high school offered.

Her life at home consisted of routine work around the house and farm, and helping with the care of three younger siblings. Each of the brothers and sisters were assigned regular farm chores, but organization and follow through were seldom consistent. As Mary Anne matured, she provided some leadership in family duty organization, and enjoyed assisting her parents with bookkeeping. The Adams family could ill afford any of the embellishments of life. Mary Anne felt stifled, sometimes embarrassed, and began to display an independent, passive aggressive nature.

As school started her sophomore year, she met Marty Starr at the 1920 Labor Day celebration in Ligonier, Indiana. Ligonier was a farm village fifteen miles north of the Adams farm. It featured grain elevators along an east/west railroad line, several stores, one hotel, two churches, a synagogue, and a farm implement center. On a typical day, the streets of this small town displayed a rich religious mix of Mennonites, Amish, Jews, Catholics, but with a preponderance of local Protestants. They all lived in harmony, with the exception of one brief spat, when area Mennonites conscientiously objected to the Great War. That had passed, and all were on hand for the Labor Day celebration.

Marty Starr was five years older than Mary Anne. Wearing his Doughboy uniform, he proudly marched in the Labor Day parade with other Army veterans. Marty had grown-up in a family situation quite similar to that of Mary Anne, and although they had never met, his home was less than twenty miles northwest of the Adams farm.

Given the fact the he was older and had been overseas with the U.S. Army, may have caused Mary Anne to view Marty as more worldly and self-assured than he deserved. However, he was more physically mature than the boys she knew at Cromwell High School.

Unfortunately, Marty's lack of ambition and life direction, common knowledge within his community, had not reached down to Kimmell. His parents had hoped that a stint in Uncle Sam's Army would help to kindle a fire under him. It did not. But, Mary Anne Adams did kindle his fire. Her long silver blond hair, pure blue eyes, and tall, well-proportioned body caught the attention of most boys. She completely captivated Marty with her good looks and appealing exuberance.

For Mary Anne, Marty was a man, a war hero. He represented a door out of, what she considered, a drab situation and a pathway to, she hoped, a stimulating life. Mary Anne was as awestruck with Marty as he was smitten by her. He stirred in her a tender recollection of a line she had just read in "Vanity Fair": "Three things shall I have till I die, laughter and hope and a sock in the eye." The style of the quote charmed her, but she paid scant attention to its full meaning.

Marty started coming by the Adams place to see Mary Anne every weekend without fail. He had a car and they could go out together; Mary Anne liked that very much. It gave her a chance to get away and no one seemed to mind. The special attention thrilled her, as did the newfound liberation from her colorless home environment. Traveling through the countryside on the seat next to "her man" was a dream come true. One Saturday they ventured to the big city of Fort Wayne, 35 miles away. The two were inseparable.

By Christmas Mary Anne was certain that she had become pregnant. Since the first time she and Marty had shared intimate relations in the front seat of his car, she speculated what it would be like to have a baby, be married; live with just one someone, somewhere different. After the first time, having intimate relations became a regular, and feverishly anticipated part of their relationship. *Although she had not overtly intended to become pregnant, it was not a shock to her, and not entirely unwanted. The desire for a change in her life would definitely take place; it could not be avoided. Mary Anne Adams was optimistic but Marty oblivious.*

At that time and place, an out-of-wedlock pregnancy, almost without fail, demanded marriage. Marriage was expected, and considered the responsible thing to do. Any other choice could, and almost surely would, bring discredit on man, woman and child. The pressure for an expecting couple to get married was self-imposed, family imposed and community imposed. Marty grudgingly succumbed to the pressure, and for the first time in his life sought, acquired, and tried to hold a steady job; a fulltime farm hand.

By New Year's Day 1921, Mary Anne was beginning to show, and would soon be forced to admit to being pregnant. Therefore, in mid January with the completion of the first semester of her sophomore year, she dropped out of Cromwell High School. She and Marty, the Adamses and the Starrs, started making wedding plans.

Marty had found a job outside his parents' farm and Mary Anne hoped to do the same. Unfortunately, she experienced severe morning sickness, and sporadic debilitating bouts of nausea. Her mother's support and assistance through this difficult time was welcomed and appreciated. Anticipating having a child together, but not actually living together, presented awkward moments for the expecting couple. Mary Anne's father stood aloof, while growing more and more skeptical of Marty's character.

Marty and Mary Anne were in no position to make or expect elaborate wedding plans. Their weak economic condition was shared by both sets of parents. Who would cover the costs of a wedding, and where were the young couple and new baby going to live; how would they make a living? These questions weighed heavily on all parties, with the possible exception of Marty. In spite of everything, Mary Anne's outward optimism concerning the future seemed boundless. However, fleeting thoughts questioning Marty's moral fiber intermittently crossed her mind. When this occurred, she would quickly brush it off, telling herself that marriage made the man, and she would always be there to help him.

As her pregnancy progressed into the sixth month, the couple decided to embark on the only viable option available to them. They eloped. Sixteen and six months pregnant, Mary Anne Adams ran away with her war hero Marty Starr. Eloping to get married seemed the expected and proper thing to do given their circumstances—young, poor and pregnant. In Marty's car, and with only the few dollars they scraped together between them, they couldn't go far, and couldn't be gone long. Their dreams and expectations for a future together may only be imagined. For certain, they were resigned to returning home promptly, at least until after the arrival of their baby.

Perched high on a bluff overlooking the meandering St. Joseph River, the massive dark brick and stone Berrien County courthouse in St. Joseph, Michigan must have frightened the apprehensive young couple. Mary Anne had never been so far away from home, but the new surroundings excited her. Holding hands, they ascended the spacious concrete steps and entered the great hall.

Mary Anne wondered if they would be allowed to marry. She took heart in knowing that others had done this before them. For as long as could be remembered St. Joe had served as the Gretna Green for northern Indiana, with interesting stories told of young couples traveling there to tie the knot.

Her question was soon answered when they were directed to the Justice of the Peace in the second floor County Clerk's office. In that office, on March 16, 1921, Mary Anne Adams exchanged wedding vows with Marty Starr. On their marriage certificate, Mary Anne claimed to be 18 years old while Marty honestly and proudly reported being a 21 year old Great War veteran. This civil ceremony took less than five minutes.

The newlyweds' honeymoon consisted of a hand-held walk on the blustery bluff overlooking a cold, dark-blue Lake Michigan. A large white fountain watched over by two sculpted Athenian maidens gave the setting a feeling of fairytale splendor. They sat on a park bench near the veranda of the famed Whitcomb Hotel, and admired the interplay between white caps and sea gulls skimming the lake surface. A chilling west wind blew horizontal tears from Mary Anne's steel blue eyes. Brushing them away, she directed Marty's attention to the sun reflecting off the sail of a boat leaving the harbor between the pier and lighthouse. As Marty's arm clutched tightly around her, Mary Anne wished for a happy future—a sail across a quiet sea toward a beautiful sunset in paradise.

From the lake bluff, the newlyweds strolled to the hotel dining room, and shared the most elegant dinner either could imagine. However, both experienced some discomfort while being served. First, neither had ever dined out in their life, and both were unsure of proper etiquette. Secondly, the hotel and dining room conveyed elegances, an extravagance beyond their limited familiarity. Were they dressed properly? Did they look out of place? Nevertheless, Mary Anne took it all in, and thoroughly enjoyed herself. She wanted this part of life, and refused to allow a single unenthusiastic thought to enter her mind, especially those of obstacles that may lie ahead. A sock in the eye; never.

Following the meal, the couple headed back to Indiana and the Starr home. They arrived at dusk to a small reception of the two immediate families. Mary Adams had made a wedding cake and the Starrs had made ice cream. The two families enjoyed a good time together honoring Marty and Mary Anne. Marty's father proposed a toast to the guests of honor. Everyone clinked their glasses of grape punch together followed by jokes about prohibition. The celebration lasted less than two hours. When the Adamses had left for home, the Starrs unveiled to Marty and Mary Anne a bridal bedroom fixed-up especially for them. Mary Anne cried. Marty enjoyed a second dish of ice cream.

From their marriage, until Donald Starr was born June 29, 1921, the day following Mary Anne's 17th birthday, the newlyweds lived with Marty's parents and siblings. Following the baby's birth, the young family moved-in with Mary Anne's parents and siblings; the two oldest of which had moved out. Mary Anne felt more comfortable depending on her mother for assistance with the baby. Of course little sister Vonda was always at her beckon call, and thoroughly loved helping care for the baby.

Both homes were crowded, and provided only tolerable living arrangements for Mary Anne. She determined to endure these circumstances as only temporary.

Marty worked steadily as a farm laborer. Mary Anne found little jobs from time to time outside the home, but remained attentive to the wants and needs of baby Donald, who she and Vonda affectionately called Little Mickey. Vonda enjoyed assisting with Mickey's care, and became a great help and confidant to Mary Anne.

It was apparent that staying in Noble County, Indiana provided only bleak future prospects. Therefore, during the spring of 1922, Marty, Mary Anne and Mickey moved to Vicksburg, Michigan where Marty obtained a job in a butcher shop. This move improved their quality of life, and relieved the stress on their parents' households as well. Their future brightened.

It wasn't long before Mary Anne discovered she was pregnant with their second child, Ruth Anne, born March 1, 1923. As the growing family struggled to make ends meet, Marty left the butcher shop, and took a job working in the Vicksburg paper mill. Mary Anne started taking part-time jobs, and soon worked fulltime in a clothing store as a sales girl, with some modeling. The young family of four projected a wholesome image of social and economic stability.

However, in spite of both working, the Starrs still experienced financial difficulties. Marty was money-wise irresponsible, and had developed a drinking habit. By the mid 1920s, his drinking became problematic. Mary Anne's persistent pushing of him to be more responsible for supporting his family only served to aggravate an increasingly difficult situation. Marty became verbally abusive.

In early 1927, Mary Anne discovered Marty cheating on her. Shortly thereafter, an argument erupted between them when Marty returned home from a late night of carousing at a local speakeasy. As their argument grew heated Marty became enraged. He crudely announced that he had contracted a venereal disease. Because of her husband's condition, Mary Anne never again shared intimate relations with Marty. However, with their options limited, the two of them continued to live in the same house with their children. Mary Anne sincerely wanted and tried to keep her family together.

While her husband squandered his paychecks, Mary Anne worked hard at poor paying jobs, trying her best to feed, clothe and house the family. Also, she suffered from an ever-increasing level of verbal, and then physical abuse from Marty. After almost seven years of marriage, and two growing children, Mary Anne started, albeit reluctantly, thinking about divorce.

Marty's abusive behavior toward Mary Anne continued to escalate until on the evening of February 15, 1928, he exploded in a savage rage. Swearing at her, he struck her several times, knocking her to the floor. Mary Anne sustained multiple scrapes and scratches, including a sever bruise on her right cheekbone.

With hers and her children's welfare at stake, she obtained a restraining order against Marty, and successfully had him removed from their home. How would these developments affect family members, and how they would react, weighed heavily on Mary Anne's mind.

Divorcing proved much more difficult for this young farm girl than getting married. However, determined to make a better life for herself and her two children, Mary Anne displayed the independent self-determination emblematic of the Flapper generation. Maybe this was her "sock in the eye."

She had cared and provided for her husband and children. She had taken a job as a sales lady for $10 a week to help supplement the $24 a week Marty received working in the paper mill. Further, she endured repetitious spousal abuse from an unfaithful husband who frequently failed to support his family in any manner.

No more! Seeing a hopeless future with Marty, one she had suspected many years earlier, but never admitted, Mary Anne committed herself to a separation. She retained a lawyer, and in March of 1928 officially filed for divorce. She wanted more out of life than the day to day drab subsistence she, Mickey, and Ruth Anne shared with Marty; more correctly, endured at the hands of Marty.

QUIET GUILT

In the official Divorce Decree, Mary Anne Starr—Plaintiff, charged Marty Starr—Defendant with verbal and physical abuse, marriage infidelity, threats against her life, and failure to support the family financially. She requested a permanent restraining order, temporary alimony during litigation, a sum suitable for the support and maintenance of the minor children both temporarily and permanently, and payment of her attorney fees. Lastly, she requested full custody of Donald and Ruth Anne Starr.

With Mickey six and Ruth Anne barely five, Mary Anne packed their meager possessions and headed for the big city—Kalamazoo. Only twenty-three and a single parent of meager means, Mary Anne's pride would not allow her to seek family or public assistance. She had requested and received a temporary alimony payment of $5 per week until the divorce was official.

Finally in control, she had no intention of relinquishing her independence. Immediate objectives were self-apparent—housing for the three of them and employment for her. When able, she would tend to legal debts. The road ahead appeared difficult, but to Mary Anne Starr, the future brimmed with alluring possibilities. Kalamazoo energized her.

On June 16, 1928, the Decree for Divorce, uncontested by Marty Starr, was filed; marriage dissolved. Mary Anne was elated. She had won full custody of Mickey and Ruth Anne. Marty was declared "an unsuitable person to have the care and custody of the minor children." Mary Anne received $1 in lieu of any claim she may have against Marty's property. The court ordered Marty to pay a sum of $5 per week for the support of minor children until they reached the age of sixteen. Also, he was required to pay $50 towards Mary Anne's attorney's fees. No alimony.

The "Age of Ballyhoo," as epitomized by the decade of the 1920s, had nearly passed her by. She had struggled to keep her ill-fated marriage together. Now, she felt certain that her divorce was the best thing for her two children, and for her. Since meeting Marty Starr, Mary Anne had not had much time for herself. She had wanted to read "The Great Gatsby."

The plan for the forgoing essay took form while having dinner with Vonda and listening to her recollections of Mary Anne's life. Even after writing this much, I knew I had only scratched the surface. Someday "Murder After Midnight" may become a full-fledged book. With Vonda lost in her memories and me mesmerized by the possibilities of a future writing project, I awoke to the fact that I needed to judiciously move both of us back into the present.

"Well, did she?"

"Did she what?" Vonda asked as if coming out of a deep sleep.

"Did she read *The Great Gatsby*?" I laughingly asked.

"Of course she did, and so did I. We had a terrific time discussing it, as we have other books," Vonda came back, half joking, half scolding.

Emphasizing her point, she went on to explain how she and Mary Anne shared their most intimate secrets, and had since they were both little girls. Mary Anne enjoyed reading, bird watching, pets, and going to the movies. Robert Eastwood took her to several movies early in their relationship. She loved movies, following the careers of Hollywood actors and actresses. After seeing the movie "Jane Eyre" with Eastwood, Mary Anne became a devoted fan of movie star Virginia Bruce. I found it ironic; "Jane Eyre" was the sad story of a strictly raised, willful young lady's bout with unrequited love. Mary Anne Starr bore a strikingly strong resemblance to Virginia Bruce, an appearance she secretly nourished.

"Mary Anne and Bob Eastwood stood-up with Zeb and me at our wedding. Honestly, I never cared much for Bob, but Mary Anne loved him," Vonda said with contempt on her face and in her voice. "He could be charming when he wanted to," she added without conviction.

"Vonda, did you believe they were man and wife?"

"Well, I had my doubts, but Mary Anne always insisted that they were; common law marriage she said. I visited Mary Anne several times when she lived in Kalamazoo, and a couple of times here in Benton Harbor. In fact, Ruthie and I stayed in this very hotel the last time I brought her up to see her mother."

"When was that? Did Ruthie think they were married? What did she think of Eastwood?"

Vonda stammered. A forlorn countenance came over her. "You...you can ask Ruthie those questions yourself. We'd better get back to the courthouse. I want to talk to Mickey and Ruthie before the trial starts." It was getting late, but there was something about Vonda and the way she moved us along that left me mystified.

We drove quietly the mile back to St. Joe. I liked Vonda and I think she liked me.

XVI
STELLA STALLWELL

Vonda and I reentered the courtroom ten minutes prior to the start of the first evening session. Mickey and Ruthie were standing behind the defense counsel table, listening intently to the conversation between Senator Pinehurst and their mother. Vonda thanked me for dinner and headed in their direction. I wanted to accompany her, but thought it would be intrusive, besides two fellow newsmen abruptly pigeonholed me. "What's this we hear about Starr's daughter not going to testify?"

"What?" I assured them that I knew nothing of this, and, like them, I had been anticipating Ruth Starr's testimony following Stallwell's. It seemed a logical strategy to me, and one shared by my colleagues. Rumors circulated that Miss Starr had been a witness, if not a recipient, of Robert Eastwood's violent behavior. Both Pinehurst and Biglow had made public statements over the weekend suggesting that the defendant's daughter would be their most important defense witness. If there had been a change of plans, we all wanted to know the reason.

The nervous anxiety that permeated the courtroom was squelched by Pile's haranguing call to order, followed by the judge's brusque gavel. "Let's get started. Would the defense please call their next witness," Judge Jackson instructed as the first evening trial session got underway.

"Yes, Your Honor. The defendant wishes to continue the direct examination of Mrs. Stella Stallwell."

Before the stately Mrs. Stallwell reached the witness stand, Pile rushed forth to waylay her. When less than ten feet away, he yelled at Stallwell, "Raise your right hand!"

The flushed witness, somewhat taken aback, submitted and was sworn again to tell the truth. As she did so, she revealed a distinct Irish accent and a hint of Irish ire. Well tailored, Stallwell wore a completely new outfit from what she had worn when she stepped down from the witness stand less than two hours earlier. This was a woman proud of her appearance.

Judge Jackson shared Stallwell's surprise at being readministered the oath to tell the truth. He grinned at Stallwell as he said, "Mrs. Stallwell, I guess you realize that you are still under oath to tell the truth?" She looked up at the judge but didn't share his amusement.

Attorney Biglow gave a quick synopsis of Stallwell's earlier testimony in preparation for continuing. He recalled that she had known Bob and Mary Anne since 1934, when the couple first arrived in Benton Harbor. She considered herself a good friend of both, had socialized with them as a couple, and was regularly in the company of Mary Anne. The two women were close friends.

"Mrs. Stallwell, in addition to the kicking incident already testified to, could you give us another example of Eastwood admitting to abusing Mary Anne?" Biglow wore a smug look.

"Oh my yes."

"Please give us just one more example."

"Mary Anne called me on the telephone the Wednesday evening before the shooting. She was crying. She needed my help. When I found her, she had been badly beaten. I helped her get cleaned-up, drove her home and ultimately put her to bed. I checked on her a couple of times on Thursday. On Friday about noon, I went to Mary Anne's house again, and saw her without the bandages. She looked better, but not great. Bob was home. He said to me, 'There it is again. Family interference and I beat-up Mary Anne.'"

"What do you mean by 'family interference?' Can you clarify?"

"I had heard it before, and always took that to mean his brother Harley Eastwood. Following a previous incident, Bob said to me, 'I'm about ready to get out of this town. If my people would let me alone, I'd get along all right. But I have a fight with them and then I come home and beat Mary Anne.' As I was leaving their house, Bob said, 'Stella, I guess you know I'm a rat by this time.' That's the last time I saw either one of them until I saw Mary Anne sitting on a jail bunk the morning after the shooting. She looked up at me kind of woozy, punch-drunk and said, 'Hello, Stella.'"

The witness blotted her nose with a linen hankie, and then chokingly continued, "That's all that was said between us because Deputy Barth had me wait outside until Sheriff Diamond got there."

Biglow got a glass of water for Stallwell. She took a sip. He continued, "Could you give us a general description of Mr. Eastwood's personality?"

"Bob was low and depressed about half the time. Whenever he was like that, he made derogatory remarks about other attorneys and county officials, and became flighty and irrational. He was erratic about his law practice; disorganized. Other times he was just swell."

Stallwell testified to her awareness of the prowler incidents that led to Bob and Mary Anne buying a gun that he intended for their protection. "Bob was especially upset about the prowler's vandalism and thievery, and made reports to the police."

Biglow announced that the defense had no more questions for this witness, and Mrs. Stallwell started to get up from the witness chair. "Please remain seated, Mrs. Stallwell. I think there may be a few more questions," Judge Jackson requested as he look toward the two prosecutors.

"Yes, Your Honor, we have a few questions," came a firm response from Attorney Robert Spears. Foster had delegated the responsibility of cross-examining Stallwell to his associate. Spears was eager to jump into the fray. This was his first case since winning the fall election for Berrien County Prosecuting Attorney. He had convincingly defeated the Democrat candidate Harley Z. Eastwood, and seemed to be feeling his oats.

Spears walked briskly over to the witness box. Clearing his throat, "Mrs. Stallwell, it is apparent to me, indeed to all of us here, that you have a strong interest in this case. You and Mrs. Starr have been close friends for several years. It's a fact, is it not, that you have been present here in the courtroom for every minute of this trial?"

"Yes."

"Isn't it a fact that you sit with the defense team, at the defense table, everyday?"

"Yes."

"Mrs. Stallwell, I was impressed by the quality and organization of the questions put to you by defense counsel."

"Is that a question?" Stallwell asked.

"No, but this is. Did you create and type-up those questions for Mr. Biglow, the ones he just completed asking you?"

"Yes."

"The questions and answers sounded very familiar, as if their ideas came from, and were crafted to support, previous witness testimony."

"Is that a question Mr. Spears?"

"No, but this is! Did you copy ideas from previous defense witness testimony to piece together the questions that were asked of you? For example, Dr. McIntosh's description of Starr as 'punch drunk?'"

"No, that was my idea. It just happens to be one shared by the doctor."

"Following Attorney Biglow's reading of the questions, when you hesitated, straining your face in deep thought as if searching for and considering your answers; that was all just an act, wasn't it? You knew the answers because you made-up the questions. "

"If that's a question, you're partly right, Mr. Spears. I did make up the questions, and I did know the answers, but not exactly how I would word them. Therefore, I always think and reconsider before answering any question."

"That's good," Spears responded with obvious incredulity filtered through his voice. "How-about you describe for us again, in your own words, your impressions of Robert Eastwood."

Stallwell's answer was essentially a recap of what she and other defense witnesses had earlier stated. However, when she described Eastwood as a nervous man, Spears barged in, "Nervous like a man who was harried by a malicious woman?" He hadn't intended for the question to be answered, and it wasn't.

"You have testified that Starr suffered physical abuse at the hands of Eastwood on a couple of occasions. Did you ever actually see Eastwood strike Starr?"

"No."

Then Spears asked a question that seemed out of place, out of context, and totally new information as far as I could decipher. "Are you aware of Robert Eastwood's oil well holdings?"

"No," responded the perplexed witness.

As I looked around the courtroom, I observed others doing the same, questioningly. A gentleman seated behind me tapped me on the shoulder and whispered, "He's planting the seed for a motive. The widow has been in court all day." I thanked him with an understanding nod, but wasn't sure of what it all meant.

Shifting subjects again, "Isn't it a fact, Mrs. Stallwell, the so-called prowler turned out to be a neighborhood dog, and that the boy who owned it found the clothes and brought them back?"

"Not that I ever heard."

Shifting again, "Isn't it a fact that Mrs. Starr was pretty good with her fist?"

"Not that I know of."

Spears asked several questions of Mrs. Stallwell concerning Starr using vulgar language, throwing furniture, and scratching and clawing at Eastwood. With each of these questions came a familiar, emotionless response of lack of knowledge.

Spears may have had more questions, but it was clear he had gone as far as he could with this witness. After enduring more than two and a half hours of grilling, Stella Stallwell was permitted to step down.

The time had come to discover if Ruth Anne Starr would be called as a witness. A flourish of agitated whispering passed through the gallery. All eyes were on the pretty fifteen year old, slender blonde seated in the first row directly behind her mother. Mother and daughter bore an unmistakable resemblance. The girl's moist, blue eyes stared at the floor.

Judge Jackson looked at his watch and reminded everyone that court would reconvene at 9:30 A.M. Then he nodded to Pile, who sprung into action.

On my way out of court, I spoke briefly to Vonda, Mickey and Ruthie who were all in a hurry to start home. A couple of others had tried unsuccessfully to talk with them. I could see that they were agitated and wanted to get away; it had been a long day. They told me they had to go to school in the morning, but may be up for the evening session. My question for Ruthie was left unasked, but answered; she would not be testifying.

I went straight to the public telephones, and placed a collect call to William Moore at the *Chicago Tribune*. We talked for 15 to 20 minutes. Billy told me that the prosecution probably wanted Mabel Eastwood at the trial because of the letters they used during the cross-examination of Starr. Mabel Eastwood had been appointed the administrator of the victim's estate, which may include oil claims; a tacit suggestion of motive. He wanted me to find out about the oil and if Starr was in fact indigent. He asked if I could call him same time tomorrow. I said I would.

"Thanks Chuck. You've been a lifesaver. Your pictures are in the mail."

XVII
OBJECTION

I patted myself on the back repeatedly during the drive home. I pictured myself as a dispassionate thinking, tireless investigator, who used cool honest logic in reporting the news; the reporter who best understood the Robert Eastwood murder case. The victim was brash, abrasive and prone to bad temper; not surprising since he was orphaned at age five when his schizophrenic parents were institutionalized. At the age of twenty he suffered gas poisoning, which led to a disability discharge from the U.S. Army. Regrettably, he found release from the pressures of daily life by lashing out violently towards his common law wife.

On the other hand, the defendant was passive aggressive. She relentlessly sought the good life and had persistently pushed upward on the social and economic ladder. Unfortunately, Robert Eastwood became the ladder to her dreams. I believed that my efforts to know Mary Anne Starr and the origins of her behavior were unrivaled.

This newly acquired knowledge allowed me to understand why the murder happened, but it did not exonerate the murderess. I had drawn a sense of self-satisfaction and confidence from what I believed was reasoned, impartial evaluation.

The Chief had directed me with several questions, and now I had the answers. If justice were to prevail, Mary Anne Starr would be found guilty of non-premeditated murder—manslaughter. It wasn't clear to me what the sentencing parameters were, or what Starr's sentence should be. I still had work to do, but at least I was objective; more than I could say for other reporters and their newspapers, all of which consistently vilified Starr.

After reading hundreds of newspaper accounts, and interviewing numerous officials and average citizens, I felt I had a good handle on all that had happened from the time of the shooting through day seven of the trial. The first two days of the trial, the days I had missed, seemed to be the last remaining gap—my next day's objective.

Shortly after eleven I pulled the Coupe into the barn. Someone had put Ginger out and she exploded past me like a bat-out-of-hell. What made this animal so happy, so full of life? Whatever it was, it always made me feel good. I was happy to be home.

Mom and Dad were still up. Mom told me that Ken seemed upset about something and that maybe I should look in on him. I wanted to talk with Ken anyway; I needed his and Josh's help with some articles for the paper.

I could see a light on in his room, so I knocked lightly and entered, finding him seated at a small desk, reading.

"Mom thinks you're upset about something?"

"I'm not as upset as John Barnes."

"How's that? Did you find out anything more about the Uncle Otto thing?"

"I don't think you know, but John and I have been in the cast for the senior play. We had tryouts in early November and we both won parts. We've been working hard at play practices and for the first time really getting to know each other. I guess you could say we've become good friends."

Trying to be the supportive big brother I said, "Well that's good isn't it? I suspect John could really use a friend about now."

"Chuck, last Friday was our first performance. We were planning to have a surprise 18th birthday party for John following the opening. When we found out at school that afternoon that something bad had happened at the Barnes' place, everything was postponed. We haven't put on the play or the party. I don't think anyone ever told John what we were planning."

"Well, how is John taking this—have you talked to him since the funeral?"

"I had a long talk with him today. We skipped school and went down to the depot. He's really taking this hard. He's thinking about running away, jumpin' a train. He doesn't want to be taken in by another family."

Holding my reactions and suggestions in check, I asked, "What do you think we could do to help him?"

"Chuck, you don't understand. He's upset because he wanted to kill his dad and now he feels that it's all his fault because he was a coward; afraid to do it. I knew he didn't get along with Uncle Otto, but I didn't know he had planned to kill him. At the depot he told me plain."

"He did the right thing. It wasn't his place to kill anyone. I hope you told him he should never do something like that. He's probably overstating his intentions, but not killing his dad certainly does not make him a coward."

"Oh, he's not a coward, that's for sure; I know him. But Chuck, if he'd killed his dad, his mother would still be alive and his dad would still be dead. To John there was no other way. No one was going to stop Uncle Otto. No one was going to help! James, John, Kelly and Aunt Arlene would have continued to live in terror. Chuck, it wasn't going to just stop! Do you understand?"

A faint knock, the door opened and Mom came in. "What are you boys arguing about? Please keep your voices down. Dad needs his rest. Go to bed. It's late."

"We're not arguing Mom. We'll keep it down."

Mom stared at the both of us, "There's a note from Maxine on the kitchen table." Then she turned and closed the door behind her.

"Ken. Thirty minutes ago I thought I knew all there was to know. Now, I don't think I know anything. But, I'm going to try to find out more about this.

I have no advice, but let me know if I can help you or John. That's about all I can say." Ken nodded and looked back at his book, but I didn't think he was reading.

In the kitchen I foraged for something to eat. Mom, in her aging bathrobe, joined me and appeared ready for bed. She told me there was some ham in the icebox and fresh bread in the bread drawer. I asked her if she knew anything more about Uncle Otto. "No, but Maxine stopped by after supper to tell you boys about a toboggan party Friday night. Her note is on the table. She's such a nice girl Chuck. I'm going to bed and you should too."

"Thanks Mom. Gotta leave early in the morning to stop-by the office."

"Dad will be up."

I made myself a ham sandwich and started to review my notes from the trial. As I was finishing my sandwich, I remembered Maxine's note. When I opened it, I was surprised to find that all it said was **"Miss U C. Drew Scott. Max."** Maxine was a master of "less is more." Although after midnight, I daydreamed of Maxine's warmth, soft damp lips, mysterious scent. I longed to affectionately molest her. However, Mom's promotion of Maxine was starting to make me feel uncomfortable.

By two, I had completed my article about the day's trial and put together a couple of school interest stories from Josh's notes. Then I sat on the floor and talked with Ginger for a few minutes. She didn't get up, but I could hear the little flicks of her tail against the linoleum floor and feel her cold moist nose burrowing under my hand each time I stopped petting her. "Good night, Ginger," and I went to bed. It was a short night's sleep.

The next courtroom day came early. There was very little activity 30 minutes before scheduled start time. That's what I had expected and wished for. My mission was to find the court recorder and ask permission to review the trial record for the two days I'd missed. At precisely 15 minutes prior to court's reconvening, Miss Beatrice Solis, the quintessential efficient *old maid*, appeared from a side entrance to make sure everything was in its proper place and ready for the call to order.

I introduced myself to Miss Solis and explained my situation and request. Without expression, she instructed me to come to her desk at the start of the morning recess. I thanked her, but before I could say more, she disappeared by the same side door she'd appeared from two minutes earlier.

A hurriedly gathering gallery reminded me of roosting starlings coming alive at sunrise. People around me were excitedly anticipating Starr's daughter testifying. I was sure Ruthie wasn't going to, and Mickey, Ruthie and Vonda were not in attendance. They'd told me they might attend the evening session.

Just prior to the call to order, Biglow announced to our second row delegation that Mrs. Starr had decided not to allow her daughter to testify. "I don't want her mixed-up in this sordid affair," Starr was quoted as saying. Pinehurst had announced 24 hours earlier that Ruth Anne Starr's testimony would be extremely important in aiding her mother's defense. Simple posturing or fact, I wasn't sure.

9:30 A.M. and Gordon Pile had commenced his high strung ten second immortality quest. Starr's day of reckoning approached. Judge Jackson pushed forward, "Is the defense ready to call the next witness?"

"Yes, Your Honor we are," Biglow responded as he rose to his feet.

"If it please the court, the defense would like to call four witnesses, each to briefly attest to the character of both the defendant and the victim in this case."

"Let's get on with it. Call your first witness."

The first two witnesses commented on Starr's good standing within the community. Biglow gave each a glowing introduction as a salt-of-the-earth good citizen. Satisfied that witness creditability had been established, he asked each how they knew the defendant followed by five to six additional questions. Each witness described Mary Anne Starr as a peaceful, quiet person—a woman with a good reputation.

Biglow then called on two more witnesses to comment on Robert Eastwood's character. Again, he gave each of them a sterling introduction as one of Berrien County's finest, followed by a similar set of questions. Noteworthy comments were as follows: "Eastwood was dangerous when angry." "Bob had a vile disposition." "I never trusted either Eastwood." One witness quoted Eastwood as saying, "I'm just as likely to kill a person as do anything else. I have no control over my temper."

Biglow dutifully turned each witness over to the prosecution for cross-examination. In each instance, Foster and Spears waived their right to cross-examine. Their emotionless deportment conveyed their appraisal of the testimony's merit.

Little more than an hour into the morning session, Pinehurst abruptly announced that the defense rested. This action took the court by surprise. The last four witnesses had added little information and had even less impact in support of Starr's defense. Could the untold testimony of Ruth Starr have energized the conclusion of the defense's case? Not knowing what Ruthie would have revealed made answering that question next to impossible. However, at the very least she would have cast her mother in a more sympathetic light.

Even though it was early for a morning recess, Judge Jackson thought it appropriate to recess before beginning with rebuttal witnesses. Appropriate or not, most observers wanted to move the trial along to find out what would happen.

As soon as Pile had recited his lines, I went straight to Miss Solis. No expression, no comment, she just motioned for me to follow her. We exited the courtroom through a side door and entered a tiny office. On a corner desk I found the trial transcript for the first three days; I had only asked for the first two. Miss Solis pulled out a chair for me. "I'll be back in 15 minutes."

"Thanks," I said, "this is perfect." Miss Solis vanished. I got right to work, certain I had only 14 minutes and 27 seconds left. If nothing else, that woman was punctual.

Upon reentering the courtroom, I headed directly for my regular seat. Never before had I concentrated so hard for 15 minutes. My notes were a mess, but I knew if I could review them promptly, I could straighten them out and add to them. The notion passed through my mind that I was not the same person I had been just one week earlier. A week ago I could never have learned so much in so little time.

"All rise!" Pile was at it again and so were we all.

Judge Jackson read thoughtfully as we waited for his instruction. Something told me he enjoyed our waiting for him more than he enjoyed his reading material. He finally lifted his head, tapped his gavel and casually looked toward Foster and Spears, "Are you prepared to call your rebuttal witnesses?"

"Thank you, Your Honor," replied Spears. "Like the defense counsel, we would like to call a series of character witnesses."

The prosecution team had prepared and called five separate character witnesses. One more than the defense team had used, but with a similar ineffectual result. Essentially each of these witnesses worked in or around the Robinson office building where Robert Eastwood maintained his law office. They reported hearing the couple in question frequently quarreling, Starr using profane language, and one witness exclaimed, "Mary Anne chased Bob down the hallway yelling at him!"

Like the corresponding defense witnesses, these too added little. That was also true of Biglow's cross-examination of one of these witnesses.

Q. —"Did you hear Eastwood use profane language?" A. — "Yes, they both did."

Q. —"Who started the arguments?" A. —"I don't know."

Q. —"Whose voice did you hear the most?" A. —"Bob's."

This was the first trial I had ever observed in person. Keeping that in mind, I decided to moderate my evaluation of both defense and prosecution work with character witnesses; incompetent beyond belief. This opinion was unanimous among the press corps. "Comic relief," Halamka wisecracked.

"The State would like to recall Deputy Aaron Barth to the witness stand," Attorney Foster announced. I thought I caught a hint of relief in Foster's voice as he led our escape from what had just transpired. Deputy Barth had seated himself in the gallery following the morning recess. Barth, in uniform, marched to the witness stand and was sworn to tell the truth.

When asked by Foster, Deputy Barth denied taking a message from Eastwood to Starr, telling Starr that she could do anything she wanted with the furniture in their Pipestone St. law office. Apparently Eastwood went out of town on business and when he returned the office furniture was missing.

Foster then repeated a question he had asked Barth during cross-examination a week earlier. "When you were preparing to finger print and photograph Starr the morning following the shooting, what did she say to you?"

"How's Bill?"

"What did you answer her?"

"Bill is dead."

"And then what happened?"

"Mrs. Starr fainted."

"And when she revived after fainting, did she inquire as to what happened to Mr. Eastwood or how he died?

"No."

Pinehurst cross-examined Barth briefly. Long enough to refresh the jury as to expert testimony that Starr's behavior the morning after was typical of an amnesia victim. Obviously, the prosecution team did not buy that story. They interpreted Starr's behavior as uncaring at best, coldhearted at worst. For the defense, it only mattered what the jury believed.

Fortuitous, I thought, that Miss Solis had provided me with the third day trial transcript. From it I had discovered why Deputy Barth had been the first defense witness. His testimony was extremely sympathetic to the defendant. Now I was left asking myself why the defense had not probed this witness more to bring out what he knew of the extent of abuse suffered by Starr. Neither did I understand why Foster would risk putting Barth back on the stand. From my vantage point, Barth could only hurt the State's case.

Next, the prosecution called Carol Floyd, the co-publisher of a shopper's guide magazine with an office next to the Eastwood law office. Floyd testified that Eastwood came into her office and told her and coworkers of an argument he was having with Starr. He said, "She's going to get me someday."

"I said, 'Leave the country and put a lot of space between you and Mary Anne.' He said, 'What's the use. She'd follow me wherever I went.'"

On cross-examination, Floyd said, "I saw no marks on Bob, but I saw bruises on Mary Anne's arm."

Following Floyd on the stand was the stepson of the proprietor of the house at 400 Parker Avenue, the house Starr and Eastwood were buying on a land contract. This young man claimed that after the contract was signed, he went over to the house to dig-up some roses and retrieve a flower box from the garage.

"Please tell this court what happened when Starr and Eastwood drove up," Foster instructed his witness.

"She came at me like a Bantam rooster and said, 'What the hell are you doing with those flowers?' She argued so much I asked Bob to quiet her down so I could explain, but he merely shrugged his shoulders and walked away.'"

Turning to the defense team, Foster said, "Your witness."

"We waive our right to cross-examine this witness Your Honor."

"In that case, Mr. Pile will you announce the noon recess and let's reconvene at 1:30 P.M."

On my way out of the courthouse, I chanced to cross paths with Deputy Barth. Realizing now that I hadn't paid close attention to his original testimony and remembering the low regard he held for me at our first meeting, I sheepishly greeted him, "Hello Deputy Barth."

He stopped, looked me straight in the eye and said, "You look hungry. Come on rookie, I'll buy you something to eat."

Riding in Deputy Barth's squad car from the courthouse to the Pegasus, he told me about differences between Benton Harbor and St. Joseph. Interesting, but I needed to know how he felt about this trial. We found an open booth and both ordered breakfast.

"Breakfast is my favorite meal."

"Mine too," I responded sounding childish.

"Are you married, Deputy Barth?"

"Why do you ask?"

Considering my answer momentarily, I decided to come straight to the point. "Because I really want to ask you about the trial and didn't want to just crudely jump into it."

"Jump away."

There was something about this six-foot plus, 200 lbs. plus, chiseled in granite officer of the law that appealed to me. He gave me the impression of a confident man who, when he spoke, spoke the truth.

"You were the first witness for the defense. It was my first day covering the trial and I know now that I was unprepared, over confident, and inattentive."

"And in one short week you have conquered all those short comings?" Barth smiled.

"No, but at least now I know they exist. This morning I read your testimony from last week. Also, I heard you testify as a prosecution rebuttal witness. It is quite clear to me that you believe Mrs. Starr and Mr. Eastwood should have gone home and worked things out." I didn't really believe that and I didn't want to offend Barth, but felt that pushing him a bit would get the conversation going.

"Lots of people listen, few hear and some only hear what they want to hear. Nothing is clear to you, Chuck. I should be a defense witness. But, the defense attorneys never ask me the right questions on the stand or anywhere else, and, of course, the prosecution attorneys avoid those questions. This trial is nothing more than a silly game, a charade, designed to accomplish nothing."

The waitress came delivering our orders, interrupting Barth's attention-grabbing lecture. We were both hungry and immediately started eating. Questions swirled in my head. Our coffees were warmed.

"What do you mean 'accomplish nothing'? Won't the trial determine if Mary Anne Starr is guilty of murdering Robert Eastwood?"

"No, you're missing the point, Chuck. Do you remember the doctor explaining that society has no help or solution for people with mental disorders like whatever afflicted Eastwood? Basically, they kill someone before they are eligible for medical help—which ends up being incarceration in an asylum for the criminally insane. Would you call that an accomplishment?"

"Have you had other cases or known other people with these kinds of illnesses?"

"Do you?"

The way Barth asked gave me the feeling that cases like Starr's were common. For a few seconds I couldn't think and then it dawned on me, "Yes! My uncle killed my aunt and then killed himself."

"Are you talking about that Fennville farmer last week?"

"Yes. Do you know about it?"

"Yes I do, and more than you can read in the paper."

"What do you know?"

"Chuck, let's be clear about all of this. We are not talking officially and you are not going to ever quote me without my permission; and you don't have my permission. Is that clear?"

"Yes."

"I have a friend who works for the Allegan County Sheriff's Department. The murdered lady was treated at the hospital there last spring, allegedly the result of a beating by her husband. Her husband was well known to authorities, both law and medical."

The waitress came to clear our plates and to warm our coffees again, but Deputy Barth declined the refill. He had to go to work and I had to get back to the courthouse. Before he dropped me off, I got the name of a contact in the Allegan Sheriff's Department, Deputy Jack Dailey.

"I have to ask you, Deputy Barth, did you ever send Starr home to work things out with Eastwood?"

"Never, that jackass beat her up several times! There was no working anything out."

Barth left me overwhelmed recounting the number of times he had witnessed Eastwood's abuse, and how common this problem was in Berrien County. His bitter frustration left me empty, befuddled. I thanked him.

Back in the courtroom the prosecutors prepared to continue calling rebuttal witnesses. The second row consensus held that closing arguments would start sometime during the afternoon session. With my notebook in my lap and pen in hand, I sat at a loss, alone in a crowded room. Deputy Barth's revelations had clouded my head; storm clouds.

Pile jolted me from my stupor. "All rise! The Honorable Court for the County of Berrien, Michigan, now stands in session. God save this State and this Honorable Court."

Judge Jackson dropped into his seat as if falling from the sky. Whack! "Does the prosecution have any more rebuttal witnesses?" It came as more of a wish for a negative response than a request for more testimony.

"Yes we do, Your Honor. If it please the court, the State calls Sheriff Donald L. Diamond. The uniformed sheriff stood up in the first row of the gallery, then made his way to the witness stand to meet Pile. He pledged to tell the truth. The gray headed, slightly stooped sheriff took his seat in the witness chair.

In preface to his questions, Prosecutor Foster stated that the purpose of his witness was to challenge the credibility of Starr's testimony. Foster then produced a transcript of Starr's police station interrogation conducted by himself and Sheriff Diamond one hour following the shooting. The interrogation transcript was placed in evidence.

Foster read each question and answer while Diamond verified the same. The prosecutor read, with exaggerated emphasis, one of Starr's answers in which she plainly stated that she shot Robert Eastwood. This interview was damning to the defendant who had previously stated that she remembered none of it.

Then Foster asked Sheriff Diamond if he knew of a jail record for Mrs. Mary Anne Starr. The sheriff came prepared. He produced such a record and Foster asked him to read it aloud. The sheriff complied, "Mary Anne Starr, 30, a model, residing in Kimmell, Ind., Charge: assault with a deadly weapon, March 5, 1934, Released by order of Justice J.W. Cullinine and Bob Eastwood."

Before Diamond finished, Pinehurst leaped up. "Objection, such testimony is highly prejudicial without producing a warrant!"

"Overruled."

"Your Honor, there is no warrant, no information, no proof, no conviction!" Pinehurst strenuously objected, raising his voice for the first time during the proceedings.

"Overruled! Now sit down, counselor, or I'll have you removed."

Pinehurst grudgingly complied, but was clearly distraught. Both his co-counsel and client attempted to console him.

Foster continued asking Diamond if he recalled another incident when Eastwood and Starr drove up to the county jail. Diamond nodded saying, "Bob complained about a fight and said she threatened him. I told them to go on home and straighten out their difficulties."

"Do you remember yet another time involving a gun?"

"Yes. It was one night when they drove up, and Bob called me over to the car and said, 'Here she is. I want you to lock her up. She has had a gun in my ribs ever since we left Berrien Springs.' Bob handed me the gun. I took it from him and threw it in the river. It was an old type gun. I doubted it worked."

"Objection, Your Honor! No dates, times, places…"

"Overruled."

"Who ever heard of throwing evidence in the river?"

"Overruled!" Jackson glared at Biglow who had replaced Pinehurst as the defense's objector. Biglow sat down slowly, but compliantly. Pinehurst appeared to be suffering great duress.

Looking toward Foster, Jackson asked if there were any further questions.

"No, Your Honor, that concludes our questions of this witness, as well as the conclusion of our rebuttal witnesses."

"Any cross?"

"Just a couple of short questions, Your Honor," Pinehurst spoke as he apprehensively rose from his seat. His tone was civil, but he clearly avoided looking at Judge Jackson.

"Sheriff Diamond, we need for you to clarify a few salient points. First, you testified that Robert Eastwood drove Mrs. Starr to your headquarters, and then told you that Mrs. Starr held a gun in his ribs all the way from Berrien Springs and wanted you to arrest her. Is that correct?"

"Yes Senator."

"Please tell us again, who had the gun?" Pinehurst raised his voice on 'who' and 'gun' to emphasize his point.

"Bob Eastwood."

"Sheriff Diamond, were you a party to this practical joke?"

"No."

Pinehurst was crafty.

"Although I don't condone this type of humor, are you aware that Robert Eastwood was a prankster and enjoyed practical jokes no matter how inappropriate?

"I was not."

Shaking his head and pulling his chin whiskers, "No more questions, Your Honor."

Seeing no indication of redirect and not wanting to encourage any, Judge Jackson instructed, "In that case, Mr. Pile will you call the afternoon recess and let's reconvene at 2:55 P.M.

XVIII
CLOSING ARGUMENTS

Chet Henry, a reporter from the *Kalamazoo Gazette*, introduced himself to me during recess. Henry claimed that he wanted to find out more about the Otto Barnes case and heard I may have the scoop. Since I wanted to know more about Glenn Biglow and Mabel Eastwood, both from Kalamazoo, I thought we might be able to help each other.

Quickly I discovered my Kalamazoo counterpart's interest lay in reporting his personal accomplishments as opposed to discovering what I had to offer. Henry did seem to have creditable information concerning the Robert Eastwood disbarment, though. According to him, Eastwood had been under investigation for corrupt practices from the time he hung out his shingle in Kalamazoo. Ultimately, it was discovered that Eastwood had forged documents, neglected to provide services for which he had received payment, and failed to represent his clients' interest. Our fact-collecting break ended all too soon.

Judge Jackson flashed a rare smile as he called the court to order once again. "Is the prosecution prepared to begin their closing argument?"

"Yes, Your Honor, we are prepared. My co-counsel and Prosecuting Attorney elect, Mr. Robert M. Spears, will handle the State's closing arguments. We, of course, reserve our right of rebuttal following the defense's closing. At this time, let me present Attorney Spears."

The tall, angular Spears rose and swaggered around in front of the prosecution's table. "Your Honor, the State would first like to extend to you our gratitude for your skillful management of *The State of Michigan v. Mary Anne Starr*. It has been our privilege to work under your watchful guidance." A blush of appreciation crossed Jackson's pale bespectacled face.

Just 31, Spears had rapidly climbed his way within the Berrien County legal community to be elected a month earlier as the county's chief prosecutorial officer. He relished his new status and wore a crisp new blue suit for the occasion. Spears' exuded self-confidence that bordered on arrogance. He was determined to make the most of his courtroom floor time to make a political statement for what to expect from his coming administration.

He turned leisurely to the jury and continued, "Secondly, we want to thank you, gentlemen and ladies of the jury, for so diligently fulfilling your patriotic and civic duty to our great county by serving for such an important circuit court trial. We extend our humble thanks to each and every one of you." Spears smiled and bowed to his captive audience of thirteen stoic faces.

Spears went straight for the jugular in a steady, forceful voice. "Send Mary Anne Starr to prison for killing Robert Eastwood!" He stared searchingly across the jury as if anticipating something miraculous to occur in response to his command. They sat unaffected.

Standing five feet in front of the jury box and as close to the center as he could place himself, Assistant Prosecutor Spears commenced his closing argument: "Well, was it self-defense or was it temporary insanity? Or, does any of that really matter? I can't remember anyway! If you have felt confused from time to time by the arguments in defense of that woman, I don't blame you; so have I. First she says, 'Please excuse me for I know not what I did, I was not in my right mind.' And then she says, 'Oh, I remember everything. I shot him in self-defense.'"

Spears spent considerable time recounting selected statements in Starr's testimony. He laced each portion of it with his contention that it was either implausible or irrelevant. He did not mask his pleasure at making light of Starr and her entourage of supporting witnesses.

"She claims devoted love for her victim, yet after she killed him she paints him as the cruelest and most contemptible person she had ever met. She claims she loved the deceased too much. Then why did she constantly nag and dog his every move; causing family conflicts with his brother, his lawful wife, his children? If she loved him, why did she kill him? Why?" His voice receded quietly as if searching for theatrical effect.

Continuing his dramatic flair, Spears rhetorically exploded, "I'll tell you why! She saw Robert Eastwood's growing desire to rejoin his family. She feared losing him. That ticket into her desired social set was drawing away. He wanted to be a real father and responsible husband. He didn't want to live in sin with an adulteress. But she kept on nagging, badgering, conniving, until he couldn't take anymore and he pushed back. This impossible relationship struggled on until the spiteful Mrs. Starr became so calloused, so malicious; she got a gun, pursued and killed her prey."

Sensing that he had captured the jury's full attention, Spears shifted his attack, lacing it with as much religious fervor as he could assemble. He lifted his gaze slightly above the jury saying, "Let us recall the Ten Commandments; simple but true. *You shall not murder. Neither shall you commit adultery.*" Raising his left arm and turning slightly, Spears directed the jury's focus toward the defense table. "I give you the murderer, defendant Mrs. Starr, an evil woman of double sin."

I wondered if the new prosecutor thought he waxed eloquent. In his next breath, he substantiated my suspicion.

Looking as humble as he could, he went on, "The voice you hear today does not belong to me. It is America speaking to you through me. America is calling on each of you to make your choice in the name of human decency. To answer that virtuous call, the only conclusion you may draw is, 'guilty as charged.'"

Attorney Robert Spears finally stepped down from his imaginary podium and returned to the prosecution table. As he did he blotted an imaginary tear from the corner of his eye. Foster smiled up approvingly as Spears took the seat beside him. As for the second row congregation, we were relieved; praying the defense could bring their arguments to a conclusion by the dinner recess.

Judge Jackson looked to the defense table and nodded to Biglow who was standing with his unsheathed tablet at the ready. Biglow took two steps forward while clearing a gravelly throat.

"Your Honor, the defense also wishes to extend our thanks to you for your dutiful direction of this trial. We are aware of the hardship it has placed upon you, forcing you to be away from your home and family for long periods of time. Pivoting toward the jury, Biglow thanked them as well. He emphasized their importance because the fate of the defendant was held in their hands. Turning partially back around, he explained to the judge and jury that he and Senator Pinehurst would share the duty of presenting their closing statement. He would go first.

A paunchy gentleman of medium height, Glenn A. Biglow appeared to be in the twilight of his career, although only 47. Dressed in an aging, rumpled, brown three-piece suit, the same suit he wore every day, he had a stodgy look about him. There were times he failed to give the trial his full attention. With only a lack luster professional life to his credit, Biglow was retained by Starr less than two days before her preliminary examination and was far from her first choice, if indeed she ever had a choice.

Biglow again cleared his throat as he swung directly toward the jury. He immediately lashed out at the prosecution's failure to offer counter expert witnesses. "Our medical experts each supported our claim that the defendant, Mary Anne Starr, shot Robert Eastwood in self-defense. They each confirmed that she did this while in a state of temporary insanity, clearly not knowing what she was doing, and now can't remember because she has experienced temporary amnesia. All the result of numerous beatings and blows to the head administered by her common-law husband Robert Eastwood. This little woman shot the man she loved instinctively, out of sheer terror for self-preservation."

Biglow waited several seconds to allow the jury to digest his opening remarks. While he paused, he made pencil checks on his tablet. I glanced at Stallwell to see if she approved.

After he graphically described several beatings by the mentally deranged Eastwood, Biglow spoke directly to the jury in a low, soft voice, "I hope that if Eastwood had a sane moment of consciousness after he was shot, he took that time to ask God to forgive him for what he had done to this innocent little woman."

"If Eastwood was sane when he committed these violent acts against Mary Anne, then he is lower than any rat who ever crawled under your barn." Attorney Biglow looked specifically from one farmer to the next, a sum representing over half the jury.

"Please think with me for a couple of minutes," Biglow requested. "Mary Anne never intended to shoot Mr. Eastwood with a pistol. For heaven's sake, she had many other opportunities to do that if she'd wanted to. Would a sane person shoot someone in front of the police station?"

Biglow told the jury that even if they concluded that Mary Anne was in her right mind when she shot her tormenter, they still couldn't convict her unless they believed she had not acted in self-defense. "Why would she do it?" he asked. "She loved him—more than that, she worshipped him, idolized him. She forgave him everything he did to her. On that fateful night, his blow to Mary Anne's temple put her in an amnesiatic state. Then, and only then, she did the very thing she would never have done in her right mind."

Attorney Biglow concluded his remarks with, "This little woman will have nothing to fear from your verdict if you allow yourselves to be guided only by the evidence as it has been presented to you during this trial, in this courtroom. I thank you for your attention to my portion of defense's closing remarks and I would request that you grant my associate, Attorney Pinehurst, the same consideration. Thank you."

The courtroom stirred in a synchronized sigh of relief. At fifteen minutes to five we had already passed our accustomed recess time. Judge Jackson had shown uncharacteristic patience during tiresome legal oratory, or was it simply his haste to complete the trial that kept him from interrupting? Whatever the reason, before calling on Pile, who seemed to be chomping at the bit, he said, "Mr. Pinehurst, I trust you are prepared to deliver summation remarks. However, we will wait until after our dinner recess to hear from you. If all goes well, I anticipate giving my charge to the jury before we adjourn our evening session. Mr. Pile, let's reconvene at 7:00 P.M." Whack!

From the courthouse, I drove directly to the Pegasus. Penny greeted me at the cash register with a smile of accomplishment. She told me that Mrs. Starr's friend was talking with another lady at table number three. "She expecting you and happy to talk with you, Chuck."

While following Penny to table number three, a feeling of apprehension passed over me, yet was short-lived. The introduction went well, thanks to Penny. "Mrs. Bell, this is Chuck." Penny introduced us with such an easy charm that we were instantly comfortable with each other. That's how I met Georgie Bell.

"Penny has told me about you. I know that you are just starting out in the newspaper business and want to know about Mary Anne Starr. Since the shooting took place, I've been at a loss for what to do. I can talk to you and maybe that will help. Let's go to my place, it's close. I'll fix us a bowl of soup, tell you what I know and you can get back to the courthouse. Penny told me you have an evening session?"

"I don't know what to say except, thank you, Mrs. Bell. I'm hungry for both, your soup and your story of Mary Anne." I recall thinking that it was Penny I needed to thank.

She laughed. "Please call me Georgie, everyone does."

Mrs. Bell told me that she met Mary Anne and her children in Kalamazoo shortly following Mary Anne's divorce. Five months pregnant at the time, Georgie had been laid-off from her job. Her husband worked for the telephone company and they were looking forward to starting a family. Since they were close in age and lived just five doors from each other, Mary Anne and Georgie became close friends.

We walked to Georgie's house, a modest but neat two-bedroom bungalow. She told me she was 38 years old and had been a widow for six years. She had lost her baby in childbirth and two years later her husband was killed in a traffic accident. At Mary Anne's suggestion, she moved to Benton Harbor in 1934 and they worked together at the Vincent Hotel. Mary Anne had gotten her the job.

Georgie fixed tomato soup and egg salad sandwiches while the story of her friendship with Mary Anne unfolded. I asked if I could help, but basically tried to stay out of her way. The meal was good, as was her story of friendship and sorrow:

"During the summer of '28, Mary Anne, Mickey, and Ruthie moved-in just down the street from us. Mary Anne and I became thick as thieves. She was so excited about living in Kalamazoo, her new job, and freedom. As I said, Mac and I were expecting, we were thrilled, and I took care of Mickey and Ruthie while Mary Anne worked. It was a good arrangement for the both of us.

A month, or maybe two went by, and Mary Anne had an opportunity to buy the small diner where she worked. With the help of her parents for a down payment, she was able to get a mortgage from a local bank and bought the restaurant, Della's Diner. Everything was great. My pregnancy was moving along fine, Mickey started school only five blocks away, and I took care of Ruthie.

The week before Thanksgiving, I lost my baby. I was told I would be unable to have children. Mac and I were devastated. Continuing to take care of Mickey and Ruthie helped but I don't think I was ever the same.

Della's Diner thrived under Mary Anne's management. She absolutely loved running that business. I'll admit there were times that I thought she was neglecting her children, but then again, it may have been sour grapes on my part. In any case, she was happy and I was happy for her.

Mary Anne's appreciation of my help flowed easily, which I think drew us even closer to one another. She did pay me for looking after Mickey and Ruthie; good kids.

Not long after Christmas, Mary Anne's loan officer started coming by Della's. Soon he wanted to talk with her a little more than normal. She told me about him. He made her feel uncomfortable but she felt she had to be nice to him, after all, she said, 'He was so nice in helping me obtain the mortgage.'

One day he asked her to go out with him. She told me she smiled at him and said, 'You must be teasing. I don't think your wife or family would care too much for that.' At which he said, 'They'll never know.'

She told him she had two children, didn't date, and if she did date, she would never go out with a married man. Unfortunately, he wouldn't take no for an answer and the whole situation got worse. He really started pressuring Mary Anne to go out with him.

This rake liked to show-off his fancy car by parking it right in front of Della's—asking Mary Anne if she'd like to go for a spin. He told her that he could teach her a few things about being successful in business, something to the effect that, 'When you do something for a customer, they should do something for you.'

Well, this got worse and worse. He made Mary Anne's life miserable. She finally decided to sell the diner. I'm not sure if that caused this guy to go away, but he eventually left her alone.

Mary Anne quickly got another job. She became the manager of the soda bar and dining area at the Madison Drug Store. That's in the Burdick Hotel building. Again, she liked that job, but that's where she met Bob Eastwood.

Just another no-account lawyer, if you ask me, but Mary Anne fell for him. I think she had stars in her eyes for lawyers, doctors and successful businessmen. I guess I can understand that. There's no question, Mary Anne worked hard for a better life than she had grown-up in. She rationalized that Eastwood was just going through a rough time with the Depression and all. But, she said, 'He'll get going again, he is a lawyer you know.' I hated it when she would tell me things like that.

She frequently told me how nice he was to her and her children; what a smart, funny guy he was. Right away I could tell she was smitten. Oh yes, she had to have known he was married, but again she rationalized that away.

I'll admit I cried with her when she told me of their exchanging wedding vows under the stars in front of her home church down in Indiana. I know it was beautiful. I wish I could have been there to share that moment with her.

Unfortunately, though, things were already going sour in their relationship. Personally, I never trusted Bob. They depended on Mary Anne for their financial support. After Bob moved in with her, they were evicted, then she lost her job and had to take Mickey and Ruthie to live with her parents. Added to losing jobs and evictions, Bob was disgraced by disbarment. He really should have been put in jail for what he'd been doing, forgery and such. Up to that point, I do not believe Bob had ever hit Mary Anne, but all things considered, they had to leave Kalamazoo.

In the spring of '32, I remember because it was about the time of the Lindbergh kidnapping, they moved to Niles and lived with Bob's sister for a few months. His brother Harley was the Niles city attorney. During the fall of that year, Harley won the election for Berrien County Prosecuting Attorney and moved to Benton Harbor. Soon Bob and Mary Anne followed, Bob hoping to latch on to a job with his brother.

Mary Anne quickly secured employment as manager of the dining room at the Vincent Hotel, but Bob became little more than an errand boy for his brother. It didn't take Mary Anne long to figure out the lay of the land here in Benton Harbor. With his brother's help, Bob got his law license reinstated.

Mac had died a year earlier. Mary Anne encouraged me to move here. As I said, she helped me get a job and eventually I ended up at the printing company where I work today. It was good to be back around her. The two of us have had a lot of good times together.

After Bob was reinstated, the brothers formed a law partnership and Harley appointed Bob his Assistant County Prosecuting Attorney. Things were looking up for Bob and Mary Anne.

It was Bob's suggestion that the two of them bring Mickey and Ruthie to live with them. Both kids started school here that fall. By November, Mary Anne had taken the children back to live with her parents. That's when I first discovered Bob had hit Mary Anne in a fit of rage. I told her she should leave him, but she said she loved him. She wanted to help him through the rough time he was having.

About the best thing I can say about Bob as a lawyer is that he was inconsistent. His brother lost reelection, in '35 their partnership dissolved and Bob and Mary Anne, mostly Mary Anne, established a private practice. That practice never went well, nor did Harley's. If you'd ask me, both Eastwoods were shysters. Divorces and trumped-up lawsuits were their stock-in-trade. They were always involved in shady deals and Bob couldn't retain clients. He had a Jekyll and Hyde personality—one day nice, next day bad.

His mistreatment of Mary Anne became more frequent. I told her she had to leave him and I'd think she was going to do it. But, then Bob would do something really nice like take her to Chicago, to a play or look at the new home she had always dreamed of, something. She'd forgive him and try to help him.

It was no use; Bob Eastwood was crazy just like his parents. Mary Anne told me both of Bob's parents had died in an insane asylum; that's where Bob should have been.

She finally shot him. She did Benton Harbor a favor. But, if you read the papers, you'd think she was the most evil person in the world. Not true, she is a good, kind person and my best friend.

Did you know that Vonda and Ruthie visited Mary Anne the weekend she shot Bob?"

"Oh my gosh!" I cut Georgie off. Looking at my pocket watch I could see that I only had fifteen minutes before the start of the evening session. I thanked Georgie for supper and for sharing the last ten years of her life. Her love and respect for Mary Anne Starr were patent, but that and five cents may get you a cup of coffee, not an innocent verdict.

"Chuck, I hope we meet again sometime. Penny speaks so highly of you."

Back in the courtroom I could feel emotion swelling amongst the boisterous spectators. Everyone expected the defense to conclude their closing arguments in approximately one hour. That would leave time for Jackson to give his charge to the jury before adjournment. "We may have a verdict and sentence by noon tomorrow," I told Halamka, wanting to know what he thought. He didn't respond.

No surprise that less than one minute past seven, the 56-year-old J.P. "Senator" Pinehurst stood statuesque before Starr's panel of judges. He meditatively stroked his beard, waiting for absolute silence. Nattily attired in a tailored dark gray suit, beige suede shoes, hair tightly braided in the familiar ponytail, the defense lawyer was the focus of attention. He wore a tie, but I couldn't see it due to his long brown and speckled grey beard. His intelligent hazel eyes carefully surveyed the thirteen attentive citizens awaiting his words. The medium height, stout Pinehurst cut an iconic figure that exuded legal scholarship.

Pinehurst was a vigorous advocate for Mary Anne Starr, a characteristic effort of his long and storied career. Returning from Texas within a week prior to the start of Starr's trial, he generously offered to take the case other Berrien County attorneys had shunned.

Pinehurst enjoyed the study of law and had a particular fascination with the insanity defense. His credits included the publication of an acclaimed legal article, outlining the importance for an insanity legal defense strategy. The subject, he reported, first came to his attention two years earlier when a mentally disturbed U.S. Congressman from Washington, Marion Zioncheck, committed suicide by jumping from a fifth floor window in downtown Seattle. The ill-fated Zioncheck died in the street just a few feet in front of a car driven by his widowed wife.

Pinehurst began his impassioned plea to the jury with, "Did Mary Anne Starr murder Robert Eastwood?" It appeared that Pinehurst mocked the opening statement of Spear's closing. "Any other crime, whether it be on the statutes of Michigan or not, is absolutely not relevant here. Adultery? Not relevant. I recall some nineteen hundred years ago. I see before the Holy Nazarene a woman brought by scribes on a similar charge. And what did He say? 'Let him who is without sin among you be the first to throw a stone at her.'" Quietly he turned his gaze from the jury to his client, to the prosecutors and back to the jury.

The defense attorney's presence and delivery stilled all other courtroom sound. When it came to the scriptures, Assistant Prosecutor Spears did not have to remind Pinehurst how to effectively call on them. To people who knew him, Pinehurst represented a biblical scholar without rival. He frequently led religious functions both within and outside the House of David.

"When this little woman called out for help at the doctor's office, at the hospital, at the police station—no one answered. She pleaded, she begged for help. Not just for herself, but also for her tormentor, poor Robert Eastwood. No answer. No help. We all know there is a lot of sin in this world. Too much sin. But, when it comes to people connected with this case, this little woman," he motioned and looked again toward his client, "was more sinned against than sinner."

Looking back at the jury, he continued, "Please give this defendant the same consideration, the same fairness you would give your own daughter." He contended that the evidence contained nothing that contradicted Starr's claim of amnesia at the time she shot Eastwood.

"Three separate, each distinguished in their profession, medical experts supported the fact that Mary Anne Starr was not in her right mind when she reacted instinctively to fend off Eastwood's attack in desperate fear for her life. For the love of God, what sane person would meet with a policeman in a police station, and then walk outside and murder someone? If that's not the legal definition of insanity, it should be! It was anticipated and logical that the prosecution would at least attempt to bring forth rebuttal medical experts. Since none appeared, a reasonable person would conclude that none could be found. But of course, what expert would fly in the face of reason? What reasonable person would conclude otherwise?"

Pinehurst sermonized a second time, offering that Starr felt defenseless and humiliated when she appeared before Berrien County officers with marks of violence all over her body. "What must this little woman have been thinking when she was repeatedly told, 'Go home and work it out in the morning.' What did she think? What do you think?"

In slightly more than 60 minutes, Pinehurst had reviewed for the jury virtually all evidence supporting his client. It seemed to me that certain elements had surpassed being redundant. From the tone of his voice, the end approached. I anticipated a crescendo of oratory and the Senator complied.

"The manhood and womanhood of the entire world are waiting to hear what you will do with this poor little woman. Your verdict of not guilty will preserve that standard of womanhood, of motherhood, you and I believe in."

Stroking his beard the defense attorney called upon all the sincerity and conviction at his command. He then made his final plea to the jury, "Please send poor Mary Anne home to her children; relieved of the shackles she has born all these years."

Pinehurst thanked the jury for their attention, the prosecuting team for their professional representation of the citizens of Michigan and Judge Jackson for his efficient management of the trial. The only thing missing was a closing hymn and benediction.

At eight fifteen Jackson requested a fifteen-minute recess.

During recess, I made a quick call to the *Chicago Tribune* to report to Billy. He thanked me for my help and told me that he would see me in the morning. "I'm bringing you a few more pictures."

Following recess most of us in row two expected Judge Jackson to begin his charge to the jury. He had given every indication that it was his intention to do so before closing for the evening. After thumping his gavel, he said, "It appears that we have completed closing arguments."

"If it please, Your Honor," Foster interrupted.

"The bench recognizes Attorney Foster."

"The State would like to exercise its right to rebut the defense team's closing remarks. It shouldn't take long Your Honor. We wish to clarify a few relevant points of evidence before the jury goes to deliberation."

"You have the floor, Mr. Foster."

"Thank you, Your Honor," Foster nodded an acknowledgement to the Judge. He then turned and walked over to the jury box.

W.C. Foster was a handsome, fit, 5' 10", 37-year-old lawyer. He was born and raised in the tiny village of Newberry in Michigan's Upper Peninsula.

Newberry was the home of popular State Supreme Court Justice Louis H. Fead. Fead had been a longtime mentor and friend of Foster's. Judge Fead presided over one of Berrien County's most famous Circuit Court trials, *The State of Michigan v. The Israelite House of David*, 1927—at the very time Foster began practicing law in Benton Harbor, fresh out of at the University of Michigan Law School.

In 1929 Foster was appointed Assistant Prosecuting Attorney, and in 1934 he was elected to his first term as Berrien County Prosecuting Attorney. As he completed his second term, he chose not to run for reelection. Foster planned to return to private practice following the trial.

Attorney Foster looked from left to right and back again across the jury box. He made it a point to look each juror directly in the eye. "An attempt has been made to becloud the real issue, to befog the minds of you jurors. The defense has tried everybody and everything but the real issue. Please follow closely as I summarize this case; a murder case."

Again Foster gazed at the people seated in the jury box. "The real and only issue is: Did she shoot Robert Eastwood or didn't she?" He clearly wanted to help the jurors view the trial in its simplest form. Ironically, three of the four attorneys began their remarks with almost the same statement—was anyone keeping score?

"First, the defense claims that Mrs. Starr was insane when she shot Mr. Eastwood. Then, they claim it was Mr. Eastwood who was insane when she shot him in self-defense." Foster, looking baffled, scratched his head. "Let's try the murder case and not get lost in the fog these attorneys have sprayed all over this courtroom."

Foster returned to the prosecution's opening witnesses and recalled aloud short statements made by each. He highlighted one, John Henry Johns, whose testimony had been the same at the arraignment—the day of the murder—as it was during the trial. "Johns, a merchant policeman, testified that Mrs. Starr looked 'bewildered and dazed' when he rushed up and took the gun away from her. Holy smokes! Who would look happy and nonchalant after they shot a man in the back twice and then put two more bullets through his brain? She knew what she was doing and she did it well."

Feigning frustration, Foster became even more emphatic. "Was she showing evidence of amnesia when she told Sergeant Jake Winters, 'I killed him, he had it coming to him for a long time!' It looks like murder to me."

Reacting to the defense claim that he failed to bring expert witnesses to counter act their experts, Foster declared it was unnecessary and a waste of the court's time. "Please remember that each expert testified that Starr 'might be' in a state of amnesia, but under cross-examination each expert testified that Starr 'might not be' in a state of amnesia. Why call more experts to simply say the same thing?"

The prosecutor addressed the hypothetical questions put to the experts by the defense. He said, "They were just that, hypothetical. Each expert admitted on cross-examination that if any of the facts in the questions were changed or untrue, their answers would not stand. Why call more experts?"

Lastly, Foster challenged the plausibility of Starr's story. "If Eastwood was coming toward her with his fist raised, why didn't she run to the police station? No, it was Eastwood running for the sanctuary of the police station when she shot him in the back. She shot him in the back. Is that self-defense? In the back. Irresistible reflex? In the back!"

"Mary Anne Starr shot Robert Eastwood just as she said she did, 'Because he had it coming to him.' By your verdict you can clearly make a point that people just can't get away with that in Berrien County."

Foster again thanked the jury, the judge and opposing counsel. He took his seat.

Judge Jackson unresponsively shuffled some papers together. "We shall reconvene at ten. At that time I shall charge the jury. Take over, Mr. Pile."

XIX
OFFICE WIFE

The Coupe started on the first try and we headed for home. From the bridge to Benton Harbor I caught sight of a light inside the Pegasus. I was tired and needed to go straight home, but I couldn't keep from stopping to see if Penny might be closing up. From what I could see through the frost incrusted window in the locked door, the diner was deserted. Good, I thought to myself, but tapped on the window anyway.

A disheveled Penny banged through the swinging kitchen door wiping her hands with a towel. I pressed my face against the window and when she finally figured out who it was she broke into a big smile, unbolted and opened the door.

"Sorry closed, have been for over hour. Come back tomorrow, please." She teased appearing put out by my imposition.

In a dejected deadpan, I turned away mumbling, "Oh, alright."

"Come in, silly and get out of cold. I thought you gone home. Did trial go late?"

"Yes, but it will go to the jury first thing in the morning. We'll probably know by noon what's going to happen to Mary Anne Starr. How come you're still here? Are you alone?"

"School out for Christmas break. I just came for evening meal and when that over, I tell Hebe go home. I clean up. She gone almost hour."

"Hebe?"

"You meet Hebe, right? My sister, she work full time, mostly in kitchen when I'm here."

"I think I saw her. She's a little older than you?"

Penny told me that her sister was seven years older and that the two of them came to America eight years ago. She asked me if I wanted something to eat, but I said I really had to get going because I had a long drive ahead of me. Penny insisted, saying it would only take her a minute to fix me something. When I was unable to tell her what I'd like, she told me she wanted to surprise me.

Penny fascinated me. Dressed in old worn clothing, the baggy wool sweater she wore had holes in both elbows and drooped over her hips. Her dark hair hung straight along the smooth angular sides of her olive-skin face. A grease smudged left cheekbone added an earthy charm to her confident manner. As we talked she put three pieces of bacon on the griddle.

"Where are you from Penny, I mean originally?"

She looked at me with amusement lurking within her dark, long-lashed eyes. "Did I say something stupid?" Not letting me feel uncomfortable, Penny rambled on telling me of how she came with her sister from Greece to Chicago when she was ten. They lived a short time with relatives in Chicago, but then were sent to Benton Harbor to work for a distant cousin. "How did you get from Chicago to Benton Harbor?" I asked.

"We rode in old truck." She paused as a reflective moment washed over her.

We were both 19 but she seemed so in control, or at least more adult than others our age. Penny's accent intrigued me, and her manner of speaking reminded me of my Nana. Nana could work in a kitchen full of children under foot while effortlessly carrying on a meaningful conversation with the farm extension agent. Penny possessed that same calm self-assurance. As if in spite of her definite old world accent, she handled English fluently, picking up nuances and implied meanings naturally.

"In a truck?"

"Ya," she smiled and told me that the two of them were given a ride in a truck hauling bootleg liquor to a speakeasy out east of town. "They want Hebe to work there but she say no. She no speak English so good and fear she get caught; we both be deported. So, we end up here." I sensed something missing in the matter-of-fact way Penny told me her story.

"Why didn't your parents come to America with you?"

"They are dead."

I could tell by Penny's abrupt tone that she wasn't interested in telling me more. She asked me to go back into the dining room and sit down. She carried a plate with something of an unpronounceable name and sat it before me. From what I could tell it consisted of toast, bacon, tomato, cheese, and a tasty spice or two. Mom needed this recipe. Good.

"What's this white stuff?"

"That feta cheese."

"Feta cheese? What's that?"

"Cheese made from goat milk."

"It's good." It really was delicious and I devoured it in no time. I told Penny that I really had to get home and asked if I could drop her off. She said she still had to finish cleaning the oven, but lived only a short distance. As she walked me to the door, Penny handed me something wrapped in a napkin.

"What's this?"

"*Baklava*, you like it. It remind you of me as you drive home." She smiled. An adult smile. A disarming smile; one engraved in my memory."

The drive home took over an hour. Patches of ice were irregularly spaced all the way making driving particularly tedious. Fortunately, it wasn't snowing or blowing. The piece of *baklava* did remind me of Penny—very sweet in a natural, stimulating sort of way.

My thoughts turned to Mary Anne Starr and the fateful night of October 17; a blink in time that had dramatic effect. That instant, a pivotal point, separated two undesirable situations. From all I had gathered from testimony, interviews, fellow reporters and old newspapers, Mary Anne Starr's life from the shooting until her trial—two months—was a long, arduous, and sensationally unfortunate melodrama. Before I reached home I had mentally sketched my next major article, "From Arrest to Trial," for the *South Haven Tribune*:

> *Just minutes after 1:00 A.M. Monday October 17, 1938 Mary Anne Starr sat at a table in the chief's office of the police station. She had been arrested for the murder of W. Robert Eastwood less than 30 minutes earlier. The Berrien County Sheriff and Prosecuting Attorney teamed up from across the table to interrogate her. The sheriff and Mary Anne chain-smoked cigarettes. Following the interrogation, she was transported to the women's ward at the county jail in St. Joseph, approximately one mile away.*
>
> *When Mary Anne awoke the next morning, she found herself being hurriedly readied to meet Deputy Sheriff Aaron Barth, assisted by a reporter/photographer from the St. Joseph Herald-Press, for photos and fingerprinting. She had a vague recollection of her surroundings as she had previously been to the county jail on legal business. She liked Deputy Barth. Not scared, she may have been apprehensive as to why she appeared to be an inmate. Was this another one of Bob's little games? Those thoughts may have crossed her mind, recalling similar charades.*
>
> *Mary Anne asked about Bob. Barth tells her Bob's dead. She fainted. Once revived, the sheriff stopped to see her and tells her that her arraignment will be at noon in the Benton Harbor Courthouse. He asked if she had an attorney. She gives him a name of the lawyer she wants to retain. The sheriff agrees to contact that attorney for her. Then he asked if she would be willing to talk to newspaper reporters. She agreed and the sheriff says he will set up his office for the interview.*
>
> *At 11:30 Mary Anne was taken from the St. Joseph jail to the courthouse in Benton Harbor where she was arraigned for the murder of W. Robert Eastwood. The judge asked if she had*

an attorney. She said no, the attorney she wanted rejected her. The judge appointed an attorney to represents her for the arraignment. That attorney made it clear that he would not represent her any further. A preliminary examination was demanded and scheduled for ten days later in the same courthouse. The judge then remanded Mary Anne back to the county jail without bond.

By the time Mary Anne returned to the county jail, more reporters packed the sheriff's office requesting a meeting with her. Request granted. Less than 24 hours following the shooting, there had been three conferences between the defendant and the news media. Evidence for and against her, mostly against, was being outlined in newspapers and a defense strategy of temporary insanity was bantered about, ostensibly initiated by Mary Anne, herself.

The time from Mary Anne's arrest through her arraignment took less than 12 hours. In light of her difficulty in obtaining counsel, this represented quite extraordinary bureaucratic efficiency. Additionally, in less than 24 hours, news reporters were engaged in a ferocious competition to capture or claim the most startling headline label for the infamous female defendant and the hapless public defender she had supposedly murdered. The curious effect of this irresponsible name game found the defendant and her victim experiencing a reversal of their public personas— deviously villainous and a compassionate helpmate—respectively.

During the ten days between the shooting and the preliminary examination, numerous conferences between reporters and defendant took place in the accommodating sheriff's office. Newspapers unanimously malign Mary Anne Starr in their headlines, e.g. **"OFFICE WIFE KILLS LAWYER," "WOMAN SCORNED SHOOTS ROBERT EASTWOOD," "SILVER BLONDE SLAYER KILLS PARAMOUR," and "SWEETHEART-SECRETARY SHOOTS BOSS."** In news articles that accompanied these salacious headlines, Starr was most frequently referred to as the **"Office Wife."** She was also cast as "The Blonde," "The Silver Blonde," and "The Other Woman." From the day of the shooting pictures of Starr decorated newspapers.

Projected trial witnesses quoted Starr as saying, "You're GD right I killed him! He had it coming to him for a long time," "I had to eat dirt; now someone else can eat dirt,"

"Take that you SOB," "I'm not sorry. I'd do it again," and "They've been calling me a GD whore around this town; now I'll show 'em who's a GD whore!" True or false, these quotes were so often repeated in newspapers that the general public parroted them on the street.

Orchestrating her own defense without the aid of counsel, Mary Anne Starr hurt herself and future trial prospects. When asked why she didn't leave Eastwood if he was treating her so badly, she repeatedly responded, "A woman does funny things when she loves a man."

Robert Eastwood's obituary reported that he had obtained his law degree from Northwestern University. His schooling had been interrupted by military service during the Great War. In 1919 he received a medical discharge, the victim of German gas warfare. In 1920 upon completion of law school, he married Mabel Otto and they had four children. Wife and children lived in Kalamazoo.

The Berrien County legal community closed down October 19th in observance of Eastwood's funeral. Lawyers, veterans and friends packed the service held in a local mortuary. Newspapers gave more attention to Mary Anne's private viewing the night before than they gave Mabel Eastwood's funeral attendance. However, both women shared the headline, **"WIDOW AND 'OFFICE WIFE' WEEP AT BIER."**

Starr finally retained counsel, Attorney Glenn Biglow from Kalamazoo, less than 48 hours before her preliminary examination. Her early sense that the Berrien County legal community was distancing itself from her proved all too true. As Biglow hurriedly prepared for the preliminary examination, he advised Starr to stop talking to reporters—good advice, too late.

The preliminary examination marked Mary Anne's second personal appearance in the Benton Harbor courtroom in just ten days. A large crowd clustered at the municipal building steps awaiting the "Office Wife." Their rowdy behavior reflected community interest and sentiment towards the woman. The defendant arrived in a squad car driven by the County Sheriff.

Municipal Judge Rankin W. Cannon, in full regalia, exacted as much pomp and decorum for the jam-packed courtroom as he could muster. The atmosphere tantalized

Mary Anne, but she maintained a reserved external appearance. True to her nature, she cordially greeted Attorney Biglow, and with quiet poise took a seat next to him at the defense table. The next hour proved a learning experience for both defendant and her counsel.

Prosecutors Foster and Spears called two witnesses, and Foster led all direct examination for the prosecution. Biglow handled the cross-examination for the defense.

John Henry Johns, merchant policeman and the first witness at the scene of the shooting, was questioned and cross-examined for 45 minutes. At approximately 12:30 A.M. he heard two shots, but couldn't identify their location until he heard a voice call for help. Johns was standing at the intersection of Wall St. and Main St. talking with a fellow security guard at the time; over 400 feet from the shooting scene.

The two men ran towards the sound. Johns saw a form in the street bending over shooting at something. He heard, but did not see, a gun. The shooter left the street walking toward the library, at which time Johns was about halfway to the scene and passing an alleyway connecting Wall St. to 6ᵗʰ St. He shouted at his companion to cover the alley he testified, "They may be trying to get away down that way." The night was dark and he could only see people when they were in the dimly lit street. A person walked from the shadows into the street, picked up the victim's hat and started hitting the victim with the hat.

The streets of Benton Harbor were poorly lit that time of night. Streetlights provided some light along the south side of Wall St., with one providing light for the municipal building steps. The north edge of the street was dark and a person stepping from the street onto the sidewalk in front of the library was virtually hidden from view. No eyewitness ever testified they had actually seen Starr shoot Eastwood. Wall St. curved from the northeast to the west, making objects on the north side of that street even more obscure from a distance.

The second or third time the defendant hit Eastwood with his hat, Johns grabbed both of her arms from behind. The defendant had the hat in her right hand and a purse in her left. Johns demanded the gun. Not seeing a gun, he presumed it was in her purse. He seized the purse. The defendant said, "Give me my purse and I'll give you the gun." He returned her purse and she retrieved a gun from her right coat pocket and gave it to him.

As others arrived at the scene, Johns reported that he told one officer to take the defendant into the police station, told another to call for an ambulance, and then he attended to the victim who was still alive and moaning. As the first officer at the murder scene, Johns assumed de facto command.

Biglow cross-examined, but only established that Johns was inarticulate.

The second witness called by Foster was Benton Harbor physician Clark A. Twitchell. Twitchell testified that he was on duty at Mercy Hospital when the victim was brought in still breathing, but that he died immediately. Twitchell described the nature and location of the four gunshot wounds. He signed the death certificate, indicating gunshot wounds as the cause of death.

Biglow's cross-examination established angle of bullets entry, bullets did not exit the body and bullets were not removed post-mortem.

Foster moved that the respondent be bound over to Circuit Court for trial at the next term thereof. Biglow counter-moved for dismissal on the grounds of failure to show premeditation or malice aforethought. Judge Cannon overruled the dismissal motion and bound Mary Anne Starr over to Circuit Court on the charge of murder. No bond was set.

In the month between the preliminary examination and her Circuit Court arraignment, Mary Anne became acquainted with her attorney Glenn Biglow, but her search for more legal help failed. She lost her home and most of her belongings. The land contract for her house had been foreclosed. She was not allowed to have all of her clothes and other special possessions at the county jail. Her cherished pets, Chocoo, a Chow dog, and Jack, a Persian cat, were taken away. Mabel Eastwood had taken control of all personal property as the designated administrator of Robert Eastwood's estate; probate estimated value $4,600.

Family members, especially Mickey, Ruthie and Vonda, and a few close friends did make regular visits. On one such jailhouse visit, Mary Anne gave Mickey and Ruthie $3.46, the last of her money.

On November 28th, Mary Anne in the escort of two sheriff's deputies crossed the street from the jail to the courthouse for her Circuit Court arraignment. *The short walk to the top floor courtroom proved longer and exceedingly more strenuous than the legal proceeding itself. Counsel had prepared Mary Anne for a quick arraignment, but this court appearance seemed frivolous in its brevity. Biglow waived the reading of the information and entered a plea of "not guilty" on behalf of his client. Disgruntled reporters and spectators, anticipating heated debate, immediately filed out of the courtroom following Judge Warren's remanding of Mary Anne Starr back to jail to await trial; date to be announced. The whole procedure took less than two minutes.*

After returning to the quiet, albeit austere, four walls of her jail cell, Mary Anne had time to reflect on what had transpired. First, at the preliminary examination and now at the arraignment, Prosecutor Foster displayed a confident attitude regarding her responsibility for Attorney Eastwood's death. She may have recalled her first meeting with Foster shortly after he had defeated Harley Eastwood for Prosecuting Attorney. She had liked him and knew the feeling was mutual. She remembered what he had said later when she reported to him that Bob had beaten her and threatened her life; "Go home and work it out." Also, when allowed to make a phone call to Foster following her arrest, she could not forget his lack of support in protecting her property. A growing feeling of betrayal by the very legal system she had enjoyed working within weighed heavily on Mary Anne.

Several reporters confronted Attorney Biglow while leaving the courtroom following the Circuit Court arraignment. Responding to their questions, Biglow revealed his intention to develop a plan for an insanity defense. Given the unusual and sensational nature of this strategy, blaring news headlines followed. However, and not coincidentally, the Berrien County Bar Association wrested front-page top billing from Mary Anne's arraignment by concurrently announcing their resolution paying highest tribute to the late Attorney W. Robert Eastwood. Several bar members, and more than one who had declined to represent Mary Anne, paid special tribute to their fallen colleague and friend. Even if their intention concerning Eastwood was genuine and heartfelt, it was an unreciprocated admiration. In fact, Robert Eastwood's relationship with fellow barristers had always been fractious and his contemptuous critiques of them notorious.

The week of the trial's start, Pinehurst returned from an extended convalescence in Texas. Attracted home by the Starr case, he met with the defendant and shortly thereafter announced in a flamboyant news release that he was considering joining in her defense. A day later and only four days before the trial began, Pinehurst teamed with Biglow to form Mary Anne Starr's defense team.

Pinehurst reported that he had comprehensively studied and authored articles concerning the insanity defense, to which he added self-defense. He immediately requested that X-rays be taken of Mary Anne's skull and demanded of her that she no longer talk with anyone about her case. Not announced publicly was Pinehurst's distain for the Eastwood brothers and in particular Robert Eastwood, who had represented two farmers in a frivolous civil suit brought against the House of David a year earlier; the Gravel Case.

Although not her first choice for legal representation, Mary Anne trusted and relied heavily on her two attorneys. The three of them held their last strategy session late on the Sunday afternoon before the trial. In only his third day, Pinehurst became the lead attorney. Acutely aware of the trial's meaning for her life, its anticipation tantalized the defendant, an emotion shared by her lead attorney.

The People of the State of Michigan v. Mary Anne Starr began on December 12, 1938 at 9:30 A.M. Fifteen minutes later, jury selection commenced and lasted a day and a half. The jury pool had to be expanded do to multiple witness challenges. Finally, just past mid morning of the second day, a jury of eleven men and two women, all married, was empanelled. At the end of the trial and before jury deliberations, one juror would be eliminated.

In his opening statement, Prosecutor Foster exaggerated and misstated several facts of the case, either unwittingly or on purpose. However, his message was short and clear, "Mary Anne Starr admits killing Robert Eastwood and we will prove she intended to do just that."

Pinehurst's opening was considerably longer and much more involved. He unmistakably enjoyed the technical nature of his remarks. Basically, the defense would prove that their client experienced temporary insanity when she shot Robert Eastwood in self-defense. This was complicated by the fact that the defendant was in a state of induced amnesia, the result

Clare Adkin

of several previous beatings and a severe blow to the head immediately prior to the shooting. Also, the defense would prove that Eastwood suffered from paranoia and dementia praecox, a progressive insanity frequently leading to homicide or suicide.

For the remainder of the second day of trial and half of the third, the prosecution paraded security guards, firemen and law officers to the witness stand. Each testified that they were either near the actual scene of the crime or had arrived there soon after the shooting took place. They all essentially agreed, with minor discrepancies, on the same set of facts. The victim's son concluded the prosecution's case.

I was fully aware that actually writing this article for submission would require a major effort on my part. As it stood it was too long, too informal, and too sloppy, but it was a task I needed to accomplish. Also, I looked forward to adding a picture or two to the final piece.

Even if it hadn't been my job—which it was—nothing could have kept me from court the next morning. Judge Jackson could be counted on to come up with something unanticipated. Whatever his instructions to them, the jury faced a difficult task. I was tired. I wanted to get home and go to bed.

Ginger met me as I walked from the barn to the house. She brought me a stick with a transparent request. I threw it as far as I could, stomped some snow off my shoes and gave a sigh of relief as I entered the kitchen.

Mom and Dad were involved in a heated discussion. I'd never seen them openly argue, but they were close. Both were raising their voice towards each other and hardly acknowledged my presence.

"What's going on?"

"Your Nana has gone into a deep depression. Won't talk to anyone, not even Grandpa. Your father doesn't think it's any of our business."

Mom never referred to Dad as your father, always Dad or Honey. She was mad.

"Now hold on, I never said that. I said that us running over to your folks wasn't going to help anything. Your parents have successfully gotten through lots of problems in their lives. They will this time too. Give'em a chance."

"Well it's my mother, and I care about her! She thinks she's responsible for what Uncle Otto did and it's just not so. I don't care what you or Ken think."

"What do you mean, what Ken thinks?" I asked, not seeing Ken as part of the discussion.

160

Dad tried to explain, "Grandpa Hunter came by after supper and told us that Nana has been sick and in bed since the funeral. She thinks she's responsible for what Uncle Otto did. She apparently believes she could have intervened before this happened. Ken was listening to our conversation with Grandpa and he agreed with Nana."

Mom interrupted, "That's not exactly what Ken said," Mom looked at me as she spoke. "When Grandpa left, Ken started arguing with your father and me that everybody knew about what was going on at Uncle Otto's and did nothing. I told Ken to be quiet and go to his room."

"That's when he stormed out of the house and took off with the car. We don't know where he is." Dad spoke in an even voice, as if not too upset.

Silence filled the kitchen as all three of us stopped talking, staring into space, thinking. Visions of Mary Anne Starr's unanswered cries for help flooded my head.

Mom broke the silence by putting a pan into the cupboard while saying, "Josh has written an article for you about the Allegan Winter Fest."

"What's that?" I said, but not really wanting to change the subject.

"I don't know, but he says it's new and important. He's upstairs. Oh, I almost forgot, Maxine stopped by and wanted you to call when you got home."

"I can't do that now, it's too late. I'll call her in the morning from the office," I sounded more businesslike than I intended.

"But that will be long distance," Mom informed me.

"Do you think I should go looking for Ken?"

"Would you? I'm worried," Mom said in a voice of exhaustion.

Dad put his arm around Mom's shoulders and nodded to me.

"First, I want to check to see what Josh has for me. Then I'll go. I think I may know where Ken is."

I drove directly to the train depot in Fennville. Ken sat inside on a wooden bench talking to the tired manager. He didn't look surprised to see me, and I could tell he was in a foul mood.

"What do you want?"

"I need your help. Do you have a line on anything I can put in the paper tomorrow?" I poorly skirted an obvious reason for being there.

"Ya, family facilitates murder/suicide."

"That's not exactly what I'm looking for, but have you heard more about what Uncle Otto did?" I just wanted to get home and go to bed.

Ken opened up and explained to me what John Barnes had told him. Otto had always been a very strict parent, but had become physically abusive the last year or so, especially toward Aunt Arlene.

"The people at school knew about it, so did the hospital and the County Sheriff. No one ever lifted a finger to help that family. They lived in fear, Chuck! And now two of them are dead and John jumped a train today for Chicago and who knows where. He's gone. So that's three gone and one wounded. Some story."

Ken looked as if he would collapse and sink beneath the dirty depot floor. I put my hand on his shoulder knowing I didn't want to extend the conversation into any of my leads. That would only rekindle his fire.

"Ken, everyone in the family is struggling with this, most of all Nana. Let's go home and try to help make sense of all of this. I know you're worried about John. So am I. I'm sure Kelly and James need help and for that matter, Nana. The trial story I'm working on for the paper has many parallels to what has happened in the Barnes family. You understand as much or more about this as any of us. Come on, let's go home."

Ken didn't look at me but got up. The now wide-awake depot manager spit on the floor, pulled a small bag of Bull Durham tobacco from his shirt pocket and rolled a fresh cigarette. Ken and I headed out the door.

XX
JURY'S IN

At five after six I'd been lying wide awake for at least ten minutes; thinking. How much turmoil and heartache could one man cause; Uncle Otto, Robert Eastwood? No problem getting up because I was anxious to get started and see what the day held in store. I knew Dad was in the kitchen waiting for, "Anyone ready to go?"

I quickly got cleaned up and dressed, combing my hair in the mirror over the dresser I'd made in woodshop. Out of the corner of my eye I saw it. The calendar. The note read—**"FIRST DATE, Sunday, October 16, 1938."** My mouth fell open in recognition. That was the day Maxine and I went to South Haven to see a matinee movie. We must have been sitting in the same theater, at the same time, watching the same movie as Mary Anne Starr. I ran downstairs to double-check my trial notes.

"What do you want for breakfast?"

"You know what I want. I gotta check something right quick." I opened my briefcase and scrambled through trial notes; there it was, Sun., Oct. 16, There Goes My Heart, Virginia Bruce, favorite.

"Eureka!" I shouted. "Dad, I was in the same theater, watching the same movie as the defendant in the trial. I wonder if Maxine remembers anything."

Of course Dad wanted me to slow down and explain what I was talking about. I tried to do so as he fried bacon. Ginger mimicked my excitement and wanted to participate in the conversation. The attention I gave her encouraged her rambunctious behavior.

"You'd better put her out."

"Do we have an old bone or something I could give her?" I looked around the kitchen, but all I found was an old piece of stale bread. To Ginger it might as well have been a steak dinner. She pranced proudly into the yard with the bread held in her mouth; dropped it and looked around as if hoping someone might challenge her for the treasure.

I scribbled off a quick note: *Maxine, I've been getting home late each night, but the trial should end early today. If it does, I'll come by tonight. We are definitely on for the toboggan party Friday. I'm working on a byline. What do you think of this? "Good evening Mr. and Mrs. North and South America and all the ships at sea. Flash—Maxine and Chuck are an item! C. Drew Scott."*

Just having fun, I hoped Maxine would recognize that I had borrowed that line from Walter Winchell's, "Gossip more than News," radio program. I loved Winchell's voice and his outlandish delivery. Maxine and I hadn't seen each other for a few days.

I folded and laid the note on the cupboard counter and asked Dad if he could get Josh or Ken to run it over to Maxine, preferably before noon. I explained to him about the toboggan party and that I hadn't been able to get in touch with her.

While eating breakfast we talked more about the whole Uncle Otto thing. Dad was concerned about Nana, but still believed that time was the ultimate healer. I told him about John Barnes running away and how upset I had found Ken the previous night. Dad assured me that John Barnes could take care of himself, but wished he had waited until he graduated, being so close. As for Ken, Dad again relied on time to bring him to his senses. "Ken's smart. He'll realize that none of us could have known Uncle Otto would go crazy. No one has a crystal ball."

My dad's way of looking at things was sure and usually comforting. However, this time I didn't find the same solace I once did, and I was unsure as to whether I would ever know what I believed in the way Dad knew what he believed in. It was as if the older I got, the less I knew.

"Dad, I gotta go. I need to stop at the office and finish up a couple of articles before I can go to St. Joe. Fortunately, court doesn't start until ten this morning, which gives me a little more time."

"Be careful driving. You gassed up?"

It wasn't much after seven when I walked into the newspaper office. There were a couple of men in the back working on the printing press, but other than that, it was pretty much empty. I went right to work on the story **FROM ARREST TO TRIAL**. As for the Allegan Winter Fest, I submitted Josh's article almost verbatim. I needed to do some Christmas shopping and Josh was at the head of my list.

The Chief came in as I was leaving. He greeted me with a big grin, "Chuck, do you still work for me? I hardly see you."

By his expression and tone, I could tell he was in good humor and genuinely happy to see me. "The trial in St. Joe ended yesterday and is going to the jury today. I'm on my way there now to see how the judge will instruct the jury.

"Good. Good. I want to read your conclusion."

The Chief meant what he said; he wanted to read what I had written. My knees felt weak. Speechless, I just stood there looking at him.

"Rose wants I should ask you for dinner tomorrow around six thirty? She says you bring a friend." A question or a command, it didn't matter, his meaning was clear.

Seconds pounded in my head. What an honor, I thought. "I'd like that Chief. May I bring something? I don't want Mrs. Mendelsohn going to a lot of trouble."

"No trouble. You will bring a guest with you?" The Chief made more of a request for me to bring someone than asking me if I thought I would. Hard to explain, but again I understood his meaning and very much wanted to comply.

"I think so, but I have to ask her; I think so." I know I didn't sound just right, but the Chief patted me on the back, "Good. Good. I'll see you then if not before," and ushered me out the door.

The drive to the courthouse started out with me in an ecstatic state. Being invited to dinner at the Chief's home had filled me with pure delight. However, before I entered Benton Harbor my mind wrapped itself around the future of Mary Anne, Mickey and Ruthie Starr. What must each of them be feeling at that very moment?

With time to spare, the Coupe came to a stop outside the Pegasus. I had time to have a cup of coffee. Hopefully, Penny would be working. The now familiar smells and sounds of the crowded diner made me feel at once welcome and anonymous; but no Penny to be seen.

I thought that the young woman pouring my coffee must be Penny's big sister. With the exception of being a little heavier and speaking with a thicker accent, the resemblance was unmistakable. She caught me staring.

"Breakfast?" she smiled.

"Is Penny here?"

She looked at me questioningly, "Penny?"

"Sorry. I don't know her last name, but you must be her sister. Hebe?"

She laughed, just like Penny, and said, "You must be Chuck the farm boy."

That took me by surprise and I didn't know quite how to take her remark. "Yes, my name's Chuck, Chuck Scott. I'm a newspaper reporter."

"Yes, Penny tell me. She work late and no come yet. I tell her you ask?"

"Ah, yeah. Would you tell her I'll swing by around suppertime?"

Hebe asked me if I'd like to try a fresh piece of *baklava*. Again surprised, an expression of understanding passed between us. "Yes, of course." Mixed and mystifying emotions coursed through me. Hebe was a stranger, but a stranger that seemed familiar and pleasingly clever. She aroused my curiosity.

Eager spectators gathered around the courthouse but were denied gallery entrance, a full hour before Judge Jackson's arrival. When admitted I managed to find a seat next to my friend Mike Halamka, as I felt confident he would assist me with trial nuances. The ninth day of trial began at precisely 10:00 A.M., no shocker. With sentinel Piles' introductory fanfare completed, Judge

Jackson forcefully swung into action with his charge to the jury. He meticulously explained jury responsibilities, although he had previously done so when the 13 jurors were initially impaneled. He again reminded jurors not to discuss the trial with anyone other than fellow jurors. "In fact," Jackson emphasized, "you will not know who your fellow jurors are until one of you is eliminated. Once that is completed, you will be allowed to discuss the trial with one another; indeed, you are required to do just that."

In a most stern and remarkably clear voice, the judge charged the jury, outlining the possible decisions available to them in light of the charges brought against, and the defense of, Mary Anne Starr. He cautioned that sentencing was not a jury responsibility, but his and his alone within the parameters established by the State of Michigan. He then listed and clarified for the jury the possible verdicts at their disposal with the range of sentencing guidelines available to him.

1. Not guilty by reason of temporary insanity—acquittal.
2. Not guilty by reason of self-defense—acquittal.
3. Guilty of murder in the first degree—mandatory life.
4. Guilty of murder in the second degree—two years to life.
5. Guilty of manslaughter—two to fifteen years.
6. "If you find the defendant was in a temporary state of amnesia at the time of the shooting, so that she was bereft of her normal mind, she is entitled to an acquittal."

Following one hour and ten minutes of instructions, Jackson requested Bailiff Pile to eliminate one of the jurors by lot. After this was completed, the jury, 10 men and 2 women, retired to the jury room to select a foreman before taking a noon recess. Court stood in recess until such time as the jury arrived at a verdict.

As the courtroom slowly disassembled, I looked around, not knowing exactly what to do or expect. Two questions ominously emerged. First, how would the jury rule? Second, how would the judge sentence? Mike helped a bit. "The jury will not come back with a decision until late this afternoon at the earliest, and maybe not until tomorrow." How he knew that I wasn't sure, but I believed I had time to drive to the office and get something in the paper about closing arguments and Judge Jackson's charge to the jury.

I said hello to Vonda, Mickey and Ruthie on my way out of the courtroom. Mickey introduced me to his Grandmother, Mrs. Adams, who seemed to possess all those good grandmotherly attributes. It was Ruthie that concerned me. She had lost weight, her skin pale and blotchy, and she had a shrinking presence about her. She looked malnourished and increasingly introverted.

They were going to have lunch and come straight back to the courtroom to wait for the jury. I told them my plan and that I'd see them later in the afternoon.

I immediately went to the bank of public phones along the wall in the first floor hallway and called the *Chicago Tribune*. Billy had not been in the gallery, and I felt sure he would appreciate a report. The sound of his typewriter clicked in the background as we talked. Even though I was the one giving Billy the trial information, I felt that it was Billy helping me to better understand the whole proceeding. He thanked me profusely for the call and asked if I might give him a call when the verdict was announced. I agreed.

Then I called Maxine to see if she would go with me to the Chief's for dinner Thursday night. It felt good to talk with her. Chipper as ever, she told me that Ken had dropped off my note and that she did remember the lady in the restaurant who looked like the actress Virginia Bruce. "That's amazing," I told her, "We'll have to explore this some more when it's not costing so much."

She disappointed me when she said she couldn't go with me to the Chief's for dinner due to a previous commitment. Speechless for a second time that day, I was relieved as Maxine marched on with details about the Toboggan party scheduled for Friday evening. "In the dunes near Saugatuck," she said.

"Sounds like a good time. Pick you up around six?"

Maxine said that would be perfect and that she looked forward to seeing me. "Me too." Nothing original to say.

There were wind gusts and snow flurries all the way up U.S. 31 to South Haven. Before going to the office, I ducked into the Dairy Diner for something to eat; I felt starving. The noon rush subsiding, I had no problem finding the exact stool I sat on the evening Maxine and I came in after the movie. I ate gazing at the table near the window where Mary Anne may have been seated. What a strange coincidence, I thought. No time for daydreaming, I had to get to work.

The office was a cacophony of noise and activity. Like all other employees, I knew where to go and what to do. I wasted no time starting an article on the day's events, **JURY DELIBERATES: STARR'S FATE IN THEIR HANDS**. Unpretentious, I thought. I really only wanted to cover Jackson's charge to the jury with possible outcomes. I prefaced the charge with a brief summary of closing arguments. Lots of work needed to be done on the Uncle Otto incident before I could submit a culminating story for that catastrophe.

While writing I worried about the jury coming back and me not being there. I had to get back to St. Joe, so as soon as I had something to submit I headed for the door. Simultaneously, the Chief came out of the printing room and shouted, "Chuck, wait a second, I need to talk to you." He yelled something to one of the men working in the back, then closed the door, which only kept out a portion of the noise.

"Chuck, I think we need a wrap up column for that Fennville story of yours. Any chance we could have something tomorrow?"

"Chief, I'll try, but a lot depends on when this jury comes back and when the judge passes sentence. But I'll try; how about for sure Friday?"

"You'll try for tomorrow?"

"Right Chief—gotta go."

There were less than a dozen people milling around the courtroom. The grandfather clock told me that it was after four. I interrupted a lady sitting in the back row reading *Gone With The Wind* to ask if there had been any word from the jury. She looked up slowly while carefully marking her place. "Excuse me?"

"Has there been any word from the jury; how are they progressing?"

"No, except that they did request the bailiff to let them look at that little pistol again."

"Was any explanation given for wanting to see the gun?"

"No, not that anyone shared with me."

At least I hadn't missed anything, I surmised. Vonda and her mother were seated at the front of a nearly empty gallery talking softly. I went over and sat down with them, but it was clear they didn't really want company; they'd rather commiserate by themselves.

"Where are Mickey and Ruthie?" I asked.

"They went for a walk. They should be back in a little while. It's cold out there."

"Mind if I go look for them? I could use a little exercise."

I figured they'd head for the lake and I soon found them shivering on the bluff near the Whitcomb Hotel.

"Lake's beautiful, isn't it?" I greeted them. Ruthie looked up startled and wiped her nose, which had turned pink and runny in the cold wind.

When she noticed me, she smiled and whispered weakly, "Yes, it really is beautiful." As she spoke with a shutter, I thought I could hear the faint rattle of teeth.

"Does it ever freeze over, Chuck?" Mickey asked.

"During the winter, ice almost always builds up along the shoreline. It helps protect against erosion. It will freeze all the way across during some really cold winters. When it does, it still wouldn't be a good idea to walk across the ice from here to Chicago."

"Where's Chicago from here?" Mickey asked.

As best I could, I pointed west-southwest across the lake. "I think we should be getting back to the courthouse and inside where it's warm."

"I agree with you, Chuck. Come on Mickey, let's go. I'm freezing."

On the walk back to the courthouse, Ruthie whispered, "What do you think the jury's going to do?"

This is the first I'd heard Ruthie say anything about the trial and the first time she had started a conversation. As encouraging as this seemed, it was a conversation I'd tried to avoid with family members, especially Ruthie. Conscious of her delicate condition, I searched for a way to avoid responding. Finally, I decided to tell the plain truth. "This is my first trial and quite honestly I don't have the slightest idea. I will say this; in my opinion Robert Eastwood had gone mad."

"He was an evil person; plain, simple, an absolute evil man!"

I stared straight ahead to avoid showing the shock I felt at hearing Ruthie spew forth with such venom. It was quite a departure from her normally quiet reserve. Until that moment she had said nothing about the trial and certainly never raised her voice in my presence. Mickey jumped in quickly, "Ruthie, don't get all worked-up again. Let's wait and see. I'm sure the jury heard the same things we heard and will come to the right decision."

"They didn't hear everything. I'm scared for Mommy," she snipped at her brother. Mickey drew his coat collar tightly around his neck and kept walking. The conversation ended.

The court appeared to be in a state of hibernation. The three of us appreciated its warmth, out of the wind and cold. Vonda and Mrs. Adams still sat worrying themselves to death. Mickey suggested they get up and walk around the courthouse; they complied as if they hadn't considered they had the right to do so.

After scouting around and talking with anyone I thought might give us some answers, I came to the conclusion that nothing would happen until after the jury returned from their evening meal, and they hadn't recessed yet. Close to five, I asked Mary Anne's family if they'd like to go to supper with me. Mrs. Adams thanked me, but said she had packed supper for the family and asked if I would join them. I acknowledged her kind generosity, but made up an excuse of having to keep an appointment. I knew they were a proud family of limited means and didn't want to compromise that. Had they accepted my initial invitation, I don't know how I would have paid for it.

As I left the courthouse, a bright idea popped in my head—Penny. It took me five minutes to get to the diner. Scanning the dining area for her, I found and occupied an empty wall booth.

"Hi Chuck," said a waitress carrying three full dinner plates to customers seated at a table near me. "Be with you soon."

Since it was Hebe, I asked if Penny was working. She told me Penny was baking pies in the back. Hair had fallen over her face and she swept it back with her right wrist and the toss of her head. "I tell her you here. Can I get you something?"

"Could I have a short stack and sausage?"

"Coming-up," and she disappeared through the swinging door.

I had almost finished my pancakes before Penny appeared. She presented me with a piece of pie while sliding into the seat across from me. Evidence of light perspiration beaded across her forehead and the bridge of her nose. It gave a flushed glow to her olive complexion. Her dark eyes flashed as she edged the pie towards me, "I want you try this and tell me what you think."

"Well, I can see it's not cherry or apple."

She ducked her head forward, lifting her eyebrows, "No."

With the edge of my fork, I sliced through the brown flaky crust revealing a white and green filling. Apprehensively, I took a small bite. In a surprising sort of way it was warm, creamy and quite good. Trying to show my pleasure by facial expression I added, "What is this? Is this what you've been baking?"

"It's called *Spanakopita*. Do you like?"

"Yes, I like, but what is it? I've never had a pie quite like this."

"It made of dough, spinach and cheese. Hebe taught me how to make. She said mother taught her. Our customers have developed taste for it."

"I can see why, Penny. It's very good, and I hate spinach!" We both laughed.

"Penny, I want to ask you a question," I said feeling unsure of exactly how I wanted to invite her. It was the first time I'd ever asked a girl out that wasn't a friend of the family. I realized that of all the people I could ask, Penny was the one person I most wanted to take.

"Uh-oh, this sound important. Are you newspaper reporter who want Greek cooking story?" As she said this I wondered if I had been a bit pretentious about my job and she was giving me a hard time. No matter, I wanted to take somebody to the Chief's tomorrow and Penny was my choice.

"No, I'm serious. My boss has invited me for dinner tomorrow evening at six thirty and I would like to take you with me. Will you go with me?" I looked straight into Penny's eyes with as much sincerity and hope as I could muster, knowing of course she would say yes.

Penny had not expected this. At first she seemed confused. Expressionless, she looked at the *Spanakopita* that I had half finished.

"Did I say something wrong?" I tried to get Penny to look at me, but I was unsure of myself and didn't want to add insult to injury—a Nana expression.

"No, nothing wrong," came her measured reply. "And Chuck, I like go with you to your boss for dinner." Penny stammered, thinking. Then she looked at me and began, "I never go out with boy before, not alone..."

"We won't be alone," I interrupted, "The Chief and his wife will be there."

"That not what I mean. We go in your car, right? To South Haven, right? Just you and me," she said looking at me as if I was asking her to go on the Lewis and Clark Expedition.

"Please, Penny, you can do this. The Chief and his wife Rose are nice people and we'd have a good time. I'll bring you straight home."

"I want to go Chuck. I must ask Hebe. She worry about me. I think she say no."

"Why would she say no?" I found myself pleading. "Go ask her, let's find out."

"She not here now, but I ask her when she come back."

This represented the second girl that had turned me down that afternoon. I knew Penny and Hebe lived together, but not much beyond that. Pushing any harder may have been self-destructive, so I did my best to bring our discussion to an amiable conclusion.

"Listen, I've got to get back to court. When I get out tonight, I'll swing by to see if you are still here; I don't know what time that will be. If I miss you, I'm certain I'll be in town tomorrow. Either way, I'll stop by."

"I'm sure I can give you answer this hour. Finish your pie," she seemed to flirt; at least that's how I chose to interpret it.

"Tell me. From my observations, Hebe is single. Does she ask you if she wants to go out with some guy?" I'm not sure why I asked that question, other than I just wanted to talk with Penny a little longer. We represented different worlds and I wanted to share mine and get to know hers.

"Yes, she ask. I'm certain I say yes, but I also certain she ask me."

Penny remained direct, self-assured and serious. Now, more than ever I wanted to take her out, and she would be the perfect person to have with me at the Mendelsohns.

"The pie was great. You'll notice not a crumb left. I'll be back." Winking at Penny I said, "This story is not over."

I thought with that I'd fade towards the sunset, but Penny came back with a sparkle in her eyes as I walked out the door of the Pegasus. "What story, Mr. Newspaper Man?"

As seven o'clock approached, a few people began wandering into the courtroom. At approximately seven fifteen the fifty or so milling inside the courtroom were startled by three short rings of the jury room buzzer giving notice to all that the jury had reached a verdict.

News that the jury was coming in spread quickly. At seven thirty, Sheriff Diamond escorted a smiling defendant to her seat. When Judge Jackson reassumed command at eight, he faced a packed house.

Formally reconvening court, Jackson announced, "The jury is about to render its verdict. There must be absolute quiet and order. There will be no disturbance, no expression of approval or disapproval of any kind. Following the verdict, everyone will remain seated until the court gives permission to leave. Anyone violating these rules will be taken into custody immediately."

Allowing for quiet, Jackson then instructed Pile to bring in the jury. As the two women and ten men quietly, but tensely, filled the jury box, each sound they made seemed magnified. When all were seated, a hush fell over the great hall.

"Ladies and gentlemen of the jury, have you reached a verdict?

A mumbled chorus of "We have," came from the uncomfortable group of twelve.

"Mr. Foreman, what is your verdict?"

Foreman Clyde Oronoko, a retired St. Joe fireman, solemnly rose to his feet. "We, the Jury, find the respondent guilty of manslaughter."

"So say you, so say all members of the jury?"

A second mumbled chorus emanated from the jury box, "We do."

A reverberating rumble instantly radiated through the gallery, but just as quickly dissipated as six uniformed officers made their presences known and appeared to be taking attendance. Mary Anne Starr showed no emotion, as if momentarily detached. Her mother seated directly behind her in the first row, wept into a kerchief. Tears flowed silently down Vonda's cheeks. Mickey showing his strength of character sat unbowed, but with strain meanly creasing his boyish features; eyes red and watery. Ruthie had stayed in the corridor, not able to bear being in the courtroom during the reading of the verdict. When word came to her, she cried convulsively, uncontrollably. Mickey hastily attended to his sister.

Judge Jackson briefly, but cordially, thanked and excused the jury from their eight days of sequester. "The respondent is remanded to the custody of the sheriff. She will appear for sentencing at 10:00 A.M. tomorrow."

Attorney Pinehurst stood up, "Counsel for the defense desires to enter a motion for suppression of sentence for two to three weeks in order to prepare a proper motion for arrested judgment and a motion for a new trial."

A weary Judge Jackson responded, "The court will take up said motion at 9:30 A.M. Baillif Pile."

This case is not over until I say it is. With that egotistical thought filling my head, I recall a countervailing feeling of being drained, empty. I didn't know what to think of the verdict or Pinehurst's motion. It was as if I'd been in a hurricane for a week and suddenly it stopped. *Was I in the eye or had it passed?*

XXI
SKOPELOS

The courtroom was practically deserted by the time I rose from my seat and wandered aimlessly toward the open doors. I was overwhelmed with a heavy feeling bordering on an immobilizing paralysis. A week earlier, I would have considered the jury's decision lenient. After the fact, I couldn't resolve my position, and felt inexplicably ill at ease. The prospect of Jackson addressing Pinehurst's appeals for a suppression of sentence and a new trial left me with a slow growing apprehensive curiosity.

A cold wind jolted me from a self-imposed lethargic trance. Mine was the only car parked on Church Street and it started right up. The little black Coupe was my true companion. *Let's give Penny a chance to lift our spirits. If she agrees to go with us to the Chief's for dinner, at least we'll have that to look forward to.*

Three customers still lingered in the Pegasus, talking more than eating. Penny straightened shelves behind the lunch counter. Industrious and efficient, she reestablished order out of the day's disarray. If aware of my presence, she didn't acknowledge such.

I caught her attention asking, "Hey Penny, are you still serving?"

"Oh, hi Chuck. Did jury come to verdict?"

"About half an hour ago. Guilty of manslaughter."

"Can you tell me about it? The grill is shut-down, but we have piece of *Spanakopita* left if you like?"

"Yes, if I may have a piece of cheese on the side? American." I took a stool at the counter.

"But Chuck, it full of cheese."

"Please?"

Penny flashed me a quizzical glance as she headed for the kitchen. She returned with an ample slice of *Spanakopita* adorned with a chunk of American cheese. "Will this do?" The fact that she seated herself on the stool next to me added a special appeal.

"It will do if you will agree to go with me to the Chief's for dinner." I confidently looked at Penny, but received no response. "Okay, it will do and I look forward to consuming it." I tried to fill the uncomfortable silence. Being turned down had never entered my mind.

"Why did you want cheese with it?"

"My Nana always says, 'Apple pie without cheese is like a kiss without a squeeze.' Now, I know this isn't apple pie, but I can always hope, can't I."

Penny laughed, "Yes Chuck, you hope." Both of us reveled in an imaginary double-meaning neither of us understood. "What is Nana? Is that like banana?"

"Nana is my grandmother, that's what we call her. I don't know where the name came from. It's just always been so."

After eating some pie and exchanging small talk, I returned to what was really on my mind. "Penny, what have you and Hebe decided; will you be able to go with me to dinner tomorrow night?"

"No Chuck, I can't. Hebe not think we know you well enough and it too far to go."

I wasn't about to beg, but I did not want to accept no for an answer. "How will you ever know me well enough? Or is that what you say when you don't want to go out with someone?" I didn't like the way I sounded, but I blurted it out without thinking. Trying to soften my words I continued, "What I mean to say is, I would like to go out with you and I want to know the proper protocol to make that happen." I didn't like the pretentious way that sounded either, but I now wanted Penny to go with me more than ever.

"If you listen, I think I help us make happen."

"How?"

"We closed Christmas Eve and Christmas Day. Some friends have party Saturday afternoon and Hebe suggest I may invite you. Will you come to party?"

"Yes!" Again, I didn't like the way I sounded, but my eagerness must have pleased Penny by the delight shown on her face.

Penny excused herself to cash out her remaining customers. Her manner with customers was more of that between friends than vendor and patron. They visibly liked Penny. Before leaving the restaurant, a middle-aged woman with an old-fashioned shawl tied tightly around her head stared at me and then smiled with intent at Penny. Penny blushed ever so slightly, "See you soon Mrs. Danapolis."

I watched Penny turn off the outside light and hang up the **CLOSED** sign. "Are you kicking me out too or can I help you close-up for the day?" I hoped for the opportunity to talk with Penny without others around.

"Are you sure Chuck? You should go home, no?" Penny's questions were genuine, not immature bantering.

"I'm not in any hurry. Are you sure I can't help do something?"

"Okay, you put chairs on top of tables so I can sweep and mop. Also, I spill grease in kitchen that need scrubbing."

Penny and I went to work and shortly I found myself on hands and knees scrubbing the kitchen floor. Penny came into the kitchen to dump a bucket of soapy water in the sink. "Chuck, what you doing?" she giggled.

"I'm scrubbing this grease spill like you suggested. What does it look like I'm doing?"

"I mean you have on good suit pants. You should not be on floor. Here, let me do."

"Actually, I'm all done," I said as I turned from all fours and sat with back against a cupboard. Penny picked-up my bucket of water and dumped it in the sink. Then she sat on the floor next to me.

"All done, but look at knees," she said pinching a wet spot on one of my pant legs.

"It's just water Penny. It'll dry and besides, I'm on my way home." It was a pleasure sitting next to her. I searched for more to say, but was completely satisfied just being there with Penny. Finally I said, "What would you like for Christmas?"

"Everyone talk about Christmas present. They so excited. Hebe and I have never given gifts, but I think it good idea. I know Hebe want radio. I save my tips to buy for her." A gleam pervaded Penny's face as she talked about buying a gift for her sister. It was clear that a strong connection existed between these two women.

"But, what do you want Penny? What would you want for yourself?"

Penny thought for a few seconds with a faraway look in her eyes. "If I have first wish, I like go back *Skopelos*."

"Back to *Skopelos*? That sounds like more Greek food."

"It is Greek island where Hebe and I were born and lived until we come America. It where we lived with mother and father. It beautiful place, Chuck." Good memories flooded Penny to the quick, as if she were adrift in some magical place.

"What happened to your parents, Penny?" I spoke in a low voice suspecting that the answer may be a delicate subject.

"We good family. Hebe and I loved father and mother. Father was fisherman and mother was daughter of wine maker. Father said we were poor, but I not think we poor, we had good life. I love go fish with father. One day father and mother go fish. Big storm come. They no come home."

The reflective sadness that welled-up within Penny sought escape through her glistening eyes. I touched her hand. "I'm sorry Penny. Someday you will go back. I'm sure of it. *Skopelos*?"

Quickly bringing her emotions under control, she turned to me and said, "Hebe told me that she think *Skopelos* nice place to grow-up, but she feel confined there; it small island. She not so interested go back. I am, it beautiful place."

"Always take time to remember Penny. Someday you will go back. I wish I had a destination like *Skopelos*." We sat on the floor, relaxing, talking; occasionally looking at each other. Our faces were no more than a foot apart. My face moved closer to Penny's. She did not move. When my lips pressed lightly against hers, she held steady. And then she pressed back.

"I'll drive you home, Penny."

"That not necessary. I live close. I walk all time."

"Then I'll walk you." I refused to take no for an answer this time. Walking next to Penny thrilled me while my wet knees chilled me. We did not touch, but I felt as her protector, even though she probably would have been more protection for me.

We soon came to a large two-story warehouse with lights on in a couple of second floor rooms. Penny told me that she and Hebe lived upstairs. When we arrived at what appeared to be a fire escape on the side of the building, she turned to me, thanked me for helping her and told me that she looked forward to Saturday.

"Me too!" That colorless phrase, the one that ended my enjoyable evening with Penny, bounced around in my brain all during the night. Surely, I thought, an accomplished reporter like myself could come up with something a little more impressive, more meaningful, more romantic.

Voices came from downstairs early the next morning. Wide awake, I got out of bed, dressed and headed for the kitchen. Dad and Mom were drinking coffee having what appeared to be another serious discussion. Ginger got up from her safe haven underneath the table and came to me, requiring a couple of pets before I could pour myself a cup of coffee.

"Dad's going to take me to Allegan to be with Nana."

"Has something happened?" I asked knowing that Allegan could only mean the hospital.

In a troubled, worried voice, Mom answered, "She's listless, just wants to stay in bed. The doctors want to keep her for a day or so for observation and tests."

Mom and Dad explained to me that Nana had been shocked and grief-stricken with the initial news of the shootings, and had never gotten over it. In fact, she had gotten worse and Grandpa was having difficulty taking care of her.

"I'll drop your mother off at the hospital and go back and pick her up this afternoon. That will give your Grandpa a break. He stayed with Nana over night. Maybe we will be able to take Nana home so she can be in her own bed tonight." Dad's concern for Nana's condition had noticeably increased. He did not mask his empathy for Mom's feelings; no more of the "be tough and this will pass" bravado.

"Dad, why don't you let me take Mom to the hospital? That will give me a chance to see Nana. I have time and it's really not much out of my way."

"I don't know, are you sure?" he said as he looked questioningly towards Mom.

"I'd really like to," as I joined Dad in looking for Mom's agreement.

"That would please Nana. Let's go, Chuck. Dad and Grandpa will pick me up around four this afternoon. Hopefully, they'll let us take Nana home." All agreed and Ginger wagged her tail.

Nana did not look well laying there in the hospital bed, withered, pale, sunken eyes outlined with dark rings. Mom fought back tears at the sight of Nana's pitiful condition. With her hands on Nana's shoulders, she bent down and kissed her mother on the cheek. Nana opened her eyes, and as her awareness grew so did a smile cross her face. She reached a feeble hand towards me.

I took it and whispered, "Do you want to know what I want for Christmas?"

Nana beamed and hoarsely whispered back, "What do you want, little Chuckie?"

"Well, glad you asked," as I winked at my Nana. "I have a present for Grandpa, a round of cheese. And I'm hoping that you will bake us each an apple pie for Christmas."

Nana squeezed my hand smiling, "Have you been good?" Then she turned her head toward Mom smiling, "You know apple pie without cheese is like a kiss without a squeeze."

"I know Mommy. We all want you home for Christmas. That would be the best present of all."

"Where else am I going to bake the pies?" Nana replied with a touch of mischief in her voice.

On my way out of the hospital, I stopped at the nurse's station and asked to speak with the head nurse. I was told that she was in the admissions office. Finding the nurse I wanted, I explained my family's confusion over the relationship between our Uncle Otto Barnes and his wife, Aunt Arlene. In fact, this was information I needed, more than clarifying any family confusion. Two things became obvious: first, the nurse believed it to be an abusive relationship and second, she wasn't going to tell me anything more. She did suggest that I talk to a sheriff's deputy by the name of Jack; "Lives over near Fennville." It sounded like the same deputy that Barth had mentioned.

It took me over an hour to drive from Allegan to the St. Joe courthouse, plenty of time to figure out where I was going to find a round of cheese. The drive itself was informative and once I got to Paw Paw, I tried to retrace the route traveled by Robert Eastwood and his friend Izzy the night of the shooting. Places, times and distances took on new meaning when visited personally.

Entering the courtroom only five minutes before the scheduled start, Halamka motioned vigorously for me to sit next to him. A welcome like that should not be taken lightly. I moved to him quickly, "Hi Mike, what's on your mind?"

He whispered that a reliable source had told him that Pinehurst would deliver a compelling argument requesting arrested judgment and a motion for a new trial. The people he had talked with in the legal community agreed that Judge Jackson would support the defense's appeal. One thing for certain, his suspicions would soon be addressed.

Court started right on time at 9:30 A.M. with Judge Jackson recognizing Attorney Pinehurst for the purpose of presenting his request and motion. Looking particularly dapper in a blue three-piece suit and new light beige dress shoes, Senator Pinehurst addressed the court. He argued his contention that the jury had been prejudiced by testimony regarding adultery, a non-issue in the case. The prosecution's use of the Ten Commandments and its labeling the defendant as a "woman with a double sin" were particularly objectionable tactics according to Pinehurst.

Continuing, he charged that expert medical testimony failed to be given proper court consideration and the verdict was contrary to the evidence on record. When speaking of records, Pinehurst's vehemence resurfaced. He charged court error in permitting testimony of a previous arrest in the complete absence of verifying records. Finally, Pinehurst concluded that the prosecution had inappropriately offered, and the court incorrectly allowed, the introduction of new evidence by rebuttal witnesses.

Judge Jackson pondered Pinehurst's meticulously crafted remarks for all of five seconds. Then he firmly declared, "The questions raised by defense counsel have been carefully considered by this court and found to be wholly without merit and worthy of no further argument. Therefore, the request for a stay of sentencing and a hearing on the motion for a new trial are hereby denied."

Before the sound of Jackson's voice dissipated, Prosecutor Foster was on his feet. "The people move for sentence, Your Honor." Foster sat back down.

Noticeably frustrated, Pinehurst reminded Judge Jackson that statute gave the court wide latitude in sentencing. "Your Honor, you are at liberty to sentence this respondent anywhere from a maximum of 15 years in prison to a minimum of probation with credit for time served. In view of this court record and the suffering already endured by this defendant, the court may quite honorably and justifiably suspend sentencing." Senator Pinehurst paused, then reluctantly gave up the floor and returned to his seat.

The packed courtroom became still, an uneasy stillness, as if something stealthily moved through the air. Jackson broke the silence, "Will the defendant please stand?"

The pretty, blue-eyed defendant stood up compliantly between her two attorneys, Pinehurst on her left and Biglow on her right. Behind them sat Stella Stallwell on the first row bench next to Mickey, Ruthie, Vonda and Mrs. Adams. Without emotion Judge Jackson asked, "Mary Anne Starr, you have been convicted by a jury of this court of the crime of manslaughter. Have you anything to say before the court passes judgment?"

Starr appeared taken by surprise at this request. She glimpsed questioningly, first at Pinehurst and then at Biglow. Receiving no reaction from either, she meekly replied "no."

The courtroom again fell silent. Then Judge Jackson asserted his authority one final time. "It is the sentence of the court that you, Mary Anne Starr, be confined to the house of corrections at Detroit for a period of not more that 15 years, the maximum fixed by the statutes, and not less than 14 years, the minimum fixed by this court. It is the recommendation of this court that you serve the full maximum term."

Pinehurst's recent plea for leniency in sentencing had fallen on deaf ears. Jackson had plainly predetermined the punishment he would exact.

Mary Anne Starr sank to her seat with head bowed. She obviously understood the severity of her sentence. It was also obvious that the sentence was totally unanticipated by attorneys and defendant. Before the stark gravity of her circumstances could fully set in, Jackson remanded Starr to the custody of Sheriff Diamond who stood at attention next to the grandfather clock.

"Whack!"

"All rise! The Honorable Court for the County of Berrien, Michigan, now stands in recess. God save Michigan and this Honorable Court." Judge Toby D. Jackson vanished. An amusing irony I thought, that Gordon Pile should have the last word. For the second time in less than 24 hours I felt totally frustrated, disappointed and perplexed.

XXII
CASE CLOSED

The noon rush was still an hour away. I had gravitated to the Pegasus for reasons that never occurred to me. Penny straightened tables while Hebe organized dishes and flatware behind the counter. "What's cookin?" I asked, although not hungry. Both women looked up and greeted me with warm smiles.

"Is trial over?" Penny asked.

"It's over," I responded with a sigh of relief, but a discontented feeling still lingered.

"I want you tell me all about it. First, come with me. You meet some very special people." I followed Penny through the swinging door. She introduced me to an elderly couple working in the kitchen. Both wore long white aprons and, they each wiped their hands on their aprons as they interrupted their work to greet me. The couple was distantly related to the family in Chicago that had helped Hebe and Penny come to America. Penny called them *Yia Yia* and Uncle K, short for *Kambelos*, and encouraged me to do the same. If not actually linked to Hebe and Penny by blood, *Yia Yia* and Uncle K were certainly of the same Greek nationality as the girls with whom they shared a reciprocated affection.

Their smiling faces were infectious and their welcome heartfelt. I had difficulty understanding their broken English. Penny effortlessly assisted our communication and I was pleased with how comfortable they were with me. Hebe joined us and I received a cook's tour of the kitchen, which all were as proud of as they were of each other. The orphaned sisters had acquired a new family in a new world.

Penny announced that she had invited me to the Saturday party. Again, everyone showered me with animated smiles and pats of welcome. By the time Penny pulled me out of the kitchen, I had in my possession a sack of unpronounceable pastries, with which I intended to become well acquainted.

"This is great," I said to Penny as we sat down at the counter. Penny again tried to explain to me the family relationships that existed between her shirttail relatives here in America. The mere fact that she wanted to take on this near impossible task made me incredibly happy. How swiftly I'd shed the empty feeling I felt walking out of the courthouse just minutes earlier.

"Penny, is a *Yia Yia* like a Nana?"

"That's-a good, Chuck," Penny beamed.

Hebe came out of the kitchen with her coat, saying she was going to get flour and would be right back. I asked if I could go get it for her and Penny added, "Let Chuck and me get flour?" Hebe hesitated, but I agreed that Penny had a good idea, and suggested we take my car.

"How much flour you need Hebe? We walk, not far, good exercise." Penny had hastily directed us away from taking my car. Hebe's furrowed brow at the mention of the car indicated her disapproval.

Penny put her coat on and Hebe gave her the money for 20 lbs of flour. Once outside the diner I said to Penny, "Well, you wanted exercise. Let's go." The sun had cracked through high white clouds, which added a blinding brilliance to the wintry outdoors. As we walked, we tried to impress each other with our visible breath. The snow squeaked under each step we took.

"How far are we walking?"

"Not far, newspaper man. You make it."

"Okay dumb dinky diner high school Harriet, I'll do my very best to keep up with you," I replied in the most cowering voice I could conjure.

Penny laughed as she hit me on the arm, "You remember?"

"I remember everything. For example, I wonder what the Greek girls at the Pegasus Diner have against a poor farm boy and his little black Ford Coupe?"

"Hmm, as you say, long story."

"This newspaper man would like to hear it."

"I don't know. Let me think about." The concern shown in her soft brown eyes and faintly creased brow left me to believe that a serious memory dwelt deep within Penny. Not usually one to pressure others whose feelings may be compromised, I still I wanted to know more of Hebe and Penny's story.

We had walked about six blocks east along Main Street when we came to a general store that sold several items in bulk. Penny asked for two 10 lb sacks of flour. When I picked up both, she insisted that she carry one. It didn't take much to make me relinquish one of the sacks. The Coupe would have made this job much easier, but I chose not to revisit the subject. However, I did consider the sense of importance and feeling of privacy the Coupe provided, especially with someone like Penny seated next to me.

"Does Hebe normally carry two of these sacks of flour by herself?"

"Yes and sometimes more. Let's speed up, slowpoke. I need get back soon."

After returning to the diner, I confirmed with Penny and Hebe that I'd pick them up at noon Saturday to go to the party. I asked about what I should wear, where we would be going, and how long the party would last. I knew I had to be home by suppertime Christmas Eve for the Scott family Christmas celebration. *Yia Yia* and Uncle K waved to me from the swinging door. *Yia Yia* shouted she was happy to meet me and Uncle K shouted he would see me at the party. At least that's what I thought they said.

The trial article that needed to be written congested my head. Still perplexed about the outcome, I wanted to get back to the office and start writing. Maybe in writing I could clarify my personal opinion, which hadn't materialized yet and I could only hope that it would as I tried to put it on paper. The details of closing statements, the charge, the verdict and sentencing ran through my brain like newsreel highlights; like bits and pieces of yesterday's dream. Organizing and presenting this story in an honest, coherent front-page column would be difficult. But, that was my job and I liked it.

Even with a busy mind, I enjoyed the wintery drive along the lake and tree-covered sand dunes lining the coast between Benton Harbor and South Haven. The gray, barren deciduous trees, interspersed with a variety of evergreens, all possessing a plastered white western side, the result of blowing snow, made for a picturesque journey. The omnipresent west wind revealed itself in other ways, but most prominently by the eastward lean of passing fruit orchards. Pegasus pastries and a Yellow Delicious apple provided nourishment for my ride.

The newspaper office clamored with activity. I went straight to my desk and trusty L.C. Smith typewriter and started hammering away. Two or three rewrites and I stopped.

MARY ANNE STARR TO GO TO PRISON
By C. Drew Scott

St. Joseph, Dec. 22—The fate of Mary Anne Starr, on trial for murdering her common law husband W. Robert Eastwood, was sealed at 10: A.M. today when Circuit Court Judge Toby D. Jackson sentenced Starr to 15 years in prison. The sentencing was based upon a jury verdict of guilty of manslaughter, punishable by 2 to 15 years in prison. Judge Jackson sentenced Starr to a term of from 14 to 15 years with the strong recommendation that she serve the full 15 years.

Last night, when the jury came in with their verdict, Starr's defense attorney, J.P. Pinehurst, pleaded for an arrested judgment. He said this would allow time for the defense team to prepare their motion for a new trial. This morning, Judge Jackson denied the motion as without merit. Pinehurst then made a futile last minute appeal for leniency in sentencing.

At the trial's conclusion, Pinehurst was asked if he would pursue any further legal actions on Starr's behalf. He answered, "It takes money to appeal for a new trail and Mrs. Starr has no money." Later he explained that the Governor had the power to

issue a commutation of sentence, but gave no indication that a commutation would be sought on Starr's behalf.

This brings to a close a drama that started on October 17 when Benton Harbor attorney W. Robert Eastwood was shot to death on the street in front of the city's municipal building. Mary Anne Starr was arrested at the crime scene with the murder weapon in her possession. The defendant never denied having committed the murder.

However, Starr's defense strategy was three fold. First, she claimed to have acted in self-defense. Second, she claimed temporary insanity at the time of the shooting. Third, she claimed temporary amnesia, the result of repeated beatings inflicted on her by Eastwood.

The state's case against Starr, directed by Berrien County Prosecuting Attorney W.C. Foster, was much less complex. Foster claimed that Eastwood and Starr experienced domestic difficulties. Starr armed herself with a pistol and went looking for Eastwood. When she found him, they quarreled and she shot him twice in the back. She then walked up to his prostrate body and shot him twice in the head at point blank range.

Several prosecution witnesses corroborated the state's account of the crime. Witnesses for the defense supported Starr's claim that she had been the victim of Eastwood's chronic physical abuse. Also, the defense brought in three medical experts who clarified and supported Starr's claims of temporary insanity and temporary amnesia.

For over two months, this murder case has piqued the interest of the citizens of southwestern Michigan and beyond. In an attempt to avoid idle conjecture and wild inferences, the following list is offered as the primary elements that have made this case fascinating and suspenseful:

1. The victim and the defendant were common law husband and wife as well as business partners— Starr managed Eastwood's law office.

2. Starr is an attractive 34-year-old divorcee with two teenage children.

3. Eastwood was legally married, but estranged from his wife and their four children for the past ten years.

4. Eastwood had practiced law, was disbarred, was reinstated to the bar, and had served as Berrien County Assistant Prosecuting Attorney under his younger brother, Attorney Harley Z. Eastwood.

5. Starr experienced extreme difficulty in obtaining defense counsel and once she did, her lead counsel's unusual hair drew as much attention as her own.

6. The murder weapon was a tiny strange four barreled 22-caliber derringer pistol.

7. The victim was shot in the back by an assailant, who claimed self-defense.

8. The defendant claimed temporary insanity and charged her victim was insane.

9. The murder took place in front of the Benton Harbor police station and courthouse.

10. The defendant had beautiful long silver blond hair!!!

There were 10 days of intense trial excitement featuring one Saturday session and three evening sessions, most of which took place before a crowded courtroom gallery. This upcoming Monday morning, the day after Christmas, Mary Anne Starr will be transported to Detroit where she is to be incarcerated in the Detroit House of Correction. This case is closed...for the time being.

Feeling a bit uncomfortable about what I'd written, I took the article to the Chief for his opinion. The Chief, busy as always, told me I hadn't got him killed yet. "Just leave it on my desk. Rose is expecting company tonight."

"I'm looking forward to it, Chief," and headed home. It was clear that the Chief was not going to read my article right away. Nevertheless, I was ill at ease as to what he would think of it, especially the last line.

XXIII
JACK DAILEY

Snow began to fall quite heavily during the drive home from South Haven. As I walked the path from the barn toward the house, Mom opened the kitchen door and sent Ginger running out to greet me. I roughed her up a bit before she took off looking for something. Born to hunt, she submerged her nose in the snow sniffing for invisible prey or lost toys. When I clapped my hands, she exploded into a full gallop, running circles around the yard and me. I stomped my feet on the back step but before I could open the kitchen door, Ginger was next to me, hind quarters wagging from side to side, ready to escort me into the house.

"Hi Mom. Where's everybody?"

"Josh and Ken are Christmas shopping in Holland and Dad is trimming at Uncle Bill's. What should we have for supper tonight?"

"Oh, didn't I tell you? I've been invited to the Chief's for supper."

"Yes you did, it just slipped my mind. Is Maxine going with you?" Mom asked more in the form of a suggestion than a question.

"No. I asked her but she had a conflict or something. So I asked a girl I met in Benton Harbor, but she also turned me down." There was an involuntary disappointment in my voice as I thought of Penny.

"Really, I thought you and Maxine were sort of going out just with each other? Who is this Benton Harbor girl?" Mom's stoic matter-of-fact questions were a clear indication of her advocacy for Maxine. I could tell she was somewhat surprised that I'd asked someone other than Maxine.

We spent the next hour or so sitting in the kitchen talking. Talking with Mom seemed easy and natural. I could always count on her to be interested, supportive, and typically non-judgmental. Our conversation ranged from Christmas shopping, Josh and Ken, my work and finally to the Uncle Otto episode. Even though Nana was home from the hospital and doing well, Mom still expressed deep concern for her mother's well being.

I was interested in Mom's opinion of Uncle Otto. Showing far less emotion than she had displayed a few days before, she told me that she knew Uncle Otto had an abrasive side to him, but she was totally stunned by what had happened. As a little girl she remembered some very happy times with her Uncle Otto at family picnics. It seemed to her that it had been only the last year or so that she had heard about him having angry outbursts. I reminded Mom of what Kelly had told me and what John Barnes had told Ken. We agreed that a family dynamic existed within the Barnes family that we did not clearly understand and probably never would. We decided to go to Allegan in the morning to finish the Christmas shopping and so I could look up Deputy Jack Dailey. "We'll take the Coupe; I'll drive."

I still had about an hour before heading back to South Haven for dinner, so I told Mom I wanted to drive over to Maxine's to talk to her about tobogganing tomorrow night and try again to get her to go with me tonight. Mom smiled her approval.

About a mile from Maxine's house, I met a car I thought I recognized. Was it the Hero's? As we passed I saw someone seated close to the driver. *Maxine?*

My heart pounded. I felt anger but couldn't clarify exactly why. Maxine and I had been going out regularly for a couple of months, but had not made any commitments to one another; I certainly had not. However, a hot iron of hurt ran through me. *Was she seeing that High School Hero again?*

I drove on for a couple of miles trying to block Maxine out of my mind, and then turned the Coupe for home, never stopping at the Martins. Before I arrived home, I had rationalized that my over sensitive imagination had jumped to conclusions about Maxine and the Hero, what's-his-name. Probably nothing, I wasn't even sure it was the two of them I'd seen. In fact, I wasn't sure that Chuck and Maxine were an item. I never knew what an "item" was anyway.

The Chief lived on North Shore Drive, the north side of South Haven, but not on the lake side of the road. His house was a nice, but inconspicuous, two story bungalow with two second floor dormer windows projecting from a gentle sloping roof. Before I could knock the second time, Mrs. Mendelsohn opened wide the door with an even wider smile. "Come in Chuck, we are so happy you could come." With that she gave me a small hug and told me to make myself to home. "Irving just got home and will be right down. I must check the oven. Be right back. Can I get you something? Please sit, relax. You men work too hard."

The living room was stuffed with neatly framed family photos, special keepsakes and tasteful, but inexpensive, bric-a-brac. The chairs, end tables and couch were old, but in excellent condition and very inviting. They may have been hand-me-downs or family heirlooms. A hard-finished wood floor revealed itself around the edges of an 8' X 10' Oriental rug of dark muted colors and off-white fringe on each end. Mom had instilled in me her interest in such detail and definitely expected a report.

"Good evening C. Drew Scott," the Chief emphasized my literary handle as he ambled into the room. "Rose has been slaving in the kitchen all day. Did you bring a friend?" he asked, looking around toward the kitchen.

"No, she couldn't come because of a previous commitment." I gave Maxine's excuse, but was thinking of Penny. "But I brought the appetite of two." A good feeling waxed through me at how absolutely comfortable I felt being with the Mendelsohns in their home. I was not at all awe struck, nor unimpressed, just comfortable and looking forward to an enjoyable evening with two genuinely good people.

"If you nice gentlemen don't mind, dinner is served in the dining room," Mrs. Mendelsohn announced in a most graceful manner. "Irving, would you mind lighting the candles?"

"What, President Roosevelt's joining us for dinner?" the Chief declared as only he could.

As we moved from the living room to the dining room, the Chief ducked into the kitchen to get some matches. When he returned, he lit three tall white candles proportionately spaced on the dining table. The table was absolutely pleasing to the eye. The intricate white lace linen tablecloth was extraordinary to behold, especially so to a poor farm boy. I was apprehensive as to where and when to be seated, but Mrs. Mendelsohn put me at ease, insisting that I sit on one side and that she and Irving would sit at opposite ends.

"Mrs. Mendelsohn this…"

"Rose," she interrupted. "Please, Chuck, call me Rose. I don't want to be treated stiff and formal."

"Thank you, Rose. But this is a most formal, and indeed, elegant table. And if the meal you've prepared tastes half as good as it smells, I'm in heaven!" I wanted to compliment Rose, but I also wanted her to know that I meant every word. She had gone to a great deal of trouble for a fledgling newspaper boy, and I was most appreciative.

The three of us shared a perfectly glorious evening. First, let me try to describe the meal Rose had prepared. We started with *Challah* bread and *Matzah* Ball Soup. The bread we broke from a sweet, golden braided loaf. Rose informed me that *Challah* was a Sabbath tradition, but that "It's Irving's favorite and tonight is special." The soup I can only describe as a light chicken broth with a dumpling floating in it; both bread and soup were very tasty. For the main course, Rose served us stuffed cabbage and a pot roast that had been marinated with lemon juice, both of which melted in my mouth. One of the side dishes the Chief called *Kugel*. To me *Kugel* was a fruity tasting pudding and it was excellent. For dessert, Rose served French hazelnut coffee with what the Chief said was Rose's signature orange sponge cake with an apricot pineapple sauce; absolutely heart stopping.

The dining experience with the Mendelsohn's ranked as a highlight of my life. Every dish presented a new dining delicacy paired with a narrative of family religious customs and traditions. The Mendelsohn's enthusiasm for sharing their cultural heritage with me was only equaled by their interest in finding out about my family roots and interest. The Chief and Rose were a sharing couple, who made me feel good about myself. It was a treasured lesson.

During supper, our conversation moved from the newspaper business in general, to the Starr trial and other noteworthy events of the day. The breadth of their knowledge on such a wide range of subjects truly amazed me and I was filled with the desire to become a more knowledgeable person in my own right. A vision of me becoming an apprentice at the feet of benevolent world scholars struck my imagination.

As we were enjoying cake and coffee, the Chief mentioned his despair with the Munich Dictate. Unsure of his meaning, using the word "dictate," I apologized for my lack of understanding. He immediately explained the Munich Conference of last September and how Czechoslovakia had been betrayed, especially by France, although critics habitually faulted England and their Prime Minister, Neville Chamberlin.

I told the Chief that I knew that Germany had been given western Czechoslovakia in return for a German promise of no more expansion.

"Bull shit, that Nazi bastard will never stop! And by what right does a country or group of countries have to give away part of yet another country?" The Chief's voice had gotten louder and louder, and it was clear to me that he possessed a profound interest in European affairs.

"Irving, please don't let's get on this subject. You know how it upsets you and we have a guest," Rose said in a pleading, yet calming voice. However, the concern in her eyes troubled me. I really wanted to hear more of what the Chief had to say, but I didn't want to cause Rose any discomfort.

"Mrs. Mendelsohn, Rose, if you wouldn't mind, I'd really like to hear more about this? It sounds to me like you both have more than a passing interest in this topic." Humbly I looked from one to the other.

After pausing a few seconds, Rose answered, "Chuck, this is a very distressing topic for both Irving and me, and I don't want this to spoil our perfectly splendid evening."

My now desperate interest could not be veiled, although I sat without saying a word. Observing me the Chief finally turned to his wife, "Rose, I promise to keep my voice down, but I would like to share with Chuck a little of our perspective on these matters." The Chief was more making a request than a statement.

Rose looked long and searchingly at her husband before turning to me, "Irving served as an Austria-Hungarian war correspondent during the Great War. I grew-up in Prague, but was attending the university in Vienna where we met. Shortly after the Armistice, Irving proposed and we married in Prague where my parents still live. In 1925 we moved to America and eventually ended up here in South Haven."

"That is very nice Rose, but Chuck wants more than our love story, as beautiful as that may be," the Chief said sharing a tender recognition between the two of them. "Chuck, the war was terrible beyond belief, Europe torn to rubble, and the people who survived, they had nothing; starving. A great turmoil followed the war and Rose and I knew that if we wanted a chance in life we had to leave."

"Yes, but things did eventually get better didn't they?" I asked wanting to encourage the Chief to tell me more about their lives. The Chief's face seemed to be at once filled with both pain and determination.

"Things did get better, I don't believe to a pre-war level. We keep up with Rose's family by mail. Although they still live in Prague, it is now in the country of Czechoslovakia; a proud country, ready and willing to stand-up to Nazi aggression."

"That's good, isn't it Chief?"

"Even in the face of this current world wide economic depression, I do believe life was improving for my relatives in Czechoslovakia; at least their letters indicated such." Rose's smooth kind voice infused a mollifying sophistication to the conversation.

The Chief followed, "Getting better is always relative. Relative to starving; okay, getting better. But not for long. The Czechs were ready to defend from German invasion and had a treaty pledging France's support in that event. All betrayed in Munich. The Allies should give away Poland next?"

"Now Irving, you know that is completely conjectural on your part. Hitler has given no indication of that intention. In fact, he pledged just the opposite."

"Rose, if you give a ravenous dog half a bone, trust me, he will be back for the rest. Prague will be part of Germany in less than a year. What's next? You tell me."

"We still have hope, don't we?"

"We have the hope of the German Jews who have been leaving Germany since Hitler came to power. What do their actions tell you? There is no hope for Jews in Germany and tomorrow there will be no hope for the Jews in Prague! We must get your family out, now." The Chief tried to moderate his voice, which only made his desperate message more disturbing to me.

"I agree that anti-Semitism is growing, but I don't know if it's because of Hitler, in spite of Hitler, or just happens to be taking place at the same time. Without question, Jews will not be able to coexist with Hitler's Germany," Rose added but clearly wanted this line of conversation to cease. "Chuck, please have another piece of cake."

"Only if I may have some more of your special sauce topping," I said as I held up my empty dessert plate. "Rose, would you explain for me the meaning of anti-Semitism? I'm not familiar with that term, but I think I understand your meaning."

Rose answered in a most charming manner, pointing out that, "anti-Semitism ranges from barely noticeable discrimination to openly violent hostility towards Jews." She sliced me a second piece of cake and passed the bowl of apricot pineapple sauce to me. The Chief poured himself another cup of coffee. Both asked me questions about farming and I found myself responding in an actively promotional manner, a manner uncharacteristic of me when it came to farming.

As I said my goodbyes to the Mendelsohns, I felt "full to perfection," another of my Nana's pet phrases. But this time I was full of more than just good food, I was full of good thought-provoking company in a satisfying, glowing sort of way.

"I thank you both for a wonderful evening. See you tomorrow, Chief. I'll have the final 'story coming out of Fennville' with me."

"Shalom."

I decided to drive passed Maxine's on my way home. Had I thought more about it I probably wouldn't have because it wasn't on the way and secondly, I wouldn't just drop-in after nine.

Christmas tree lights gleamed through the parlor windows of the Martin house. I seriously reconsidered stopping until I spotted the strange car in the driveway. It was the same one I had seen during the afternoon, positive. The thought that Maxine might be sharing some of her hot chocolate with the Hero bothered me. I went home.

Mom baked cookies while everyone else engaged in Christmas preparation of one sort or another. Dad popped corn and we all sat around the tree as I recounted my dining experience at the Mendelsohns. Mom especially wanted to know what we ate and it pleased her that I had been so observant of the table setting and home furnishings.

"I don't suppose they had any Christmas decorations up?" Mom asked noting that from the sound of their names they were probably Jewish. I confirmed that the Mendelsohns were Jewish and displayed no Christmas decorations, but that I had learned about Chanukah, the Menorah and other Jewish traditions.

"Have any of you come across the term "anti-Semitic?" I asked. Ken told us that his world history teacher had explained it in class when they were studying the Black Death plague of the 14th century. Ken said that in some towns of Europe the plague was blamed on Jews.

"Hostility towards Jews is actively promoted by the Nazi Party and the Mendelsohns fear for the safety of their European relatives. The Chief and his wife emigrated from Austria several years ago. They are both very worried about what is happening in Europe."

"Leave Europe to the Europeans. We have enough problems here to choke a horse," Dad said with his typical finality. Ken pointed out that the world was becoming more interdependent, like it or not. From the tone of the conversation, I could see that the Scott family would revisit this topic. Everyone wanted to know more, including Dad.

Before going to bed, Mom and I agreed that we would go to Allegan right after breakfast. She asked me when I had seen Maxine last. "It seems like a year ago but I know it's not more than four or five days. I'll see her tomorrow. We're going to a toboggan party in the dunes."

The next morning Mom and I arrived in Allegan around ten. A hustle and bustle of last minute shoppers added a festive excitement to the small town all dressed up for the holidays. I dropped Mom in the business center to shop, while I headed for the sheriff's office. To my good fortune, Deputy Jack Dailey had just reported for duty and a plump, gray-headed lady behind a clean office counter introduced us.

Deputy Dailey suggested we get a cup of coffee and use the interrogation room to talk. That sounded good to me and I was particularly pleased that he seemed to want to talk with me too. Dailey appeared to be in his mid-twenties and when he told me that he had graduated from Fennville High School, we had some readymade common ground. My experience had been that common knowledge and acquaintances help to break the ice and establish mutual creditability.

After getting the social niceties out of the way, I went straight to the heart of what I needed to know. "Can you tell me why the Allegan County Sheriff's Department did not intercede in the Barnes family domestic problems before the murder/suicide? It's my understanding that you had received multiple reports and requests for your intervention over the past two years."

"Hold on, Chuck. Your understanding is shot full of holes. First of all, no one ever came to the sheriff's office to file a formal complaint, ever. Secondly, the first I personally heard of any potential problems between Otto and Arlene Barnes came to me from a friend who works in Fennville. He told me that Arlene Barnes had shacked-up with a neighbor of his while Otto Barnes was deer hunting up near Grayling a little more than a year ago. I believe one of your uncles may have been in that hunting party. Anyway, it's none of my business and nothing we would investigate." Dailey reported this to me just like the more senior officers I had talked with in Berrien County, strictly by the book. And I could easily checkout the deer hunting scenario.

"But I have it from a reliable source that Arlene Barnes came into the sheriff's office last spring and reported that Otto had beaten her up and broken her arm. She was told to 'go home and work it out.'" Certain I was on solid ground, I pressured Deputy Dailey to find out exactly what law enforcement did to ameliorate this assault. I had heard the "go home and work it out" advice too many times.

"Stop. Your head has been filled with misinformation. Let me tell you what I know about this case. I happen to be the officer assigned to find out what was going on in the Barnes family." Dailey's mildly defensive factual review of the events that led up to the shooting at the Barnes farm definitely had a convincing ring of authenticity. I occasionally wrote down a note or two, but I knew intuitively that I would remember every word verbatim.

Dailey briefly consulted a manila folder labeled: **BARNES, Otto and Arlene (1938)**. "On March 25th our office received a call from a nurse at the county hospital reporting a suspected assault. I was assigned to go to the hospital and investigate. When I got there, I found Arlene Barnes pretty battered-up with a broken arm in a shoulder sling. Otto Barnes had brought her to the hospital and he was pretty banged-up himself. Both had received facial stitches."

"After receiving a preliminary report from the reporting nurse, I interviewed Otto and Arlene separately. As I started with each one, I told them that if their stories varied, I'd know who was lying. Guess what? Their stories matched almost perfectly. And I believed them."

"Please continue. As I said, I need to know what really happened." Try as I may I couldn't conceal my anxiousness for this account. Why do police officers typically take their time when reporting? Finally Dailey proceeded:

"It seems that on the day in question, Otto Barnes had planned to go to Michigan City to pick up a load of fertilizer. He was to be gone most of the day. However, a few miles south of South Haven he had a flat tire and decided to return home and try again the next day. When he arrived home several hours early, he found another man in the house with Arlene. Neither wanted to tell me exactly how he found them. The two men got into a fight and eventually Mrs. Barnes' guest left.

Then Otto and Arlene got into it. This fight ended when Otto slapped Arlene hard across the face, which severely cut her upper lip. He brought her to the hospital for stitches. Otto tried to steady his wife as they climbed the front steps of the hospital. She didn't want his help and swung at him, losing her balance and falling down the steps. You guessed it—she broke her arm.

Arlene Barnes did not deny she had been having an affair. Although she did not love the other man, neither did she love Otto. She said she felt, 'Between a rock and a hard place. I don't want to break up our family, yet I don't want to live with Otto either.'

Otto Barnes admitted to me that he had exploded into an irrepressible rage when he accidentally discovered his wife with another man. He revealed to me that he had suspected his wife had been cheating on him for several months. However, he had never confronted her with his suspicion, praying it would stop and feeling embarrassed by his personal inadequacies. It seemed to me that the whole situation had depressed him beyond his ability to fully explain.

A more dejected man I have never witnessed. He cried uncontrollably in front of me for several minutes. When he began talking again, he told me that he suffered from diabetes. For almost two years he had been unable to have sexual relations with his wife. For the past year he felt certain that his wife had no interest in him whatsoever. Further, he told me that his relationship with their children had deteriorated to such a degree that he was certain they no longer held any respect or love for him.

Before I let them go, I had a long talk with Otto and Arlene together. I didn't really know what to say to them, but I didn't want them leaving the hospital wanting to kill each other. The longer they talked, the more they convinced me, and I believed them, that they wanted to work through this for their children's sake. As we left the hospital, I reminded them that I would be stopping at their farm to check on their progress every once in awhile."

"And did you do that? And what about their children making reports of abuse at school?" What right I had to interrogate this officer, I wasn't sure, but believed it needed to be done. I didn't want to offend Deputy Dailey, but the tenor of my voice could have easily resulted in that. Fortunately, he started again as if unaffected.

"I added visits to the Barnes farm on my calendar. Every other week I would make a stop at their place on my way to work. I made it a point to talk face to face with at least one of them, but frequently both were present. In my opinion, they were making progress. All outward signs indicated so. Less than a week before the shooting, I stopped to see them. Arlene wasn't home. Otto said that Arlene and their daughter Kelly had been working together at the canning plant in Fennville during the fall and were just finishing up that morning. He told me about their oldest son having a part in the school play and that he looked forward to seeing it. He even invited me. I think it was going to be on the coming Friday night, the day of the shooting."

"Then why did he go crazy? He killed Aunt Arlene and apparently tried to shoot Kelly before he killed himself. That's what I want to know. Can you tell me why?"

"Chuck, I don't know if it's possible to know the answers to your questions. I want to know these answers too, it's my job. I will tell you this, and no more. What little more I know would not be helpful to you."

He collected his thoughts for a long moment and then continued:

"Immediately following the shooting we were called to the Barnes place. The actual shooting took place just about the way newspapers reported it: Otto and Arlene argued, Otto got his shot gun and shot and killed Arlene as she sat at the kitchen table, Kelly ran for the neighbors, Otto went outside and shot at and wounded Kelly, Otto went back into the kitchen, reloaded, stuck the muzzle in his chest and pushed the trigger.

After doing everything we could at the farm, I decided to pay a visit to the man Otto had caught his wife with last March. When I found him, he acted suspicious. I'll admit to you now, but never again, I scared the living shit out of that asshole. Finally, he admitted to me that he and Arlene had rekindled their affair. He did not think that Otto knew that he and Arlene had been sneaking around. I checked up on his alibi for the day of the shooting and am satisfied he never went to the Barnes' place. That's all, Chuck."

"Thank you, Deputy Dailey. But, please can you answer one more question? No one has ever mentioned what happened to the Barnes' livestock."

Dailey sat silently for what seemed an eternity; then he grudging mumbled, "He slaughtered everything on the place before turning his gun on his wife. The children that were still at school were fortunate." Even though this was a shocking revelation, it was not unexpected. Common sense told me something must have happened to the cows and team of horses. I acknowledged my appreciation with a somber nod.

"I have to write a story for the paper about this shooting. If you would like to read it before I turn it in, I'd be happy to bring it by."

"I don't think that will be necessary. For my two cents, I don't think it would help anyone to speculate about Arlene Barnes' affair or the bloody details of the shooting in the paper or anywhere else."

Considering Dailey's parting words, I realized that he was at least partly right. However, these problems will not go away because we choose not to talk, write or read about them. I knew that writing this story would represent a major obstacle for me.

From the sheriff's office, I walked without a specific destination into the hectic business district. What Deputy Dailey had shared with me about Uncle Otto and Aunt Arlene seemed reasonable considering what I already knew about their situation. Dailey had no reason to mislead or exaggerate, and it gratified me to know he'd been monitoring the case for several months prior to the shooting. Contrary to my earlier judgment, the sheriff's department had not ignored my aunt and uncle's volatile state of affairs. Who was Aunt Arlene's romantic consort? Dad would say, "Let bygones be bygones." Still I wondered.

"Hey Chuck, can you help me with these packages?" Mom hollered from across Main Street. She had her arms full of what I believed to be presents. I helped her carry them to the car. "Where have you been? I would like your advice in picking out shirts for Josh and Ken."

I explained that I had been talking with Jack Dailey at the sheriff's office and that I felt better about the whole Barnes thing, "Just one of those tragedies that we may never fully understand." I chose not to tell Mom about Aunt Arlene's love tryst, at least not at that time. "What did you buy for me?"

"You'll have to wait for Santa Claus," she laughed. "It's almost one. Let's get something at the Soda Shop before we head home?" Mom asked in such a way as to indicate that we would be doing something really special.

"Sounds great to me, but I have a little shopping I need to do before we go home. Where's the best place to buy a radio?"

Mom and I had a nice time together in Allegan. When we returned home, she rushed around wrapping presents and getting supper. She wanted to eat early so that I could eat and not be late picking Maxine up for tobogganing.

"The story coming out of Fennville" was not going to be completed as I had promised the Chief. I felt forced to call, apologize and ask for more time. The Chief had other things on his mind and told me that Monday would be soon enough. He wished me a Merry Christmas and hung up. The abrupt end to my phone call left me confused, but it wasn't nearly as confounding as deciding what to write about Otto Barnes. Oh well, I had Maxine to look forward to.

Like a picture from *Look* magazine, Maxine wore just the right coat with matching gloves, snow pants, boots, scarf, and hat. A stylishly stuffed sweater remained to be seen. Even though there was no evidence of the gorgeous feminine body hidden beneath all these winter clothes, I knew it existed alive and well. We tied the Martin's toboggan to the Coupe's rumple seat and were off to the Saugatuck sand dunes.

Upon exiting the Martin's driveway I asked, "Maxine, do you remember the night we first went to a movie in South Haven? I've been thinking about it because we may have seen the defendant in the trial I just covered for the paper. I think I asked you about this once before. Have you thought about it?"

"I remember your blue mouth and spinning on those little bar stools!" she giggled.

"No Maxine, I'm serious. Didn't you see someone in that restaurant that looked like the actress from the movie?" I cajoled Maxine to try to get her to concentrate.

"I recall a woman seated near the window that had hair like the actress in the movie. Don't you remember her?" Maxine asked as if everyone would remember.

"No, I don't think I ever looked at the other people who were there." I absolutely did remember what was on my mind the night of the movie and it had nothing to do with Mary Anne Starr who was now sitting alone in her cell at the Berrien County jail.

"It was a long time ago, but I do remember her. It seems to me that she was talking to someone. I can't be for sure." Maxine's voice faded, indicating no real interest in the subject.

The quaint, tiny village of Saugatuck was all decked out for Christmas. Christmas trees trimmed with multicolored lights could be seen through the frosted windows of family homes. Streetlights and telephone poles were laced with evergreens and red and white ribbons, garlands hung along rooflines and wreaths made of grapevines and evergreen boughs adorned front doors.

At the foot of the designated sledding dune north of town we rendezvoused with 12 to 15 other winter recreation enthusiasts. Climbing the dunes was never easy, but pulling a toboggan up steep snow covered inclines was almost impossible. Of course no real man would balk or fail to meet the challenge. Laughing, joking, stumbling and sliding backwards, all added to the fun of this winter wonderland.

By the time we approached the top, I could feel damp warmth on my skin beneath the heavy coat. This sensation always bothered me because I knew how quickly it could turn to an uncomfortable cold.

At the summit of the dune we were sheltered on three sides by large pine trees. The open side, the result of wind and shifting sand, faced Lake Michigan. Our party gathered at the apex of a large triangle whose base, several hundred feet below, could only faintly be made out in spite of the bright moonlit night.

The slide to the bottom was fast, breathtakingly fast. The snow covering the sand was thin and lightly crusted. Nervous chatter served to further excite tentative sliders. Three, four, or five persons piled on each toboggan. Finally, one hardy, or foolhardy, crew set sail. Amidst shouts, screams and cries for help, they disappeared into the dark below. In a matter of a few short seconds, we could hear their distant voices shouting from the bottom, encouraging the rest of us to join them. We did.

Maxine sat in front with me behind. My feet were securely placed beneath her bent legs. Maxine held on to my legs and I held on to Maxine. A second couple did the same seated behind us. With the four of us ready and clinging desperately to each other, somebody helped push us off. The last words I heard from Maxine were, "Oooh Nooo!" I'm not sure of my last words, but they may have been, "Our Father..."

Suddenly we were at the bottom, all screaming with delight, "Let's go again!" And up the dune we headed, stumbling, laughing, pulling, pushing.

In addition to a white crescent moon, millions of stars displayed their tiny lights across the sky. The top of the dune felt like the top of the world and the dark skyline seemed to disappear into the earth's curvature. One of the girls claimed she could see the northern lights. I didn't and I didn't think she did either.

A couple of the guys had flasks of whiskey. We men all took a jolt. Not all of the girls did. Someone said it tasted like anti-freeze. Others agreed. I had never tasted anti-freeze, but believed my chances of seeing the northern lights had improved.

After the third run, most had had enough, others were simply too exhausted. A few hardy souls went back for one last run.

We were all invited to the home of a fellow tobogganer for hot chocolate. "I hope it's as good as yours," I whispered in Maxine ear.

With a knowing grin she mischievously whispered back, "Have you been a good little boy?" Maxine was sexier than my imagination, which could be quite erotic. I began to understand that if I gave Maxine an opportunity, she would counter with a pleasant surprise.

It turned into an exciting social gathering. One of the couples had mixed two large bowls of holiday punch, one red, and one green. The red punch packed more punch. Another reveler mixed up eggnog. You could have yours with or without extra nog. Add a little jazz from a Victrola and lots of cigarette smoke, and a good party became a real bash. At times you could not hear the person standing next to you. There were definitely more people at the house party than tobogganed down the sand dune.

When Maxine and I left around midnight, we were both feeling the "extra punch" and welcomed the clean cold air. As we walked to the Coupe, we could clearly hear the happy voices and loud music coming from the house. Tranquil, the outdoors was quiet and fresh. Stillness cloaked the rural landscape, while moon light cast a pristine glow on the crest of snow covered fields.

Starting the Coupe shattered the serene environment, but it had to be done. Maxine snuggled close to me as we made our way home. We talked some, but in the main quietly basked in the evening's afterglow.

Parking the Coupe in front of the Martin's front door I observed no lights except the front porch light. I put my arms around Maxine and pulled her towards me anticipating a romantic embrace. She did not disappoint me, meeting my advance with warm, eager lips. Heavy coats and gloves did suppress an element of sensual pleasure, but they served to heighten optimistic visions of things to come.

Maxine drew back and asked me if I would come over tomorrow. "Of course. Name the time." Then I remembered Penny. "Oh, I'm sorry. I have to go to Benton Harbor during the day and we usually get together with the Scott family on Christmas Eve."

"The trial is over isn't it? You work all the time Chuck and tomorrow is Saturday, Christmas Eve. I want to see you; please?" she pouted. "Maybe in the afternoon?" Maxine requested in a playfully begging tone of voice.

"I really can't. I promised someone I'd go to a function in Benton Harbor." My mind raced as I looked for a graceful conclusion to our conversation.

"Chuck, are you seeing someone in Benton Harbor. Are you going out with someone else?" Maxine's voice took a more serious tone as a questioning frown covered her face. Her question took me completely by surprise. I felt befuddled as I searched for an unoffending answer.

"Well, it's not like that. I promised these two girls I'd go with them to a community party and I can't very well back out now."

"Why not? It was you that said we were an item and I believed you!"

Why had I written that on the note? "Maxine, it's not like that. It's not a date. Besides, didn't I see you out with an old boyfriend?" As soon as I said that, I wanted to take it back. Too late.

"What are you talking about?" Maxine scolded. "Oh, you just go to your party with your girl friends." Maxine started crying. "I guess I had the wrong understanding. You need not walk me to the door, I can find my way." With that Maxine jumped out of the Coupe, walked stiffly to the house, up the three steps, across the porch and through the front door, never looking back. I waited for a light to go on inside but none did, and then the porch light went out.

I sat in the dark trying to make sense of what just happened and mulling over possible options available to me. Dad says that, "failing to plan is planning to fail." But I liked surprises; at least I used to. When I began to get cold, I started the Coupe and headed home, unsure of how I wanted our misunderstanding resolved.

XXIV
GREEK MAIDENS

The drive from home to the newspaper office had never taken more than half an hour. My little Coupe cut through snow better than any car on the road. It never failed to start on cold mornings, had a great heater and everybody wanted to ride with me. We were a team.

This particular morning afforded little time to reflect on my good fortune. Once again, Josh had saved the day by coming up with two new story ideas for me to edit and elaborate on for the paper. In the final analysis, Josh was the true journalist in the family; he had a knack for writing short stories. But, what I needed was someone to help me write the "Story out of Fennville," or at least give me a suggestion as to an appropriate theme. The few ideas that had so far come to mind were instantly squelched by multiple personal objections.

As I parked in front of the *Tribune* office, I saw the movie theater marquee down the street. Maxine came to mind. Oh well, at least she wasn't dominating my thoughts. My distress at our parting seemed to have quickly dissipated and, quite selflessly, I hoped it had for her as well.

When I pulled the chair from under my desk, I found a gift wrapped packaged with my name on it: **For C. Drew Scott—to be opened immediately!** I was skeptical but quickly obliged. To my surprise, I found an Argus Camera model C2. Two of the reporters that I had met in St. Joseph had cameras just like it. It was brand new, the latest edition, and everyone wanted one. They called it "The Brick" because of its shape. Wow, how I could use this camera, I thought.

Underneath the camera I found a little white envelope containing a card made out to me, **C. Drew Scott**. The message: **Your first Chanukah present. We hope it brings you lots of joy and happiness. Shalom, Irving and Rose.** I was filled with a feeling of overwhelming gratitude and wondered how to thank them. The Chief came storming in from the printing room at that very instant.

"Vhat do I do? That damn press has broken down again! Vhere's my phone?" the Chief demanded as if someone had hidden the phone that sat prominently amongst his desk debris. He had a habit of substituting 'Vs' for 'Ws' when he was upset.

"Chief, what have you and Mrs. Mendelsohn done?" I said holding up the camera. "You have given me such a wonderful gift. I want to thank…" The Chief cut me off.

"You should bother me now?" the Chief barked holding the receiver to his ear. "Oh, that's for you," he said as if clarifying my understanding of some esoteric issue. "If you should use it in your employment, that's up to you. Rose wanted you should have it." Pulling the receiver from his ear and looking at it he shouted, "Vhy is there no...who is this?" and the Chief motioned for me to leave his office, not letting me say more.

How lucky could I be? If I should view the gift as something really nice, then he wanted me to credit his wife as the thoughtfully generous member of their family and credit him as just a humble unconcerned bystander. However, he wanted me to understand that the camera could, or should, be considered a professional investment. *What a guy, the Chief.*

I touched up the articles Josh had written and turned them in—a snow sculpture contest in the village of Bangor and a winter carnival in Holland. Then I headed for Benton Harbor by way of South Haven's North Shore Drive. I wanted to stop by and thank Mrs. Mendelsoln personally, although I knew the Chief was as much, if not more, responsible for my gift.

Rose was as pretty and vivacious as ever. I insisted that she be the subject of my inaugural photo and she playfully consented, but only if I'd take a loaf of freshly baked rye bread to my parents. I agreed.

Driving on, I could hardly wait to have Rose's picture developed. The bread's succulent aroma permeated the Coupe. I doubted I would wait long enough to share it with Mom and Dad.

My heart began to race as I entered Benton Harbor. Could going to a Greek holiday party be that stimulating? I wondered if I was dressed properly and if English would be spoken. It's not that I was scared, just a little apprehensive. I did look forward to seeing Penny.

Benton Harbor was busy with what I suspected were more Christmas shoppers. A slightly askew **CLOSED** sign hung in the Pegasus window. Parking near the warehouse, I decided to leave the present I'd brought tucked safely inside the closed rumble seat. That may have lessened a potential awkward situation, plus then I'd have a chance to find a more appropriate time to present the gift. Climbing the exterior metal staircase to Penny's apartment, I remember asking myself if I'd be invited in and if so, what would I find?

On the first knock I heard a squeal and scurrying within the apartment. On the second knock Hebe unlocked and opened the door. "Come in, Chuck, we're just a minute ready. Are you little early?" Hebe asked with a particularly delightful style.

Stomping some snow off my shoes on the landing, I stepped in, "Honestly I haven't paid any attention to the time. I can come back in a little while if you'd like?"

Hebe insisted that I come in and have a seat; they would be ready in just a few minutes. Not knowing exactly what was expected, I took off my shoes and left them on the doormat. Hebe pointed for me to sit in the room's only easy chair before she walked hurriedly into a bedroom, although she personally appeared to be ready.

The sisters' squeaky-clean apartment held two bedrooms and a main room that served as both living room and kitchen. At one end were a small sink, cook stove and icebox. The outer wall contained the main room's only window around which were hung floor length shear white linen curtains. A small square table containing a framed wedding picture stood in front of the window. It was set for two, but had three chairs. The fourth chair stood at the far end of the room next to a steam heat register. On the inter wall were three Greek Orthodox religious icons, the middle of which was a two foot tall wooden crucifix. From what little I knew and what I was learning, I considered the apartment to be simply decorated, but with a touch of good taste. Listening to the two young women dressing in the adjoining room held more of my attention than did the furnishings of their humble warehouse apartment.

When they emerged from what I surmised to be Penny's room, I found myself dumbstruck. These two strikingly pretty young women were dressed in what I would describe as ornate, artfully colorful, traditional Greek party dresses. They were not twins, but they were sisters, unmistakably.

"You ladies are beautiful! Are you sure you want to be seen with me, and for that matter, am I dressed appropriately to go to a party with the two of you?" They both giggled and Penny assured me that I was dressed just about the way all of the other men would be dressed.

"We go. Don't want be late," Hebe said, sort of confusing me since she had just a few minutes before implied that I had arrived early. More than likely she had simply searched for something appropriate and polite to say, not intending anything judgmental.

"Let's go," I said and bumped Penny on the arm. "Oh no! Wait right here. I want to show you something." With that I slipped my shoes on and ran down to the Coupe to retrieve my new camera.

Returning I proudly displayed the camera that the Mendelsohns had given me as a Chanukah present. I explained Chanukah as best I could. "It would be an honor to take a picture of the two of you as my very second subjects; Mrs. Mendelsohn, my boss' wife, being the first."

Hebe and Penny cheerfully agreed. I took two pictures of them inside the apartment and one on the landing outside their apartment door. I didn't know much about proper lighting and wanted to make sure I got a good picture of these Greek maidens in their beautiful dresses. Penny made me promise to show them the pictures as soon as they were developed—my original intention, of course.

The three of us had fun driving to the party. We were packed in the front of the Coupe with Penny squeezed in between Hebe and me. I wished I could have taken a picture of that. Although Penny kept her legs well out of the way of the shift rod, the thought of her legs did tantalize me. Also, it pleased me to notice how comfortably Hebe joined in our friendly back and forth chatter. She really was charming. How had she stayed single for so long?

The party was held in the basement of a Methodist church on the southeast side of town. Approximately 80 people attended, mostly small families with men and women of all ages. Women, dressed in traditional Greek party dresses, provided their favorite dishes. Hebe had prepared a large basket of *baklava* for which I had unsuccessfully begged for an advance sample. Older women busied themselves setting the tables and arranging the food. Older men, more conservatively attired, talked and joked in small groups; most men smoked cigarettes or pipes. Young children noisily chased one another back and forth for no apparent reason. Young teenagers segregated themselves by sex while older teens and young adults exhibited a welcome tolerance for members of the opposite sex. Penny and Hebe alternately served as my escort, but chiefly Penny, who told me that all Benton Harbor Greeks attended.

Immediately upon our arrival *Yia Yia* came over to welcome us, especially me. Uncle K hailed me from across the room and came quickly to shake my hand. Penny reminded me to address them as *Yia Yia* and Uncle K, which was good because I had forgotten their last name was Kambelos. Uncle K asked for my help in carrying another table down from upstairs. Once Penny translated for me what he was trying to say, I gladly assisted him. Both *Yia Yia* and Uncle K introduced friends, some who did not speak a word of English, but all went out of their way to make me feel welcome.

We were soon asked to be seated. I ended up sitting across from Penny and in between *Yia Yia* and Hebe. A perfect location, for I had women on each side of me making sure I had enough to eat, and Penny directly across, who was very easy to talk to and admire. Three or four older women waited on the tables, although not assigned or required, to make sure the food circulated to everyone. The din of jovial fellowship perfectly accompanied the mountain of good food.

This party marked my second ethnic style meal in just three days, and the second in my entire life. *Did this make me a Renaissance man?*

Following the meal, the women cleared the dishes and the men broke down the tables and pushed back the chairs. A woman sang what I understood to be a favorite Greek love song. A man gave an exhibition of an ancient Greek dance with intricate footwork. We all clapped rhythmically, while a few chanted. It had obviously taken him a good deal of practice to prefect the dance's complicated steps.

Two men brought out a violin and a lute and were promptly accompanied by a woman with a *Bouzouki* and a tambourine. The *Bouzouki* looked like a pear-shaped guitar. We were all instructed to arrange ourselves in a large circle holding hands. As the music started playing, people began singing and dancing in a counter clockwise direction. The Greek lyrics left me smiling, but with my mouth shut, not wanting to compound my ignorance. With Penny's help, I quickly caught on to the dance steps. All were drawn in, from the very young to the elderly, and all had an uproarious good time. Some may have found me amusing, but if that was my contribution, I wasn't the least bit embarrassed.

Although I didn't want to leave, by mid-afternoon I told Penny that I'd have to go because the Scott family traditionally had a gathering on Christmas Eve. "I could drop you and Hebe off at your apartment or if you would like to stay longer, do you think you could find another ride home?"

Penny briskly reacted, "Wait here," and she hurried off to talk with Hebe. They spoke earnestly for a short time and I could feel an uneasiness grow within me. However, when both came toward me smiling, I felt things had worked out well.

"Chuck, we are happy you could join for party," Hebe said as she patted me on the arm. "If you drop Penny at home, I ride home *Yia Yia* and Uncle K. We have meeting to build church and we want attend."

"Hebe, I had a great time and thank you for including me. I'll take Penny straight home," I assured her as if talking to a concerned parent.

As I drove Penny back into town, I couldn't help thinking about Hebe and Penny's interesting behavior towards one another concerning my car and me. Maybe it was because of the fact that I was definitely not Greek, had no sisters, and felt that I sometimes stuck out like a sore thumb—another of Nana's pet expressions. My curiosity artlessly surfaced when I asked Penny pointblank why her sister was so reluctant to let her ride in the car with me. Since I was probing anyway, I decided to continue and asked why Penny paid so much deference to her sister. "Penny, you're 19 years old. Your sister is not that much older than you. Please don't think me judgmental, and please don't think me offensive, but I believe you are old enough to be deciding things for yourself."

Penny grimaced at me. Thinking I had over-stepped my bounds, I quickly offered, "I'm sorry Penny. I don't have any right to pry into your private life or offer any of my personal advice."

Thoughtfully hesitating, Penny eventually replied, "No, it not that Chuck. You did not do something wrong."

"What is it?" I said in as soft and compassionate a manner as I could muster. Penny was very much an adult; I knew that. Yet she was not at liberty to be carefree. Losing her parents at an early age probably had affected her in some way. Whatever she held inside, it appeared to inhibit her, make her guarded.

"Chuck, I know I not have tell you, but I want." After a long, pondering silence during which I simply sat quietly, Penny unfolded a dark memory she and Hebe shared of a horrifying event. She spoke deliberately:

"I did not tell you whole story about when Hebe and I come to America. Do you remember that we rode with load of bootleg liquored from Chicago to Benton Harbor? After unloading at speakeasy, they wanted Hebe become cocktail waitress, but she refuse. The driver was to take us to Kambelos family—we had never met. Hebe and I not know where live *Yia Yia* and Uncle K, and when driver turn off road and follow farm lane, Hebe worry. Driver say we not pay him for ride to Benton Harbor. In best English Hebe try explain cousins take care of money, we have no money. The man no care; no want money. He say I go first and drag screaming from truck. Hebe jump on back hitting and scratching, try make him let me go. Big sweaty man laugh. He release me, grab Hebe by her hair and hit many times. 'You go first!' She scream for me run for help. I saw man throw her in back of truck. He hitting her and I could hear screaming and pleading. He on top of her, pin her arms over head. I helpless, terrified. I hide behind big tree not far from lane. I try think what do.

When he done with Hebe, he got off her and push her off truck. Throw our clothes case on ground. Man look around. He call me. I not move. Hebe moan in pain and man call me come help sister. I not move. Finally, he turned truck around and drive away, nearly run over Hebe."

"Wouldn't you think the trucker would have worried that you'd bring help and he'd be arrested?" I feared that I sounded cold or uncaring.

"He not know Hebe send me for help. She yell in Greek. I not know which way to go. I lost, in strange place and I want stay near Hebe.

After man go, I come from behind tree and try help Hebe. Her eyes swollen, cuts and marks on face. Blood in hair. I help her stand. Blood on her torn dress. She seventeen. We decide follow truck and try walk back to road. I help Hebe and carry clothes case.

It long time but we find road. We saw motorcycle coming. We both scared and crying. Hebe hold me tight against her although she could no stand by self. We both crying and shaking. Uniformed man on loud motorcycle stop next to us. We both stiff in fear, afraid look at him. That is when we meet angel."

"You met an angel?"

"Yes, Deputy Aaron Barth. He switch motorcycle off and try comfort us. Then he ride get help. He come back with car and drive us *Yia Yia* and Uncle K. We not know them, but Deputy Barth know. They good to us, especially me *Yia Yia*. Deputy Barth stay with us for long time after we cleaned-up and Hebe bandaged. Deputy Barth did much. He know how dress Hebe's wounds.

Hebe was afraid what will happen to us. She said we not talk to police. She certain we deported or worse. When Deputy Barth ask questions, we tell him Hebe fall by accident off farm truck but not hurt bad. We thank him for help."

"Did Deputy Barth believe you?"

"No, sure he did not, but he new at police and believe there nothing he could do. We so scared, but now, I still no believe Deputy Barth could do something unless he see man beating Hebe. If that happen, I think Deputy Barth do justice there. Now, it long time passed. I try forget, and I certain Hebe have bad memories. She always insist we stay close each other. Hebe take Mother's place; I wanted and needed. She worry for me and I honor her, for all life.

This help you understand Hebe's worry for me riding with you in car and why I will try follow her wish? From time parents die, Hebe watch close for me and most time I need and welcome her. It is sure I never dishonor Hebe."

Penny's heartfelt story helped me to understand things I had only superficially observed. And more than that, I gained awareness, empathy for society's vulnerable, especially concerning the plight of young women.

How long had we been sitting in front of the warehouse Penny called home? Penny's story hadn't been particularly long, but it seemed a year since we left the party to go straight home.

"Can you come up for minute?" Penny asked, which helped relieve us both from her unnerving account of her sister's savage rape.

"Okay, but just for a minute." Regaining my composure I said, "I think Santa Claus left something in the rumble seat for the Greek girls." I opened the rumble seat and took out the present I had originally wrapped for Hebe.

"What Santa Claus? What this Chuck? You should not bring presents."

"Well, it's not presents. It's a present, only one. And, if I shouldn't have, then I didn't. It's from Santa, and he has the right to give presents to good little girls and boys." I knew that I had simply signed the present **Merry Christmas, from Santa** because I didn't know Hebe's last name and was embarrassed by my ignorance. Now, I could turn that ignorance into a gift for both Hebe and Penny, and no one would know the difference; quite clever I thought.

Penny unlocked the door to the apartment. We both took our shoes off and Penny hung her coat on a hook near the door. She offered to take mine, but I declined, saying I really couldn't stay. I felt the need to be gone before Hebe arrived.

I placed the gift in the middle of their table and enjoyed giving Penny a few instructions. "When Hebe comes home, tell her the present was already here, but that you waited so that you could open it together. From then on you may tell Hebe whatever you please. As you know, I received a surprise gift today that made me very happy. I want you both to feel that same happiness when you open this gift."

"We will, I promise." The excitement in Penny's eyes made my heart throb. She literally squealed with delight.

"Penny, may I ask you a question?" I asked meekly while in my mind I thought to myself, better now than later.

"Sure."

"What is your last name?"

Penny laughed, "Why Chuck, you mean you not know my name?"

I just stood there smiling at her, waiting. What could I say?

"My name is *Penelope Melaina*. Now, may I ask you question?"

"Sure, Miss *Melaina*."

Penny stood quite close with her hand on my chest and dark smiling eyes looking into mine. "When will you show me pictures of Hebe and me? I would like to see you and pictures, soon," she whispered.

XXV
TRADITIONS

The drive home from Benton Harbor passed quickly. Hebe's savage rape and imagining how it must have compounded the heartbreak and desolation that had already befallen the two young immigrant women, weighed heavily on me. Trying to extend my sympathies seemed hollow in light of the horrific attack Hebe and Penny had survived so long ago. My concern for their wellbeing was not expected by them and clearly not required. But I couldn't shake a desire to be viewed as somehow more essential in the *Malainas'* lives.

Penny had told me that Hebe would like to marry someday, but would only consider marrying a fellow Greek. Hebe had always thought her marriage would be traditionally arranged—*proximinio* Penny called it. I understood how that might be easier for Hebe, being more steeped in Greek mores than Penny. However, there were not many marriage-eligible Greek men living in Benton Harbor. Both *Malainas* looked forward to becoming naturalized United States citizens.

In contrast to Hebe, Penny possessed a strong desire to return to Greece and the island of *Skopelos*, the place she was born and where her parents had lived and died. She made a strong effort to keep those early formative years vivid in her mind; green mountains that were greener and the blue waters that were bluer than anywhere else in the world. Her descriptions of the quaint coastal village of her childhood home were idyllic and alluring—enough so that I was interested in visiting there, someday.

It had turned dark by the time I reached home. Every light in the house was on and there were several cars in the driveway. I knew that a full house of Dad's side of the family awaited me. Mom and her sister-in-laws were having fun getting in one another's way preparing a family feast. The dining room table was set for twelve. That meant that three to five Scotts would have to eat in the kitchen. I was pretty sure that I qualified to sit with the adults in the dining room.

Ginger had snuck into the living room where the men congregated. They didn't seem to mind having her around. When she saw me, she came to me head down, wagging, as if she knew she was getting away with something. Mom had tied a large green bow around Ginger's neck. The bow against her shaggy deep red coat provided an interesting novelty to our holiday spirit. I patted her shoulders and whispered that she had better not let Mom catch her. Ginger wagged her tail slowly as if she understood. She drilled her muzzle under my hand, wanting more attention.

I took roll mentally determining that we had ten adults, three tweeners, and five children with ages ranging from four to nine—no absentees. Mom would have to use all her diplomatic skills to seat everyone without hurting anyone's feelings. She excelled at this art form.

After Mom had everyone in a suitable dining location, impeded by the fact that the four year old had to be extracted from an upstairs closet he had taken refuge in during an impromptu game of hide and seek, she called on Dad to offer a blessing. For as many years as I can remember, her request totally surprised Dad. His pretentious demonstration of perseverance amused most. By the look on Ken's face, he had tired of this annual charade. Considering my recent experiences with holiday meals, the preservation of traditions pleased and intrigued me.

The Christmas ham dinner with all the fixin's, all the Scotts, and accented with great merriment was an eternal family tradition. The meal's finale featured a choice of fresh baked apple, cherry or pumpkin pie, with or without homemade ice cream. When I requested a piece of cherry pie, Mom proudly announced to everyone, "That comes as no surprise. Miss Maxine dropped by this afternoon to deliver us a Christmas cherry pie, but I think it was really a present for Chuck." Everyone laughed knowingly as they looked at me. I smiled appropriately, but internally I felt mixed emotions. For some inexplicable reason, I resented Maxine for doing this and wondered if her motive surpassed simply spreading Christmas cheer. Also, Mom could be irritating at times and her interest in Maxine had reached that point.

Following the meal we exchanged gifts, the result of having drawn names at Thanksgiving; another tradition. Uncle Bill brought in his famous popcorn balls and Grandma Scott contributed her special homemade Christmas candy. Before the evening ended, Grandma suggested that she would play the piano if we would all join her in singing Christmas carols. Following the carols, Grandma recited "Twas The Night Before Christmas" for all those who believed in Santa Claus. Everyone listened with rapt attention.

Long before midnight the last Scott had gone home and the last "Happy Christmas to all and to all a good-night" echoed with laughter throughout the house. Mom's satisfaction showed all over her and everyone pitched in to help clean up. As we did we shared observations and interesting news we had learned about the Scott family and its individual members. Ken pointed out that no one had said anything about Uncle Otto, which resulted in no response. He had obviously gotten our attention, judging by the uniform silent look of reflection.

Finally turning out my light and getting into bed, I lamented that Christmases were not as thrilling as they once had been. Maybe getting older or the annual routine had dampened my spirit. I did look forward to going to Grandpa and Nana Hunter's in the morning, but even that had lost its usual fervent anticipation. My busy mind mulled over the plight of Mary Anne Starr and her children Mickey and Ruthie. Before I fell asleep I dreamed of how good it felt sitting beside Miss *Penelope Melaina* on the diner floor.

By mid-morning Christmas Day, all of my family; Dad, Mom, Ken, Josh, me and Ginger; were at Nana's house on Upper Scott Lake a mile east of Pullman. I looked forward to seeing everyone on the Hunter side of the family, even though I knew it would be pretty much a duplicate of what it had been in years gone by. I had not calculated how I would excuse myself so I could travel to St. Joe to visit Mrs. Starr, but had driven the Coupe to Nana's so that at the earliest opportunity I could leave discretely.

To my astonishment, Kelly Barnes and her youngest brother James were there. Of course Nana had thoughtfully invited them, they being her niece and nephew, and I was happy to get the chance to see Kelly. Nevertheless, I was concerned that something may be indelicately said that would upset one or both of them. Kelly walked with a pronounced limp, undoubtedly the result of the shooting. After thinking about their situation briefly, I reconsidered. Life goes on with or without us, so we may as well meet it head on, and what better place for Kelly and James Barnes to get on with their lives than around Nana's table at Christmas.

Being second cousins of about the same age, it didn't take Kelly and me long to find a chance to talk semi-privately. She said she was doing well. She had been offered and accepted a fulltime job at the cannery and hoped that by next summer she could be living completely on her own. Possibly by the start of the next school year she could afford to have James come live with her. That was her goal and I admired her for it.

Kelly had received a letter from her brother John who was living on a ranch near Madera, California. He was hoping he would be hired on there as one of the regular hands. Kelly felt that John was okay, but wanted him to come home to complete his senior year. She did not think that he would because he felt responsible for what had happened and embarrassed to be seen by old friends. "I tried to reason with him, but he has made up his mind. He is very hard headed, just like Dad."

When Kelly said that, I could tell that she wished she could take it back. I quickly changed the subject. "I've been working for the South Haven newspaper and recently I've been reporting on a courtroom trial. It's interesting work but I don't think I want to make a career out of it."

Kelly was fascinated by the Starr trial and asked me lots of questions. She fixated on the similarities between what her mother had suffered and Starr's experiences. As she quizzed me, our conversation began to make me feel uncomfortable. I found myself thinking about, but avoiding the term, "justifiable homicide." Explaining that term would prolong our increasingly painful conversation, although, in the case of Mary Anne Starr, that was exactly what I was thinking.

We were fortunately interrupted by Nana, who wanted everyone to open the present that she and Grandpa had placed on or under the tree for each of us. They were small inexpensive gifts, but Nana had taken great care in selecting or making each one. Each of us received a present, but Nana never allowed anyone else to give gifts in her home. No one really knows why she insisted on observing Christmas in that manner, but that was her way. It was tradition. Nana gave me an old weathered duck decoy that her father had played with as a little boy and later used hunting ducks on Scott Lake. "Thank you Nana. I'll keep it forever and ever."

The Hunter family Christmas Day gathering was a little smaller than the Scott's Christmas Eve celebration and all of us were able to squeeze around Nana's dining table to enjoy the annual roasted goose dinner. Grandpa Hunter provided the Christmas goose. Nana's signature dishes included a moist goose dressing with rich dark gravy, and her much loved scalloped potatoes loaded with cheese. No one ever left Nana's table hungry, but my appetite had disappeared as had my attention to the carefree dinner conversations. I remember thinking that my allegiance to family traditions just wasn't what it had been in the past. I wondered if the time was coming for me to start building some traditions of my own.

Voices seemed to rise and fall as if I was falling asleep. I found myself increasingly preoccupied. Never before had I wanted to avoid or cut-short a family gathering, especially one at Nana's. But, that's exactly what I did. Following the meal, I excused myself and was soon on my way to St. Joseph.

While driving, I speculated about how my explanation for leaving early had been taken. Delicate family situations like that in the past had led to severely hurt feelings. The offending party may not be informed of his transgression immediately, but he eventually would be informed and it would not be a pleasant experience. The explanation that I gave, I had to go to the office to complete some work for Monday's paper, seemed reasonable to me. Lord knows the adult family members believed in the responsibility of work. My trepidation stemmed from two facts. First, it was Christmas at Nana's—sacred—and second, my story was not exactly full disclosure. In Allegan County, less than the full truth was a "bold-faced" lie.

I decided to go straight to the county jail and request permission to see inmate Mary Anne Starr. Talking with Starr directly had been my goal since I had first seen her on the witness stand. After the trial was over I experienced an increased sense of urgency. The duty officer granted me permission and directed me to wait in an outer office while a trustee was sent to see if the prisoner would agree to see me. I waited for almost thirty minutes before the officer returned and led me to a small interrogation room. "Take a seat; Mary Anne is on her way." While waiting I asked myself what I'd most want to know from this lady.

Mrs. Starr was led into the room. We were told that she could have 30 minutes with me. I stood as she entered and started to introduce myself, but she interrupted, "Of course, I feel like I know you, Chuck. I saw you talking with Mickey and Ruthie at the courthouse and understand you've been getting to know each other. How nice of you to come. How are you doing? Please, sit."

Her warmth and civility humbled me. Seated directly across the table from this lady affirmed my first impression of her, stunningly beautiful. Mary Anne Starr possessed movie star good looks and a personal countenance that at once attracted and intimidated men. After staring at her for an embarrassing moment, I stuttered trying to say something, anything, that wouldn't sound stupid or immature.

"Chuck, it's nice of you to come see me, but what are you doing here?" She asked incredulously. "Don't you live somewhere up north? Surely you're not working today, it's Christmas. Don't tell me that you drove all the way to St. Joe just to visit a prisoner you hardly know?" She smiled and spoke easily to me as if speaking to an old friend.

Dressed in a white blouse with the media-famed Scottish dog broach fastened at the neck and tailored navy blue skirt, I wondered if there wasn't a standard prison uniform. If so, was she accorded preferential treatment? There wasn't a hair out of place in her golden locks, but from the slight puffiness around her red-rimmed blue eyes, I suspected she might have been crying. There were no external signs of the beatings she had allegedly suffered.

"I've always wanted to talk with you personally and I thought that maybe you could use a visitor at Christmas time." How could a person in her situation appear so relaxed, natural? "Have you had any visitors since the trial ended?"

"Oh, I've had several visitors. You just missed Ruthie, Mickey and Vonda. I hear you've gotten to know my three best friends? They brought me Christmas dinner and some presents. Sheriff Diamond let us use his office to have dinner and spend some time together."

"I'm sorry I missed them. I've gotten to know them over the past two weeks and visited at Vonda's home last Sunday. I even went to basketball practice with Mickey. He's pretty good. You have a nice family."

"Thank you Chuck, but please, call me Mary Anne, everyone does. If you had gotten here earlier, you could have eaten with us. Vonda is a fantastic cook. Also, you could have seen Ruthie in the dress I made for her while waiting for the trial."

"I wish I could have, but Ruthie would look good in an old brown flour sack. She takes after her mother." Before it came out, I wished I could have taken that comment back. The last thing I wanted to do was appear to be sweet-talking Mrs. Starr or be viewed as having an interest in her daughter.

"That's nice of you to say. I think she looks good in green. I knitted her a green dress. It fit her perfectly. Ruthie is such a wonderful little girl; not so little anymore." Her face filled with worried emotion.

"Mary Anne," I started, but before I could finish my question Mrs. Starr burst into tears, putting her head on the table and crying convulsively. At first I thought about calling for help, but just sat helplessly mesmerize. Then I tried to assist her by offering my handkerchief. Eventually her crying became sobbing and then sniffling as she tried to regain her composure.

She slowly sat up straight. With tears still tumbling down her cheeks she struggled to speak, gasping for short breaths of air. Looking at me through watery eyes, she said, "I've never had a break in life, never. This is just another whack I'll have to take. I don't know if I can go on anymore. I don't know if I want to." Her voice faded into another world.

"Please don't say that. You can make it, Mary Anne, you must. Mickey, Ruthie and Vonda are all depending on you. You will survive this, for them, for yourself. You must." Talking without thinking, that's what I did. I searched for something compassionate to say, something that would resonate. The pitiful woman teetered on the verge of hopeless despair.

Though I believed I had come a long way in just two short weeks, I had a lot to learn about life as well as our judicial system. The only thing I knew for sure was that I didn't know a whole lot. I was still not absolutely clear in my mind if I believed Mary Anne had received justice at her trial. Had she lied on the witness stand? Somebody had. How is it that so many people in the world can be absolutely sure of themselves, yet occupy absolutely polar positions from one another? I had pondered that idea previously. Had Starr committed a justifiable homicide?

Speaking calmly and quietly I asked, "Mary Anne, are you going to request a pardon or appeal your case for a new trial?"

Dabbing her cheeks and nose she answered, "Senator Pinehurst says that he is going to prepare a request that the verdict be vacated or that I be given a new trial. He is a good man and I know he will eventually get me out of here."

"Mary Anne, have you heard of the murder/suicide that took place near Fennville little more than a week ago?"

"Yes, I read about it in the paper and Senator Pinehurst and I talked about it."

"Did your attorneys consider drawing an analogy from that case to support their closing arguments for your defense?"

"No, they told me that the Fennville case would detract from our line of defense and would only serve to confuse the jurors." On this point I was in total disagreement, but it would serve no purpose to discredit Mary Anne's attorneys.

"How well did you know Prosecuting Attorney Foster before this trial?"

"Pretty well, we were definitely on a first name basis. I knew him as Bill and he called me Mary Anne."

"I gathered from your testimony that you didn't like Izzy Genoa. Why?"

"I had heard that he was a bootlegger during prohibition, and when it ended he was involved in shady dealings; always having problems with the Michigan Liquor Commission. I was told that he operated a blind pig on the east end of Benton Harbor. Bob and Izzy were friends and that friendship never served Bob well. In fact, Izzy, Bob, Harley and one of their cronies at the courthouse got into a big mess with the Liquor Commission while Harley was the county prosecutor."

"What's a blind pig?"

"Oh, it's a joint that sells booze after hours."

"Can you tell me anymore about this Liquor Commission mess?"

"No, Bob didn't talk to me about that, but I do recall that right after it was settled Bob was appointed Assistant Prosecuting Attorney."

"How did you select your two attorneys?"

"I couldn't get an attorney to take my case and finally Glenn Biglow was more or less assigned to me. I never knew exactly how or why. As for Senator Pinehurst, he read about my case when he was on vacation out west. He said he was fascinated and came home to talk with me about it. He asked me if he could represent me and I gladly accepted. He's a good man; smart."

At that point I thought I had interrogated Mary Anne long enough and didn't want her to feel uncomfortable with my visit, but I had to ask one more question. "Mary Anne, you answered this question several times during the trial, but may I ask you one more time for my personal clarification? Did you really experience amnesia?"

She looked at me pensively. "Yes Chuck, I did. The last thing I remember of that night was Bob running at me. The next thing I remember is Deputy Barth telling me the next morning that Bob had died. I never had an experience like that before and I hope I never do again. People testified that I said and did things during that time that I just don't do, never. I loved Bob and he loved me. He never meant to hurt me. It was his disease that caused him to do those awful things."

"Thank you Mary Anne for sharing all of this with me. I know it's not easy for you."

As subtly as possible, I turned our conversation away from the trial and to experiences and memories we held in common. We both enjoyed discussing the personalities of animals. How we came to the subject of Seabiscuit has escaped me, but we enjoyed remembering how that ungainly, but big-hearted racehorse defeated the magnificent and invincible War Admiral. She laughed when she told me she had received several gifts and eight proposals for marriage since she had been in jail.

"Mary Anne, your time is up. Mr. Scott, you will have to leave now." Our half hour had passed in a blink of an eye. Mary Anne told me that Sheriff Diamond and his wife would be driving her to Detroit in the morning. Oddly, she looked forward to a wintery cross state drive. With that we said goodbye, wishing each other a Merry Christmas and Happy New Year.

As I drove across the bridge towards Penny's, I was acutely aware of the tempest of emotions that churned within me. It struck me as strange, wishing Mrs. Starr a happy New Year; somehow out of place. I rationalized that my next stop would not be as emotionally strenuous as the last. Penny expected me, although I'd been unable to promise her an exact time. We had become quite good friends, but I was still nervous and a little unsure of myself. It was hard to imagine that the two of us had gone to a party together little more than 24 hours earlier.

Penny opened her apartment door almost before I knocked. "Hi Chuck! Come in, I watch for you."

"Hey Penny, Merry Christmas." Penny took my coat and hung it next to hers by the door. The new radio played softly on a shelf near the sink. Penny looked especially Greek, dressed in what may have been a new dress. Her hair was combed back loosely around her head and clamped in the back. Nice, I thought.

"Where's Hebe?"

"Hebe has date! Can you guess who?" Penny asked bubbling with excitement.

"How would I know? I don't know many Greek men and I don't think I met any at the party that would be eligible or that Hebe might be attracted to."

"He is not Greek."

"I thought you told me Hebe would only be interested in marrying a Greek."

"It is alright to be interested without marrying, no? It is just date."

"Okay, do I know this person?"

"Yes," Penny said smiling from ear to ear. Plainly she was thrilled for her sister and could hardly contain her delight in teasing me.

"I give up. I know very few people around here; mostly people I've met at the courthouse. And I don't think she'd go out with Bailiff Gordon Pile."

"Deputy Barth, Aaron Barth, that is who. He tried for long time to get Hebe to go out, but she always make excuse. A week ago he told her he had been invited to Christmas party, but he would not go unless Hebe go with him. Hebe say yes. That-a great, no?"

"Yeah, that's really neat. They're both nice people and I think they'd make a handsome couple. Do you know where they went?"

"It is at home of Deputy Barth's friend in St. Joe. It strange seeing Deputy Barth dressed not in uniform. He look real nice when he come for Hebe."

"I'll bet Hebe looked real nice too. Say, did you guys like your Christmas present?" I asked as I looked toward the radio.

"Yes, yes, we both very pleased. Did you hear I have radio playing? Hebe said you should not do this; it cost too much money. But I tell her you are newspaper man and could afford." Penny chuckled, obviously having fun with me, and much to my pleasure.

"Santa Claus, not me, and I think he got a real good deal for the radio." Penny squeezed my arm and gave me a quick kiss on cheek. So quick that I hardly knew it happened. However, I immediately perceived that being alone in Penny's apartment enhanced our romantic possibilities. Before I could move closer, Penny offered a suggestion.

"Let us go to beach. I love beach."

"Penny, it's winter time," I protested.

"So? I love go to beach, anytime, and now is great time, before sun go down."

"Okay, I'm with you. Let's go." We got our coats and boots on and Penny put a scarf around my neck. Then she stepped back and took a long questioning look at me, as if sizing me up.

"You missing something. Oh yes, Santa leave something for you." With that Penny handed me a small colorfully wrapped box tied-up with red, green and white ribbons, **For Chuck—From Santa**.

Looking at Penny I sighed, "Penny, you shouldn't have done this." Not letting her respond, I went on, "Okay, it's from Santa!" and I tore open the package handing Penny the ribbons. To my surprise I found a bright red flat touring hat, the style of the ones worn by the men of the House of David. I could either sit it on top of my head or pull it down over my ears. I tried it on, "I like it! I love it!" And I really did like it. I visualized driving my little black Coupe with this distinctive red touring hat; quite roguish I visualize.

"Let's see what it looks like on you," and I popped the hat on Penny's head. I did this as a pretext for pulling her close and kissing her. For a moment I thought she was enjoying the encounter, but all too quickly she drew back, plopping the hat back on my head.

215

Looking at me with playful eyes she said, "I think it look better on you," and gave me another phantom peck on the cheek. "You will need. The beach cold, windy. We go?"

Little did I know we would be walking to the beach. I had presumed I would drive. It was at least a mile away, over the bridge and through St. Joe. Penny explained that she had not talked to Hebe about riding with me alone in the car, and although it would probably be fine with Hebe, she didn't feel comfortable without her knowing in advance.

I did not question Penny any further about this subject. We walked and talked. Penny reminisced about her childhood on the Greek island of *Skopelos* in the Aegean Sea. She described how she and her mother frequently walked the beach looking for shells, enjoying the beautiful sunsets while feeling the sand between their toes. She painted a picture of lengthening shadows slowly climbing the mountain backdrop. It sounded so vivid, so *"once upon a time,"* that I absolutely understood Penny's longing to return. Listening to her convinced me that I must at least visit there someday. I was certain that *Skopelos* lingered somewhere in my future.

As we were both letting ourselves dream about sailing away to Greece, Penny stopped and, as if reassuring herself, stated that she must first become a naturalized United States citizen and she must graduate from high school. Both of these events were already on her schedule. Penny's plan included making sure that Hebe was safe, secure and happy; a tall order I thought. Then she could go to Greece she said. "But, I must first earn money for trip."

Penny displayed a keen interest in where I was from, how I grew up, how the Scott family made a living, and what plans I had for the future. I evaded my nonexistent personal future plan, but enthusiastically accorded her a guided tour through Scott family history. Taking Penny to visit the farm seemed like a good idea, maybe during blossom time.

When we arrived near the south pier, the red sun was sinking low on an unusually clear western horizon. Snow fences placed along the beach had corralled smooth undulating sand drifts, now covered with snow. Stalactite columns of ice clung to the catwalk, which ran the length of the pier to the lighthouse. A significant amount of shoreline ice had built up in rough mounds and although tempting, would have been hazardous to traverse. Cold dark blue water salted with millions of whitecaps commenced approximately 50 yards out from the natural shoreline, now covered by ice and snow. The outer rim of ice rhythmically rose and fell with lake swells coming ever shoreward. Occasionally, a beam of sunlight slanted through the ice crystals to find Penny's glowing face. I could not imagine a more perfect winter panorama. Penny had it right when she proclaimed her love of the beach.

Reaching into her coat pocket, Penny pulled out the colorful ribbons that had been tied around the present she had given me. "When I was little girl, I wanted kite like other children on beach. Mother gave me ribbons that we hold up in wind. I remember. Very proud. We run along seashore with ribbons flying in wind." Penny shared her tender story in just a few short, but touching sentences. "Economy of words," the Chief would describe it. She handed me a share of the ribbons and we both held them up into a stiff west wind. Penny untied her scarf and tilted her head to the wind. She luxuriated in the feel of the cold air on her face and her hair blowing freely.

Our back and forth chatter lessened. We both sought to inhale the natural wonder of the winterscape. Penny told me that she always marveled at Michigan's four distinct seasons. It reminded her of nature opening and closing doors. She asked a question or two about the lake and the ice, but in the main she just immersed herself in the time and place; so did I.

By the time we made our way back to the apartment, the sun had gone completely down and the streetlights outlining Main Street revealed a few snow flurries in the air. There were no streetlights near the warehouse and it was quite dark finding our way, giving me a good reason to hold Penny's hand. She didn't mind. We welcomed the apartment's warmth, both nearly frozen to the core. The weatherman on the radio called for 10 above zero and a 10% chance of seeing the northern lights in a clear night sky.

As Penny prepared a little something for our supper, I couldn't help admiring her and feeling guilty for comparing her with Maxine. Maxine had smash-you-in-the-face good looks, and although she didn't flaunt it, neither did she conceal her many natural assets. Penny, on the other hand, appeared quite plain. She never did the slightest thing to knowingly draw attention to herself, no make-up, no jewelry, common clothes, and no perfume. Under close scrutiny her olive complexion revealed a smooth, flawless skin texture, the perfect complement for her dark clear eyes. Almost shoulder length straight dark brown hair, encased an oval shaped face.

Penny didn't overtly mask her natural features; she simply did nothing to accentuate them. The sexiest she ever appeared was when she wore her navy and white waitressing outfit, and that would never adorn the pages of a fashion magazine. To me she was a diamond wrapped in butcher's paper.

She was fun to be around, easy to talk to, never demanding, but interested and encouraging. While we were sitting at the table eating the toasted cheese sandwiches Penny had prepared, I formulated a strategy for how to move our relationship in a romantic direction. As we cleared the dishes, I put my right hand on the small of her back. She guardedly turned toward me, intently looking deep into my eyes. I felt a rush of sensual anticipation. Penny whispered softly as if listening, "I think I hear Hebe coming."

Damn, I thought. Why did Hebe pick this time to come home? Less than a minute later Hebe opened the door as she shouted over her shoulder to someone at the bottom of the stairs, "I had good time Aaron, see you in morning."

"Hi Chuck," Hebe said as she closed the door, stomped her feet on the mat and hung-up her coat. "You two here long time?" She inquired, looking at the two of us standing near the sink. She spoke not in an interrogating voice, but as someone happy to see us. By her expression, Hebe was happy. Penny wasted no time in questioning Hebe about her date with Deputy Barth. Hebe put her sister off, but judging by her flushed complexion, she held pleasant memories of the time spent with Deputy Aaron Barth.

Changing the subject, Hebe said, "Chuck, look what Santa bring Penny and me for Christmas." She pointed at the radio. "We love it. Does this mean we good girls this year?" she said with a giggle.

"Well, that must be true. I know it is in America. Does Santa Claus make stops in Greece?"

The three of us laughed, joked, and generally had a good time working on an extremely difficult jigsaw puzzle picturing ocean, sky and seagulls. The Greek sisters clearly held puzzle superiority over the peach-pickin' newsman. Shortly after nine, Hebe excused herself saying that she had to open the diner early in the morning. We both said good night as she went to her room and closed the door.

Penny turned to me, "Chuck, you start for home. I worry you making long drive at night." Her concern was unadulterated, not idle conversation.

"I can make it home with my eyes closed. Right now I want you to close your eyes." As I said that, I put my hands on Penny's waist and pulled her close to me.

"I want to see what I taste," she responded softly as her lips met mine. For a long moment we simply held that position. I pulled her tightly against me until I felt her body heat. My eyes were still closed when Penny released her lips from mine, "That was good Chuck. I am glad you come to see me."

"No more than me, Penny. I had a great time." With another quick kiss on her warm full lips, "I've got to work tomorrow, too." As I said that, the Barnes story flashed through my mind and I remembered my promise to turn it in first thing in the morning. I had miles to go before I sleep, figuratively and literally.

"Chuck, there New Year's Eve party at high school next Saturday."

"Yes?" I answered as if expecting, hoping, that something else was coming. "Do you think I should write a story about it for the newspaper?"

"No, silly. I hope you take me. Will you? I know it long way for you to drive, and…"

"Yes," I interrupted. "I'd love to, Penny. Just tell me what to wear, time and place, and I'll take you. Do you think Hebe would mind if we took my car?"

This time, Penny pulled me to her as she reached up and initiated a very firm and hungry kiss. Her advance met with my full cooperation, but not overly so. I wanted to encourage Penny, not scare her. She was taller and stronger than Maxine, but I suspected fragileness beneath the surface that I wanted to be sensitive to. "You always close eyes?"

The drive home took a full hour, but passed quickly. My head was filled with the two women I had intended to see that day and neither had let me down. Both left me in an emotional turmoil, but for different reasons. Mary Anne Starr was going to prison, but I was convinced she was no more a threat to society than my Nana. My interest in a deeper understanding of Mary Anne was waning while my support for her freedom increased. Contrarily, my interest in Penny had increased exponentially. The adjective combinations that I conjured up to describe her, young/mature, mysterious/common, fun loving/serious, strong/fragile, naive/wise, self-assured/apprehensive, all seemed to compete with each another. I couldn't figure this girl, woman out. But I had a compelling urge to discover more of Penny *Melaina*.

A familiar car was pulling out of our driveway as I slowed to turn in. We both stopped and I got out believing that it must be Maxine.

As I approached her car, Maxine rolled down her window and said, "Hi Chuck. Merry Christmas. I stopped by to drop off something for you. I think you're going to really like it." She smiled up at me.

"But Maxine, this is a complete surprise," I said, confused by this meeting and a possible gift.

"I know. I'm sorry about the way I acted the other night. We should have stopped and talked it out. I'm sure there is a logical explanation for everything."

The sight of Maxine through the car window, all bundled-up in a heavy winter coat, still held me spellbound. "I'm sorry, too. I didn't mean to upset you." Memories of that parting still crystal clear, I recalled that I was upset, but not devastated.

"If you have time to follow me home, I could make us some hot chocolate and we could, maybe, talk this out?" After a short pause, she smiled, "Maybe even kiss and make up?"

She was absolutely the most tantalizing, enticing woman I'd known. That mysterious sent wafted lightly on the air. The memory of Maxine's hot chocolate with melted marshmallows had a compelling sensuous pull.

"Good idea, I'm right behind you."

I got back into the Coupe, but only watched as Maxine's taillights disappear down the snow covered country road. For a couple of minutes I simply sat there in the dark, thinking. Maxine's feminine charms were undeniably enticing, and the opportunity for an intense intimate encounter lay only a couple of miles down the road. I possessed a vain pride in viewing the two of us as the perfect couple. I knew for sure that Mom felt that way. She would welcome Maxine Martin into the Scott family in a heartbeat. "Someone will scoop up the opportunities you miss," so said Dad. Plans are nice, but reality gets the last word. Everyone loved Maxine. *Was I crazy?*

I put the Coupe in the barn and went to the house. "Here, Ginger?"

XXVI
ONE YEAR LATER

It was hard to believe that a whole year had passed since Penny and I had shared that first innocent kiss on the floor of the Pegasus. From that time forward we dated quite regularly until June, when I left for California. By regularly, I mean seeing each other once every week or two. A promising romance was difficult since we lived so far apart and I worked full-time at the paper, while Penny completed her senior year and worked after school and on weekends.

I had lived in California for over five months and was anxious to get home for Christmas. But it was seeing Penny again that mattered most. We had exchanged a letter or two, but I hadn't heard from her since last August. The little time we had shared will forever live in my heart.

We were together on a secluded beach one warm summer evening and decided to climb into the Coupe's rumble seat to watch the sunset and the night sky leisurely fill up with stars. Playfully, we competed to discover shooting stars. Before our search of the celestial heavens had ended, Penny and I shared the most intimate, tenderly affectionate experience of our lives. Whispering, laughing, crying, snuggling, we fell asleep wrapped in each other's arms and didn't awake until after midnight, covetous of each other's body warmth in the cool night air. Together we searched for a unique significance in the misty yellow halo gilding the moon. We mutually agreed that we had added new meaning to the term "struggle buggy." Forever and ever...and ever.

Our last date was spent enjoying the excitement of the Silver Beach Amusement Park, dancing in the Shadowland Ballroom, and walking hand-in-hand along a moonlit beach. Together at the beach was always our favorite time. Sadly, that last beach walk had become increasingly uncomfortable until it came time to say goodbye. As if by tacit agreement, the most delicate feelings for each other were left unspoken; months later we even stopped writing. We were in the wrong place and time in our lives.

It came as no surprise that Maxine had reconnected with the high school Hero or that she taught in a little country school. However, I was somewhat suspicious when Mom informed me that Maxine had recently announced a January wedding. With a concerned expression, Mom said in a questioning tone, "It seems quite sudden." Mom may have wanted a reaction from me, but I avoided giving her one. I was certain she believed I had lost a golden opportunity with Maxine. In a strange sort of way, I felt relieved that good-looking, safe and predictable Maxine Martin was no longer a possibility in my life.

221

I responded to Mom in my most deadpan, unconcerned manner, "Does this mean there will be no cherry pie over the holidays?" There was a hint of disappointment in Mom's laugh. As expected, she inquired about my current dating life. "Well, I've been keeping company with lots of cows, horses and mules, but very few women. There was an unconfirmed female sighting about six weeks ago, but it was just a mirage. I am planning to go to the Seattle World's Fair when I get back. They say there are women at the fair." Mom looked at me only mildly amused. She couldn't disguise the fact that nothing would please her more than for me to find a nice girl, marry and settle down—and give her grandchildren she could help raise. Mom had never been thrilled with me living and working in California.

The day after Christmas I stopped in at the *Tribune* to see the Chief. I was startled to find Rose working there. Gracious as I remembered, she invited me into the Chief's office so that we could talk and catch up. The office appeared much cleaner and more organized than I remembered. There were pictures on the walls and the Chief's desk displayed an intricate inlayed grain of highly polished mahogany. For all the litter, I had never before seen the top of the Chief's desk. A phone and a framed picture of Rose were the only objects on the desk.

"Hey, that's the picture I took of you."

"I know," Rose smiled sentimentally as she picked it up. "Irving was so proud when you gave it to him. He had it framed and always displayed it on his desk."

"Where is the Chief?"

"Please sit down Chuck. It's a rather long story." With that Rose told me how the two of them became desperately concerned for her parents' welfare after Germany had invaded all of Czechoslovakia last spring. I remembered that because the Chief had told me that Rose's parents had moved only weeks earlier to Katowice, Poland, where he was born. "We decided that Irving would go to Katowice and escort my parents here to live with us. About the time Irving arrived in Katowice, the Germans invaded Poland. Travel in Europe became very dangerous, if not impossible for Jews."

With a face full of despair, Rose's voice broke, "I have not heard from Irving since the first of November. I've talked to Congressman Hutchinson, I've written letters, I don't know what else to do?" She looked and sounded hopeless. I wanted to reassure her, but I too felt her anxiety.

We talked for a while; both of us attempted to be optimistic, but found it next to impossible. Rose Mendelsohn's wide-ranging knowledge of news events, international affairs, astonished me once again. The ease with which she acerbically satirized the "phony war," appeasement, isolationism, America

Firsters, and even our national hero, Colonel Charles Lindbergh, rivaled that of her husband. However, Rose sallied forth with a surgeon's precision while the Chief plied his craft with the delicate force of a blacksmith's sledgehammer.

Talking with Rose was at once enlightening and emotionally draining. More than once I felt tears welling up within as I observed Rose's dread of losing her family. Working may have been a life saving therapy for her. She was resolute and capable. As I readied to leave she asked, "Chuck, you will do something for me?" Her syntax reminded me of the Chief.

"Chuck, there will be a hearing on the Starr case Friday. You, more than anyone here, are familiar with that case. Will you cover it for me and write up an article for the *Tribune*? It should take only a couple of hours."

I was thankful, indeed grateful, for this unexpected opportunity to do something for Mrs. Mendelsohn. "Of course I'll do it. I want to do it. Please leave it to me."

Finding out about the status of Mary Anne Starr immediately assumed a high priority on my home visit agenda—right after Penny. And I had an official capacity. I knew with all certainty that favorable possibilities hung in the balance for the Starr family. I hoped to see all of them at the hearing. Finding out about the hearing seemed a most fortuitous evolution of events.

On Friday, December 29, 1939, I drove the yet dependable little black Coupe to St. Joseph. I hadn't been in the area since the previous summer, the last time I had seen Penny. I was determined to stop and see her following the hearing. "Absence makes the heart grow fonder," my Nana would say. Remembering, I smiled to myself, thinking how ridiculous my response had been, "Out of sight, out of mind." Not true.

A bitter west wind rushed off the lake and prohibited snow from effortlessly falling to earth. December in St. Joe had not changed. The ominous courthouse looked the same, as did the majestic top floor circuit courtroom. The faint varnish smell welcomed me and when I heard the floor squeak as I located a seat in the familiar second row, I felt right at home. I looked around for a recognizable cast of characters; I wasn't disappointed.

Old friend Mike Halamka slid into the seat next to me and without missing a beat brought me up to date on the Starr case. "Pinehurst has been seeking a new trial since the day Starr was sentenced. In November he filed a formal motion for a new trial. The hearing on that motion has been scheduled and canceled twice by Jackson who appears to be dragging his feet."

"Why is he doing that?"

"I don't know, but as the original presiding judge, Jackson must conduct a hearing on the matter or risk being discredited."

"What do you think is going to happen at this hearing?"

"I'm not sure." Halamka coughed, "Curious isn't it, Jackson scheduled this hearing for Friday afternoon before the long New Year's weekend. I bet it'll be quick."

At precisely 1:30 P.M. Judge Tobey D. Jackson made a curtain call in the Berrien County Circuit Court. After bringing the hearing to order, Jackson declared that the proceedings would be swift, only entailing oral arguments by the defense and prosecution attorneys. Jackson hadn't changed. He then told J.P. Pinehurst to present his claims on behalf of Mary Anne Starr. Six weeks earlier Pinehurst had prepared and delivered to Jackson a brief, a meticulous outline of seven such claims.

"If it pleases the court," Pinehurst began, "I would like a minute to inform all present of my client's current disposition." Jackson nodded. "Since her incarceration, Mrs. Starr has been a model prisoner. At present she is working in the administrative office of the Detroit House of Correction doing routine clerical work. However, she has had to be excused from her duties sporadically due to a chronic nervous condition that is reported exacerbated by a left eye defect. This problem eye has caused her much discomfort and led to repeated prescription changes for her spectacles. Her present illness is the reason we did not request her presence here today." Without stating so explicitly, the bearded attorney made it clear to everyone that Starr's medical problems were the result of Robert Eastwood's beatings.

"I shall commence a reasoned explanation of defense's motion for a new trial by reminding the court that the trial of Mary Anne Starr, December last, was hastily conducted. In addition to the regular trial schedule, sessions were conducted during the weekend and several evenings. Impending holidays may have contributed to that hectic pace which commenced when, less than two weeks before the originally scheduled start; the trial date was moved up one week. Consequently, this timetable left insufficient time for the defense to investigate testimony and other state's evidence. It placed the defense at a distinct disadvantage."

"Now, let us revisit the mental condition of Robert Eastwood, which precipitated the incident in question here. And allow me to remind the court that at the time of said incident, it was Eastwood that confronted Mrs. Starr on her way home." From there, Attorney Pinehurst spent considerable time portraying Eastwood as the victim, not of Starr, but of paranoiac dementia praecox, "The most treacherous form of insanity, often ending in homicide or suicide. Unfortunately, it is not easily diagnosed."

Pinehurst then read for the court a scholarly journal article on the disease. The article had been researched and authored by Pinehurst. In support of his claim, Pinehurst introduced a certified copy of Eastwood's personal application for admission to the University of Michigan Hospital in Ann Arbor. "In Eastwood's petition, and in his own hand, he stated that both of his parents died in an Ohio insane asylum." Pinehurst interpreted Eastwood's petition as unsolicited self-incrimination, being that Eastwood knew he had inherited mental defect.

In addition, Pinehurst revealed that several months after the trial the prosecution's medical and psychiatric advisor had phoned him personally to make him aware of this document. The said document had been delivered to Prosecuting Attorney Foster prior to trial. According to Pinehurst, this physician, Dr. J.C. Parkman, stated to him over the phone, "Yes, Senator Pinehurst, I scuttled your case by not making you aware of Eastwood's application for medical help."

"Your Honor, this is the most flagrant suppression of evidence I have ever witnessed in my long career before the bench. Because it was suppressed, it must be considered new and exculpatory evidence." By Jackson's expressionless face and prosecutor Spears casually cleaning his fingernails, I judged Pinehurst's passion for this argument far exceeded theirs. When the defense attorney tried to draw a parallel between Robert Eastwood and the fanatical escapades of Washington Congressman Marion Zioncheck that ended in suicide three years earlier, all agreed the suppression argument had run its course; at least in Jackson's courtroom.

Pinehurst submitted and summarized for the court an affidavit signed by prosecution witness John Henry Johns, a merchant policeman. As the first person on the scene, Johns stated that it was he who shouted, "Don't shoot! Don't shoot!" He never heard Eastwood say anything at all. This directly contradicted the state witnesses who reported that after the first two shots, Eastwood shouted, "Don't shoot! Don't Shoot!"

A second affidavit was presented. This one had been written by a juror, stating that she was convinced that clemency should be shown the respondent, but had been pressured to vote for manslaughter. To make herself perfectly clear on this point, she stated that, "I was not coerced, but did feel pressured by the other jurors into agreeing with them."

Halamka and I looked at each other in disbelief. Neither of us offered an explanation of the juror's distinction between "coerced" and "pressured," nor did she.

With the two affidavits as a buffer, Pinehurst moved to his expert medical witnesses. "It is my seventh and final argument that each of the three medical witnesses, and the testimony of each, was accorded great prejudice within this courtroom, and thus discredited in the eyes of the jurors. My client's defense required proper attention to expert medical testimony."

Pausing momentarily to look around the courtroom, the neatly bewhiskered jurist concluded, "For these seven trial errors to be properly addressed and for justice to prevail, my client deserves a new trial, or at the very least, a commutation of sentence. Thank you, Your Honor."

Without invitation, Prosecuting Attorney Robert M. Spears rose and submitted his own affidavit to Judge Jackson. This one was signed by the three firemen at the scene. All three stated that none of the firemen shouted, "Don't shoot! "Don't shoot!" Spears then asked, "If they didn't say the words, that only leaves Robert Eastwood."

I recall thinking to myself, *am I deaf or what? Didn't the John's affidavit state that he, Johns, yelled "Don't Shoot?"* It didn't seem to matter to anyone that Johns wasn't a fireman and therefore, fell outside the parameters of the prosecution's affidavit. Halamka shared my disbelief.

Spears continued, "Pinehurst's arguments are based entirely on evidence that is cumulative and reiterative, and as such, have no creditability as arguments for a new trial. Eastwood's prior medical condition is absolutely irrelevant to the time the respondent pulled the trigger, that shot the gun, that fired the bullets, that killed Robert Eastwood." Spears turned, looking at Pinehurst in a one-ups-man-ship sort of deportment.

Spears smirked, "Perhaps Mary Anne Starr's health isn't so good. But let me further state, without attempting to be humorous in the least, that Mrs. Starr materially affected the health of Robert Eastwood."

"In answer to the defense's contention that the trial had been conducted hurriedly, I say the attorneys for the respondent might have asked for a continuance at any time during the proceedings. They did not do so—their choice. Neither did defense offer additional charges to the jury when Judge Jackson so graciously inquired if they cared to suggest any at the trial's conclusion. They did not do so—their choice." Satisfied, Spears returned briskly to his seat.

Judge Jackson looked back through the brief that Senator Pinehurst had so proudly and painstakingly prepared. He methodically turned from one page to the next. While he was doing this, I looked over the half filled gallery. There were several familiar faces from a year ago. How had I missed Mickey, Ruthie and Vonda? Mickey and I made eye contact, waved and with gestures agreed to meet following the hearing. Ruthie seemed to have physically matured more than expected in just one year; she was 16 and a high school junior.

Jackson cleared his throat. "I have studied the defense's motion very carefully. It is well organized and well reasoned. I have listened thoughtfully to the oral arguments concerning this motion. The defense has contended that there has been a miscarriage of justice in *The State of Michigan v. Starr*. I am not so impressed. However, I am satisfied that the jury had all available evidence in this case, and that they arrived at a fair and appropriate verdict. At that time I considered the length of the sentence very carefully. Nothing has happened since that time to change my mind. If I were properly called upon to pass sentence in this matter again today, it would be exactly the same."

Almost as an afterthought, Judge Jackson denied Pinehurst's motion for a new trial. At the same time he refused defense counsel's alternative plea to have Mary Anne Starr's sentence commutated. Attorney Pinehurst shook his head in disbelief.

Following the close of the hearing, I moved quickly to speak with Ruthie and Mickey. Before I could get to them, they were surrounded by three or four other reporters. It was obvious that Ruthie was the focal point of attention. How would she be portrayed in tomorrow's papers? As interested as I was to talk with the Starrs, I was able to capitalize on an opportunity to speak directly with the defense counsel. A crestfallen Senator Pinehurst willingly gave me a couple of usable quotes.

"At this time, we have not planned for an appeal to the Michigan Supreme Court or a request of Governor Dickinson for executive clemency." Pinehurst went on to indicate, "These avenues remain open, but neither will be pursued immediately." Avoiding further comment, a totally dejected Pinehurst slowly made his way to a side door of the courtroom where two familiar young men waited.

As I headed for the main courtroom exit, I met up with the Starrs. Each was disappointed, but not devastated the way they had been a year earlier. Vonda had assumed complete responsibility for her sister's children. She outwardly maintained a strong positive demeanor. Still, the pain suffered during the past year clearly showed in her face. There existed a stoic resignation to fate on the part of both Mickey and Ruthie. They told me they had visited their mother several times during the year, but I sensed these visits were difficult and depressing for all. Although courteous, they understandably wanted to get out of the courthouse and drive back home. Vonda wanted to talk about the hearing's result with me, but succumbed to the wishes of her niece and nephew. Mickey, Ruthie and Vonda wished me well.

The Pegasus had been painted and a new neon sign hung in the front window; **OPEN**. Entering the door brought back memories of smells and noisy chatter. There was an open booth along the wall that I promptly occupied. I didn't recognize the waitress that came to take my order, but she smiled when I told her I'd like to see the *Melaina* sisters. "Penny's not here, but I'll tell Hebe someone's here to see her. May I take your order?"

"I'll take your best breakfast with a piece of *baklava*." I watched the waitress to see if she would indicate that breakfast after noon was strange or not possible. She didn't blink as she wrote down my order. She was definitely not Greek.

Moments later I saw Hebe peering from behind the swinging door. When I caught her eye, she came promptly over to my booth. As I stood to meet her, she gave me a big hug, told me to sit, and slid-in across from me. "Where you from Chuck? What you been doing?"

"Well, that's a long story, but basically after I quit working for the newspaper, I went to California and have become a lonesome cowboy. Right now I'm home for two weeks and plan to go back after New Years. But, tell me what you and Penny have been up to. Where is Penny?"

"Which do you want first, me or Penny?" she smiled.

"Okay, tell me about you first."

"I'm married!"

"What?" I asked in amazement. "Who's the lucky guy, and where did you find him?"

"Oh, he come in regular?" Hebe teased. "Deputy Barth. Aaron Barth. We marry last August."

"That's great Hebe. I knew you had been seeing Deputy Barth. He is an impressive man. I wish you a long happy life together. But, didn't Penny tell me that you would only marry a Greek and then only by '*proximinio*?'" I tried to give Hebe a hard time.

"Isn't it American custom 'beggars cannot be choosers?' Aaron pretend Greek! And thank you Chuck. We are happy. Aaron will always be officer. Together we buy Pegasus. *Yia Yia* and Uncle K get old and they want me take over."

"This sounds terrific, Hebe. Now, tell me where I can find Penny?" I didn't want to change the subject too quickly or seem rude, but I really wanted to see Penny.

"Penny in Greece; her dream. She left right after wedding and now she can't come home. The war cause travel restriction and I fear worse. We worry Chuck, but I receive letter last week. Penny said she fine and on list for people to leave country. She says not worry." Hebe's voice told a different story and I know she had every right to be worried, as did Rose Mendelsohn. Did this explain why Penny's letters stopped? Europe was fast falling into the abyss of total war. No safe country existed on that continent.

It was good seeing and talking with Hebe again, but I confess that when I found out there was no possibility of seeing Penny, my interest waned. The drive home from Benton Harbor brought back memories, especially in light of my day's experiences. As the miles passed I evaluated what I had learned. First, I was happy for Maxine. She had, or was soon going to, achieve her goals in life. For sure she would make a terrific wife and mother. Second, I worried about the Mendelsohns. Without question, the Chief and his in-laws were in grave danger. What could I do? Thirdly, Mary Anne, Mickey, Ruthie and Vonda had all lost again. Their situation should have given me an inspiration to do something good. Maybe write their story; I had lots of material and I missed writing. Lastly, I was happy for Hebe and Deputy Barth. An interesting twist, I thought, when considering the circumstances of their first meeting along a lonely country road east of Benton Harbor.

Where is Penny, what is she doing? I think I longed for her more after discovering she was unattainable—in Greece. And I remembered back when I thought Fennville to Benton Harbor was a long distance. It would be nice to again walk along the beach with her—even in winter.

"Concentrate on those things for which you have some control and don't worry about those things outside your control," so said Dad. Every time I thought of that advice, I could see a self-satisfied look on Dad's face, thinking he had magnanimously passed along some sage wisdom that only he, and maybe Socrates, truly understood.

With that thought in mind, I began mentally outlining the piece I'd submit about the hearing for a new trial. I stopped at the South Haven office to write and turn in Rose Mendelsohn's assignment. *"This case is not closed for this paper until I say it is! Now, get-the-hell out of here and let me get some work done. I'm late for supper!"*

XXVII
THE PRINCIPALS

SAME COURT SAME VERDICT
Mary Anne Starr to Stay in Prison
By C. Drew Scott

St. Joseph, Dec. 29—Yesterday in reunion fashion, the principals in *The State of Michigan v. Mary Anne Starr*—Dec. 1938 reconvened in the Berrien County Circuit Court for a hearing to consider a petition for a new trial. Last month, Attorney J.P. Pinehurst filed a motion with the Circuit Court for a new trial or a commutation of sentence on behalf of his client Mary Anne Starr. Pinehurst represented Starr last December when she was found guilty of manslaughter for the murder of her common law husband Attorney W. Robert Eastwood, a past Assistant Prosecuting Attorney for Berrien County.

Presiding over the hearing was Hillsdale Circuit Court Judge Tobey D. Jackson, the judge of record in the original trial. Prosecuting Attorney Robert M. Spears represented the State as he did assisting Prosecutor W.C. Foster one year earlier. With the exception of defendant Starr, who did not attend due to illness, the cast of judge and legal adversaries remained nearly intact.

The original verdict, guilty of manslaughter, had been anticipated and was initially accepted by all parties. However, Judge Jackson's sentence of from 14-15 years in prison with a recommendation of serving the full 15 years had shocked many, appearing unduly severe.

The hearing began with Pinehurst outlining his reasons for filing the "motion for a new trial, or an alternative order of reduction of sentence, and probation—Nov. 10, 1939." The defense counsel provided details supporting several complaints of original trial errors as well as the discovery of new evidence. His justifications for a new trial are summarized as follows:

1. Affidavit of John Henry Johns (merchant police officer) stating that on the night in question he was the person that cried "Don't Shoot! Don't Shoot!" These were not the cries of Robert Eastwood. Additionally, there was no loud and

boisterous talking or disturbance on the street between Starr and Eastwood before the shooting; the street was quiet.

2. Affidavit of Linda Stover (housewife and juror) stating that she wanted a verdict of "Not Guilty" but was pressured by other jurors to agree to a compromise verdict of "Manslaughter." With that verdict she, and she believed other jurors, wanted to recommend leniency. They were informed that the jury could only determine guilt or innocence, not degree of punishment. Stover further stated that being a first time juror, she deferred too much to the opinions of the other jurors.

3. Rushing the trial's conclusion was an error. Less than two weeks before the trial's scheduled start, December 19, 1938, it was moved up to December 12. Holding weekend and evening sessions afforded defense counsel no opportunity to verify the veracity of testimony given by State witnesses.

4. Five State witnesses were introduced during rebuttal that were never indorsed and were a total surprise to the defense counsel. This was a clear violation of statutory mandate and put the defense at a distinct disadvantage.

5. The State failed to offer expert rebuttal testimony as to the mental and physical condition of the defendant and the victim. Prosecution's claim that it was too expensive for the taxpayers and that juries didn't pay attention to medical experts anyway was clearly prejudicial as was their labeling the defendant "A Woman with a Double Sin." These errors justified correction by the Court.

6. The State possessed knowledge of exculpatory evidence, the victim's application for admission to the University of Michigan Hospital for psychiatric evaluation, which they withheld from this Court, the defense counsel and the jury. This behavior was a clear violation of legal precedent, ethical conduct, and statutory law.

7. Affidavit of J.P. Pinehurst in which he corroborates his first six claims based on his personal knowledge. This statement included his observations of Starr before, during and since the trial. In his deposition Pinehurst admits to defense's failure in more vigorously objecting to the hurried nature of the trial.

> Prosecutor Spears countered claims justifying a new trial with affidavits in opposition to those submitted by Pinehurst. He declared that defense's "new" evidence was merely a redundant display of "old" evidence reviewed by the Court during the original trial. In total, it did not rise near the level required for arguments supporting a new trial.
>
> As to the previous mental health of Robert Eastwood, Spears argued, "Eastwood's condition in the past had absolutely nothing to do with the time the respondent committed the murder. It matters not whether he was the epitome of health or a helpless invalid. If real, I sympathize with the defendant's health problems, but who can deny that her health is infinitely better than that of her victim?"
>
> Spear's ten-minute rebuttal of Pinehurst's hour-long plea concluded with a direct attack on Attorney Pinehurst. "How, after a year's time, can defense claim that his client suffered a rushed trial? The defense never once objected, nor did they request a continuance of the proceedings, although they had ample opportunity to do so."
>
> Judge Jackson informed Pinehurst and Spears that he had patiently considered both claims and rebuttal. When it came time to render a decision, Jackson moved with deliberate speed. He found there to be no miscarriage of justice in the Starr trial. Therefore, he denied the motion for a new trial. As to the alternative motion for a reduction of sentence and immediate probation, the judge denied that as well saying, "If I were to pass sentence today, it would be exactly the same."

I had wanted to hand the piece to Rose personally, but by the time I finished she had left the office for the Synagogue, her Friday night custom. Saying goodbye in person would have been a strain for both of us. A simple note was the best I could do. I placed note and article next to her picture on the Chief's desk and headed for the farm.

The day that had started with such promise had left me filled with angst. I was convinced that Mary Anne Starr had not received justice—not in her murder trial or in the hearing for a new trial. An overpowering urge roiled within me to write for publication my appraisal of the characters associated with her case, laying bare their strengths, shortcomings and foibles; albeit, the effort would have been challenging and the remuneration paltry.

But, if I had made such an effort to analyze the trial principals, I would have started with the impeccably credentialed prosecution team of W.C. Foster and Robert M. Spears. At the time of the Starr trial, Foster was stepping down as prosecuting attorney in favor of his handpicked successor and assistant prosecutor, Spears. Foster was not retiring nor leaving his legal career by any means. He chose not to run for reelection in order to prepare for a future run for a Circuit Court judgeship. He aspired to someday sit on Michigan's Supreme Court, a career destination he shared with his law school roommate, and a post achieved by his hometown hero and mentor, Judge Louis H. Fead. It would not look good on Foster's resumé to lose his last, and possibly most high profile, case as county prosecutor.

Foster and Starr were well acquainted. He had privately expressed an admiration for her but despised her husband, opinions he shared with and held in common with colleagues. Bob Eastwood's inconsistent and, at times, despicable personal and questionable professional behavior was common knowledge among Berrien County's legal community. His prior disbarment was not without cause and his reinstatement suspect.

Harley Eastwood's legal reputation was no better than his older brother's, and most were convinced that Harley won the county's prosecuting attorney position as an unfortunate accident; swept into office as the result of the 1932 Democratic landslide. It pleased Republicans, especially Foster and Spears, that Harley ran for reelection three times. Foster had defeated Harley Eastwood in two elections and Spears defeated him in the last.

Mary Anne Starr's trial put Foster in a conflicted position. The fact that he had prior knowledge of the physical abuse Starr suffered threatened to call attention to his ambivalent response to her pleas for help. The high-profile nature of Starr's trial made it one Foster could not delegate and could ill-afford to lose because of its implications for his future aspirations. Lastly, he felt the need for maintaining a reputation of being strong in the crusade against crime, a position he expounded upon during his closing argument. That monologue resonated like a campaign speech. Concluding with a stern jury solicitation he proclaimed, "This trial boils down to whether or not Starr shot and killed Eastwood. We all agree, she did. Are we going to approve of that, or are you, by your verdict, going to say 'you can't get away with that in Berrien County!'"

Given the lame duck chief prosecutor's more general trial tact, the newly elected Spears eagerly embraced his prosecutorial role of trial attack dog. He vigorously seized the opportunity to establish himself as Berrien County's chief law enforcement officer. The regionally significant Starr murder trial provided Spears the forum for fulfilling his campaign promise of being tough in the fight against crime and corruption.

Just three years out of law school, Robert M. Spears hailed from an old and well-established Benton Harbor family that stood ready to assist with his career advancement. His youthful enthusiasm was only enticed by such a winnable case. If clouded judgment is ever justifiable, his may be attributable to sheer lack of experience. This was never more glaring than when he pretended rage toward the defendant or when he endeavored to wax biblically eloquent by calling up Bible chapter and verse with which to hold Starr accountable. His law school theatrics fell flat in the courtroom. Spear's saving grace was the fact that he was prosecuting an open and shut case. Starr shot and killed Eastwood, and never claimed otherwise.

Spear's amateurish shortcomings were surpassed by those of Judge Tobey D. Jackson, the youngest Circuit Court judge in the state of Michigan; having risen to the bench by appointment, not election. Jackson began and ended the trial of Mary Anne Starr trying to justify his station and prove his power; setting rules, pounding his gavel, and repeatedly threatening to clear the courtroom. If his punctuality appeared defiant, his sentencing decree was blatantly vindictive.

Jackson's support of the prosecution was never in doubt. He consistently overruled defense objections while sustaining those of the prosecution. He only lightly disguised his irritation at being assigned to travel to St. Joseph to preside over the Starr trial—an irritation that grew as Christmas drew near. Jackson determined to complete the trial before Christmas, gave Starr the harshest sentence available, dragged his feet scheduling and rescheduling a hearing on a motion for a new trial, and never honestly considered granting a new trial or a commutation. Finally, his rescheduling the hearing for Friday afternoon, the last day of court before the New Year's recess, leaves no room for speculation as to his determination for closure. Insecurity would not allow him to do anything that would place his decisions in question or challenge his authority. Ego and self-doubt haunted the Hillsdale judge.

Turning to the defense team, it must first be emphasized that no Berrien County lawyer had wanted to take Starr's case. Not wanting to defend someone accused of a crime against one of his or her own most likely contributed to this shunning. Starr's age, glamorous appearance, and regular presence within the Berrien County legal society may have frightened some attorneys. Also, if newspaper headlines and coverage serve as a barometer, her case was unwinnable. Area citizens generally agreed that the defendant was a fallen woman, guilty of murder.

Attorney Glenn A. Biglow agreed to represent Starr just prior to her preliminary examination. He began his practice of law 15 years earlier in and around Kalamazoo. He was married with four children and owned a home on scenic Gull Lake, just a few miles northeast of Kalamazoo.

Obtaining Biglow as counsel should be viewed as an assignment to the defendant, rather than a selection by the defendant; her first choices summarily rejected her requests. Biglow did not maintain a thriving law practice even by Depression standards. He needed work.

In the main he acquiesced and succumbed to his client's directions for her defense. He was greatly relieved when Senator Pinehurst joined him as defense counsel just four days prior to trial. As the trial progressed, Biglow's role declined until he completely absented himself from the motion and hearing for a new trial. The most that may be said of Biglow's efforts to defend Starr is that he did not get in Pinehurst's way.

As for J.P. "Senator" Pinehurst, he sincerely believed in his client and the strategy he crafted for her defense. Although a man of accomplishment, he had been a frustrated jurist for almost two decades. Since leaving both law and politics in California to join the House of David religious commune, he had few opportunities to practice his legal craft, though he did become a member of the Michigan Bar.

During the 1920s he participated as part of the legal team defending the House of David in various civil litigations, but did not practiced law outside the colony. With the passing of the colony's religious leader in 1927 and the coming of the Depression, Pinehurst's executive responsibilities grew exponentially, forcing him to relinquish most legal duties.

Nevertheless, the most famous of Pinehurst's legal cases was the one he argued in 1929 before the Michigan Supreme Court. In that case the court ruled in his favor and overturned the 1927 Circuit Court ruling of Judge Louis H. Fead (Foster's mentor) to dissolve the House of David as a "public nuisance." Also of note, he represented his religious colony in a civil dispute with two area farmers over a gravel contract. The two farmers were represented by W. Robert Eastwood, described by Pinehurst as "a blind squirrel hoping to find an acorn." Before joining Biglow to defend Mary Anne Starr, Pinehurst had not officially practiced law for three years.

Two years earlier, Pinehurst had suffered a heart attack that forced him to curtail his active professional life. However, his scholarly reading schedule accelerated and he became a self-proclaimed authority on the insanity defense. He became intrigued when reading about the Robert Eastwood murder and Starr's difficulty in obtaining counsel. Ever the champion of the underdog, Pinehurst visited Starr in her jail cell to offer his services.

After joining Starr's defense team, his interest in the insanity defense became an obsession. He worked day and night building a defense strategy that incorporated temporary amnesia and self-defense with the claim of temporary insanity. The success of this strategy depended on an informed judge and jury, and creditable medical testimony. Educating the judge and jury was the responsibility of Pinehurst, with the help of his expert medical witnesses. This would have been a formidable task even if the trial had not been hurried along, and even if Ruth Anne Starr had testified. Pinehurst was counting on the daughter's testimony to counter balance that of the victim's son, as well as provide an emotional corroboration of the savage beatings inflicted upon her mother. Ruth Anne Starr's testimony was to be the Senator's *coup de grâce.*

Pinehurst's tunnel vision eliminated alternative avenues of defense and thus, compromised his client's best interest. For example, in his personal affidavit submitted in support of a new trial, Pinehurst revealed that Starr had rejected a plea bargain offer. If she had pled guilty to manslaughter before the trial, the prosecution offered to recommend the minimum sentence be imposed as well as early parole. Accepting that offer would have resulted in serving two years maximum. One is left wondering how, or if, Pinehurst presented this offer to his client. Was the affidavit revelation of a plea bargain an attempt to cover his ill-advised tracts? Did his fixation on temporary insanity cause him to ignore the best interest of his client? Not surprisingly, Pinehurst continued to work for his client's release, *pro bono.*

When evaluating the main players in *The State of Michigan v. Mary Anne Starr*, the defendant must not be overlooked. Starr's behavior before, during and following the incident of 12:30 A.M. October 17, 1938, was curious. Why had she cohabited with an abusing married man for eight years? Why was she carrying a gun? Why had she so willingly talked with reporters less than twelve hours following her arrest? In that jailhouse "press conference" she suggested a justification of temporary emotional insanity based on her total lack of recall of the incident. Was she aware that just such a defense strategy had been successfully plied two years earlier in Berrien County during a love triangle murder case? And lastly, why did she refuse at the last minute to allow her daughter to testify in her defense? Pinehurst's frustration spilled forth at this apparent enigma.

Given the many unanswered questions about Mary Anne Starr, she may forever remain a captivating mystery. A few facts serve as a window into her elusive character. Of humble beginnings, she was intellectually bright, and socially and economically energetic. Given those character traits, her motives become clearer, although not completely so. Starr had viewed Eastwood as a ladder into the lifestyle for which she aspired. She also viewed him as a person who needed her to achieve both economic and social success. Starr and Pinehurst shared an intense social status consciousness.

Starr managed Robert Eastwood and his law practice. Without her there would have been no law practice. Because of Eastwood's professional position in Benton Harbor, Starr enjoyed membership within the social set she coveted. The only thing standing between Mary Anne Starr and her economic and social aspirations was managing Eastwood's mental demons—a task that became ever more challenging over time.

The cast of minor characters enthusiastically added spice, confusion and contradiction to a preordained flawed trial. Eyewitness testimony emanating from the Benton Harbor police station was the rival of any Keystone Cops farce and reliably unreliable. No two witnesses ever gave completely compatible accounts; many contradicted one another, and a couple committed unintentional self-indictments.

A remarkable resemblance between testimony and previous newspaper accounts resonated throughout the trial. Frenzied news reporting greatly influenced a shallow law enforcement investigation. Just like old Will Rogers, the sheriff's department "only knew what they read in the papers." Newspaper headlines of a scorned woman's vicious murder of a selfless people's defender were at once grossly misleading and sensationally popular. At the very least, a change of venue should have been requested. County lawyers speciously grieved for their fallen brethren while spurning the scarlet woman. The Circuit Court judge wisely voluntarily recused himself.

After losing her petition for a new trial, Mary Anne Starr's future appeared bleak. Without gubernatorial intervention or the removal of Judge Jackson from the bench, her possibility of a sentence reduction or early parole ranged from slim to none. She had become a pariah within Michigan's legal system. Even her physical appearance, or the memory thereof, stood against her. With the lone exception of J.P. Pinehurst, no one sought to advocate for Mary Anne Starr.

Before heading back west, I picked up Kalamazoo and South Bend newspapers to compare my coverage of the hearing for a new trial with those written by others. The featuring of Starr's blonde hair was to be expected, as was the lack of mention that Starr had not been in attendance. On the other hand, I was surprised and irritated by descriptions of Starr's children at the hearing. And why was it necessary to focus on Ruth Starr's "attractive appearance?"

The more I thought about the nature and effects of faulty or misleading news reporting, the more upset I became with the profession I had given-up; probably a good decision. I had always enjoyed creative writing, but would never have considered its existence in a newsroom, much less on the front page of a newspaper. It startled me to think that just one year earlier I had such pride in researching and writing articles for the *South Haven Tribune*. More than a job, it was a responsibility that I had taken very seriously. "The pen is mightier than the sword," my history teacher used to say, and I believed it. Though limited, my experience with the newspaper profession had left me a cynic. The incentives for sensational reporting were great, whereas the truth relied on personal integrity. Does integrity sell papers or advance journalism careers?

I pondered the solutions to these questions the following day as I turned the Coupe onto Route 66 heading southwest out of Chicago. I figured the trip west would take me at least four days. On the seat beside me lay a copy of *The Grapes of Wrath*.

XXVIII
THE LETTER

It was late April of 1949 and the freshly blooming landscape gave notice of another door opening. The drive from California had been pleasant. I looked forward to returning home to the farm and seeing everyone. As anxious as I was to see Mom and Dad, I knew it was going to be a bittersweet visit. Nana had passed away and I expected that Mom would be taking it hard. I hadn't been home since being discharged from the Navy following the war, almost four years ago. I felt guilty for not visiting more often, but I was determined to make a success of myself and looked forward to reporting my good fortune, especially to Dad.

The views along Chicago's Lake Shore Drive and around the southern shore of Lake Michigan were inspiring. The excitement of Chicago had thrilled me, as it reminded me of America's big bustling rural city. It truly was, as Carl Sandburg portrayed, "City of the Big Shoulders." After clearing the pungent, gray smoke of Gary, Indiana—even more so than I remembered—I entered Michigan near the sleepy hamlet of New Buffalo. I continued north along the sand dune fortified coast of Lake Michigan. Large forests, small lakes, and geometric fruit orchards all conspired to fulfill the mythical Michigan of my memory.

As eager as I was to get to Fennville, I knew at least one stop was necessary. From the bridge entering Benton Harbor, I spotted the Pegasus diner. Once inside I found the interior had been completely remodeled and expanded. It had become more of a full-fledged restaurant than the dinky little diner I use to frequent. A memorable symphony of aromas made me hungry. I looked around to see if I recognized anyone. I really wanted to see Penny and felt an uneasy anticipation. The passage of time had lined and creased her picture but never dulled my fancy. I often wondered where she might be or what she may be doing. We had lost touch completely after she became stranded in Greece ten years earlier. Travel restrictions had been lifted following the war. I was certain she would have made it back home. Most likely she would be married, I thought.

"Is Hebe *Melaina* here? I'm sorry, I mean Hebe Barth." A portly middle-aged woman led me into the kitchen, new door—still swinging, and to a rear office.

The door was open. I could see a woman working at a desk with a uniformed man seated across from her eating a sandwich. I knocked on the frame and they both turned towards me.

"Chuck!" The woman screamed as she jumped up and rushed around her desk to me. It was an affectionate reunion of old friends. Hebe gave me a tight hug of joy while Deputy Barth vigorously shook my hand and patted me on the back. A bit older, they both looked good and were indisputably happy to see me, as I them.

We sat and talked, catching up with each other's lives. Ten years had passed, the Depression had ended and a world war had come and gone. Hebe and Aaron had done well for themselves. They had two children and were proud of the new home they had built south of the city limits. The Pegasus thrived, with an established reputation of "where the neat meet to eat." Deputy Barth, now Detective Barth, had his eye on running for Berrien County Sheriff. A good man, he'd make a good sheriff.

I told them that a friend I'd met in the Navy and I had started a ferryboat operation in California. We were partners in the business of hauling people and freight between Long Beach, just south of LA, and Santa Catalina Island, approximately 26 miles. Business was good and I liked California.

They told me that Penny had been trapped in Greece during the war. She met a *Thessaloniki* businessman who had taken refuge on *Skopelos* ahead of the Nazi takeover. He was several years older than Penny, but they eventually married and, after the Germans withdrew, moved from *Skopelos* to *Thessaloniki*. They tried to reestablish his trucking company near that port city. Their plan was to move to America when the war ended, but even before it ended a civil war erupted between the existing government and the communists. To further complicate their situation, Penny became pregnant and gave birth to a baby boy.

"Penny name baby for Uncle K," Hebe proudly informed me.

With a forlorn look in her eyes, Hebe ended her tumultuous account relating the last information she'd received. "Almost year ago, friend of Penny write us, tell us that trucks commandeered and Penny husband murdered. Penny and little boy disappear. That all we know. Not know if alive or dead. We hear nothing more."

Disturbed by what Hebe had told me and knowing the conversation could really go nowhere, I struggled to move us in another direction. Fortunately, an observant Detective Barth saved Hebe and me from our doom and gloom by injecting, "Guess what Chuck, you'll never guess who received an appointment to the Circuit Court last year?"

"Senator Pinehurst?" I smartly quipped.

"No, not hardly. Pinehurst passed away over a year ago. Bill Foster, you remember Foster don't you? He got lucky. Old Judge Warren died and the governor appointed Foster to fill the vacancy."

"Really? Is Robert Spears still the Prosecuting Attorney?"

"No, private practice. But, I know something you'll be even more interested in. Who do you think is managing the House of David Hotel just down the street from here?" Not waiting for my answer, Barth exclaimed, "Mary Anne Starr!"

"What! So she finally got out of prison. Why would she come back here?" I asked in disbelief.

"Well, I think I can answer that for you, but why don't you ask her yourself? You met her, didn't you?"

"Yes, once or twice. Do you think she would be at the hotel right now?"

"More than likely, she runs it. Her apartment's on the first floor."

Saying my goodbyes to the Barths was difficult. They felt like family to me. Hebe wrote down Penny's last address and gave it to me. I hadn't thought of asking for it, but felt good that Hebe would want me to have it. "I still have picture you take of Penny and me. It only picture of Penny I have."

Could she be found? Was she still alive? Reports were that the civil war had plummeted Greece into utter economic devastation and absolute anarchy; worse than the war. I worried for Penny and wondered if there was anything I could or should do. As I walked over to the hotel, I visualized walking down that same street beside Penny one winter day, long ago.

The House of David Hotel supported a large block-lettered wall sign that faced westward down Main Street and could be easily seen from the front step of the Pegasus. The fresh warmth of the bright spring day made my short stroll quite enjoyable. Main Street had been the route of the annual countywide Blossom Parade until the war forced its cancelation. Benton Harbor looked much the same as I had remembered.

Upon entering the hotel, I saw Mary Anne talking with one of the guest. A good feeling came over me when she obviously recognized and hurried over to greet me. She was the same attractive and cordial lady I had last talked with years earlier in the jail. I hoped that the town's people had received her the same way she had received me, but I doubted it. A little older, she was still impressive, fashionably dressed and not a blonde hair out of place.

"Chuck, you put on a couple of pounds since I last saw you. You're not a skinny farm boy anymore." She laughed, putting me completely at ease.

We talked for several minutes before she asked me if I had eaten lunch. "No I haven't. It would be my pleasure to take you out for lunch?"

"Don't be ridiculous, I'm taking you and were not eating here; it's only vegetarian," she whispered. "I always liked the dining room at the Vincent Hotel and I've not been there since I got back. We'll go there." Mary Anne's resolute manner told me that she was making some sort of esoteric statement by returning to the Vincent Hotel.

"Don't you just love these delicate linen napkins?" Mary Anne commented as we were being seated. As we talked it became obvious that her observation powers were just as acute as I'd remembered. During lunch Mary Anne carried the conversation which was fine with me. I enjoyed hearing her voice. It came as welcomed surprise when she described her life in prison and on parole. Her story tugged at my heartstrings. She began:

"My first two years were the most difficult. While being processed in, the matron in charge of inmate welfare gave me paper and pencil and instructed me to write out a confession of the crime for which I was committed. I told her, 'I cannot do that, because I have no recollection whatever of the shooting, or murder of Robert Eastwood.' That is true to this day, Chuck. I'm certain amnesia resulted from Bob's hitting me just before the shooting. Need I say the matron severely reprimanded me for not complying with her wishes?

Feeling unjustly imprisoned, and then unreasonably punished, I suffered a nervous breakdown before serving out my initial thirty-day quarantine period. Headaches have haunted me since the night of the shooting, but never such excruciating pain as I went through those first two years. My vision has declined and I've lost all hearing in my left ear.

I was so weak, I had to spend considerable time in the prison infirmary. When I was able, I held some of the best assignment available to inmates. Several times I served as the cook for Warden Gillies and his family. Mostly I've worked in the administrative office processing inmates in and out of the prison. Working, more than anything, saved my life.

After being turned down for a new trial, Mr. Pinehurst and I agreed that as long as Judge Jackson handled my case, I didn't have much chance of getting out early. In the fall of 1942 Pinehurst wrote and told me that Jackson had lost in a bid for reelection. My hopes were lifted and with the New Year we again started working for early parole. Judge Warren, you remember the judge who requested that he be replaced as my trial judge, assumed responsibility for my case. Senator Pinehurst told me that he had known Warren for a long time and believed that Warren would try to help us. The Senator knew everybody who was anybody, if you know what I mean?"

"I know what you mean. Senator Pinehurst was a well known and respected leader in this area and a man of considerable accomplishment." Mary Anne smiled her agreement and continued:

"By a twist of fate, the previous summer I met a woman who had been sentenced by Judge Warren on a perjury conviction. To my surprise, this woman and her boyfriend, both married to different people, had been encouraged by their attorney, Harley Eastwood, to lie about their place and length of residence. They were applying for divorces so they could marry each other. Would you believe they were arrested on their wedding night and taken to the Berrien County jail?

Following their trial and conviction, Judge Warren discovered that Harley had suborned perjury—encouraged them to lie! Warren started a movement for Harley's disbarment. In the mean time Warren successfully petitioned for the parole of the newlyweds he'd sent to prison for perjury.

As you can tell, I am overjoyed to share with you that they finally caught up with Harley. In order to avoid the embarrassment of disbarment, Harley gave up his law license and moved to California. If I were a profane woman, I would describe Harley in more dramatic terms. I'll simply say he's the most avaricious man I've ever met.

Judge Warren didn't like Harley either, and he probably didn't like Bob. He liked Senator Pinehurst who cajoled him into advocating for my parole. I saw the letter Warren wrote to the Parole Board in July of '43. He said my sentence was too severe and had I taken the plea bargain, I would have already been out. But, and that was the problem, but! He said he feared infringing on the board's jurisdiction and would support whatever action they took. It took the Parole Board a whole year to deny my parole and tell me that I would have to serve at least eight years, four months and six days! At that point, I gave up."

"I guess I can understand why. It sure looked hopeless."

"When I came up for parole in the spring of '47, who do you think strongly supported it?"

"Judge Warren?"

"No, he had passed away. The judge appointed to fill Warren's seat on the bench; Bill Foster! Yes, the man who prosecuted me, the man who told me to, 'go home and work things out in the morning.' Bill Foster. Life is funny, isn't it?"

"It really is. Yours is an unbelievable story, Mary Anne."

"Well, at least prison is behind me. I'll admit there were times I didn't think I'd make it. I missed both Mickey and Ruthie's graduations, their weddings, the births of my grandchildren."

"Did people write to you; visit you?" I asked with great concern, remembering what Dad once told me, "The only thing worse than death is being forgotten."

"It didn't seem so at the time, but Vonda, Ruthie and Mickey came to see me every other month. Vonda came several times by herself. Senator Pinehurst came a few times and I did receive lots of letters. At least I had a few friends who remembered me."

"Mary Anne, during your hearing for a new trial, it was revealed that you had been offered a plea bargain that would have resulted in a much shorter sentence. Did Pinehurst make you aware of the prosecution's offer and do you believe he gave you good advice?"

"They say hindsight is 20/20. Senator Pinehurst visited me the day before the trial started. I remember because I had a splitting headache. He told me that Foster suggested I plead guilty to manslaughter. If I did, he would recommend a sentence of two to seven and a half years with a recommendation of early parole; possibly out in two. But, how could I plead guilty to something I didn't remember doing? Pinehurst believed I would be exonerated, and that our defense strategy would prove it. I agreed. The Senator stuck with me to the day he died. He gave me this job; he's the reason I'm here today. He was a good man." The conviction with which Mary Anne spoke left no doubt as to her loyalty to Senator Pinehurst.

"When were you paroled?"

"Two years ago, next Wednesday. And as of Wednesday, I'm a free woman!"

"That's great Mary Anne. Did you say Vonda and Ruthie are visiting?"

"Yes, they went shopping. I'll let them tell you what for. The three of us are going to a movie tonight. They should be back at the hotel by now. Shall we go see?"

Mary Anne insisted on paying for our lunch, which I'm sure was quite expensive. However, I couldn't even remember tasting my roast beef sandwich. As we left the Vincent Hotel and crossed to the other side of Main Street, I tried to recall the inside of that magnificent structure. Mary Anne's story had held me so spellbound that the only physical thing I could remember was the linen napkins.

Vonda and Ruthie were standing in the lobby holding several packages between them. Being together under markedly better circumstances invigorated all of us. All three women were full of news and of course wanted to know all about what I'd been doing with my life. A youthful reflection of her mother, the now garrulous Ruthie was married and mother of two. And talk of another impending wedding did pique my curiosity.

A year earlier, Mary Anne had been introduced to a successful Chicago businessman, thirteen years her junior. He stayed at the hotel while visiting relatives in Benton Harbor. Ruthie described him as, "a dashing Rhett Butler look alike." They had fallen in love, but were prohibited from marrying until Mary Anne completed her parole. The wedding date was set for May 13th in Chicago, where the newlyweds planned to make their home.

I felt grateful to have been included in a portion of this happy time with people who had been dealt far more than their share of life's misery. Judging by their affectionate good humor, these women convinced me that Mary Anne

Starr was on the threshold of having her dreams come true; a fate she so richly deserved.

As late afternoon approached, I explained that my parents were expecting me and that I should be heading for Fennville. We all agreed to stay in touch. As I left the hotel, warm feelings of happy endings mingled with an eager desire to get on home.

I started toward the Pegasus, but hadn't walked 20 feet when I heard a voice behind me, "Wait-up Chuck, I'll walk you to your car." Vonda stepped quickly to catch up. "Do you remember taking me to the Vincent Hotel for dinner?"

"How could I forget? That was a long time ago. Mary Anne and I just ate lunch there."

A strained appearance came over Vonda. I could see that something was troubling her. She wanted to talk with me, privately.

"Chuck, it has been over 10 years since that horrifying nightmare began. It will never end for me, but I trust you Chuck, and," Vonda stopped talking staring blankly, first at me and then straight ahead. I could feel a damp chill in the late afternoon air. She seemed a woman full of unshed tears. When she started again I knew I was about to hear something she had wanted to talk about for a very long time. Then, an avalanche of pent-up emotions burst forth. As we walked Vonda spun a story that found me holding my breath, totally astounded.

"The day before the shooting, Sunday, Mary Anne had called me early in the morning, wanting me to come to Benton Harbor. She seemed almost frantic. She thought she had to separate from Bob. In fact, he had left the day before and she didn't know where he had gone or when or if he would return. She wanted to talk with me, wanted me to come.

At the time I thought, 'Thank God, my sister has finally come to her senses. She has been mistreated long enough. Is that what she means? Finally, she's going to get out?' Understand Chuck, I hated Bob. What he did to Mary Anne, what Ruthie had witnessed; it was horrifying.

I picked up Ruthie, who was visiting her grandparents, to go with me to visit her mother. I knew they would like seeing each other. We met Mary Anne around noon at the Vincent Hotel, where she had reserved a room for Ruthie and me. She never wanted us to come to their home. I could tell by her face that Bob had beaten her again. She said she fell while raking leaves, but knew better. Later, Mary Anne suggested we go to South Haven to see a movie. We had a good time, we always did.

After returning to the hotel, Mary Anne told us she had some work she wanted to finish at the office and left the hotel at about eight. I wanted her to go home with us in the morning and I think she may have, but she wanted to talk with Bob before she did.

Sometime around eleven, Mary Anne stopped back. Ruthie and I were in bed. She said she was going to go out looking for Bob one last time. She would go home and be back to see us first thing in the morning.

I laid awake thinking about Mary Anne and the beast she had been living with. I couldn't sleep, so I got up, dressed and went for a walk. In front of the hotel, I saw a man and a woman cross Main Street a block ahead of me. It was Bob and Mary Anne. I decided to parallel them by walking down 6th. When I got to the library I stopped, seeing the two of them crossing the street and entering the police station. Good, I thought, maybe the police will do something to protect her this time.

I sat in the dark on the bottom library step. Shortly, Bob came out by himself and started across Wall, heading for 5th. I was sure he didn't see me; there were no streetlights on my side of the street. Then Mary Anne came out and headed across the street in my direction.

The next thing I saw was that brute violently attacking Mary Anne. I ran to help her. She was lying near the curb. He had a gun. When he saw me coming he dropped the gun on Mary Anne and turned, heading toward the police station. Actually, I think he dropped the gun before he saw me because as he did he said something to Mary Anne. I picked up the gun and fired it at him. Mary Anne was withering in pain at my feet. That's when I went over and shot him in the head.

When I got back to Mary Anne, she was trying to stand up. I helped her. Crying, she took the gun from me and told me to go get Ruthie and go home. 'Don't say a word about this. I'll take care of it. Don't say a word. Don't run. Go!' I'll never forget. It's played in my head thousands of times. She was protecting me, just like she always had."

"You mean Mary Anne did not shoot Robert Eastwood?" I asked in utter disbelief.

"No, I shot that bastard. I hated him, Chuck." Vonda's whole body shook. Tears streamed down her red-blotched face.

Trying to muster a calm voice I asked, "Mary Anne must know you shot him. Didn't the two of you talk about it?"

"I believe that she knew at the time of the shooting, when she took the gun away from me and told me to leave. But the next day, and to this day, I don't believe that Mary Anne has any memory of the actual shooting; she's blocked it out, it's not there."

"Did you ever consider confessing to protect your sister?"

"I thought about it long and hard Chuck, I still do; always will. To this day, I'm ashamed of what I did. I was pregnant at the time with our second child.

Mary Anne was convinced that if she did shoot Bob, it was justifiable, legal. Her attorney believed she would go free. He believed she shot Bob. I never thought that my sister would be behind bars for eight long years."

Vonda took a slow determined breath. "In my mind she had a far better case than I would have had. However crazy it seems, she loved Bob; I hated the man. I don't mean to make excuses; I'll always be ashamed for what I did."

"Vonda, I am not going to judge you for what happened, nor shall I share your confession with anyone; ever. Sometimes decisions must be made when a good choice does not exist. I think Dad told me something like that years ago, and I believe it. Personally, I believe that Mary Anne is looking forward to her future and that she treasures you and your support. You're a good person, Vonda, and so is your sister."

Vonda gave me a faint tear-filled smile and tried to assure me that they were happy. Letting out a deep sigh, as if in relief, she said, "Mary Anne's marrying a nice man. We're all happy for her. She's taking Ruthie and me to the Liberty Theater for a movie tonight. We'll have lots of fun."

"That does sound like fun; just the three of you. What movie are you going to see?" I couldn't help thinking of the calamity that followed the last time the three of them went to a movie.

"It's something starring Bette Davis. I think she said it was **The Letter**."

"Oh Vonda, I don't think you should go to that movie. Maybe you could suggest something else?"

"Why?" Vonda responded with a puzzled expression. "Mary Anne is a big fan of Bette Davis. She loves going to the movies."

"I saw that movie, Vonda. Bette Davis plays a spurned adulteress who shoots her lover in the back. The movie is tension-packed and shocking. Please, promise me you will not go to that movie."

With a head full of questions, I set out for Fennville. Years had passed, but I was again following a familiar road with a familiar murder trial churning in my head. Wanting nothing to interfere with my reunion at the farm, I decided to come to terms with the Mary Anne Starr case before I arrived home. To amuse myself I devised a plan in which I served as both the interrogator and the witness.

I. —Why didn't Mary Anne leave Eastwood? W. —From the day they met, she had taken care of and defended him. She did not want to give up hope. Leaving him was the same as admitting she'd failed in love for a second time.

I. —Why was Eastwood carrying a gun the night of the shooting? W. —Not sure, but it was Eastwood who wanted

the gun, not Mary Anne. When he threw the weapon on her prostrate body, he was promoting the suspicion he had created of Mary Anne's habit of threatening him with a gun. I am sure that Mary Anne was not carrying the gun; she never had before and it certainly wasn't fashionable. The gun wasn't found in her purse or her hand, but in her coat pocket.

I. —Why didn't the police conduct a thorough investigation? It would have uncovered the presence of Vonda and Ruthie, and may have uncovered the Izzy Genoa connection or other unseemly situations within the legal community. W. —Because the police believed Mary Anne shot Eastwood; open and shut. They had seen it coming and some wondered why she had taken so long. Eastwood was crazy. Investigations cost money and budgets were tight. And lastly, when it comes to 'uncovered,' I think you answered your own question.

I. —Why didn't officers and other officials come forth and reveal those facts, e.g., Izzy Genoa, Liquor Commission scandal? W. —They were members of a community of interest, maybe holding their breath lest they be implicated in some way.

I. —Why did Berrien County lawyers and judges shun Mary Anne's case? W. —Because the case could be damaging to their careers. Newspapers had already convicted the evil woman and the public had lined up against her; they viewed it as a no win, indigent situation.

I. —Why did Pinehurst come forward to defend Starr? W. —Because he believed in her case, it was his case, his area of expertise, and provided him a venue for showcasing his legal prowess. Additionally, Pinehurst's House of David religious cult had experienced a similar shunning by the Berrien County legal community in their 1927 civil trial as a public nuisance. And, the Senator savored the limelight.

I. —Why didn't Vonda come forward? W. —Initially Mary Anne told her not to. As time passed, Vonda evaluated her chances and thought Mary Anne had the stronger case. Also, Vonda was pregnant with her second child at the time and already responsible for Mickey and Ruthie.

I. —Why wouldn't Mary Anne allow Ruthie to testify on her behalf? W. —Ruthie had witnessed her mother being beaten by Eastwood. It had been extremely traumatic for the young girl and Mary Anne did not want her daughter forced to relive that event. Pinehurst wanted Ruthie to testify for the very same reasons.

I. —Why had prosecutors worked so hard at trial to convict Mary Anne of first-degree murder? W. —Actually, the prosecutors wanted to work out a plea bargain for a lesser charge and sentence. However, when the case went to trial, they were simply doing their jobs with their respective careers in mind.

I. —Why such a severe sentence? W. —Jackson wanted the appearance of a strong law and order judge. Judgeships were political position and Jackson had to run for reelection. Jackson was insecure.

Dad had a new orchard tractor sitting next to the barn. The moment I opened the car door I could smell the fragrance of apple blossoms comingling with fresh turned earth; I was home. The cherry orchard that ran out from behind the barn had grown significantly. Walking around to take a closer look I noticed a white cross. It stood about three feet high and was placed under the spreading branches of the old Elm tree we use to climb.

I hesitated to allow emotional feelings to settle before I walked closer to read the marker's inscription. Mom had written me that Ginger had died, but seeing the marker made it real. "Ginger, Faithful Friend and Companion 1934-1947." What more could be said of anyone?

The kitchen door slammed and I turned to see Mom running towards me. While Mom bear-hugged and kissed me, Dad happily shouted from the open door, "Come on, Chuck, we're hungry!" as if this was just another suppertime.

At the table, we talked about everything and everyone we had ever been related to. Ken, Josh and their families were doing well and would be at the funeral. Ken was farming and Josh was teaching high school English. The inevitable question loomed and then Mom, as if trying to be funny, came straight out with it. "When are you getting married Chuck? You know you've got to keep up with your little brothers."

I smiled and chuckled, but put Mom off with, "I don't know many eligible women, but rest assured Mom, I haven't given up looking."

When I asked about Uncle Otto, Mom said they'd rather not talk about that, but the children were doing well for themselves. Dad told me that out of respect for Nana the whole extended family simply never brought up the subject of Otto Barnes. The message was clear, so I let it go, even though to me this didn't seem healthy.

The following morning, Dad and I walked around the farm. Dad served as my tour guide, as if I'd never before seen the place. He was rightfully proud. I loved every step. Farming was a noble profession. When we got back to the house, Mom insisted we hurry and get ready to go to the funeral.

The church was full, attendance the equal to that of an Easter Sunday service. Everyone who knew Nana, loved Nana, in my mind a truly great lady. I decided that my memorial to her would be to think of her whenever I requested cheese with a piece of apple pie.

From the church we traveled in a car caravan to the McDowell Cemetery for a short internment service. While standing respectfully and listening to the minister, but not hearing, I spotted the headstone of **"OTTO & ARLENE BARNES, Husband and Wife."** *What had the minister said at their funeral? Had they been forgotten?*

Following the benediction, Mom asked Dad to invite everyone to join us at the Grange Hall for a potluck dinner honoring her mother, Wilma "Nana" Hunter. This was a customary chain of events for a rural funeral. The hall was full by the time we arrived. Several of Mom and Nana's friends had everything setup and more than ample food for all who attended. Many old and familiar faces greeted me, and several I was certain I had never met before. One and all expressed their deepest sympathies to Mom.

Mom, Dad and I agreed as we rode back to the farm, it was a fitting and well deserved community tribute. Nana had lived in and contributed to her community for **88** years. *Nana, you made the world a better place and we will never forget you, never.*

I stayed for only a couple of days, feeling pressure to get back to my business. As I left early on Tuesday morning, I told Dad that I had never remembered the farm looking so good. Mom made me promise to be home for Christmas, "The whole family will be here and you must." I promised. Mom cried.

On my way to Chicago to pick up Route 66, a tradition, I looked in at the newspaper office in South Haven. Rose Mendelsohn had sold the paper following the war. The people working there didn't know where she had moved; Chicago, maybe.

When I crossed the Indiana border, I stopped to gas up and look at my road map. *I wonder what sunsets are like on Skopelos this time of year?*

XXIX
SUNSET

It took me two days of hard driving to get to New York City. I booked passage on an Italia Line ship scheduled to sail May third for Naples, Italy—in two days. Immediately I called my partner in Long Beach to see if he would be willing to buy my share of our ferry line business. I quoted him a very good price. He accepted, told me I was crazy, wished me luck, and said he'd wire me the money by Western Union.

I then called Dad and Mom to let them know what I planned to do. "Why are you doing this?" "Why now?" I couldn't answer their questions, at least not to their satisfaction, but neither tried to dissuade me. Dad cautioned that I might be sailing into a civil war and Mom made me promise to be home for Christmas, to which I promised for the second time.

Then I called Hebe to let her know I was going to look for Penny and ask her for any information she could give me, such as names and addresses of friends, anything. Also, I wanted to know where their original *Melaina* home was and what might be the best way to get there. Hebe exploded with excitement. I could hear her crying on the other end of the line. She told me I would have to take a ship to Athens and from there a bus to the city of *Volos*. From *Volos* I was on my own, but maybe a ferry or fishing boat could transport me to *Skopelos*. Hebe gave me a very detailed location of where to find their little village toward the north end of the island. It lay on the west side about eight to ten miles across the channel from the island of *Skiathos*; maybe forty miles from *Volos*.

I assured Hebe that I would walk if I had to, swim if I must, but that I was going to *Skopelos*. That's where I would start my search for Penny thinking she may have been in contact with someone there, the beautiful place she had dreamed about to me.

Briefly, Hebe told me what she knew about the Greek Civil War. She feared that travel would be dangerous, but that civil unrest had subsided and only lingered in the mountains along Greece's northern border. "Greece ravaged, depressed country. I told people starving there. Be careful. I pray for you find Penny and little boy. He four years now."

Before shipping out, I had one more thing to do, which I dreaded. I had to sell my little black Ford Coupe. She had been good to me for 11 years. The dockhand I sold her to really wanted her; he thought she was an antique. The Coupe was 20 years old. I explained that she was solid and dependable, and that I couldn't part with her for less than $150. We settled on $120, which I believed was the buyer's very last dollar. The cash that I acquired from the sale of the Coupe and the ferry business would serve as an insurance policy for my trip to Europe. I patted the Coupe on her rumble seat before she drove away with the happy stranger.

Crossing the ocean reminded me of my time in the Navy. I enjoyed being on the water. Traveling by ship was an unhurried existence. It gives a person plenty of time to sit, read and think, all healthy activities that could be engaged in concurrently. I had purchased two books for my journey: Daniel Defoe's *Robinson Crusoe* and Mark Twain's *The Innocents Abroad.* Both books seemed appropriate. Also, I knew that anything written by Twain would be amusing and I needed to read *Robinson Crusoe* since long ago I had claimed before a high school literature teacher that I had read it. Guilt still lingered after all those years.

Half way across the Atlantic some of my fellow travelers complained of suffering from the voyage's tiresome repetition. Trying to avoid a similar fate, I busied myself reading, meeting and talking with fellow passengers, walking the decks, and outlining my philosophy of life; the latter a noble enterprise, I fancied. With an increasing frequency I found myself thinking of Penny.

After 13 days aboard ship we arrived in Naples. Before landing I had learned from the captain what I should do in order to best book passage to Athens. After less than two hours ashore, I had secured a place on a cargo vessel routed to Athens the following morning.

The trip from Naples to Athens took three and a half days. It was a scenic voyage, through the Strait of Messina, across the Ionian Sea, and passing countless picturesque islands until we reached the Greek port of Athens. I spent most daylight time next to the railing taking in the views and asking myself, why this irresistible impulse to find Penny, and why now? Time passed quickly.

By the time I landed in Greece I had convinced myself that the chances of finding Penny were remote, but I had to push forward. Greece had experienced a decade of turmoil, devastated by war, foreign occupation, and civil unrest. I recalled that the war had stranded Penny, who later married and moved with her husband to *Thessaloniki.* Her husband had been murdered. I feared Penny had likely suffered a similar fate. If not, she may have been kidnapped or if fortunate enough to escape, where would she have sought asylum? She obviously hadn't made it back to Benton Harbor, hadn't contacted Hebe, past friends didn't know what happened to her, and the list of dead end leads mounted.

If she had escaped, would she have stayed in Greece? I doubted it. And if she had made it out alive, she may have remarried. If someone was chasing her, she certainly would not return to a place she had previously lived. Penny was smart; far from the terror struck child that had witnessed her sister's brutal rape.

I deliberated day and night, evaluating endless scenarios, all of which ended poorly. Traveling in a crowded, smelly old bus from Athens to *Volos*, I resolved again that I was going to go straight to *Skopelos*. I'd walk the beach that Penny dreamed about; I'd view the sunset, and feel the warm salty breeze on my face. *Was my objective clouded by faulty memory or active imagination? Was I remembering or imagining the times Penny and I had shared?*

My plan was to track down people who remembered the *Melaina* family. Hopefully, someone still made the wine that Penny told me her grandmother made. I wanted to taste it. After exploring *Skopelos*, I'd take a boat to Thessaloniki and see if I could determine Penny's whereabouts at the time of her husband's murder and her disappearance. That was my plan.

Two leathery brown *Volos* fishermen who regularly plied the waters of the northern *Sporades* island group agreed to drop me on *Skopelos* near the village of *Glossa*. They knew that area well, they said. When fishing was good, they typically stopped at *Glossa* to sell fish. From my notes, the place where the *Melainas* had lived was a mile or so south of *Glossa*.

As we approach the island, I thought to myself that Penny's descriptions were not at all exaggerated. The lush blue-green hills rising behind the shore were matted by a clear blue cloudless sky. The sky was several shades lighter than the blue water of the Aegean. With the sun moving ever lower in the western sky, the water changed color depending on the direction viewed, from jet black, through various turquoise shades, to shimmering silver in the blinding sun line. Sailing northward along the island's western coast I saw only two or three tiny white stucco homes tucked into the thick vegetation covered hillsides awash in the late day sun. Pristine, I thought. This must be the right place. When I passionately exclaimed to my two weathered seafarers how spectacular the setting was, they both smiled at me and spoke rapidly, nodding to one another. We honestly didn't understand each other, but all three of us laughed together and pretended we did.

One of the men pointed ahead saying, "*Glossa, Glossa!*" I thought I could make out the entrance to a small harbor in the distant. Knowing that my destination was nearing, I could feel a mounting nervous anticipation. From approximately 75 yards off shore I could see rocky outcroppings separated by open stretches of golden sand. The only people on the beach were two women casually walking along the shore in the same direction we were sailing. The younger of the two seemed tall and supple while the older one was short and round. They could have been mother and daughter, sharing the day and comfort of each other's company. The taller of the two held her head up, feeling of the wind move across her face. Her long dark hair waved freely in the ocean breeze. As my heart raced, I casually signaled a far-off hello. Both women squinted in our direction, but did not acknowledge my salute. They continued walking as I gazed at them, savoring the serenity and wondering.

Trying to catch up, a small child ran splashing along the water's edge. He spotted our boat, stopped and looked in our direction, then continued his chase while holding up a fist-full of brightly colored ribbons to blow in the wind. My heart stopped as I stared in silent disbelief. The younger woman turned with one hand on her hip as she beckoned to the little boy. *"Kambelos, me akolouthis?"* "Are you coming, Kambe?"

Clare Adkin

ABOUT THE AUTHOR

Clare Adkin was raised on a fruit farm in Allegan County, Michigan. After graduating from Michigan State University with a degree in history he embarked upon a 38 year career in teaching and coaching. He has been thinking about Mary Anne Starr, the subject of **Quiet Guilt**, since he discovered her while doing research for his first book **Brother Benjamin** (1990). True to his mantra, "History is interpretation, the essence of which is research and writing," he has persistently endeavored to instill the same in his students. Adkin and his wife Sally make their home in Durham, North Carolina.

**For more information about the author please visit him at
WWW.CLAREADKIN.COM**

LaVergne, TN USA
29 November 2010
206633LV00004B/1/P

9 781886 057586